JIRVALLA

JIRVALLA

BOOK ONE

Wick Pearl

RESOURCE *Publications* · Eugene, Oregon

JIRVALLA
Book One

Resource Publications
An Imprint of Wipf and Stock Publishers
199 W. 8th Ave., Suite 3
Eugene, OR 97401

www.wipfandstock.com

PAPERBACK ISBN: 979-8-3852-7198-6
HARDCOVER ISBN: 979-8-3852-7199-3
EBOOK ISBN: 979-8-3852-7200-6

VERSION NUMBER 01/23/26

Contents

1

The Shepherd of Fish

Jaspen chirped out a series of clicks and whistles, a warning cry familiar to every sea beast that roamed these waters near Jirvalla. It was a signal to all that the Shepherd of Fish was gathering his flock. And that he was prepared to battle until death those daring to thieve even the smallest Lesser-Fin from his shimmering flock.

Slither-Tail, alone, ignored Jaspen's call and the fish slipped through the current to draw closer to the Shepherd's growing shoal. It was unusual to see one as immense as this so near the shallows—its length three times Jaspen's height, its head as wide as the boy's outstretched arms. Named for its resemblance to the jungle's Slither-Belly, Slither-Tail moved through the water in a wavy, rippling manner similar to its forest-dwelling cousin. Jaspen caught the monster's beady black eyes and sounded out his cautionary message a second time.

Yet the creepy fish simply opened its mouth in an act of aggression, flaunting its two rows of spiked teeth before clamping shut its jaws with a menacing *clack*!

Fool, thought Jaspen and raced toward Slither-Tail.

Jaspen's neck prickled with fear and the awful tingling spread to the base of his spine. He had never opposed a beast so deadly or huge. He brushed a finger over the lance he had carved from Spear-Snout, ten suns ago. The boy reminded himself that he could swim as fast as Double-Tail, dive as deep as Shell-Back, and leap from the sea to heights as great as Long-Nose. He beseeched his god, the Always, for the courage, strength, and wits to conquer Slither-Tail. Still, he quivered with fright.

Reaching the fiend's long powerful body, his hands and heart trembling, Jaspen pulled himself onto Slither-Tail's thorned back. A red stripe rose along the Shepherd's chest and his blood spiraled up into the water. He seized the weapons fixed to his wrists and chirped out a final caution, trying to sound brave—*leave now*!

Never before had Jaspen surrendered his flock to an intruder. Never before had he wanted to swim away and admit defeat. Yet he could not bear the notion of returning from his duty empty-handed. Nearly twenty of Cove tribe's poorest families relied upon Jaspen for sustenance. Without the boy's help, most would have starved seasons ago.

Jaspen closed his eyes and pictured old man Chokli, stump-footed Plimpoc, and Azo, the tiny infant—a few of the many who depended on him for nourishment.

Tightening his grip on the lance, Jaspen punched it deep into Slither-Tail's sinewy back.

The beast jolted and whipped its sinister face toward Jaspen. Its tail thrashed and body bucked, determined to cast its rider.

Jaspen plunged his other weapon, a lustrous pearl knife, into Slither-Tail and clung to the hilts of his lance and dagger—struggling to remain on his mount. He pressed his knees deeper into the muscles that rippled along each side of the creature's spine. More blood spilled from the inside of Jaspen's thighs. He watched, concerned, as crimson strings rose from his legs before diluting in the seawater.

Fresh blood drew ocean scavengers like a forest carcass drew Tiny-Black-Wings. An insatiable swarm would soon appear, sniff out the source of blood, and attack. If Jaspen failed to vanquish Slither-Tail prior to the horde's arrival, his troubles would become much more perilous than those posed by a single beast.

The monster's next jarring effort flung Jaspen from the fish's back and into open water.

Slither-Tail veered to face Jaspen. And bolted straight for him.

Its double-rowed maw of piked teeth wide open.

2

Slither-Tail

JASPEN SCRATCHED AT THE water, kicking and squirming, anything to escape the path of Slither-Tail's jagged teeth and terrible jaws . . . but the fish was too fast.

The beast tore into Jaspen's upper leg. Due to the Shepherd's unusual coloring, however, as well as the boy's swift reactions, Slither-Tail's teeth only raked across Jaspen's thigh.

Since the day the ocean's hand had set Jaspen upon Jirvallan shores over two hundred round moons ago, the boy had never seen another who claimed the same strange markings as he. A blackish-brown hue flowed like a dark, rolling wave from the nape of Jaspen's neck all the way down his back, seeping over to shade the edges of his ribs and the horns of his hips. When the deep shadowy color met the backs of his legs, it gradually began to fade to lighter and lighter shades until reaching his ankles. Conversely, Jaspen's front—his face, chest, abdomen, thighs, and shins—was a tint akin to the sandy beaches where the Cove lived in their grass and twig huts. It was as if the Shepherd was a distant relative of Day-Belly Night-Fin, the second most feared predator in the sea.

Head spinning, senses frayed, the gash on his thigh gaping wider—burning as if set aflame—Jaspen assessed the damage. The pain was bone-deep and spreading fast, ranging now from hip to knee. The bite, however, wasn't large enough to render his leg useless. A bigger issue was the volume of new blood that poured from his wound into the ocean. The Shepherd gathered his wits just in time to see the serpent charging again.

The monster would not miss a second time.

Jaspen's webbed fingers dug into the sea, frantic. Dashing for the safety of a coral forest, his hand grazed something tethered to his good leg by a length of braided sea grass. In all the mayhem, he had forgotten about his latest invention. It was a crudely constructed jug fashioned from the stem and bulb of a strand of whip kelp. He had yet to test it. Though he knew the merest malfunction would result in his death, there was no other choice.

Jaspen glanced back. Slither-Tail was closing fast.

One more second, he thought. *Just a little . . . bit . . . closer . . .*

Slither-Tail broadened its colossal jaws and a powerful in-rush of water nearly sucked Jaspen into the behemoth's mouth.

Now!

He stabbed a finger into the opening of the whip-kelp jug and prized out the moss plug he had packed into the container's narrow, tube-like neck.

A wispy, black cloud streamed out of the container and stained the water. It spread like fog and soon the smoky haze was upon its target— Slither-Tail's cavernous mouth.

Jaspen shifted direction and shot for the surface. He was hoping the ink he had teased from Eight-Legs would confound Slither-Tail as it had confounded him last season, when the dark toxin scrambled Jaspen's senses so severely it took him a full sun to recover. Even if the poison failed to frustrate the monster's sight and smell, it would—at the very least—serve as a smokescreen to afford the Shepherd a few precious seconds to flee to safety and plot another attack.

Five strokes from the surface, Jaspen peeked back to see his enemy flapping its face as if Jelly-Limbs had scourged the beast across the snout with its venomous tentacles. The ink was working. Jaspen clacked his tongue and Slither-Tail jerked its great head toward him. Though befuddled, the monster blasted toward the sound.

Jaspen looped around to gain a position behind his foe. He grinned, for the savage was speeding for the ocean's surface.

The Shepherd accelerated and burst into the air, five or six arm lengths from Slither-Tail's wide snout emerging from the sea. He flew toward the beast at a slight angle as the creature surged out of the water, higher and higher. At the apex of his flight, Jaspen snatched the long, bone spear lashed to his back.

Slither-Tail was dazed and off-balance, still fighting the poison, and the fish plummeted backward toward the waves, exposing its soft underbelly.

Jaspen upraised the spear, with both hands, high above his head.

The creature's black gaze caught Jaspen and the boy sneered at the beast. Slither-Tail seemed to realize its vulnerability and its dark eyes widened with panic.

Arching his back, Jaspen throttled the bone harpoon tighter and drove the spike downward with every shred of force and muscle he could summon. The spear's tip knifed into the underside of Slither-Tail's jaw. As the beast fell backwards, belly toward the sky, the weapon's barbed head gored through the floor of the monster's mouth. It gouged through the serpent's tongue and split the hard, bony palate above it before boring into the creature's brain.

Slither-Tail stiffened, in shock. A shudder rolled down its spine like an ocean swell journeying toward land. The convulsions set in. The churning and writhing and frothing. The beast thrashed its head—enraged, demented—in a final effort to dislodge the spear pinning shut its mouth.

Yet the Shepherd's bone spear held.

Jaspen grinned to himself. Today, the Cove in his care would eat.

The fish's gaze wheeled from side to side, then up, and down. Its fins twitched. Gills opened and shut. The nostrils pinched and the body swayed gently, gracefully . . . powerless. Slowly, Slither-Tail halted all movement and began to sink. Vines of blood crawled from its mouth to twine around the spear before the current swept them away like smoke in a breeze.

The first of the scavenging mob arrived as Jaspen had forecast. The feeding frenzy began at once, the hungry legion stripping away great swaths of flesh and fin, and tongue and entrails, as Slither-Tail descended into the shadows of the sea, its heart still beating, its black eyes still broad with dread.

The boy loosed a fearsome cry of victory into the sea; a howling call alerting all within earshot that the largest Slither-Tail in the whole of the sea had fallen victim to the bone spear and pearl knife wielded by Jirvalla's one and only Shepherd of Fish.

3

Kama

KAMA DREW A DEEP breath and pressed her shoulders, back, buttocks, and calves into the rough trunk of an Arrow Bark tree.

Her younger brother, Shim, counted, "Six, seven, eight . . . " both hands covering his eyes.

Kama focused all of her attention on absorbing the balmy warmth of the bark, willing the rich, brown color and saw-toothed grain to flow into her.

" . . . nine, ten!" Shim's eyes sprang open. "Ready or not, here I come!"

As her brother spun around, Kama pushed her back and legs deeper into the tree. She looked down and smiled. She had done it again! For the second time this morning, Kama had urged her flesh to take on the exact hue and texture of the Arrow Bark tree. With rigorous practice, and many seasons of study, Kama could very well become a Cloaker.

Kama watched, grinning, as Shim prowled about for his quarry, keeping his footsteps soft and breathing shallow, like Night-Stripes on the hunt. And when Shim's little, tanned feet dented the sand an arm's length from Kama, she snickered.

"Ha!" Shim whirled toward the noise. "I'm gonna fiiinnd yooouu," he caroled, but looked right past his sister into the trees and huts behind her. "I can heeeaaarr you." He placed his hand on the tree, but a finger's breadth from Kama.

Smiling to herself, Kama locked on to her brother's hand.

"Yaaaaaa!" howled Shim, straining to pull his hand away. "The tree's eating me! Help! Kama! Heeelllp! Mom! Mohhhmm!"

Kama stepped away from the tree, laughing as her natural honey-colored skin, dark brown hair, and green eyes returned. "You're such a *waigu* little brother!" she chuckled. "Crying out for your Mommy like baby Azo over there."

"No I wasn't! I was just . . . pretending. Saw you the whole time."

"Okay *waigu*, whatever you say."

"I did! I was only playing like I didn't see you so— Jaspen!" Shim brightened at the sight of the Shepherd of Fish emerging from the sea with an overflowing basket, shimmering and wriggling with the sea's bounty.

Kama rested against the tree and crossed her arms as hungry children rushed in from every direction to swarm Jaspen like a hive of Stinging-Red-Legs.

"Come here you nasty, little sand-biters!" roared Jaspen, chasing them. "Born of Slither-Bellies, you are. Slither-Bellies and Side-Walkers!"

Jaspen pushed and pulled and taunted the children to their great delight. Catching Shim, he held the child to the sand and patted the little one's tummy.

"Mmmm," Jaspen licked his lips as Shim squealed with mirth. "Salt-ed Cove boy, yum!" Jaspen flashed a wild grin before playfully nipping at Shim's belly.

Charmed by Jaspen's antics, Kama reminisced about the days when he used to play with her like that, just eight moons ago. But over the past three seasons so much had changed, Jaspen growing taller and stronger, and Kama maturing into a lovely young woman.

She angled toward the children, anxious to speak with Jaspen. It had only been one round moon since he had buried Widow Yadha—the childless healer who had found Jaspen the day he had washed up, alone, on Jirvallan shores. The widow had raised Jaspen, from toddler to young man, as if he were her very own. Soon after the old woman's death ritual, Jaspen had built his own dwelling nearer the sea. Kama missed Jaspen living next door. For fourteen rainy seasons, she and Jaspen had spent nearly every day together—exploring, laughing, fighting—and Kama hated how infrequently she saw Jaspen since he had moved away.

Kama allowed Jaspen and the children to frolic for a while longer before clapping her hands.

"That's enough, now," she said, tugging children off Jaspen. "Time to choose your meals, little Covies."

She glanced at Jaspen, smiling, taking note of the thin streams of blood oozing from the sea leaves wrapped about his thigh. Kama was not overly concerned. Neither was she troubled about the crimson smears on his chest and arms. This morning's injuries were not much worse than usual. A rare day it was when Jaspen returned unscathed from shepherding fish.

"Go on," said Kama to the children and sent them to the basket of fish, their colorful scales glistening in the island sun.

"Cowards!" Jaspen called after his retreating attackers. "Like frightened baby Rope-Tails, you are. Scurry away, now. Scurry, scurry!" He grinned at Kama and approached her. "Hallo hay, Kama." He extended an arm, his flat palm facing her.

"Hallo hay, Jaspen." She pressed the back of her hand to his palm and let it rest there, enjoying his touch while peering into his smiling eyes.

While Kama's gaze inspected the Shepherd's many wounds, Jaspen caught himself gazing into the girl's soft face and wishing she would lift her green eyes, the color of a new leaf. His heart was sprinting and he fought the impulse to caress her tanned shoulder. To let his fingers play with her hair. To press his cheek to hers and feel her warmth.

What's happening to me? he thought.

How he missed the days when he would wrestle Kama to the sand or toss her into the sea. A part of him hated that she was growing up and becoming so pretty. Another part wished he were brave enough to obtain the blessing from Kama's parents that would allow him to court Kama properly and, perhaps, one day even ask her to become his dwelling-mate, his Forever-One.

"Come on." Kama took Jaspen's elbow and pulled him toward her family's hut. "Mother hasn't stopped talking of you since the day you moved away." She peeked back over her shoulder, flirtatious at first, then glanced again at the grated flesh on Jaspen's legs, chest, hands, and arms.

"What?" Jaspen hid his bloodied forearms and knuckles behind him.

Kama rolled her eyes. "Who was it this time? Little Gold-Fins?" She spread her thumb and forefinger to indicate the size of the fish. "Or did you swim into a rock again?"

Jaspen squinted at her and showed a small smile. "It was just Levaioth."

"*Just* Levaioth?"

"I stabbed out his seven eyes and cut from him three of his black hearts."

"Levaioth would swallow you whole."

"How else do you imagine I got to his hearts?"

Kama laughed until Jaspen spun her around and snaked his arm around her throat, a playful headlock.

"Would you like me to show you how I accomplished it?" He drew his pearl knife and pressed it softly to Kama's chest. "Perhaps your heart is as black as Levaioth's? Shall we find out?"

Reveling in the heat of Kama's back pressed against his torso, her soft throat against his upper arm, Jaspen closed his eyes and quietly took the scent of her hair into his nose—his heart speeding.

"Take it," sighed Kama, "It's all yours. It always has been."

"Jaspen!" Shim approached, struggling to walk while holding a large, writhing fish. "Are you eating with us tonight? At MoonFeast? Pleeeeease say yes!"

"I don't know, Shim," said Kama, still locked in Jaspen's hold. "There might not be room at the tabl—" Kama stamped on Jaspen's foot, escaped his grip, hooked her ankle around his and shoved him to the sand. "For slowpokes anyway!" and she sprinted for her family's hut, Jaspen just two strides behind.

4

Sun-Side Tribes

"How is it, young shepherd," asked Kama's father, "that you were so near to *ten* Huntressi yet none impaled you with their fabled arrows? Are they not savages?"

"I was veiled from their view, elder Kogobod," answered Jaspen while sipping coral-grass tea with Kama and her parents in the family's small hut. "Behind a sea boulder, I was. One thick with reeking Bark-Fins." He sniffed. "I smell them still."

Two round moons ago, a pair of officials from the Hall of Shells had arrived at the hut where Jaspen had been dwelling with Widow Yadha, only eighteen suns prior to her passing. The men, Quillen and Ertu, were well known to both Jaspen and his caretaker. For each of the kindly officials had made a practice of visiting the impoverished healer and her adopted son at least once each moon since the Day-Night Cove (the name by which many called Jaspen) had mysteriously appeared upon Jirvallan shores. Quillen and Ertu had always been kind, generous, and friendly. On this instance, the two men had come to ask Jaspen a favor; to measure the boy's interest in scouting every shore, sandbar, beach, watchtower, and harbor residing on the island—for the good of Jirvalla, for the good of the Cove.

Jaspen had agreed to complete the task with two conditions. One: upon his return, Jaspen had made Quillen and Ertu promise to send the royal physician to evaluate (and improve, if possible) Widow Yadha's troubled health. And two: Jaspen would assess the coastlands only if he could do so from an offshore position. For the Shepherd of Fish did not trust his natural stealth in the ocean would translate to land.

The royal officials had acquiesced, thrilled. Jaspen's assignment was to gather cultural insights and heed anything that could be construed as battle preparations. He was also to tell them of any large building projects that were within his line of sight from the sea.

"But judging from what I have seen of the Huntressi," said Jaspen to Kogobod, "those women—as fierce as they seem—love their children no less than any Cove father or mother loves theirs."

The Huntressi tribe ruled the island's northern beachlands. The warrior race, comprised wholly of dark-skinned females, also governed a third of the isle's western coast. They were known to be fearless hunters, next to invincible in combat, and experts with knives, bows, and the long-spear.

"This is welcome news." Kama's father grinned. "We Cove rarely hear of the Huntressi's goodness. Only of their ruthless battle tactics and merciless cruelty."

It had taken Jaspen, swimming at the steady pace of a Spike-Tail, three full suns to circuit the island. He had spent two nights at sea, slumbering in concavities of ocean boulders, a stone's throw from shore.

Jaspen had reported to the Hall of Shells that just over half of Jirvalla's perimeter was composed of white-, pink-, or red-sand beaches. Three shores had golden sands, two beaches were black-pebbled, and one shined with clear gems that sparkled when sunlight filled them. Between the bays, coves, and sweeping dunes were bone-colored sea bluffs, gray-bouldered tidelands, jungle shrubbery, and vast stretches of rocky shoreline where deep-green trees stepped down sheer cliffs to plant their roots into the gritty mud of high-tide waters.

Both Quillen and Ertu had been pleased to discover that Jaspen had not encountered anything that could be deciphered as battle training.

Jaspen smiled casually at Kama then said to Kogobod, "I saw also five Udok."

"You did not!" cried Kama while Kogobod's eyes grew nearly as wide as his mouth.

The Udok were the tribe of which the Cove saw least. Though the half-giants possessed the land just beyond the Cove's northwestern boundary, they spent the bulk of their time near Smoke Mountain, either in the Flame Lands or Emberblack; both a long journey from Cove beaches. Baggy fleshed and bald headed, Udok males were at least an arm's length taller and wider than the largest of Cove men. Each could tear a fully grown tree from its earthen nest—roots and all.

"They are as strong and massive as you imagine them to be," said Jaspen.

"But still no match for you," Kama grinned at Jaspen then explained to her father: "Earlier today, Jaspen stabbed out three of Levaioth's black hearts."

Jaspen squinted at Kama, only to get lost again in her leaf-green eyes.

"And what of our allies?" asked Kogobod. "Any events of note among the Treef and Faijen?"

Jaspen shook off the pleasantly numb stupor that so often resulted when his eyes bonded to Kama's intoxicating, green gaze.

"Nothing remarkable," said Jaspen.

The Cove had been allied with the Treef and Faijen for generations. The pact between the three tribes came in response to an earlier peace accord struck between the Huntressi and Udok.

The Treef were a tall, thin insectile race ranging in color from yellow to green to brown to black. Each Treef had bulbous, black eyes, a naturally armored thorax, and at least one sharp, cutting pincer. They inhabited the majority of Listening Hoof Wood, which bordered Cove land to the north. The fertile timberlands sprawled from east to west to cover almost one-fifth of Jirvalla.

Jaspen was happy to have been found by a Cove woman instead of a Treef all those moons ago, when alighting upon Jirvallan shores for his first time. He could not imagine living without the ocean near. The lengthy strip of beach where the Cove lived along Jirvalla's southeastern edge was ideal for the Shepherd. The Huntressi were the island's only other tribe who dwelled upon a sandy seashore. Their lands on the isle's northwestern coast were very similar in size and shape to Cove territory. Both tracts required a full day's walk to cross, from their eastern edge to their western border.

The Cove's other allies, the Faijen, were a small, aquatic race who commanded the lands from the base of Mount Everwater all the way up to its summit. That is where the Croaking Throat Lakes fed Jirvallans with the island's largest source of fresh water. The Faijen also reigned over the six rivers that sprang from the Croaking Throat Lakes to flow down Mount Everwater in all directions. Most Faijen fluctuated between shades of blue and green, depending how the light played upon them. Yet a small number were the color of clean water cupped in the hand—nearly invisible—with just a hint of turquoise. Each Faijen boasted a pair of gauzy, transparent wings on their backs and another smaller pair jutting from each ankle. Though most of the proud race were as thin as a toddler's arm and grew to heights no taller than a Cove man's hip, the Faijen believed themselves to be superior to all other Jirvallan tribes.

The island's sixth tribe was the Gort. They belonged to the Under-Down and ventured sun-side only to traffic their prized steel blades—swords, daggers, axes—along with finely crafted jewelry, studded with gemstones. The Gort yoked themselves with neither the Udok and Huntressi nor the Cove, Treef and Faijen, fearing a pact with either allied force would hinder trade with the other.

5

MoonFeast

JASPEN, KAMA, SHIM, AND a few dozen others from their poor village crowded around a long, wooden table. Each gazed in awe at the platters heaped high with sumptuous fish, wild game, fresh fruit, vegetables, nuts, juice, and island wine.

"Let us bow our heads and pray," said Old Man Tuttum.

The villagers closed their eyes and joined hands, solemn. When Jaspen's fingers met Kama's, a tingle rushed through him.

Tuttum began, "All praise to you, Levaioth, god of Jirvalla."

Jaspen unshut his eyes and raised his chin. Disquiet creased his face.

"You, Levaioth, and only you," continued Tuttum, "prevent the sea from rising to overwhelm our lands and huts. You alone, Levaioth, graciously provide us with sustenance from your bountiful waters."

Through clenched teeth, Jaspen whispered to Kama, "Levaioth is no god. He is but a stupid fish. A big, ugly one."

"Shh!" Kama reproved him with a sidelong look.

"Each of us offers to you thanksgiving," said Old Man Tuttum, "for your many gifts to the Cove." He raised his open palms. "We stand as one in a show of respect for your power. We ask that you receive the *polog* we are to present to you on the morrow as a blood-tithe."

The eyes of nine men at the table sprang open at the mention of the word *polog*. There had not been a blood sacrifice offered to Levaioth for six seasons. Each gaze consulted the others, hoping to earn a hint as to why the Cove had reinstated the hideous ritual.

"And we pray," resumed Tuttum, "that the *polog* quenches your lust and earns for our tribe your abundant mercy for yet another moon. All praise to Levaioth!"

The villagers refrained, "All praise to Levaioth!"

All save Jaspen.

Tuttum smiled a wide, gap-toothed grin and cried, "Let MoonFeast begin!"

The natives cheered and the chaos of burdening plates with provender and wooden goblets with various spirits ensued. Stomachs were filled, songs were sung, and jokes were told. Toasts were proposed, pipes were smoked, legends recounted, and sly endeavors by young boys to sneak sips of island wine were met with sneers from their mothers and encouraging winks by their fathers.

Jaspen and Kama fell into easy converse, as in seasons past. Yet whenever Jaspen's elbow or knee grazed that of Kama's, a flare would ignite in the Shepherd's heart and a few seconds of nervous silence would build between them.

Toward the finish of the festivities, as the sun plunged deeper into the sea, a rustling of what sounded like a small army in the nearby forest drew every villager's eye. Apprehensive, men rose from their benches . . . until the familiar report of the royal conches, heralding the arrival of the Mutahn's court, eased their agitation.

A dozen emissaries from the Hall of Shells, Cove tribe's royal residence, stepped out of the forest to advance upon the MoonFeast.

Children's mouths fell agape with wonder at the regal attire. The bare-chested delegates were accoutered in feathered leggings, kilts of sea reeds and palm fronds, thick sashes of vibrant fish scales, pearl headdresses, animal-tooth necklaces, and bracelets of bone, coral, and shell. Four of them—the warriors—each bore a curved shield forged from the hard sheath of a large Shell-Back. Their sharp, Gort swords glistened in the torchlight and failing sun.

Kama's face lit and her head swiveled in every direction, her sharp eyes casting about in a wild quest for something.

"What is it?" asked Jaspen, drawing his pearl knife. "What do you—"

"There! I knew it!"

Jaspen looked to where Kama's eyes were fixed, his dagger at the ready.

"Do you see him?" Kama indicated a boulder rising from the earth where the thinning forest rimmed the beach. "The gray stone."

Jaspen squinted. "I spy only a boulder. And trees beyond."

"Come on, Two-Tone. Look harder. At the rock, where light and shadow meet."

Jaspen peered closer and finally spotted a royal Cloaker with his back and arms pressed against the large, gray stone. He was nearly invisible.

"Amazing." Kama studied the Cloaker. "Perfect coloring. And his texture work . . . Incredible."

She grinned and it was evident that Kama was dreaming of the day when she would be invited to join the Mutahn's esteemed league of royal Cloakers—a covert group exclusive to the Cove. One that has, thus far, remained secret from all of Jirvalla's other tribes, even their allies.

"Hallo! Hallo! Hallo!" cried the messenger as he rattled a hollowed-out gourd half-filled with shells and pebbles. "Tidings from the Hall of Shells."

Jaspen and Kama turned to the herald. Flanking him were a conch blower, a scribe, and a pair of sword-wielding guards. Sorazin, the Mutahn's sole heir, puffed his chest to stand tall and proud beside the others.

"Today," cried the messenger, "at five hands from sunset, Mutahn Pehlni breathed his last."

Gasps rose, eyes misted, and women tugged their Forever-Ones closer.

Jaspen bowed his chin in commiseration then raised his eyes to Sorazin. The Mutahn's son had the wide shoulders, dark hair, and sharp nose of his father while the intense eyes and pompous smile were those of his mother. Though he was born just two rainy seasons prior to Jaspen's appearance on Jirvallan shores, Sorazin was much, much larger than Jaspen.

As children, Jaspen and Sorazin had encountered each other but a half-dozen times. Each meeting saw them at odds. Sorazin ridiculed Jaspen for his unusual coloring and affection for the sea. Jaspen usually ignored Sorazin's taunts of 'outcast', 'interloper' and *mahkifo*, the Jirvallan word for the dirt-brown sea foam that often blew in with hurricanes. They had fought once, five wet seasons ago, the battle-trained Sorazin narrowly defeating his smaller opponent.

Despite their past, Jaspen looked with compassion upon Sorazin. He had buried his own stepmother recently and was acquainted with the pain and confusing loss Sorazin must be bearing at this moment.

"Evidence suggests a natural death," the herald continued. "The Mutahn passed in his sleep."

It had been twenty round moons since Mutahn Pehlni lost his wife to the shivering sickness. His mounting heartbreak had become more and more blatant with each setting sun.

"Messengers have been dispatched to inform our allies. The Hoodoah has also been consulted," resumed the herald. "He has agreed to elect a new Mutahn on the morrow by sunfall. For those unfamiliar with the ancient canon, any Cove with at least two hundred moons is permitted to seek the Throne of Pearls. Candidates wishing to be considered are to gather at Three Rocks immediately following tomorrow's blood-tithe. If none wish to vie for the position, island law stipulates the former Mutahn's eldest son will ascend to our royal throne."

Sorazin's eyebrow jumped and he showed an arrogant smile.

The messenger stepped back, clasped his hands behind him, and held the gaze of each village elder for a few moments—as was the custom for inviting inquiries from the villagers.

When none spoke, the messenger clapped his hands twice and bowed his head. "May the favor of Levaioth be with us all."

6

Levaioth

TWO THARSOOL WERE BINDING a young, dark-skinned girl to a wooden post that rose from the tip of a long, crude, timber pier, a few arm lengths above the sea.

"She has fight, this one, I will give her that," said one Tharsool to the other, struggling to fetter the girl's legs to the place they called The Thumb. "Levaioth will be well pleased with her."

The holy man peered upward and to the sea, due east, where a morning sun hung low in the sky. He closed his eyes to its warmth, its brilliant rays.

"If only she knew the blessing it is to be chosen as *polog*." The other Tharsool rubbed his neck, fingers pausing to examine the red, diamond-shaped tattoo beneath his left ear—the mark identifying him as a member of the Cove's priestly class. "I often dream, brother, of the lot falling to me." A faraway look washed over him. "Oh! to be the blood-tithe . . . and become one with our great Levaioth!"

"*Pir sont dizzen!*" The girl spat at one Tharsool then the other.

"One cannot blame her. She is Huntressi. Spirited they are."

The pair finished securing the girl to The Thumb and turned to shore.

Hundreds of Cove were huddled on beach sands and along the forest's edge, watching the *polog* wage war with her bonds, sweat glistening on her dark face, bare shoulders, abdomen, and thighs.

The two Tharsool returned to the beach to kneel in prayer beside forty of their brethren.

Soon, the chanting began. The eerie drums. The haunting monotone voices calling for Levaioth to honor them with his mighty presence. And approve of the blood-tithe by devouring the girl completely.

Kama was mimicking the packed mud, twigs, shells, and leaves that made up the interior walls of Jaspen's hut. She watched, smiling, as Jaspen slumbered, recalling with fondness the many times they had napped together. How she missed the silly stories they would tell. The laughing and singing, just the pair of them. And curling up into his warm flesh. Kama leaned in close and breathed deep Jaspen's wonderful sea-scent. Her eyes wandered the dusky black of his back into the strip where his color lightened to gray then grew paler until fading into the creamy hue of his front. So fascinating. So beautiful.

He looked a bit like a sleeping child, even with the new muscles that rippled along his neck, shoulders, arms, and chest. Kama could have spied on him all morning, mesmerized by the steady rhythm of his torso rising and falling with each breath. She might have stayed there forever had it not been The Day. The Day after the round moon. The Day of the newly restored blood-tithe ceremony.

"Jaspen, come on!" said Kama from her camouflaged post along the wall. "Get up you lazy *waigu*. It's almost time."

Jaspen moaned and pulled the animal-fur cover to his chin before rolling over.

"Hoy, Two-Tone! The *polog* walks already." Kama edged along the wall while keeping her many textures and colors intact, no easy feat. "Up with you, quick! Before Levaioth arrives!" She nudged him with her foot. "If you miss the blood-tithe, they'll blame you for any poor fishing."

"Levaioth . . ." Jaspen's eyes struggled open. "That monster does not provide our meals, I do." He snorted and reached for a pot of urchin oil on the shelf next to his sleeping pallet. "Tell me, Cloaker," he worked the healing unguent into the many cuts and bruises over his arms and thighs, "if I were to kill that ugly sea-beast"—he grinned as his eyes hunted for Kama—"what reward would I earn?"

"You can't kill a god."

Jaspen's gaze shot to the spot from where Kama's voice had come. But she had swiftly ducked and stretched upon the ground, her flesh now the exact tint and texture of the hut's swept-dirt floor.

"If Levaioth is a god then so is Wide-Eye and Slither-Tail." Jaspen paced to where he believed Kama was hiding. "There is only one true god." He ran a hand over the wall, feeling for her. "And he isn't a stupid fish."

Kama stole silently across the floor to the wall opposite Jaspen. She stood and whispered, "Tell me about your god," then dropped again to the floor, her color and texture shifting as her body passed from wall to floor.

Jaspen whirled towards her voice but failed to see her. "I call my god the Always. Because he has always been and will always be." He inched toward Kama, eyes darting. "The Always has been alive forever . . ." Jaspen's nose twitched, clearly striving to catch her scent, " . . . and he will never taste death."

On the floor near Jaspen's approaching feet, Kama held her breath.

"The Always created first the sea and everything in it." Jaspen's eyes and nose continued to prowl. "And the mere width of his smallest finger spans the lowermost depths to the high-most waves. After finishing the ocean . . . "

Kama arched her ribs away from Jaspen's nearing toes.

" . . . the Always sighed in satisfaction, pleased with his achievement—"

He turned quickly toward a sound. Yet it was only an ornery limb from an outside tree, conspiring with Kama to distract her pursuer.

"And from his breath," continued Jaspen, "the sky and everything in it was born."

As Jaspen's feet loomed nearer, Kama squashed her back even further into the angle where floor met wall.

"Then the Always took a part of the sun and a part of the moon and he molded them together. He packed and stretched them until they became one firm, dry mass. He cast it upon the waters and called it land."

The words settled soft and beautiful in Kama's ear. They seemed ancient and mystical, from another world, yet somehow familiar.

"The Always dressed the land with mountains, valleys, forests, and flowers. He filled it with every animal that lives upon its rocks and peaks and woodlands and plains. And he loves each and every one of his creatures, feeding them with rain and berries and roots and seeds. He warms them with the sun and cools them with his sweet breath—the island breeze."

A murmur of pleasure escaped Kama's lips.

Jaspen yanked his face toward the sound. "But the Always saved his greatest creation for last: us—the Cove and Udok, the Huntressi and Gort, the Treef and Faijen, as well as my kind." He squatted down, slow and quiet. "To create such wonderful creatures, the Always reached deep into his heart and pulled from it a small sliver. He mixed this part of himself with island sand and ocean spray to shape the very first of our island kin."

Rapt by the words, Kama closed her eyes and a warm tranquility overtook her.

"And even today," said Jaspen, "the Always places a piece of his heart into every new member of every tribe that makes any of the Jirvallan isles their home."

Though Kama could sense Jaspen's soft steps drawing nearer, she remained in place, spellbound by the elegant beauty of the words from Jaspen's mouth.

"That is why the Always loves us more than all else," said Jaspen. "Because only we have a small share of the Always inside of— Gotcha!"

Kama's eyes flung open at Jaspen's touch.

He plucked Kama from the floor and stood, cradling her in his arms.

Without her hands or feet or back upon the floor, Kama's natural colors returned. Her grass skirt and top of woven reeds also took back their native hues.

Kama gazed into Jaspen's face, smiling. Catching herself, she pulled her eyes away and hopped down from his arms, embarrassed.

"I l-like your god," she said, brushing dirt from her hands, her top and skirt. "Where did you learn of the Always?"

Blushing too, Jaspen cleared his throat. "I have tried but cannot recall. Perhaps the Always told me of himself in dreams. Or my parents taught me of him before the sea snatched me away and set me upon Jirvalla. In my heart, however, I know the Always to be true."

"Why do you suppose your god made you like that and me like this?"

"The Always makes each of us different so that one person or tribe can do what another cannot. The Always wants us to have need of each other."

Kama nodded and gestured for Jaspen to follow her outside.

"The bigger the differences, the stronger the village," said Jaspen.

He gnashed his teeth at the sight of two Tharsool binding a young Huntressi to The Thumb. The long pier upon which they stood was but a short walk from where Jaspen, Kama, and the rest of their poor village had celebrated Moonfeast last night.

"Do you find her beautiful?" Kama studied the tall girl straining at her bonds.

The drums of the Tharsool began.

Jaspen's face hitched at the sound. "What does it matter? She will be among the dead before the sun is two hands high."

"We better go."

Jaspen shook his head.

"There are rules, you know." Kama folded her thin, tanned arms.

"I will no longer pretend to believe in something I do not."

"If you don't come, they—"

"We would not arrive in time anyway."

"What are you talking about? Levaioth isn't anywhere near—"

"Even now, he comes." Keeping his eyes on the pier, Jaspen waved a lazy hand towards the ocean behind him.

Detecting a slight ripple, far offshore, forming upon the ocean's surface, Kama said, "That's only wind. If it really was—"

A monstrous, black tail—the shape of a crescent moon—emerged from the sea. It rose higher and higher, craggy and moth-eaten, like a mammoth Cave-Wing soaring upward.

"Levaioth . . . " Kama whispered, shivering with fear.

7

Three Rocks

THE PLACE WHERE THE Thumb and *polog* had once stood was now only ocean. Levaioth had decimated more than half the pier. A late-morning sun blazed its rays on chips of timber that were scattered across the sea-top like crushed leaves on a forest floor.

From the foot of the splintered pier, Sorazin shielded his eyes against a bright, late-morning sun and grinned at the destruction. *If only I had such power as Levaioth's,* thought the son of the deceased Mutahn, *how they would respect me then.*

The royal conch sounded, followed by a trio of loud handclaps.

"Hallo, Hallo, Hallo!" cried the herald. "Those wishing to seek the throne seat of Cove tribe are to show themselves at Three Rocks without delay."

Sorazin strode to Three Rocks to find four others who deemed themselves worthy of the Throne of Pearls. He gauged his competition: a gray-bearded elder, an overfed Tharsool, a lowly farmer, and a pathetic flute-carver who spent his days singing to the forest plants and animals. Sorazin swelled with confidence, his superiority clear.

The herald arrived. He scrutinized each of the Mutahn applicants with care, thoroughly, judging them in silence. His stern manner gave away nothing. Unimpressed, he shook his head and heaved a heavy sigh.

"The journey to the Hoodoah's dwelling-place is renowned for its treachery." The herald was marching now, back and forth, before the seekers. "Many a life has been made forfeit along the route; to sinking-sands, to forest beasts, to iron-jawed traps, and abduction by the Gort."

He halted before the over-bellied Tharsool. "Most of you," he scanned the holy man, up and down, in plain disapproval, "lack the *physical* wherewithal or mental dexterity to survive this quest."

Leaning in closer, the herald fixed the priest with a steely gaze.

"Those deficient in either category," the herald drew back a finger and flicked the Tharsool's paunchy stomach, "should they choose to continue, will likely suffer an excruciating death."

Kama elbowed Jaspen, her eyes bright. She had convinced him that it would be a grand adventure to follow the Mutahn hopefuls to their destination.

Come on! she had pleaded. *It'll be like old times!* referring to their many former travels—into enemy lands even—when they were younger. She was also eager to sharpen her cloaking skills while trailing the Mutahn aspirants.

They looked on, along with a few dozen others, as the herald continued to torment the abdominous Tharsool.

Clasping his hands behind him, the herald tipped forward until his nose was nearly one with the Tharsool's. "Do I make myself clear?" he asked.

The priest broke. Smiling meekly, he swabbed away the growing pools of perspiration on his brow and stepped back, bowing his head, to vanish among the crowd.

Sorazin snickered, drawing the herald's ire.

The herald approached the youth. Appraising Sorazin, his eyes stopped at the sword lashed to the handsome young man's waist.

"How numberless the calamities wrought by the blade of a fool who knows not when to sheathe it." His grim stare bored into Sorazin's haughty face.

Yet Sorazin simply lifted his chin and grinned, as if he had already won the Cove's coveted throne seat.

"Dismiss him!" grumbled Kama, unable to suppress her acrimony for the brash son of the Cove's deceased ruler. "He's no Mutahn," she whispered. "Throw him out!"

Though if island tradition bore any weight at all, Sorazin—as the former Mutahn's son—would return from the Hoodoah's dwelling-place as the tribe's ruler.

The herald shook his head at Sorazin and paced to the aged graybeard.

"The all-wise Quillen." The herald smiled.

Quillen dipped his face in respect.

"If only you had as much muscle and vigor as wisdom, old man, the Throne of Pearls would surely be yours. But your back stoops, your knees creak, and your shoulders sag. And if, by the narrowest of chances, you survive the forest, the seawall will not be so kind. Reconsider, please, my friend, and live to enjoy another moon by my side."

The pair held an extended stare.

Quillen refused to relent.

"Fine." The herald backed away from the wise man to survey the throne seekers a final time. "Your blood will not be on my hands."

Treading to the water's edge, the herald made a show of thoroughly washing his palms, knuckles, wrists, and each individual finger in the sea.

Returning to the contenders, the herald said, "The Hoodoah's cave lay in that direction." His limp hand implied that the dwelling could be found somewhere to the east or north. Then, bowing, he said, "May the favor of Levaioth be with us all."

8

Sorazin

IT HAD BEEN TWO hands since the Mutahn hopefuls had set out in search of the Hoodoah's cave. Sorazin had been quiet, using the time to secretly estimate the strengths and weaknesses of his competitors.

He concluded that Fuertl, the farmer, was the lone adversary with a modicum of courage and sense. He was also the sole challenger accustomed to killing. Fuertl had battled only animals, the largest being Black-Claw, for devouring his livestock. But at least the farmer knew the importance of lethal force.

"My condolences, Sorazin." It was the old man, the so-called sage; Quillen.

Another half-witted peacemaker, thought Sorazin (for Quillen's pacifistic views were known throughout the isle). *A weakling too fearful to fight.*

"Your father was a good man," said Quillen. "A worthy Mutahn with a calm and even hand."

"Too calm in my view," said Sorazin.

"Is that right? How so?"

"For all my life I have watched you men of peace fight with words and treaties when swords and spears would have achieved a better result."

Quillen spent a few moments to weigh Sorazin's perspective. "You are angry. Your father, and hero, is dead. When grief is new, it can feel much like wrath. Your emotions are understandable, Sorazin, expected even. Your rage will pass."

"I hope not, old sage. When rage is virtuous, as is mine, it becomes the foundation upon which kingdoms are built."

Quillen's brow furrowed. "If you imply that war is a better builder of societies than peace, then I could not disagree more, Sorazin. For it is only peacetime that can breed—"

"Peacetime breeds only fools. Minstrels, poets, and painters. Sluggards, all. Men at truce are idle, wise Quillen. Prone to drink too much and hunt too little. Even we who have not yet earned the title of 'sage' are clever enough to know that a tribe that lacks conflict is a tribe that grows soft."

Quillen turned the idea over, taking his time. "Since your birth, Sorazin, you have only experienced the false promises, fruitless deliberations, and unsigned treaties of our island's brittle peace. For one born into our history during such an age, your frustration is sensible. Yet even those with but a few moons recognize that Jirvalla's current state of fragile calm is much preferred to war. Do you not agree?"

"No. It is my conviction that brittle peace is no peace at all. Because at the boundary of our imagined security, fear prowls. To me and others who have but a *few moons*, the lukewarm stench of your fragile calm is unbearable."

Quillen frowned, perplexed. In time, he said: "I have lived through times of peace and times of war as well as through this delicate state in which our tribe now finds itself. My life, so far, has taught me that any type of peace, no matter how feeble, is vastly superior to the rampant slaughter of innocent life . . . to the combat-torn faces of young soldiers. If the echoing cries of children who have lost their brothers, their fathers, had ever reached your ear, Sorazin, then you, too, would agree that even the faintest peace is worth protecting."

Spoken like a true coward, thought Sorazin, then said: "To each his own."

"I am also quite certain, dear boy, that if the Cove finish what your father began, Jirvalla will once again see island-wide peace. True peace. Lasting peace. Though it may not appear so, progress is being made. This I assure you."

"What you call progress, sage, I call decay. It is not peace that goads men to greatness. It is contention. There is nothing like war to make men of boys. To spur the strong to become stronger still. It has been too many seasons since a warrior has graced the Throne of Pearls. You men of peace have had your day. And accomplished nil."

Sorazin's neck rouged with rage. Drawing a breath, he checked his wrath.

He smiled at Quillen. "I trust that my youthful enthusiasm has not given you the wrong impression, good sage. I am young and learning still to tame my passions. Though our philosophies are at odds, dear Quillen, I respect your dogmata, as antiquated as I believe it to be." He placed a friendly hand on the old man's back. "I intend no disrespect and hope my opinions have not offended you."

That should still his suspicions, thought Sorazin.

For later this day, he might be coerced into cutting Quillen's throat. If the sage exhibited the qualities of a Mutahn, Sorazin could not chance a miscalculation by the unpredictable Hoodoah.

For reasons Sorazin did not understand, nor respect, an ancient mandate had granted Cove tribe's spiritual authority—the Hoodoah— the exclusive power to elect the tribe's incoming Mutahn. It had been this way since the days of old and it vexed Sorazin that none had been bold or wise enough to question the superstitious practice.

How fortunate for the Cove, thought Sorazin, *that I love them so much.*

To rescue his tribe from an unworthy ruler, from certain annihilation, Sorazin would place himself in harm's way to dispatch Quillen. For the sake of the Cove.

"Enough with politics, good Quillen," said Sorazin. "Let us move on to other subjects. I understand you were close to my father."

"We were, yes." He grinned. "It does not seem so long ago that he and I were treading these very paths together."

Sorazin hated Quillen's earnest smile, his false humility.

"I was in your father's company when the Hoodoah chose him, instead of me, as Mutahn." Quillen stroked his beard. "She made the right choice, the Hoodoah. I was unprepared at the time to represent the Cove as their sovereign."

"I admire your courage," Sorazin lied. "To contend for the throne twice. Are you not concerned about a second failure?" He repressed a snicker. "To return defeated, again, might very well threaten your standing as village sage."

Quillen chuckled. "I am far too old to concern myself with how others judge me, Sorazin. Besides," he smiled at the young man, "the Hoodoah invited me to return. After I had grown a beard and watched it turn silver."

9

Huntressi Arrows

KAMA PRESSED HER TORSO and hips into Jaspen's back, driving the Shepherd's chest, stomach, and thighs deeper into the rough bark of a tree trunk.

"It's not working!" huffed Kama. "Look." Her finger indicated the light strip of Jaspen's flesh running down his side that Kama was too thin to obscure. "A blind man could spot you!" She stepped back, her tree-like color and texture fading back into her natural flesh. "If only I were fatter."

"They won't see us." Jaspen turned to face her, his back to the tree. "They are so far off it would—"

"Cloakers save hostages, Jaspen. We sneak them out of enemy camps. Unseen, Jaspen. *Un*-seen. If I can't even hide you, then—"

"Shhh!" Jaspen pulled her close. "Cloak me!" he whispered. "Quick!" He canted his chin toward a fallen log but twenty-five paces away.

Kama swiftly pushed her chest and thighs into Jaspen's, her color and texture becoming as bark.

A young Huntressi, with a bow and quiver of arrows strapped to her back, squatted behind the fallen tree. Her braids, tight to her head, were as dark as a moonless night and her skin just a shade lighter. The girl's eyes burned with fury as they glared at the Mutahn hopefuls. Slowly, she stood, hunched, and crept closer to Sorazin, Quillen, and the others, exploiting the trees and brush as cover.

Though an experienced Cloaker would have had their eyes spread wide, studying the Huntressi, Kama's were closed. It had been many moons since she had felt Jaspen's chest against hers, their hips as one,

their waists locked and their cheeks pressed so tightly together. The pre-
eminent thought of an experienced Cloaker would have related to mask-
ing their charge. Kama's one all-consuming thought, however, was how
she could furtively roll her mouth to Jaspen's. His lips were so near.

"Kama," whispered Jaspen.

She smiled, far away, her neck tingling at the sound of her name on
Jaspen's tongue.

"Kama!" he repeated, louder this time.

The volume of Jaspen's voice jolted Kama from her reverie.

"I can't see her," said Jaspen. "Slide over."

"Oh," Kama blinked, clinging to her dream. "See . . . who?"

"The Huntressi!" Jaspen bobbed his chin toward the girl.

"Right. Yeah. I know." Kama spotted the girl and the pair edged
across the tree's trunk until they both could view the Huntressi without
obstruction.

The young warrioress was crouched behind a curtain of thick vines
that veiled her from the Mutahn candidates. Staring hard at the would-be
Mutahns, the Huntressi was unaware that Kama and Jaspen were watching her.

"She looks just like the *polog*," said Kama.

"Perhaps it is the younger sister."

"Only a few rain seasons older than Shim. She practices her skills,
like me," said Kama. "Spying on our tribe-mates. A harmless game."

"These are Treef lands," whispered Jaspen. "Enemy of the Huntressi.
She takes quite a risk to play a simple game— Ho!"

The Huntressi withdrew an arrow from her quiver and quietly
nocked it. With the arrow in place, she parted the vines before her, drew
the bowstring to her ear, and put Sorazin in her sights.

"No!" cried Kama and burst toward the Huntressi. "Don't shoot!"

She'll ruin her life! thought Kama. *And if Sorazin survives, he'll kill
her.*

"Kama!" Jaspen reached out to stop her . . . yet she was already beyond his grip.

As Quillen regaled the others with the tale of his long-ago encounter
with the Hoodoah, Sorazin's keen eye caught the sight of a small, dark
figure at the edge of his vision. It was a young girl with a bow—Huntressi,
perhaps—struggling to conceal herself behind a wall of hanging vines.

Sorazin's battle-trained senses tingled but he remained calm. He was accustomed to feigned attacks by lesser foes.

Sorazin kept the sighting a secret from the figure with the bow as well as the others in his party. He was loath to give the Huntressi any satisfaction by showing concern, as the girl surely intended. As she was not a serious threat, Sorazin decided against alarming his tribe-mates of the youth's presence.

When the girl drew back the bowstring, however, Sorazin nearly dove to the forest floor. Yet before leaving the dullards in his company to fend for themselves, it dawned upon Sorazin that Quillen could be of service. The old man was privy to the paths leading to the Hoodoah's cave.

Sorazin vaulted onto the sage and pulled him to the safety of the earth just as the Huntressi's arrow split the air where Sorazin had been standing.

Though the arrow missed its target, it found purchase elsewhere. The dart's tip gouged into Fuertl's throat, halting when a finger's length of the shaft jutted out the back of the farmer's neck.

Fuertl sputtered and gurgled, eyes wide, stumbling back. He turned in a slow, dizzy circle while his jaw worked up and down, like a fish on the sand gasping for life. Plunging to his knees, the farmer glimpsed the arrow's guide feathers projecting from his throat. He seized the bolt and strained to pull it free, nearly toppling with the effort. Yet the farmer's calloused hands slipped off the blood-slickened shaft, again and again. He raised his eyes to the flute-carver, desperate, beseeching him for help.

Yet the gentle musician was paralyzed by what he saw. He stood and watched in horror as a thick crimson stripe oozed from Fuertl's neck to flow down his chest and all the way to the farmer's loins.

Fuertl swayed on his knees, mumbling, nonsensical, spewing lymph . . . until collapsing, face down, into an exposed root of a tree. The arrow snapped in two when it met the earth. Moaning, abysmal, the dying man finally surrendered to his fate and allowed his body to soften and settle deeper into the soil.

A farmer and his dirt, at long last they were one.

10

Gort Holes

THE HUNTRESSI STOOD MOTIONLESS, a sculpture. Face calm, legs spread, bowstring held taut at her ear by two steady fingers.

"Kama stop!" cried Jaspen.

Though desperate to catch her, eager to place himself between the Huntressi and Kama, Jaspen was failing to gain any ground on the girl he loved. For his toes, feet, and legs were unfamiliar with the lumps and dents of the forest floor—a terrain nothing like water. And he fell.

Jaspen rose just as the Huntressi's arrow took flight.

"No!" screamed Kama, still racing for the girl.

The Huntressi spun towards Kama, Jaspen right behind her. The young girl fumbled through her quiver, nervous, finally catching a dart.

Jaspen was at Kama's shoulder now and he launched himself into the air toward the Huntressi.

She labored to nock the lance, her dark fingers quivering, refusing to comply.

The arrow dropped to the ground.

The Huntressi's brow knit and her pupils grew vertical at the sight of this strange, black-and-white creature hurtling for her. In that moment, Jaspen knew that Fuertl had been the first man the young girl had ever struck down.

Compassion swelled in Jaspen's chest. This Huntressi was a mere youth, unprepared for the anguish that came with the act of forever dousing the divine spark in another. Though endeavoring to appear dignified and confident, the girl's face tremored and her stouthearted facade crumbled beneath the ponderous burden of the farmer's life.

Nonetheless, she urged herself to stand taller and aimed a poised, fearless look directly into Jaspen's eyes. She could have run. But cowardice was not the Huntressi way.

Jaspen considered the girl's likely kinship to this morning's *polog*, the Huntressi consumed by Levaioth just a few hands ago. Jirvallan law stated that justified retaliation was allowed, island-wide—a life for a life.

Empathy dilated in Jaspen's heart and his wild, attacker's glare softened. A sorrowful look washed over him. The girl's panic suddenly calmed and she peered back at Jaspen with a gaze that seemed to address him as friend rather than foe.

Colliding into the girl, Jaspen and the Huntressi careened to the earth. They slid over the slippery grass toward a steeper slope. Jaspen belted his arms around her torso. The warrioress offered no resistance.

Is that— No! thought Jaspen as they hastened towards three, short pillars of stacked stone.

It was a common marker, one signaling the site of a Gort hole.

If Jaspen and the girl could not escape plunging into the pit's gaping maw, it would be a life of slavery for them both.

The Gort began digging their deep holes in Jirvallan forests generations ago. Initially, the underground race drew upon the hollows to capture game. A mesh of sticks, mud, and leaves were spread over the openings to hide the steep-walled pits from unwitting fauna. Framing the mouth of each Gort hole were three, short columns of stacked stone, to alert the sun-side tribes of the locations of the hidden burrows.

Over the seasons, Gort holes developed a second use: brigands on the verge of arrest began to seek refuge within them. The naturally greedy Gort were zealous to employ these despicable hole-seekers as their slaves. And they did. Until the other tribes discovered the deceit of the UnderDowners.

Seasons of inter-tribal bickering followed. It was eventually agreed that the tribe from which the criminal hailed would be awarded twenty Gort blades for each slave the Gort took into their custody.

Many suns later, the Council of All Tribes voted to reduce each outlaw's sentence from a lifetime in the UnderDown to one hundred full moons. After serving out the term, the rogues could opt to remain in the earth for another hundred moons or return to the tribe into which they were born, to face the penalties for the crimes that led them to seek out a Gort hole in the first place.

11

Treef

Sorazin hauled Quillen over the rising hump of a smooth boulder and the sage tumbled to the soft earth, safely behind the large rock.

Muffled shouts rose from where the girl had loosed the arrow.

The rallying cries of the Huntressi, thought Sorazin. *They are gathering forces to press their attack.*

Sorazin unsheathed his sword. He peeked around the boulder to assess the enemy's strength. Catching a flurry of motion behind the screen of green vines, he saw that two additional adversaries had joined the young Huntressi who had fired the arrow. Undoubtedly, more were en route.

"This way." Sorazin jabbed his chin in the opposite direction from where the arrow had come.

While scrabbling away, Quillen asked, "What of the musician, Perpeht? And Fuertl?" He motioned to the flute-carver, crying and rocking, the farmer's slack head lolling in his lap. "Surely you—"

"Shh!" Sorazin lifted a finger.

Danger neared.

Sorazin prostrated himself upon the earth.

Quillen followed suit.

Forty paces away, the long, loping strides of a Treef scout cut through the trees. He was racing toward the place where the arrow had been unleashed.

Jaspen clutched the Huntressi tighter and impaled his heels into the slippery grass . . . but the ground was too slick. It was well known that the Gort often greased the down-slope surrounding the mouths to their deep, dark holes.

The girl and Jaspen slammed into one of the three stacks of stones, capsizing the pillar. Another arm's length and into the pit they would plummet.

Jaspen held fast to the warrioress with one arm while using his free hand to scratch, rake, and claw at roots, stems, vines, rocks . . . anything to prevent them from descending into the Gort hole. Yet their bodies continued to sail unimpeded over the slickened grass.

"Kama!" screamed Jaspen, spotting her running toward them, hysterical.

"Jaspen!" she cried.

He clung to the sound of his name on her lips. It could become the last utterance he would ever hear from the girl he wished would one day be his Forever-One.

For death amongst Gort slaves was far from uncommon.

Jaspen and Kama locked eyes. *She will surely marry another,* he thought, his gaze misting. *To wait a hundred round moons . . . It is all but impossible.*

An earsplitting screech tore through the forest.

Jaspen swung his face to the din. A greenish blur was careering toward him and the Huntressi. It whooshed past.

The scudding pair suddenly struck something firm and rigid, halting their advance. Crumpling against the blockade, Jaspen folded around a pole-like barricade; just a few paces from the awful opening of the Gort pit.

Jaspen and the Huntressi gaped at each other, puzzled as to what had rescued them.

They peered up at a tall, green, stick-like being. Its thin, stake-like arms and legs stabbed into the grass between them and the Gort hole. It had been many seasons since Jaspen had beheld a Treef. He had forgotten how much the forest-dwelling species resembled the insect he knew as Green-Hop.

The Treef scout cocked its head one way then the other in quick, twitching movements. His bulbous eyes were glassy and convex and they explored Jaspen and the Huntressi with interest.

"Huntresssiii put feathered-twiiiig into Cove-man's swallowinnng plaaaaace." The Treef's voice had the creaky rasp of a bough in the wind. "Trrryinng, she is, to esssscape jussstice for her criiiiime." The creature's mandibles snapped together with a sharp *clack*!

"I kill Cove! Yes!" The warrioress set her chin, proud, and scowled to the dead farmer. "*Pir fol siyen!*" she snarled at the corpse then spat in its direction.

The Treef glared at her, cold. "A liiiiiiffe for a liiiiiiiiiiffe."

Before the Huntressi could blink she had been snatched from Jaspen's grip and hurled through the air. She slammed into the forest floor and the Treef scout was upon her in an instant, the keen points of an open claw spearing into the earth on either side of the Huntressi's throat. Throwing back its head, the Treef shrieked out a terrible roar.

Three more Treef emerged—one from a bush, another leaping down from a lofty branch, and the third rising from a mound of leaves.

"She is with me!" Jaspen rushed to the Huntressi and posted himself between her and the coming Treef.

Kama! he suddenly thought and his eyes hunted for her.

Yet there was nothing but earth and bush and tree and sky. He feared a hidden band of enemy Huntressi may have carried her away.

Then he spied her, pressed against a tree trunk in a perfect copy of its bark.

The green Treef restraining the Huntressi swung the spiny point of its other pincer to Jaspen's chest. "Back awaaaayyy, ssstraaanger, or her neck ssspliiitsss. Treeeeef law is Treeeef law. A liiife for a liiiiiiffe."

Jaspen backed up a step as the three other Treef neared. Two were built for war, short and thick, with heavier claws and larger mouths than the tall Treef that had saved them from the pit. The other, as black as a burnt log, appeared much like the green Treef—slim, lanky, and even taller than the scout restraining the Huntressi.

The brawny soldiers—the shorter one earth-brown and the other the faded yellow of an autumn leaf—squinted their domed eyes at Jaspen as they passed, noting his unusual coloring. Their leader was the thin, dark Treef.

The foursome conversed in their aboriginal tongue. From Jaspen's time in the sea, eavesdropping on thousands of squeak-whistling conversations, he could almost understand the clacks and pops that made up Treef speech.

The tall scout with its claw at the Huntressi's neck leered at her and said, "Enemy Huntressssiii wiiilll be kiiilllled. Deciiided, it has beeeeen. Treef law is cleeeear."

"It my law too!" The Huntressi squirmed against the pincer. "One Cove take Zuwansa, I take one Cove. Avenge my sister death. To honor her." Tears grew larger in her eyes. "That *Huntressi* law."

Zuwansa . . . thought Jaspen, *the polog*. His heart went out to the girl. If an enemy tribe had murdered Kama, Jaspen would have likely sought revenge as well.

"She speaks true." Jaspen's eyes travelled from one Treef to the next. "I was present when Levaioth took her sister." He glanced down at the Huntressi, her cheek wet with sorrow. "I am sorry for your loss and apologize on behalf of all Cove. We had no right to take Zuwansa."

Baffled, the Treef regarded each other then looked Jaspen up and down.

The Shepherd's black-and-white markings prompted the pale yellow Treef to query, "Yooouu are Cooove?"

"I am."

"Appeeearr as one sea-born, yoou dooo. Can anyyy sssecond your claaaaiim?"

Kama pushed away from the tree, an evident bid to confirm Jaspen as her tribe-mate.

Spotting her, Jaspen held out his palm toward Kama. He subtly motioned for her to remain cloaked. Huntressi may be close. Should a skirmish ensue, Kama's concealment might offer an advantage.

12

Contest Between Gods

"FOR TEN AND TWO hundred moons I have lived with the Cove," said Jaspen. "Since the day the sea delivered me to Jirvallan shores. I have resided each sun under the rule of Mutahn Pehlni. Until yesterday. When he breathed his last."

The green Treef spoke briefly with the dark, Treef leader. After considering his subordinate's words, the black Treef nodded.

"Cooove-maaan," The Treef leader bowed his face to Jaspen. "I aaam Tarkis."

"Jaspen." He bent his face to Tarkis.

"Yoooou are welcome heeeere, Jasssspen, ally annnd friend to the Treeeeeef."

"Thank you," he said, then lied: "Cove law states that in the absence of a Mutahn any Cove is authorized to pardon an act of violence against a tribe-mate."

The four Treef considered each other with looks of bewilderment.

Jaspen kneeled at the Huntressi's side and smiled at her. "I am Jaspen," he whispered.

"Shokku," she whispered back.

Louder, so the Treef could hear him, Jaspen said, "Shokku, your law has been fulfilled and justice served. Please accept Fuertl's death as proper settlement for the crime the Cove committed against your sister." Jaspen's eyes showed both sadness and anger. "On behalf of all Cove, I beg your forgiveness for the unlawful act carried out against your kin. I release you from any wrongdoing concerning the death of the Cove farmer, Fuertl."

Shokku was staggered by the apology; so rare was it to hear such a willing confession of wrongdoing from an enemy tribe.

"When it comes my time to enter the Everlasting Lands of Kiriath-Dae," resumed Jaspen, "I hope to meet your Zuwansa there, Shokku. I await with joy the morning we hunt together in a place where pain and sorrow and strife amongst tribes are no more."

Shokku pressed her palm to the flesh of Jaspen's inner forearm and wrapped her fingers around it. In turn, Jaspen did the same. With a slight shake, they sealed the accord.

"Cleverrr," said Tarkis. "But Cove law appliesss not on Treeef landsssss. The Huntresssi'sss sssentence ssstaaandssss. A liiife for a liiiiiffe!"

"Her death profits no one." Jaspen's hand edged to his waist, slowly folding around the hilt of his pearl knife.

Yet his grip on it eased at the quickening of a sudden thought—a cunning ploy.

"Tell me of your god, Tarkis. Is he kind? Merciful? Or war-like, as you?"

Enraged by the insult, Tarkis leapt upon the Shepherd and dragged him over the forest floor until slamming Jaspen's spine into the tree Kama was cloaking.

"Even annn allllyyy isss not permitted to ssslander another'sss god," rasped Tarkis. "Yoouuu will now payyy for your disssresspect for our greeeaat Manteez!" Drawing back a claw, Tarkis thrust it at Jaspen's swallowing place.

Yet a hair's breadth before the pincer gored into Jaspen's throat, Tarkis parted his claw and the two sharp tips of it gouged into the bark on either side of Jaspen's neck, splinters scattering.

An arm's length away, Kama looked past the pincer to Jaspen, taking great care to keep the Treef blind to her presence.

Jaspen asked, "Is he powerful, your Manteez?"

The Shepherd's many ocean battles had taught him to recognize the elements that expose an attacker's true motive: Tarkis had no intention of killing Jaspen. The Treef was bluffing.

"The mossst powerful of all gods." Tarkis snapped his jaws, spittle spewing.

"Except mine."

"RRRRAAAACKRRRCCKKKKCRRR!" Tarkis speared his other claw into the tree, a finger's width from Jaspen's ear.

"Runnn him throoooouugh!" hissed the yellow Treef.

"Ssssplit him noooww!" grated the brown.

"Allow me to prove it," said Jaspen. "My god versus yours. A contest."

The four Treef regarded each other. A refusal to defend Manteez and his power would undoubtedly incite the god's wrath.

"What do yoouu propossse, Cove-Mann? Your Levaioth ssleeeeps in the sssea while our great Manteeeeez iss watching usss and every island foressst right now."

"Levaioth is nothing but an ugly fish."

"To whooom then, do yooouu prayyyy if not Levaiotthhh?"

"His name is the Always." Jaspen stood taller. "And he is with me even now."

"I sseeee nothinnng . . . but liiiees."

"The Always is like the wind. You spy him not, but he is here. And if she is worthy," Jaspen's chin indicated Shokku, "my god will make her invisible too."

"Imposssssssibllle!"

"Heee jesssssstsss!"

"Free me and I will show you."

A smile crept over the black Treef's face. He released Jaspen from the tree, plainly relieved that Manteez would not be put to the test.

"Veryy weelll." Tarkis nodded. "If yoouur god makes her dissap-peeear, then frreeee to go she isss."

Jaspen rubbed away a smear of blood left by Tarkis's claw on his neck while stealthily gesturing for Kama to slowly edge her way to the rear of the tree's thick trunk, out of the Treef's view.

Tarkis grinned. "When your god faaiilsss, Cove-mann," he leaned in and sniffed Jaspen, "we kiilllll and eeeat the sssweeeet meat of the Hunt-ressssi *and* yoouuuuu!"

The other Treef joined Tarkis in the ominous clacks and hissing that was common to their kind.

13

The Vanishing

JASPEN TOOK SHOKKU BY the hand and led her to the tree that Kama was cloaking. The Huntressi followed, hesitant. Yet Jaspen's warm gaze and self-assured manner put her at ease.

"My Always." Jaspen uplifted his face and hands to the sky. "I thank you for delivering your loved one, Shokku, from death. For turning her into wind."

"Loved onnnne?" The Treef consulted each other, concerned. Then creaked and clacked with nervous laughter.

"Prove to all who doubt your power that you are mightiest of all Jirvallan gods." Jaspen took Shokku by the shoulders and gently pressed her back to the tree. "Show these unbelieving Treef that they are meant to worship you, my friend, and not Manteez."

"Friennnd?" The soldiers shared another round of anxious glances, for the Treef deity was evidently too grand and proud to be considered a friend.

"If you love them as much as you love me, my Always," Jaspen worked Shokku into position, placing her shoulder next to Kama's, "prove it to these four Treef by showing yourself."

With perfect timing, a light breeze sent a few leaves scurrying across the forest floor.

"Look!" Jaspen's broad eyes darted from the Treef to the blowing leaves. "The Always comes!"

"It issss onlyyy wiiinnd."

"Heee ssstalls."

"Dooo it, Cove-mannn."

"Vanish herrr now or diiiiieee."

I apologize, my Always," prayed Jaspen, *for this ruse I've devised to save Shokku. But I know of no other method of rescue.*

Jaspen faced Shokku, his eyes bounding between the Huntressi and Kama.

"Take her, my Always, and make her yours!" Jaspen threw wide his arms and turned his back to the Treef, obstructing their view of Shokku. "Turn this Huntressi into wind." He caught Kama's eye. "Now!"

Kama pushed away from the tree, being careful to remain unseen by the Treef.

Shokku's gaze widened with terror. It appeared as if the tree had come alive and a girl composed of bark was holding out a hand to her.

"Zon tuwaka siyyin!" squealed Shokku, backing away from Kama.

"Cove-maaann's god!" whispered the yellow Treef. "Heee hasss cooomme!"

Cautiously, the four Treef inched towards the back of the tree, at once curious and fearful to behold the Always.

"It is the Always!" cried Jaspen and he pushed Shokku into Kama's arms.

Kama seized Shokku and tried to envelop her completely.

Yet Shokku kicked and squirmed and refused to yield to this monster forged of tree bark.

Jaspen watched as Shokku continued to vie against Kama. It was a curious sight. The tree trunk appeared to swell and ripple then shrink, then bulge again . . . all while an occasional dark arm or leg came shooting out from the bark, only to be quickly swallowed up by the tree again.

The Treef slowed their timid steps. Each twitched with fear. For the repercussions of a mortal gazing directly into a god's face were often lethal.

Sensing the Treef's apprehension, Jaspen cried, "See that I have turned my eyes away from you, my Always!" He shut his eyes. "So unworthy am I to—"

"Foolsss," said the black Treef. "Hiiides, she does, behiiind the treeeee." Tarkis pushed past Jaspen. "I wiillll prooove that—" Yet upon arriving at the tree's far side, the Treef's bulbous eyes saw nothing but bark and limb and leaf and sky.

"What issss iiit?" The brown Treef hurried to his leader's side and gazed, speechless, at the tree trunk.

Jaspen grinned to himself. Kama had managed to tame Shokku and was cloaking her entirely. Yet while considering Kama, Jaspen noticed her camouflaged form straining to remain still under the scrutiny of the Treef.

"Vanishhhed, she hassss!" exclaimed the green Treef.

"How true he speaks!" cried Jaspen and placed himself between the Treef and Kama. "It is as promised. The Always has made Shokku into wind! If any disbelieve, scout the forest." He waved an arm at the trees and shrubs in an effort to divert their eyes from Kama. "Examine each stone, peek under each leaf."

"If sheee had ruuunn," said the yellow Treef, "weee would haaave seeeen."

The black Treef's eyes scanned the trees, probing into every shadow.

"Becomme the wiiiiinnnd, she hassss!" exclaimed the green Treef.

"Cove-maan's god is truuuuue!" cried the brown.

Dubious, the Treef leader continued to peer in all directions, alert to every sound, attentive to every movement. Yet Shokku was not to be found. As Tarkis slowly accepted the truth of Jaspen's god, his black pincer came together with a quiet *click*. Then, bowing his head, he fell to Jaspen's feet.

"Bow not to me, good Tarkis. I am no god." Jaspen pulled the Treef leader to his feet. "I accomplished nil. It was the Always."

How sorry I am, my Always, if I have become a stench in your nose by crediting this simple deception to you. But how else was I to save Shokku?

Tarkis wiped away a tear. "The Alwaayyysss . . . It is yoour god's naaaamme, yesss?"

"It is. But the Always is not my god alone. He is your god as well. And god to all who make Jirvalla their home."

Tarkis nodded and a slow smile lengthened until it cut his dark face in two. A hearty laugh followed. His head began to sway, slow at first then faster, and he leapt, low to begin with, then higher . . . A moment later, all four Treef were immersed in the wild whirling, twisting, springing dance that was the Treef's customary manner of worship.

Guilt pecked at Jaspen's heart for the hoax he had carried out.

While the Treef shrieked and danced and leapt and cried, Jaspen crept to Kama. Her face etched with concern.

He whispered to her, "Is all okay?"

Kama shook her head. Something had gone amiss.

Jaspen made certain the Treef were still occupied in their worship then quietly asked, "Wh-what is it?"

Kama arched her torso slightly away from the tree.

Shokku was not there.

"But . . . " Jaspen checked again on the Treef then ran his hand over the bark where Shokku should have been. "Where is she?"

"Th-the Always . . . " said Kama. "He turned her to wind."

14

To Scale the Sea-Wall

SORAZIN AND QUILLEN PEERED up at the sheer, rock face of a steep sea-wall. A man's length beneath them, waves crashed, briny spray dampening them like heavy mist.

"The Hoodoah's cave is there." Quillen indicated a cleft high on the white cliffs. "Let us tarry, half a hand." He looked beyond Sorazin, into the distant forest.

"Perpeht has returned to the Cove," said Sorazin, frustrated. "Three hands it has been since the farmer's death. Now come. The Hoodoah awaits."

"I pray Levaioth the minstrel is safe." Quillen forced a smile.

Sorazin, in contrast, hoped the musician had fallen into a spiked pit or trod into a steel-jawed animal trap. The idle dreamer lacked battle skills. And his influence upon the children—caroling dull songs and reciting silly poetry—was dangerous. Perpeht's piddling rhymes of love and compassion were not talents that would help expand the borders of Cove tribe.

When Sorazin returned as Mutahn, among his first edicts would be to banish impractical forest wanderers like Perpeht. The flute-carver's hut, as well as the huts of those like him, would be repurposed as dwellings for soldiers-in-training and weapons makers. Sorazin's innate knowledge of what was best for the Cove, along with the courage to carry out those obligations, was among the many reasons he knew he would soon be hailed as the greatest Mutahn in Cove history.

"The climbing path . . . " Sorazin glanced up at the cave, "can you recall it?"

He felt sorry for Quillen, so feeble and ugly. With slouching flesh, wilted muscles, and faltering eyes. Though Sorazin doubted the decaying sage had the mental resources to summon the cliff route leading to the Hoodoah, he hoped the old man could manage it. It would make for a faster climb. If time had erased from Quillen's memory the convolutions of the passage, Sorazin would slay the graybeard now. It would be a simple thing to toss him off the rise upon which they stood to be wracked upon the rocks below. But if Quillen could recollect the way, Sorazin would allow him to live . . . until they reached the mouth of the Hoodoah's dwelling place.

Sorazin did not view his decision to sacrifice one of his own as a small matter. For the sake of the Cove, however, he would set aside his personal feelings and dutifully put Quillen to death. Not only would Sorazin be exterminating an unworthy competitor for the throne, he would be thinning his herd of a weak member. His heart warmed in admiration for his keen insight, his selflessness, his astonishing maturity.

What an honor for Quillen, thought Sorazin. *A grand finale to an otherwise pathetic life.*

In death, the village elder would undoubtedly gain fame from the tales that would rise about Sorazin the Great. Bedtime fables would feature an aged sidekick who fearlessly blazed a cliff-trail for Sorazin to follow. Just before entering the Hoodoah's cave, however, the selfless sage would throw himself from the cliff, to die a hero's death. For the humble Quillen feared that a mistake from the Hoodoah would place the lesser man at the helm of the Cove. And forces mysterious had already revealed to Quillen that his role was only to guide a superior soul to the throne, never to rule the Cove himself.

Sorazin grinned at the tale. If only all lesser men had the sense to lay down their lives for greater men. If only all were as unselfish as Sorazin. If only more were willing to do anything to support their righteous Mutahn . . . what a powerful people the Cove would become.

"The way . . . " Quillen scanned the cliff, reacquainting himself with the crags and ridges, "begins here." He took hold of a narrow ledge and the climb commenced.

Upon discovering that the Always had transformed Shokku into wind, Jaspen dropped to his knees and began to weep. Soon, he too was dancing alongside the Treef in praise of his god. The Miracle of the Wind, as the event would come to be known, marked the first time the Always had presented himself to Jaspen in a physically tangible manner.

The Shepherd went on to tell Tarkis and the others what little he knew about the Always. Jaspen wished he had more knowledge about his god, wished he had borne witness to other wonderworks that verified the god's inimitable power and love for Jirvalla. But at least, now, there was the undeniable miracle of Shokku's vanishment. The Treef heeded Jaspen's every word, rapt, and vowed to report everything they had seen and heard to the whole of their colony.

Jaspen and Kama located Sorazin and Quillen swiftly. For moons and moons, Kama had been practicing her tracking skills—a typical Cloaker task—and she was pleased to demonstrate her newfound talents. They had trailed the Mutahn applicants in reverential silence: a prolonged state of awe due to the astonishing Miracle of the Wind. While eavesdropping on the aged sage and Sorazin, Jaspen and Kama had discovered that Perpeht had voluntarily ushered Fuertl's body back to Cove shores, to inform the farmer's three children and his Forever-One what had occurred.

At the sea-wall, Jaspen and Kama were presently scaling the cliffs just a dozen hand- and footholds behind Quillen and Sorazin. Kama placed herself between Jaspen and the Mutahn aspirants, becoming as one with the white rocks so as to prevent the pair above from looking back to spy Jaspen's dark back.

Kama glanced over her shoulder. "Two-tone!" she shout-whispered. "Flatter. Or they'll spot you." She pressed her open hand to the rock. "Like this."

Jaspen nodded but when Kama turned aside he grimaced in pain. The jagged rocks had opened up the wounds that Slither-Tail had inflicted upon the Shepherd just yesterday. Every touch of Jaspen's thighs, chest, palms, or fingers upon the dry, ragged cliff brought forth a spate of stinging, throbbing pangs as well as streams of fresh blood. How he longed for the cooling touch of the ocean, the curative salt of the sea. Rock was so firm—so course and unforgiving—not at all like water.

Suddenly: "Sorazin!" shouted a voice. "No!"

It was Quillen, from the opposite side of a large outcropping, just beyond Kama and Jaspen's vantage.

"Unhand me now!" demanded Quillen, his voice fearful amidst sounds of an escalating scuffle.

"Your time has come old man." Sorazin's tone was calm. "You have served your Mutahn well."

The *hiss* of a sword escaping its scabbard spurred Jaspen to intercede. Ignoring his many wounds, he pushed past Kama.

She reached out to grab him.

Jaspen shook off her hand.

A metal blade clanked against the rocks ahead.

Jaspen rounded the boulder.

"No!" Quillen's panic was rising. "Sorazin! Stop! You don't—"

Jaspen peeked around the outcropping: Quillen's back was flat upon the rocks and his hands were pressed to his throat, as if choking himself. His chafed knuckles were smeared in crimson and blood was pushing out from between his fingers, slow at first, then widening into a red stream that gushed from his wrists to his wizened elbows. Quillen's round, glassy gaze held Sorazin's, seeming to ask why . . . why?

The sage's eyes fluttered and his body began to peel away from the cliff, gradually, part by part. His blood-streaked arms fell slack to his sides and his face drooped forward, toward his chest. The weight of his sagging head provoked his shoulders to separate from the sea-wall. Quillen's torso and upper spine flaked away next. Then his upper body sloped forward, downward, followed by his waist and hips. Before long, the whole of Quillen was free of the cliff.

Jaspen ducked out of Sorazin's sightline and peered down to see Quillen's body falling and falling . . . until it broke against the rocks. The force of the fall contorted him cruelly. His joints craned in every direction. The old man's frame slumped atop a craggy sea-rock, motionless . . . before the sea reached up and swallowed him whole.

15

Hoodoah

SORAZIN HEAVED HIMSELF UP and into the mouth of the Hoodoah's cave, Gort sword at his waist, proud smile on his face. Thirty paces into the hollow's murky depths, a fire burned. Shadowy tongues licked at walls, rising and falling, shifting, dancing. A large, dark figure was sitting upon a rock, hunched over the flames, tending the blaze. The cave dweller appeared to be part man, part beast. A towering rack of antlers sprouted from the head and the furred pelt of Tree-Horns covered the man-thing's shoulders and back. The dark arms and big hands were human.

"Hallo hay," Sorazin called into the cave.

An echo ... The *pop* of the fire ... Patter of scampering cave-vermin.

Yet the creature at the fire did not move.

Sorazin marched into the gloom, shivers prickling at his back and neck, despite the day's warmth.

A sudden *whoosh* at Sorazin's ear sent his hand to the hilt of his sword. His face spun toward the sound and he crouched, blade at the ready.

Filthy pest! thought Sorazin, squinting at the Cave-Wing that flapped past him and toward the fire to perch upon the man-beast's shoulder.

Once settled, the albino Cave-Wing mewled sweetly, nuzzling its master.

"How worried you have had me, Flumflum!" The Hoodoah stroked his pet's tiny, white head. "Two suns it has been. Is it your wish to break my heart, little loved one?" He scratched the Cave-Wing beneath its lifted chin and rubbed at Flumflum's ears until the animal ruffled its milky wings, cooing in delight.

Sorazin inspected the Hoodoah from the bonfire's opposite side. He was indeed a man, with dark skin, a broad nose, full brown lips, and wide-set eyes. His face was smeared with soot and a necklace of bone, beak, tooth, and talon hung from his neck. The rich, tawny-brown hide of a Tree-Horns was draped over his shoulders and the beast's entire head—its branching antlers, black eyes, nose, and perked ears—sat atop the Hoodoah's scalp.

Pathetic, thought Sorazin. *A simple costume to conjure the aura of a seer.*

Growing impatient with the man and his silly pet, Sorazin cleared his throat. Yet the Hoodoah continued to whisper into Flumflum's ear, ignoring Sorazin while running his thick finger over the length of the Cave-Wing's delicate, white fur.

Sorazin shuffled his feet and sniffed. He rolled his head a half dozen times.

Finally, the Hoodoah turned his eyes to his impatient visitor.

Sorazin puffed his chest and stood taller.

The Hoodoah's stare was as intense as Sorazin had ever beheld. When the firelight illuminated the bright whites of the man's eyes, they flashed and burned with an otherworldly brilliance that stiffened the hairs on Sorazin's arms.

Estimating Sorazin, the Hoodoah's lips pinched in disapproval. He swerved his eyes from the youth and leaned forward to reach into the flames. His fingers rootled through the glowing ash, searching for something, indifferent to the heat. Closing his eyes, he chose four bones from the blaze, none larger than his finger.

The Hoodoah snapped one of them in two and said to Sorazin, "Your hand."

Sorazin surrendered his palm and the Hoodoah swept the splintered bone over every crease, knuckle, and hump.

If the Hoodoah was intending to thrust the ragged bone's tip into Sorazin's hand, the Mutahn hopeful promised he would not even blink. It would be a privilege to suffer for the good of his people. So brave was he.

The Hoodoah did not stab Sorazin. He casually tossed the half-bone into the bowels of the cave then pitched the other three bones into the flames.

Instantly, the fire snuffed. The cave plunged into darkness. Even the sunlight that had been filtering in from the cavern's mouth had somehow extinguished. Magnifying the den's foreboding air, every previous drip, scrape, whisper of wind, and scurry of rodent in the stony lair had been silenced.

A small flame, as tiny as an infant's tear, sparked amid the bones. Growing slowly, it flickered and swayed, its faint light casting a sinister glow onto the Hoodoah's face. The flame lengthened and thinned. It slithered over the bones, under and around them, hissing while entwining them. Seeming to study their every nob and divot. Finished with its cryptic task, the flame described a burning orange circle around the trio of bones. A short hedge of fire flared to shed light upon the three items at its center.

The Hoodoah took a long, curved tusk from the floor near his feet. He poked it into the ash within the ring of fire, careful not to upset the pattern of the bones.

"I see a boy," he said, his voice deep and resonant. "The only son to his parents." He moved the tusk to indicate a short bone between two longer ones. "Agile of mind, this child. Strong of arm and rich in heart."

Sorazin swelled with pride at the compliment. A pleasant warmth filled him.

"His mother and father wait for him in the Other Place." The Hoodoah tapped at the two taller bones that symbolized the boy's parents.

All that Sorazin had been feeling, and hoping for, had been validated.

"Almost from birth, the boy feels different."

Sorazin's mind retreated to his early years. He had always felt superior; to his peers, to his elders, to everyone—even his mother and father.

"He serves his people already. Selflessly and at great peril to himself."

The polog, thought Sorazin.

He had captured the Huntressi the evening before his father's death. It had been against Jirvallan law as well as Cove statutes but Sorazin knew any law that opposed his view was outdated. Capturing the warrioress while her younger sister looked on, tethered to a tree, had made the experience even more significant. It felt right to strike the girl; Shokku she was called. After bloodying her lip, Sorazin had sent Shokku away with a message for the Huntressi: The Cove are coming.

Peering at the bones, the Hoodoah's face pleated in confusion. He mumbled to himself while reaching into the fire with the tusk. He prodded at the bone signifying the boy. It began to glow from its center. The single dot of amber-red gleamed, brighter and brighter, hotter and hotter . . . until the bone burst into flame.

"Pain comes. A test."

The bone combusted into a spray of fragments.

"The boy feels trapped. As if entombed in the earth." The Hoodoah indicated a shard of bone beneath the ash, invisible but for its dim glow. "So heavy is his burden." A tear striped his cheek. "Enough to break even the most valiant of men."

Sorazin was unconcerned. He was too strong and clever to be lured into a trap.

"Yet the greater the conflict, the greater is he who overcomes it." The Hoodoah tapped at the dying light within the buried bone.

The bone flickered and burned redder, hotter. Pearls of fire spouted from the cinders to paint scarlet crescents in the air. The beads of flame kept coming and coming. Trails of red faded in the wake of each graceful arc. Soon, a dazzling fountain of sparks was shooting to the cave's ceiling and into every corner.

The Hoodoah smiled at the beautiful crimson glow that bathed his hollow from wall to wall. "He wins the favor of every tribe, this child." He peeked to the ceiling where a shower of glowing white ash was drifting down upon him, as softly as dewfall. His grin broadened. "Even the realms above support his cause."

Sorazin pictured himself cutting down Huntressi, Faijen, Treef, Udok, Gort—all opposing him. He smiled as he envisioned the enslavement of each survivor.

Kneeling, Sorazin dipped his face to the Hoodoah. "I am ready, sir."

"Ready? For what, pray tell."

"To become Cove tribe's next Mutahn."

"Mutahn?" The Hoodoah waved a hand at the bones. "The fire speaks nothing of a . . . " Something about the ash and bones caught his eye. He peered closer.

"No Mutahn?" Sorazin's teeth clenched. "You have made a mistake, old man." He stood, threatening, fingers hovering over his sheathed sword.

"It cannot be . . . " The Hoodoah drew in the soot, appraising the bones from every vantage. "But it is! Flumflum, do you see it? Tell me you see it!"

The Cave-Wing squeaked and the Hoodoah laughed. Long and loud.

"He has come, my friend!" He plucked Flumflum from his shoulder and embraced the pet as best he could. "The Destroyer of Thrones is here! The King-Crusher has come! Oh, how long have we waited, Flumflum? And now the God-Slayer stands in our little hollow. The one of whom the ancient scrolls speak! The one higher than any Mutahn."

The Hoodoah gyred and laughed and coiled and sprang while prancing about the fire. In response, the blaze surged—leaping, crackling—as if it, too, were celebrating the advent of this person who was now, at last, in their midst.

Sorazin's heart billowed and he eased his clutch upon his sword. He had always known he was more exceptional than anyone he had ever met. But to become a ruler even mightier than a Mutahn was beyond even his imaginings.

Sorazin kneeled again at the prophet's feet. "I will lead them well, master."

Master . . . scoffed Sorazin. *He will soon know that I am his!*

The Hoodoah looked upon Sorazin. "Lead whom?" He chuckled.

"The inhabitants of Jirvalla, Great Hoodoah."

"You?" The Hoodoah laughed. "Oh, listen to him, Flumflum." His finger drew lines in the soft down of the Cave-Wing's white head. "Perhaps the little man jests." He glanced at Sorazin. "This coward is not fit to lead a nest of baby Rope-Tails!"

Furious, Sorazin leapt to his feet. "I am the boy in the bones, you fool! The God-Slayer!"

"What an ill disposition, eh Flumflum?" He set the Cave-Wing on an antler. "Such a temper. Not at all like you, my little Love-Flum."

"Of whom do the bones speak then? Your filthy, white-winged devil?"

The boy in the bones," the Hoodoah peered to a section of wall behind Sorazin, "is there."

The fire shifted to shine upon the rock wall at which the Hoodoah was gazing.

Sorazin glanced over to see nothing but stony crags and undulating shadows.

"Step into the light, cloaked one," commanded the Hoodoah. "You have shrouded yourself long enough."

The Hoodoah and Sorazin watched the wall, expectant.

When nothing unusual occurred, Sorazin snickered then sniffed in derision.

"Come on out now, son," said the Hoodoah. "There is no need to fear."

In the murky brume, the stone wall seemed to ripple and sway.

The fire roared—snapping, popping, vaulting—in anticipation, splashing more and more light upon the strange, moving stones.

A part of the rock wall began to open, slowly, like a thick, narrow door.

Out of the boulders, stepped Jaspen.

16

To Become Less

JASPEN GLANCED AT KAMA as she stiffened and swung herself outward, striving to appear as similar to a stone door as her talent would permit. Though she was the perfect texture and hue of the wall, Jaspen could still distinguish Kama grinning at him. He shook his head in warning, urging her to ignore the desire to help him.

The pair had struck an earlier accord. Kama would remain hidden regardless of how perilous the mission grew. Jaspen refused to allow Kama to place herself in potential danger for his sake. Unless he was seriously wounded, Kama had agreed not to intervene should hostilities mount between Jaspen and Sorazin.

In like manner, Jaspen had consented to keep Kama's cloaking powers a secret to all else in the cave. Even if he was forced to flee the Hoodoah's dwelling-place by himself, Jaspen was not to expose Kama and her camouflaged position—no matter how dire her circumstance appeared. She had explained that genuine Cloakers were often sent on official commissions by themselves. She felt it vitally important to learn how to escape danger without another's assistance. If Kama endured a grave injury, however, then—and only then—would Jaspen be allowed to reveal Kama and her cloaking talent, in order to help her evacuate the cave.

Jaspen sidled out of the small opening that Kama had made for him. He stepped out of the shadowy rock wall and into the cave's firelight.

"*Mahkifo?*" Sorazin glared at him.

"At long last he appears." The Hoodoah beamed at Jaspen, as would a proud father welcoming home a beloved son.

He looked the boy up and down, pleased at the youth before him.

"Handsome, isn't he Flumflum?"

Flum peeped in agreement from her antlered perch.

"Come in! Come in! Please!" The Hoodoah bumped past Sorazin and toward Jaspen. "What an honor to host a servant of the Boundless One! Of the Peace-Bringer, the Soul-Healer, the Joy-Maker! A servant of the Always-Loving-Friend."

He knows the Always! thought Jaspen.

"Many names has the true, high god of Jirvalla," continued the Hoodoah. "Including the one of which you have grown so fond: the Always."

Hungering for answers, Jaspen asked, "Can you tell me more of him, this Boundless One I call the Always? I know so little."

"Of course." Reaching Jaspen, the Hoodoah descended to a knee. "But first things first." He bowed low, in worship.

Jaspen lurched back. "I have done naught to warrant reverence, Great Hoodoah. A mistake, there has been. I am not the boy of whom the fire speaks."

"The bones are true, son." The Hoodoah was still bowing to Jaspen.

"But I know nothing of crushing kings or thrones."

"In the moons to come, you will. As you will also know my Pahlu. When you meet her," the Hoodoah raised his happy eyes, "tell her that with all of my heart and soul I love her. Then tell her that *her* time has come. That—"

Sorazin's blade chafed out of its sheath and tore through the air, straight for the Hoodoah's neck. The Gort steel was nearly to its target when . . .

The Hoodoah's hand lifted and caught the fleet sword as if it were a feather. Though an ordinary palm would have been cleaved in two by the weapon's keened edge, the Hoodoah suffered no harm.

Sorazin stared at the Gort blade in the Hoodoah's unscathed fist, stunned.

The holy man stood up, tall and broad and threatening. He twisted the sword from Sorazin's grip, cast it into the flames then removed the antlers from his head. He used the tips of the sharp, branching tines to force Sorazin to the nearest wall.

Once the boy's back met the rocks, the Hoodoah placed Sorazin's throat between the two antlers. He drove the forked points into the stone to pin Sorazin to the cave wall. With a final push, the Hoodoah shoved the tusks even deeper into the rock, to assure that the angry man-child was securely fixed in place.

"My apologies for the interruption," said the Hoodoah to Jaspen, pacing back to him. "Please, let us continue our—"

The Hoodoah's eyes grew suddenly puzzled and he snapped his gaze to the ceiling . . . to the walls . . . to the cavern's mouth.

Tilting an ear toward the belly of the cave, the Hoodoah seemed to be heeding a voice he alone could detect. "Are you certain?" he asked the unseen speaker. Then, grinning, he said, "I miss you as well." He laughed. "As you wish!"

Flumflum, who had apparently heard the mysterious speaker as well, squeaked and flew to the familiar perch of her master's finger.

"I knew that you would hear it too, my cherished one!" Gently pinching his pet's outstretched wing between his thumb and forefinger, the Hoodoah slid his careful fingers over the Cave-Wing's soft, white limb, again and again.

Flumflum squeaked and bleated, sounding at once both comforted and sad.

"Worry not, my little Love-Flum." The Hoodoah kissed the Cave-Wing's fuzzy white head. "I promise to visit often."

"Visit?" Jaspen asked.

"I am to depart. Soon. For many moons, good Shepherd, I have beseeched our Always-Friend to safely return me to my original home. A moment ago, our loving god has, at last, granted my heart's wish."

"To where will you be traveling?"

"To the place of our birth."

Our birth? Jaspen's heart drummed and his face grew hot. *Do we hail from the same place, he and I?* His vision blurred and the Hoodoah's dwelling-place seemed to tremble, the stone walls swelling then shrinking. *Does he know of my parents?*

"Do you and I share the same homeland?" asked Jaspen. "Were you, too, lost as a child? Stolen, perhaps?" His hope surged. "Did you wake one morning to find yourself on Jirvallan shores?"

"Yes." The Hoodoah smiled then upheld a thick finger to stop Jaspen's query before it could emerge. "For everything that lives was born in the Lands of Kiriath-Dae prior to being set here, upon earth. This is the home to which I am to return."

Jaspen's face fell and he bit back tears. If only he could have learned something of his birthplace; about the mother and father he could scarcely remember. How it pained him that with each passing moon, Jaspen's parents seemed to be getting further and further away.

Sorrow filled him, like a jug filling with water. His body felt so heavy, his heart drowning. Jaspen was so overburdened with woe that he failed to realize the Hoodoah slowly backing away from him, retreating toward the fire. Neither had Jaspen fully grasped the meaning of the Hoodoah's words about returning home . . . until he watched the holy man step into the fire's center.

"No!" cried Jaspen as the flames began to swirl around the Hoodoah, suddenly crackling, leaping, spinning, sizzling.

"I must become less," said the Hoodoah, "so that you, Shepherd of Fish, Shepherd of Jirvalla, may become more."

"But I— I don't know how . . . " the blaze twined about the Hoodoah's legs, his waist, his torso, his neck, like vines crawling up a tree trunk, " . . . I know nothing!"

Greenish tendrils of smoke issued from the Hoodoah's flesh. The curling, green wisps seemed to be consuming him now, from the ground upward. His feet had already disappeared and the thin strands were now devouring his legs. As each moment passed, more and more feathery curls rose from the holy man, stretching to the craggy ceiling.

Before long, all that remained of the Hoodoah were his chest, neck, and face—floating above the flames, ghostly.

"Forget not to tell my Pahlu," he said as the green coils took his chest and shoulders, "that *her* time has come. *Her* time."

"Don't go!" pleaded Jaspen. "I need you to—"

The inferno suddenly swelled with a roaring *whoosh!*—snapping, hissing, sparking. It spread rapidly, the green fog mixing with the crimson blaze to reach from wall to wall, from floor to ceiling.

Then, as swiftly as the firestorm had escalated, it diminished to the modest size it had been when the Hoodoah first strode into the flames—a rough circle of fire the height of Jaspen's waist.

Nothing remained of the Hoodoah. Not even a small mound of ash.

"But I need you," said Jaspen. "I need you to . . . "

Jaspen was abruptly overcome by a scent so powerful and insistent—an aroma resembling freshly cut forest wood—that it chased every other thought from his head. Never before had Jaspen experienced an odor so poignant and thick, as palpable as dewfall. Nor had he encountered a redolence so pleasant and all-conquering that it decimated all of his other senses.

The scent of the Always, thought Jaspen, somehow knowing the truth of it, *descending to privately escort his friend to the Everlasting Lands.*

Flumflum's piercing shriek expelled every last trace of the Always-Friend's aroma. The potent essence retreated as quickly as it had come. Though Jaspen's nose hunted in earnest for the comforting bouquet, it found nothing. As if the scent had been a figment, a childish game of make-believe.

A moment later, the forked antlers that had been bolting Sorazin to the stone wall clattered to the floor. Flumflum beat her wings, frantic, squawking in alarm. Dashing to the fire, she circled the air above where the Hoodoah's face had been hovering prior to its exodus. After three quick loops, the Cave-Wing shot into the deep of the cavern, squalling all the while.

Jaspen watched, frozen, as Sorazin converged upon him, his shortsword drawn, the blade still powdered with bone dust from where he had hacked himself free.

17

Short-Sword Versus Pearl Knife

Jaspen raised his pearl knife, training it on Sorazin, following his every move.

Sorazin chuckled, "Whatever will you do with that twig, *mahkifo*, when I hold the entire tree?" He lashed out with his blade.

Jaspen dodged it, barely, but his foot caught upon a jagged stone. Stumbling to the floor, he cursed the pitted ground. If only they were in the sea.

The short-sword came again.

Jaspen veered out of harm's way, Sorazin's Gort blade striking the rock floor. Flint-sparks flared from the stone like shooting stars.

Jaspen pounded a fist into Sorazin's sword arm and scrambled to his feet. He dashed to the edge of the fire opposite Sorazin.

They circled the flames, weapons drawn, eyes locked. The width of the blaze was just enough to place Jaspen a hair's breadth beyond the range of Sorazin's long knife.

"How much longer can you tarry, *mahkifo*?"

Sorazin attacked.

Jaspen arched back to evade the slashing steel.

"Soon, you slippery Croak-Neck," Sorazin glared at Jaspen, "the fire will wane and I will cross the embers to slit your throat."

Jaspen was outmatched. Sorazin was a trained warrior and the Cove's most feared swordsman. If only Jaspen could get to the sea.

Come quick, my Always, prayed Jaspen, continuing to orbit the thinning fire. *Show me what to do.*

"It will not be long now." Sorazin shifted his knife to the other fist. "A quarter hand at most. Then you will be dead and I will be Mutahn."

"I will die before I permit a false Mutahn to rule the Cove."

"As you wish." Sorazin leapt over the weakening flames—swift and sudden—Gort steel hacking.

Jaspen arced away. But the short-sword notched a ditch across his chest, the shallow trough filling with blood.

Whether it is I who dies this day—Jaspen's pearl knife sped toward Sorazin's heart—*or this murdering Rope-Tail, let it happen as you wish, my Always.*

Sorazin bashed the hilt of his sword into Jaspen's fist, knocking the pearl knife into the fire.

"Your time has come, *mahkifo.*" The tip of Sorazin's blade pressed into Jaspen's throat. He backed him against a wall.

Then, suddenly panicked, Jaspen cried, "No!"

From behind Sorazin, Kama had come away from the wall. She was stealing toward them with a rock in her fist.

"Stop!" Jaspen's voice was desperate. "Please," he begged Kama. "Don't."

For if Sorazin saw her, she too would fall to his short-sword.

Sorazin grinned, as if Jaspen's cowardly pleas were for his own life, not another's.

A high-pitched squeak startled Jaspen, crying out near his ear.

Flumflum hurtled past the Shepherd and into Sorazin's face, white wings beating at his brow and cheeks.

Jaspen glanced to the cave mouth. A shaft of sun was lengthening toward him across the rocky floor. The lighted path halted at his feet.

With Sorazin consumed with the Cave-Wing flapping in his face, Jaspen shoved the short-sword from his throat and sprang toward the cavern's mouth.

Sorazin cursed while swatting at Flumflum, slashing blindly at Jaspen.

Sprinting over the sunlit route, Jaspen's eyes met Kama's.

"Jaspen!" she screamed.

He held out his hand for her to grasp. "Take it!"

Yet Kama shook her head and melted back into the wall, becoming one with the rock again.

Jaspen recalled his promise to Kama. How forcefully she had pled with him to allow her to practice evading danger without the assistance of anyone else. As real Cloakers must often do.

"I'm fine," whispered Kama from somewhere within the crags. "Go."

Jaspen knew how stubborn Kama could be. Nothing on Jirvalla would convince her to part from the wall and join him in his escape.

Speeding over the stones toward the cave's exit, Jaspen pumped his arms and legs as hard and fast as he could. Never before had he jumped from such a great height. It would demand all of his power to clear the sea-wall's projecting rocks. One hesitation or misstep and Jaspen would find himself on the same pointed stone that had broken the old sage, Quillen.

His leg muscles bunched and his fingers tightened into fists. Mustering every shred of his strength, Jaspen's whole body coiled as he prepared to thrust himself out into the open sky. His every thought and sinew focused on height and distance.

Exploding out of the cave mouth, Jaspen launched into the air.

18

To Remain Cloaked

KAMA WOULD HAVE TAKEN it back if she could have. Cloakers, while immersed in a mission, were forbidden to act on impulse. A real Cloaker would have been suspended, dismissed even, had they revealed their position to an enemy as Kama had just done. How reckless she had been to cry out Jaspen's name.

She hurried back to the wall, absorbing the colors and texture of the stones once again. Looking to the cave mouth, Kama watched as Jaspen leapt into the sky—arms spread wide, chest arched, legs straight—and asked his god, the Always, to keep him safe. Her eyes remained upon him until he vanished from sight.

Pivoting her face back to Sorazin, she was pleased to see that he was still contending with the Cave-Wing. Kama hoped he had been so engrossed with Flumflum that he had failed to hear her voice over the animal's flapping wings, scratching talons, and squawking chirps. Yet the moment Flumflum pushed away from Sorazin's face and soared out of the cave, Sorazin spun towards Kama.

Calm down, she thought, *you'll be fine. And silence your breathing.*

"Who spoke?" Sorazin's eyes raked the walls, diligent.

Yet the dwindling firelight barred him from spotting anything unusual.

"It is Kama, isn't it?" Sorazin sheathed his sword and took a half-burned branch from the fire to employ as a torch. "The would-be Cloaker." He dragged his hand over the stony walls, feeling for her. "*Mahkifo's* only companion."

He was angling directly for her, Sorazin's fingers on a course to brush over Kama's shoulder in but a few paces, when a rasping noise behind him drew his eyes.

Kama ducked.

Sorazin caught the movement and jerked his eyes back toward Kama. Unsheathing his short-sword, he poked the wall with its tip, missing Kama by a finger's width. He prodded and prodded, just missing Kama's shoulder, ribs, thigh.

"Show yourself, coward!"

With his next jab, Sorazin pushed his blade's tip into the bone of Kama's hip.

Kama grimaced, struggling to remain still, to keep silent, to push down the shrieks of pain rising to her throat.

Sorazin removed the sword's point from Kama and continued to stab at the wall, believing he had hit rock instead of Kama's pelvis.

A skittering noise from the cavern's deep drew Sorazin's glare.

"You are good," he muttered to Kama, withdrawing from the wall to move towards the noise.

But a hushed splash of Kama's blood dropping upon the cave floor urged Sorazin to return to the stone wall.

He waved the torch in pursuit of the source of the splash. Sorazin kneeled at Kama's feet, unwittingly holding the fire so near to Kama that the flesh of her legs began to singe.

Fingering the blood on the ground, Sorazin whispered, "It is that of *mahkifo*."

Kama squeezed the rock in her fist. *Do it now*, she told herself, fighting off the searing pain of the torch at her thigh. *His head is right there!*

She lifted the rock.

19

A God Who Comforts

ONCE AIRBORNE, JASPEN RELAXED. How free it felt to finally unchain himself from mountain and rock. Sky was much more like water than earth and stone. It held no boulders that bruise, crags that cut, or clumps that catch the foot.

He smiled at the sea sprawled beneath him—the rolling swells, whitecaps, winking reflections of sun, and the exhilarating openness of a blue ocean as far as he could see. His flesh tingled, eager for the salted waters to swab away the blood from rock-torn knees, a blade-slit chest, and root-tattered feet. To feel the sea again, cradling him whole, in a perfect embrace . . .

Yet Jaspen's bright outlook suddenly darkened.

Kama, he thought. *You should have remained with her,* he told himself. *She is worth far more than any pact.*

Descending faster, Jaspen peered to the rocks below. They speared out of the sea like piked teeth, chipped and gray. His leap had been strong. He would clear the stony pyramids.

What a fool I am! Is it too late to return to her? Yet he knew it was. *Be with Kama, my Always. Increase her cloaking skills. Protect my Forever One, I beg you.*

Jaspen sliced into the ocean and an immediate rush of pleasure, of belonging, overcame him. Saltwater pushed into the shallow trench across his chest with a curative sting. The healing waters soothed his tender palms and chafed thighs. It invigorated his muscles and strengthened his soul. It was a feeling as familiar and comforting as stepping into

Widow Yadha's hut, back when he was a youth. For a moment, all was fine and good.

Knifing deeper beneath the swells, Jaspen wondered if there was any truth to the rumor that these were Levaioth waters. He had swum to these parts but once. It was then, a few suns following his adopted mother's death, that Jaspen set out to find his blood-family.

After moving into his own hut, Jaspen's grief over his caretaker's passing had cast him into deep depression. He felt empty of everything but loneliness and sorrow. Though Kama would visit and make efforts to cheer him, Jaspen was reluctant to encumber her with his joyless face and wretched gloom.

Each night upon repairing to his sleeping pallet Jaspen had felt an urge to pray. Yet he knew of no god with the power to console him. He yearned for a compassionate and forever-friend who would not only listen to his supplications but respond by dispelling his crushing loneliness.

Soon after discovering that Levaioth was but a fish, Jaspen had spent sun after sun contemplating the secret identity of the divine being that ruled over all of Jirvalla. He had hoped—with a desperate, burning hope—that the deity worshiped by one of the other tribes would be mighty enough to replace the anguish in his heart with love and hope.

It was shortly after sunset that Jaspen had set out, under the cloak of a moonless night, and slipped into Udok lands. Kneeling at the stone altar of Vinoko, Spirit Chieftain of the Udok, Jaspen had clasped his hands and offered his petitions. But he had received no consolation, no feeling or change in atmosphere to indicate the presence of an immortal drawing near. This god of the volcano was no better than Levaioth.

Upon the next moon—a slim, grinning sliver—Jaspen had stolen into the kingdom of the Huntressi. He prostrated himself before the timber statue of Thaliana, her fist enclosed around a long, graceful bow. Upon her back, a quiver of deadly spears. Yet neither could this goddess of the hunt satisfy Jaspen's need.

The deities of the Treef and Faijen proved just as incapable. Lacking access to the UnderDown, Jaspen had to assume the Gort's Fire-Breath was as feckless as the island's other false gods.

Without a divine being on all of Jirvalla to calm his torment, Jaspen came to believe the only deity designed to meet his needs was to be found in his homeland. The god who knew Jaspen's parents, who had known Jaspen since the day of his birth, only this immortal would know how to ease the young man's burden.

Yet Jaspen had not the faintest notion of where to find his motherland.

For the ensuing twenty suns, Jaspen swam as far as he could in quest of his native people and the god who cared for them. Each day he would journey in a new direction. On four separate occasions, he had spent a night or two on an uninhabited cay or atoll to rest before pressing onward to the next isle.

The morning prior to his excursions, Jaspen would shepherd three times as many Fin-Folk as was customary, to fulfill his oath to feed the poorest of the Cove. He had shared with Kama the purpose of his unusual expeditions and instructed her to allocate smaller portions to those in need, so the provisions would bear the demands of hungry bellies until his return.

An additional eighteen suns passed and, still, Jaspen searched. The more he scoured the sea for his homeland, the more he yearned to reunite with his people. He longed to meet his parents. To feel their love for him, regardless of how deep he could dive or how many Lesser-Fins he shepherded that morning. Jaspen yearned to see the adoring eyes of his mother and father smiling at him, for no reason at all.

Home. Jaspen missed it more than he thought possible. His heart hungered for someone to love him as only a parent can. He craved for another to treasure him purely for who he was; and nothing more. Only home could provide such an evasive thing. Only home could give love freely, willingly, honestly, and constantly.

After another fifteen suns, Jaspen had given up his mission to find his people and their god. Lying upon his sleeping pallet, he forged a plan to end his life. He could not endure another sun living with the growing void of loneliness within.

On the morrow, at three hands past sunrise, following his final delivery of Fin-Folk to the Cove's poor, Jaspen would venture into the forest to where the Killing-Leaf grew. He would eat the red-spotted foliage until his eyes shut and his breath stopped.

Just before falling into slumber, however, Jaspen had pleaded in desperation for the god of his people, the one true god of all Jirvalla, to make himself plain. Hours later, Jaspen was awakened by an extraordinarily soft and beautiful light that filled his hut from wall to wall, ceiling to floor.

The round moon, he thought, smiling at the serene glow.

Jaspen paced to one of the squares he had cut into three of his hut's four walls. Prior to peering out of the opening, he perceived an odd change within. His loneliness had waned. In its former place was the waxing hope that tomorrow would bring something better than today.

"The moon god has heard me!" laughed Jaspen and looked to the night sky.

Yet the moon had yet to rise or, perhaps, it had already set.

Rushing to the other two cutouts, Jaspen confirmed that this cloudless night held nothing other than a few faintly twinkling Night-Sparks. He turned in a circle, stunned by the impossible incandescence flooding his hut. He was overcome by an inner tranquility previously unknown to him. Plunging to his knees, Jaspen had worshipped whatever god was responsible for this inexplicable marvel.

He had awoken the following morning uncertain of exactly what had passed during the night. Had it been a dream? Yet never before had a Night-Vision enrobed Jaspen with such lasting serenity. For the kindling warmth that had filled him last night was still burning in his chest.

He amended his plot to flee Jirvalla for the Lands of Kiriath-Dae. Jaspen would put off his meeting with the Killing-Leaf to see if this curious god would show again.

Over the next forty nights, the Always (as Jaspen would come to call his god) visited the young man with unpredictable intermittence. The deity had made himself manifest—always in a strange, abstract manner—mostly when Jaspen's yearning and loneliness for home had grown to such a great weight that he could no longer bear the hardship alone.

At each visitation, the Always would reveal something of himself to Jaspen. Yet the facts gained were akin to distant memories or vestiges left behind from long-ago dreams. Mornings saw Jaspen awakening to immediately cast his mind back to his moonlit reveries. But the words and images so vivid in his Night-Visions had drained away like water through a fist when exposed to the light of day. Still, his heart's knowledge of the Always was as real as anything the boy had ever seen, heard, or touched. Never before had Jaspen felt such a fullness of peace and acceptance. Never before had he known a being who loved him simply because it was a pleasure to do so.

Soon Jaspen's loneliness had been replaced by a powerful hope and newfound ease within his heart. There was also a wonderful feeling that his unseen god was accompanying him no matter where he traveled, always as near to Jaspen as his own breath.

And, now, by virtue of the Miracle of the Wind, as well as the confirming words of the Hoodoah, the Always had proven himself to be the one true god of all Jirvalla.

20

A Young Heart Stops

Kama was taking great care to lift the rock in her hand slowly, so as not to draw Sorazin's eye. It was a feat made more challenging by the flames of the torch, flames that were raising large, boiling blisters upon Kama's thigh.

The stone finally reached the ideal height and position. Focusing on a single point just above Sorazin's ear, Kama commanded herself, *Now*!

Yet as Kama's fingers tensed around the rock in preparation to thrust it downward with all of her force, Sorazin suddenly lifted his nose to sniff at the air.

The formerly stationary target was now in motion, shifting every second, rendering it impossible for Kama to strike with any precision. Sorazin's eyes were also much closer to the stone in Kama's grip. Any movement now and Kama would imperil herself by exposing her position.

Kama inhaled—silently, patiently—in an effort to detect the scent Sorazin had caught. It was burning flesh: hers.

Sorazin rose to his full height and turned to the small bonfire behind him in search of the odor's source. The torch moved with him, mercifully angling away from Kama's scorched leg. Within the dwindling fire, flames licked at what appeared to be the remains of a small, verminous cave-creature. Sorazin swung his short-sword up and around his body to sheathe it before striding to the blaze to eliminate the source of the smell.

Kama had been so preoccupied with remaining perfectly still that she believed the sudden burn along her middle was due to hunger. When the fiery pain began to thump with more ferocity, Kama peered down at a thick stream of blood flowing from a deep gash. When sheathing his blade, Sorazin had unknowingly gouged Kama's abdomen, splitting her open from hip to navel.

Somehow, she held the excruciating agony at bay while Sorazin approached the burning cave-vermin. He had yet to notice the fresh blood staining his sword's sheath.

Kama pressed her hand over the chasm across her womb. But her efforts did little to staunch the gush of blood. Fighting back the black-and-white spots flashing before her, she cast the stone in her fist well into the cave—a desperate effort to divert her enemy's attention.

Sorazin raised his torch toward the sound. He quickly pushed the smoking cave-creature out of the flames then set off in the direction of the tossed stone, into the depths of the cavern.

Kama inched along the wall to the cave's mouth as fast as her abdomen would allow. Time was precious. Sorazin would return shortly. Though she was doing her utmost to muffle her suffering, Kama's squeals and moans grew louder with each movement. She reached the cave's egress, woozy. The world spun before her.

She yearned to lay down and rest. She was so tired. With the great loss of blood came exhaustion. Yet as much as Kama longed to sleep, she would not allow it. Once Sorazin retraced his steps back to the cave's fire, he would discover the crimson trail leading to Kama. Once he tracked her down, it would be her end.

Kama peered to the sea rocks below. Each pointed its lethal tip toward her. She searched for Jaspen. He was not dashed against a pointed outcropping. He had made it safely into the sea. She surveyed the climbing route down to the foot of the sea-wall. Even with her injury, Kama believed she could manage it. But the descending cliff-path was long and winding. And every moment was crucial. She once saw Jaspen pass out from blood loss after delivering a basket of fish to her fellow villagers. If Kama took the down-route, she might blackout before reaching the cliff's base.

She gazed upward. The climbing path to the cliff's summit was much shorter. There was only a dozen or so holds to the top, where the rocky cliff receded into a grassy ridge.

Kama stretched for the first handhold and cried out as pain slashed across her middle. Her arm recoiled before gaining the position. With her reach hampered, she would have to search for holds that did not require her to extend her arm more than a forearm's length. This new restriction would lengthen the time it would take to win the summit. She sought a foothold only a hand's breadth from where her toes were dug into the seawall. She lifted a knee and screamed in agony again. This instance, however, she continued moving her limb while shrieking through the pain . . . until her foot reached its goal.

She inspected her wound. A new flood of blood was coursing out of the laceration and down her thighs.

Every day, Jaspen arrives with his basket of fish with cuts all over him.

Kama yelped, loud and harrowing, like a dying animal, as she moved from one hold the next.

If he can defeat the pain, thought Kama, *so can I!*

She kept ascending. Each exertion was more grueling than the previous. Grunting, weeping, coughing, wailing, leaving a wide swath of blood on the cliff rocks beneath her, Kama finally earned the sea-bluff's brow. With one long and final shout, she hauled herself up and onto a patch of lush, green grass.

Her lungs burned. She was lightheaded and nauseous. A shadowy pitch, as dark as the talons of Crowing Black Wing, pushed in from the edges of her vision. The long blades of grass were inviting, cool, and soft. Kama wanted nothing more than to shut her eyes and drift off, if only for a short while. Yet she knew if she gave into the temptation, she may never rise again.

Kama goaded herself to stand. Slanting her body downhill, she stumble-walked—exhausted, wobbling, half-blind—until her legs failed. She careened down the slope, semi-conscious, her arms and legs flailing as she tumbled and crashed through thistle, thorn, scrub, and brush. When she came to a halt, Kama pried open her eyes. She was not far from the site where she and Jaspen had watched Quillen and Sorazin begin their ascent of the sea-wall.

She struggled to a knee, head swirling, wound gaping, blood pouring. She swayed, the whole world blurred and spinning, then fell. Her torso hit the earth, followed by her cheek.

A tear streamed over her temple. She was weakening swiftly, her life ebbing away. The climb had been too much and the toil had stimulated a new flow of blood from the mortal wound at her gut.

Death stretched nearer and Kama sensed its coming.

With her last shred of strength, she clawed her way to a large tree and curled around its base. Kama replicated the trunk's color and texture. She hoped her body would remain hidden after she died—Kama did not want to give Sorazin the satisfaction of knowing that another threat to his reign had been erased.

Thoughts of Jaspen, of Shim, of her parents . . . came and went. For reasons mysterious, she yearned to speak with Jaspen's god. What had he called him? Her thoughts were so fuzzy. How amazing that he had made that girl, the Huntressi—what was her name?—disappear.

Kama dozed in and out of consciousness, unaware of anything but her desire to speak with the Always. She wanted to confess her shortcomings to him. She wanted to thank him, but for what, exactly, she could not recall. She wished she had met him sooner.

"I'm sorry," she mumbled, tears streaming. "For everything."

The chill took her feet and ankles first, freezing them until she could feel them no more.

"I shouldn't have followed them. Forgive me, please."

The sharp cold climbed to her knees, over her thighs, into her hips.

"Jaspen . . . " Her tears increased. "I, I . . . "

The chill pierced her stomach . . . numbed her ribs . . . then seeped into her lungs, smothering them with frost until Kama could no longer draw breath.

" . . . Jaspen . . . " she wheezed . . .

. . . just before the biting cold stopped her heart.

21

Invitation to Battle

JASPEN QUICKLY SWAM TO the surface and looked up to the cave, his thoughts on Kama.

She is okay, he told himself. He had to. The opposite would be too much to bear. *Sorazin could never locate a Cloaker of Kama's skill in such a dark cave.*

Nonetheless, Jaspen yearned to call out to her, to make certain his Forever-One was safe. Yet if he did, Sorazin would surely hear the Shepherd's call and redouble his commitment to hunt and kill Kama.

Sorazin . . . He would stop on nothing to acquire the Throne of Pearls. How many more would he butcher on his ruthless crusade to rule the Cove? He must be stopped. Before his return to the village.

Jaspen raced through the water. The sea-route to where he and Kama watched Quillen and Sorazin commence their climb to the Hoodoah's cave was much shorter than the land path. Sorazin would have to pass by that place on his way back to Cove shores.

A few random words of the Hoodoah refrained in Jaspen's head as he sped along the sea-top. He wished he had listened more intently while being cloaked in the cave. But Jaspen had been consumed with the physical bliss of being pressed so snugly against Kama: the warmth of her cheek against his, the soft pressure of her breasts against his chest, and her hips pushing flat into his pelvis.

Some words Jaspen could recall were: " . . . *his mother and father wait for him in the Other Place.*"

At the time, Jaspen believed the Hoodoah had been speaking of Sorazin's parents. Now, Jaspen knew it was his own mother and father about whom the holy man had spoken.

The Other Place, thought Jaspen and his stroke slowed. *They must be dead.*

He wondered how he could miss them so much. They had only been together for two, perhaps three, wet seasons.

One of the only memories of his parents played in Jaspen's head: Young Jaspen was hurrying along the shore with short, nearly straight-legged, toddler strides toward his mother and father. He was laughing, as children do, contagious and exuberant. The sun was bright and there were smeared images of others in his tribe, each colored in a similar black-and-white pattern. His parents were both kneeling, with wide grins of anticipation for their son to leap with trustful abandon into their waiting arms.

Jaspen's strength withered as a weight settled in his heart. His tears mixed with the sea.

The voice of the Hoodoah sounded in his ear: "*The only son to his parents . . .*"

Jaspen saddened even more. How awful for his mother and father to have lost their only son. Had they died in the incident that had driven Jaspen to Jirvalla? Or had they searched for him, season after season, until heartbreak overtook them.

The Shepherd waded toward the sand. He wished Kama were beside him. She always listened so attentively: quietly and without judgment. She was the only person on the whole of Jirvalla who Jaspen could talk to about anything of import.

More words from the Hoodoah came to Jaspen: *King-Crusher, Destroyer of Thrones* and *God-Slayer*. What did it mean? Was Jaspen supposed to kill Sorazin? It was all so puzzling.

It is untrue anyway, thought Jaspen. *I am no king, let alone a king crusher. The Hoodoah has erred*, he told himself, *if only this once.*

"What might Kama say?" he muttered but already knew her answer. "She would say the Hoodoah speaks true."

She would say the Always intends for me to become more than a Mutahn, he thought. *And should I shun the course that fate has wrought, my soul and life and purpose would wilt into nothing.*

"For you, Kama," muttered Jaspen, "will I pursue this path of God-Slayers and King-Crushers with all of my heart and soul and strength. For you."

A tremendous splash erupted behind Jaspen and he turned to the noise.

A pod of frolicking Long-Snout, he thought, *or the Gray-Mountain-Beast.*

He squinted at the huge, black fin of Levaioth cutting through the shallows, following the curve of the coast. Though far off, Jaspen could reach the monster in but two- or three-hundred strokes.

The Shepherd glanced in the direction leading to Sorazin. Then his eyes snapped back to Levaioth. He should kill the beast now. He could return to the Cove with a few of the behemoth's teeth and couple of its many eyes. With such spoils, the village elders would believe him when he apprised them of Sorazin's endeavor to kill the Hoodoah.

Jaspen delved within for a small voice, a feeling, a nudge. He drew a deep breath and steadied his heart. Even without his pearl knife or bone spear, he wished to swim the distance and attack the Cove's counterfeit god. Something advised him to stay his desire, however, to tarry until a more suitable time presented itself.

Scowling out at Levaioth, Jaspen shouted, "Run away, *waigu!*" He kicked at the water to send a spray of ocean toward the distant killer. "But upon your return, Tatter-Tail, I will be here! Mark my name, minnow: I am Jaspen, Shepherd of Fish!"

He plunged his face beneath the water and clicked out his threat in the undersea tongue.

Levaioth slowed, as if Jaspen's call had reached the monster's ear. The savage's tail turned toward the shore where Jaspen stood and he watched the dark, moth-eaten fin travel in a lazy circle, seemingly inviting the Shepherd to a duel. Save for its ragged tailfin, nothing of the creature broke the surface.

"Another time, Seven-Eye," cried Jaspen. "Until then, enjoy the few moons you have left. For the day we meet again will be your last."

22

Boggfrogg

JASPEN STOLE TO THE forest's edge and concealed himself behind a tree. He peeked around the trunk, eyes and ears searching for Sorazin. There was neither sight nor sound of him.

Good, thought Jaspen. *He remains far off.*

Jaspen crept from one tree to the next, closing in on his destination. His best chance at victory was to take Sorazin by surprise. He intended to launch his ambush from a site a few hundred strides away—where he and Kama had spied Sorazin and the graybeard commence their climb up the sea-wall.

Along the way, Jaspen gathered items to use as weapons—a branch resembling a long staff, dried bones and beaks, a broken Huntressi arrow . . .

When the moment arrives, he wondered, *will I even be able to . . . to . . .*

The only lives Jaspen had taken were those of the Fin-Folk.

Hunting for a good stone to throw, Jaspen's eyes caught upon an image so ghastly and unexpected that it thieved his breath and halted his legs. He gaped in shock at a large, bodiless face ogling up at him from a shallow concavity in the soil. Rumors were rife that this region of the Treef forest was home to bizarrely gruesome creatures and otherworldly spirits. Until now, Jaspen had not believed the reports.

Peering closer at the fleshy, white face and sky-blue eyes staring up at him from the earth, Jaspen could not establish whether the macabre visage was alive or dead.

Then the large eyes blinked.

And the mouth said, "Hallo hay."

Jaspen leapt back and stumbled over an exposed root. Scrabbling to his feet, he slowly approached the strange face buried in the dirt. Upon a thorough study of the creature before him, he sighed in relief.

The eyes, nose, cheeks, and mouth visible above the leaves and twigs were those of an Udok submerged in a camouflaged pit of Sink-Earth. If the half-giant had not been tilting his face upward, he would have been breathing sand and foliage instead of forest air.

I have not the time to contend with this clumsy Udok, thought Jaspen.

He quickly scanned his surrounds to ensure the half-giant was not playing the part of a decoy in an elaborate enemy trap.

"Boggfrogg is alone," said the Udok.

Jaspen inspected him, cautious, careful to remain quiet. In addition to the Udok's great size and strength, the hostile tribe was known for their pitiless barbarism. Again, Jaspen's eyes cast about the trees in search of hidden Udok.

"Boggfrogg gives his word that not one has followed him. Boggfrogg is unworthy to follow. Boggfrogg's family is the least of all Udok and Boggfrogg is the least of his famil—"

"Provide me a reason why I should not dispatch you this instant, Udok."

Though the half-giant appeared harmless, and his humility genuine, Jaspen could not discount the chance of subterfuge.

"The black-and-white sea-person interrupted Boggfrogg. Boggfrogg's mother would not be pleased with the black-and-white sea-person. Manners are very imp—"

"Has a Cove-man passed by?" Jaspen glanced toward the sea-cliff then back to the Udok.

The puffy, white face staring up at Jaspen furrowed in thought, as if struggling to solve a riddle. "How unusual that the black-and-white sea-person has interrupted Boggfrogg a second time. Is it the custom of black-and-white sea-folk to interrupt others while they are speaking?"

The question was earnest and without guile or sarcasm. It shamed Jaspen.

"No," said Jaspen. "Accept my apology. I have been rude. Boggfrogg is it?"

"Boggfrogg's mother and family say Bogg," he explained. "Though Bogg's full name is Boggfroggbigbogganbiggle. The black-and-white sea-person may also say Bogg."

Why does he extend to me such kindness? thought Jaspen, guilt prodding his conscience for treating this innocent Udok so gruffly.

"I am Jaspen." He bowed his face. "Jaspen of the Cove. Shepherd of Fish. It is a pleasure to meet you, Bogg."

"Hallo hay, Jaspen-of-the-cove-shepherd-of-fish."

"Jaspen. It is simply Jaspen."

"Bogg is pleased to meet Jaspen-it-is-simply-jaspen."

"Jaspen." He wanted to add *it's just plain Jaspen* but knew Bogg would misunderstand.

"Hallo hay, Jaspen."

"This is Treef land." As gentle and good-natured as Bogg seemed, Jaspen still required answers. "Do you frequently visit enemy soil?"

"Bogg would ask Jaspen the very same if Bogg discovered Jaspen's face in a bowl of Sink-Earth on the Huntressi plain. Jaspen would certainly not have traveled to Huntressi lands for the food. The tribe have no talent for herbs and spices. Or cooking in general. Huntressi meals are dry and flavorless. Not at all like the delicacies prepared by the celebrated Udok chef, Poggfroggpigpogganpiggle, Bogg's very own father. If only Jaspen could sample Poggfrogg's roasted dirt with boiled pebbles. Oh, what—"

"Bogg." Jaspen's expression encouraged the Udok to answer his query.

"Oh. For Bogg's tendency to ramble, Bogg is sorry." He drew a breath. "Bogg was compelled to enter the Treef woodland because it is— Uh oh."

The Udok's soft-blue eyes widened in alarm as a Water-Walker set down on a nearby branch and ruffled its snowy-white feathers. The creature had tall, thin legs with wide, webbed feet, and a curving beak, long and sharp. It hopped from limb to limb, descending, until it reached the forest floor.

"Bogg must express how greatly appreciated Jaspen's intervention would be at this very moment." His gaze grew more urgent as the Water-Walker stepped onto the Sink-Earth. "If Jaspen is capable of haste, Bogg would value that as well."

Amused, Jaspen grinned at the Water-Walker's wide feet striding atop the surface of the Sink-Earth as if it were dry land.

"Bogg would be forever in Jaspen's de— Away!" Bogg spat at the approaching fowl. "Please, Jaspen. Bogg rather enjoys his eyeballs, lips, and nose."

"Well, I do suppose . . . " Jaspen spoke slowly, "if your reason for trespassing upon Treef lands is sound, I may be persuaded to save you from the terrors of tha—"

"Be gone!" Bogg glared at the oncoming bird. "Shoo! Shoo!"

Jaspen reached out and lowered his staff-like branch so that it rested on the Sink-Earth between the winged creature and Bogg.

The Water-Walker squawked in displeasure and pecked at the bothersome tree limb obstructing its path to a meal of Udok cheek and tongue.

"To Jaspen, Bogg gives many thanks." The Udok breathed in relief. "Bogg would very much enjoy expressing his gratitude for Jaspen's saving act by preparing for Jaspen a delectable meal of sautéed Skull Dipped in Fresh Forest Dung. It is a rare specialty of Bogg's."

"Provide me with a valid reason as to your presence on enemy soil." Jaspen lifted the branch and the Water-Walker advanced a step toward Bogg. "Or shall I allow this famished fellow to—"

"Away! Shoo! Go!"

Again, the winged scavenger complained with an irritated screech as the branch dropped to thwart its afternoon repast.

"Once more, Bogg offers his gratitude to Jaspen."

"Answer please. Now." Jaspen glanced to the sea-wall, checking for Sorazin.

"Bogg passes through the Treef forest because it is only by way of this woodland that Bogg can reach the Hoodoah's cave-place."

The Hoodoah. Jaspen recalled the image of the holy man standing in the midst of the cave's fire, saying, *I must become less, so that you, Shepherd of Fish, Shepherd of Jirvalla, may become more.*

"And for what reasons do you seek the Hoodoah?"

"The Hoodoah visited Bogg in a night-story. Not once, but on three occasions over the past four moons. The Hoodoah convinced Bogg to journey through Treef lands to a cave-place high upon a sea-cliff." Bogg smiled. "This is a good reason for Bogg to be in the Treef forest, yes?" Bogg smiled wider.

Expecting Bogg to continue the tale, Jaspen broadened his eyes so as to compel the Udok to resume.

Yet Bogg simply lifted his eyebrows, his grin widening even more.

Jaspen asked, "Have you any idea *why* the Hoodoah invited you to his cave?"

"Bogg does." He bounced his eyebrows. He did not elaborate.

"And . . . " Jaspen's hand implied that Bogg should resume his tale.

After a moment . . . "Oh, Bogg understands! Jaspen's fingers flicking inwards toward his palm is a nonverbal gesture indicating that Bogg should explain the reason why the Hoodoah summoned Bogg to the Hoodoah's cave-place."

"Yes, Bogg." Jaspen wiped his forehead in frustration. "That is correct."

"The Hoodoah found a friend for Bogg! The new friend waits to meet Bogg in the Hoodoah's cave-place. The friend has a very strange name. Bogg cannot be entirely certain if the Hoodoah in my night-story recited it correctly."

When Bogg failed to volunteer the name, Jaspen asked, "And what name would that be?"

"Oh, Bogg understands. Because Jaspen is flicking his fingers toward his palm again. Jaspen of the Cove is tiring of Bogg's incessant speech and is desperate to know the name of Bogg's friend at this very moment." He grinned, victorious.

"Yes, Bogg. Again, you are correct."

"Bogg enjoys being correct. The strange name that Bogg believes the Hoodoah said is Destroyer of Thrones King Crusher."

23

Into the Void

BOGG LATCHED ONTO JASPEN'S staff-like branch and pulled himself across the Sink-Earth.

Was it you, my Always, thought Jaspen, *or your servant, the Hoodoah, who gave to Bogg the dreams? And what is it that you want of me? To befriend this good-hearted Udok? I cannot discern the benefit.*

"If Jaspen does not enjoy Crunchy Horn Hotpot," Bogg reached the pit's edge and dragged himself out of the mire, "perhaps a lovely braised Hoof and Lava Medley would be a more suitable act of gratitude. For saving Boggfrogg's life."

"Shhh," whispered Jaspen as his eyes perused the woods for Sorazin. "There is a very bad Cove-man I must ki . . . capture."

"Bogg is sorry," he whispered while wiping away the viscid Sink-Earth that clung to his plump, bald body. Upon finishing the chore, Bogg stood to his full height.

Peering up at the Udok, Jaspen was surprised to find that Bogg was not nearly as tall as he had imagined. The half-giant had no more than a hand's breadth over Sorazin.

The Udok read Jaspen's expression and said, "Bogg is shortest of all Udok. Bogg is sorry to disappoint Jaspen."

"Shhh," reminded Jaspen, still scouting for Sorazin. "I am not disappointed."

Already he is a burden, thought Jaspen.

Locating a thick tree, Jaspen positioned Bogg at the trunk's rear so that he could not be seen from the spot where Jaspen expected Sorazin to enter the forest.

"Your dream . . . " Jaspen placed himself behind Bogg, "what more can you tell me of it?"

"Bogg is pleased to tell the whole night-story to Jaspen. But perhaps Jaspen and Bogg should ask if she requires any help first." Bogg motioned to a tree in the near distance.

Jaspen looked to the tree. The only other person he knew that referred to trees as *she* and *he* was the Cove's flute-carver, Perpeht.

Jaspen studied the bark, leaves, roots, and branches. "She appears fine to me."

"She bleeds. Jaspen cannot detect it? There expands a puddle near the root bumps. It gives quite a wonderful savor to the root-dirt, but is generally not so wonderful for the one from whom the blood flows."

Noting the large patch of wet, dark soil near a bulging outgrowth at the tree's base, Jaspen peered closer at the bulbous hump at the foot of the trunk. His eyes widened.

"Is that . . . " Jaspen broke out from behind Bogg and stepped toward the tree.

The Cloaker appeared to be embracing the bottom of the tree, its back to Jaspen. Whoever the Cloaker, he was very talented—perfectly simulating the bark's texture and color.

Jaspen studied the shape of the shoulders, the slender neck, the graceful curve of the hip . . .

"Kama?"

Jaspen edged closer.

"Kama!" cried Jaspen and he raced toward her.

Jaspen's heart pinched and his legs tremored when Kama did not even twitch at the sound of his voice. He was three strides away from her when the earth beneath his foot gave way. Stumbling, Jaspen cursed the forest floor for its secret dips and hunches.

Jaspen waited, impatient, for his knee to meet the ground. He would then roll out of his fall and reach Kama with only a brief pause. Yet Jaspen continued to plummet.

And plummet.

"Kama!" shouted Jaspen as he plunged deeper into the unmarked Gort hole. "Kaaamaaaaaa!"

24

New Mutahn

NIGHT WAS FALLING WHEN Ertu, the Cove's royal advisor and cousin to the recently deceased Mutahn Pehlni, hobbled into the Hall of Shells.

"Sorazin?" Shocked, Ertu gaped at his nephew lounging casually upon the Throne of Pearls, a leg slung over an armrest. "How dare you!" The former Tharsool hastened toward the youth on chubby legs and swollen feet. "In the name of Levaioth," he seized Sorazin's elbow, "withdraw at once!"

"Or what, Uncle?" Sorazin had arrived home from the journey to the Hoodoah's cave just as the sun was dipping behind Smoke Mountain. "Pray tell." He jerked his arm free of Ertu's feeble grip. "Will you call the guards?" He sneered in disgust at how fat his uncle had grown. "Have them lash your new Mutahn to within an inch of death?"

"Mutahn? You?"

"Indeed." Sorazin grinned, smug. Extending a hand, he dangled it before the old man and fluttered the finger upon which the Mutahn's ring was placed.

Ertu considered the jeweled band. "Have I missed the banquet?" He referred to the ceremonial Feast of the Ring: an event culminating with the incoming Mutahn slipping the imperial ring upon his finger for the first time.

"Always thinking of food, eh Uncle? I have postponed the feast, little Ertu. How it must break your heart, I know, but we have not the time to squander on archaic formalities. Now, you may press your lips to the Mutahn's ring."

"Kissing a royal's ring was an absurd practice even prior its abolition over a thousand moons ago. Pretentious and arrogant is how the villagers view it."

"The custom has been restored. Now kneel and kiss your sovereign's ring."

Ertu returned his nephew's glare, suspicious. "Forgive me, Nephew, but my gaze has grown dim of late." His eyes scanned Sorazin from head to heel. "The totem the Hoodoah bestows upon each new Jirvallan ruler . . . I am certain my failing vision has simply skimmed over it. Can you please present the item to verify that the Hoodoah has chosen you to rule? They are each so lovely and different. I cherished the sight of your father's amulet."

"I have no need of a talisman to prove my legitimacy as Mutahn. In the event there are no contenders for the throne, as is the case at present, Cove law states that the former Mutahn's eldest son shall be appointed as ruler. Even idiots know this, Uncle. To ease your anxious heart, however," Sorazin's hand disappeared into his robes and returned with a small, white item, "the token you seek is here." He held it before Ertu but pulled it back when the old man reached for it. "Not before you kneel, old man, and kiss the ring of your Mutahn."

After a long moment of thought, Ertu grunted then slumped to a knee. He lowered his face and begrudgingly pressed his lips to the ring. Pushing aside Sorazin's hand, Ertu struggled up to a standing position.

Sorazin handed to his uncle the small, white totem.

Ertu gazed in confusion at the shard of bone resting in his palm.

"It is an antler's tip," clarified Sorazin, "from a rather immense Tree-Horns."

Knowing that he would be made to produce a totem from the Hoodoah confirming his right to rule, Sorazin had cleverly hacked a run of tusk from the holy man's headdress prior to exiting the cave.

"Mine eyes have never beheld one so plain," said Ertu.

"It is a symbol to remind me of the divine task with which the Hoodoah has entrusted me: To run through all enemies interfering with the expansion of Cove lands." Sorazin grinned at the anguish gathering about Ertu's eyes. "We are to begin immediately, by pressing into Udok territory."

"Kill the Udok?" asked Ertu. "You must have misunderstood, Nephew. Eight moons ago, at the Council of All Tribes, the Hoodoah advised each tribe to seek peace with its adversaries. He even proposed a border-less island, where each—"

"Apparently, dear Uncle, the Hoodoah has changed his mind."

"Have I your permission to send a footman to confirm the Hoodoah's—"

"The Hoodoah is dead."

"Pardon?"

"That sea-thing, *mahkifo*, slew him."

"Our Shepherd of Fish?"

"He tailed us to the cave. The moment the Hoodoah announced me instead of him as Mutahn, that filth drew his knife. He took Quillen first, then the Hoodoah."

"Quillen? My dear friend is dead?" Tears filled Ertu's eyes and his gaze descended. "But young Jaspen was not even a Mutahn candidate."

"In his distorted mind, *mahkifo* believed that he was. Were it not for my training, Uncle, that slimy fish might have slain me as well." Sorazin rose to his feet and unsheathed his blade. He peered down the Gort sword's impressive length. "Worry not though, little Ertu, I have placed a large bounty on the heads of both *mahkifo* and his silly playmate; Kama."

"Kama? She is a child."

"She accompanied that dirty stray to the cave, as his accomplice. A team of trackers combs the island for them even now. I expect both to be in my custody by sunfall tomorrow. Dead or alive."

Sorazin's anger flared at the sight of Ertu's disapproving face.

"Pray tell, Uncle, what would you have me do? Allow the fugitives to wander Jirvalla until turning themselves in? Then issue to them a pardon for murdering the island's most revered prophet? You men of peace are so predictable. Always an excuse to grant a second chance."

"Oh, Sorazin . . . " Ertu looked upon him with pity. "My only cousin's beloved son . . . With violence there is no end. Perhaps, in time, you will understand. It is only peace that can promise—"

"The Cove will be feared again!"

"Nephew . . . " Ertu's pity swelled. "Have you not yet learned? Fear is a weapon employed only by the frightened."

Sorazin struck his uncle fiercely across the cheek.

Ertu nearly toppled to the floor.

Sorazin brought together his hands in two booming claps.

Four hulking guards stalked into the Hall of Shells through a curtain of reeds at the rear of the Mutahn's throne. They strode to Sorazin and posted themselves at attention, two on either side of their monarch.

To his royal guard, Sorazin said, "This man is to be arrested at once. The charge is insurrection."

The butt of each guard's spear clouted the stone floor as one. The sharp report echoed throughout the royal hall, ominous.

The guards marched to Ertu and surrounded him.

Sorazin pressed his face close to his uncle's. "As for your sentence . . ."

"Nephew, please, I have—"

"On the morrow, at sunfall, you will face The Dome."

25

Gort Hole

JASPEN PLUMMETED THROUGH DARKNESS, downward and downward, legs kicking, arms spiraling—stretching, grasping—desperate to clutch anything to stop his fall. Yet the walls of the Gort hole were far too smooth and steep.

As the sheer, vertical walls of the pit finally began to slope inward, Jaspen leaned his body into the dirt wall. His flesh chafed and burned as it grated against the earthen chute, flakes of skin coming away from his chest and thighs like flower petals in the breeze. But his speed was decreasing. Jaspen stabbed his feet into the earth and clawed at the slanting walls with hooked fingers. The deeper he thrust his hands and toes, the more he slowed. One last powerful push into the narrowing dirt funnel and Jaspen's efforts would succeed in halting his descent.

Yet before he could drive his fingers and feet any deeper into the earth, the walls widened and grew vertical again. Jaspen was freefalling once more.

A moment later, Jaspen's feet and ankles were sinking into something soft and warm. The sensation quickly spread up to his thighs and waist. It was as if he were plunging into a large, deep nest of baby Puff-Tails. The feathery, lightweight matter thickened around and beneath him until, at last, Jaspen arrived at the bottom of the dark, Gort pit.

He opened his eyes yet saw nothing. He passed a hand before his face but could not distinguish it.

Kama . . . he thought and sprang to his feet.

"Kama!" he cried into the chute above. "Kaamaaaa!"

Protect her life, my Always, please, he prayed while stepping carefully across the hollow with his hands pushed out before him to defend against a collision with whatever else this pitch-black lair might hold.

The animal pelts, feathers, dead grass, and leaves that broke Jaspen's fall rustled and crunched underfoot as he continued to call out *Kama! Kama!* while searching blindly for a wall.

After seven careful half-strides, his hand finally brushed against a dry, dirt wall. He walked the perimeter of the earthen dungeon. It was a rough circle and similar in size to his hut by the sea—six long strides from wall to wall. Jaspen pressed his palms into the wall's firmly packed earth. Stretching high his arms, he drove his fingers as deep into the hard dirt as he could manage. He hoisted himself upward then dug his toes into the vertical wall. After ascending an arm's length, however, the wall began to slope inward. The severity of the angle increased with Jaspen's next handhold. Grip failing, he plummeted to the pit's floor.

Again and again Jaspen tried to scale his way out of the Gort hole. Sweat was soon coursing down his torso, arms, and legs. Fatigue burned in his thighs and shoulders. Yet no matter how he strove, each bid concluded with Jaspen sinking again into the feathery floor.

"Tell me she lives, my Always." He rolled onto his side and pulled his knees to his chest. "Tell me her wound is but a scratch."

Tell me you would never take her life from me, he thought.

He lifted his face to the shaft above. Yet his eyes were no better than a blind man's. At least the soft wind breezing down the long chute carried with it hushed sounds of sun-side life. The quiet rumple of leaves and pelts beneath him were soon joined by murmurings of faraway Gort and their slaves going about their toils.

Jaspen rose to a kneeling position and clasped together his hands. "Free Kama from death and I vow to care for her every day until my last. I love her." Tears fell. "Heal her and I promise that the day I hold Kama again is the day I will entreat her to become my Forever-One."

A scuffling from above, along with a call of alarm, sent Jaspen scrambling to the lair's edge. To remain in the den's middle would invite a sure crushing by the Tree-Horns or Long-Claw presently careering down into the Gort hole.

A great bulk smashed into the feathers, fur, and leaves a mere foot's length from Jaspen. He softened his breathing and mantled himself with the animal skins, soft down, and foliage to mask his scent. Many were the dangerous beasts that traversed the Treef wood above. Without his pearl knife, Jaspen was defenseless against the razored claws of Spotted-Pelt or the piercing fangs of Howling-Moon.

He peeked out from the leaves and feathers bunched about him. Opening wide his eyes, he gawped into the dark with hopes of catching a shadowed outline of the beast that had just become his unwelcome pit-mate.

A voice broke the silence: "Hallo hay. Jaspen?"

"Bogg!" Jaspen threw off his covering and leapt to his feet.

Though a small part of Jaspen was soothed by Bogg's voice and presence, a larger part wished the half-giant had remained with Kama. To care for her. To ferry her to the Cove healer.

Jaspen asked, "The girl, Kama. Is she alive?"

"Bogg does not know the answer. Jaspen rescued Bogg from a pit of Sink-Earth. Bogg now has a life-debt to pay to Jaspen. So Bogg entered the Gort hole and will rescue Jaspen from the UnderDown. It is the Udok way."

"There is no need, Bogg. Consider the life-debt paid in full. Count us even."

"Bogg is very sorry but Bogg cannot accept Jaspen's request. Any debt an Udok acquires, an Udok pays. This is the Udok way."

"The girl against the tree," said Jaspen, "the bleeding one . . . "

There was so much blood, he thought.

"She was my closest friend."

I loved her, Jaspen wanted to say. But he scarcely knew the Udok.

Thankful for the dark, Jaspen permitted tears to flow.

"I am a coward, Bogg," Jaspen found himself saying, unable to tame his tongue. "All of my life I have loved Kama. Never once did I summon the courage to tell her. Now she will never know. Because she is dead." Tears spilled.

Bogg's enormous hand found Jaspen's arm and patted it clumsily while working its way to the Shepherd's shoulder.

"Never again," said Jaspen, "will I allow fear to block my tongue from speaking truth." He wiped away his tears, pushing back the lake of them that had yet to be cried. "At least Kama lives now in the Everlasting Lands. Perhaps the Always will allow me to meet her there this very day."

"Bogg does not know what Jaspen means when Jaspen says the always."

"The Always is my god."

"Bogg has always adored stories featuring gods and welcomes the occasion to listen to Jaspen reciting the saga of the Always. Though it is doubtful that the Always is as robust and formidable as Vinoko; who can walk through a mountain's base and pound out great valleys with only fists."

God-Slayer . . . Jaspen recalled the Hoodoah's words. *Is it the holy man's wish for me to rid Jirvalla of its many false gods? Is that what the Hoodoah—* Catching himself, Jaspen shook his head. *I am no more the boy in the bones than this Udok.*

"However," said Bogg, "this moment is unsuitable for such a thrilling tale. For Bogg hears the approach of Mudkin chains."

"Mudkin chains?"

"Mudkin are the shortest and strangest of Jirvalla's under-earth tribes. They are made up of roots and mud and bark and bugs. Mudkin use chains to gather up those found in Gort holes and deliver them to the Gort to serve as slaves."

The jangling of the chains grew closer.

"Bogg only knows this because many meals ago Bogg's Uncle Tigg sought asylum in a Gort hole. It was shortly after Tigg's Moldy Root Sweet Bowl caused the Udok chieftain to go ill. There was much groaning that night. Uncle Tigg could not abide the shame. Oh! the pressure of a chef's life!"

"Let the Mudkin come," said Jaspen. "And kill me where I lay."

"Apologies, but Bogg cannot permit Jaspen to die until Bogg saves Jaspen. Bogg has a life-debt to pay. Bogg also believes the Gort prefer their slaves alive and strong. This is because a dead slave does not accomplish as much work as a living slave. Bogg also knows that if Jaspen and Bogg battle the Mudkin with great strength and skill, Jaspen and Bogg might overpower the Mudkin and their chains."

"I am happy to attack them," said Jaspen.

But after a few blows, he thought, *I will lower my defenses and invite the killing stroke.*

26

Mudkin

"Bogg and Jaspen will burrow beneath this soft pile of animal pelts, feathers, and leaves. When the Mudkin move close," Bogg's whisper dimmed even more, "Bogg and Jaspen will attack the Mudkin in great surprise and vanquish the enemy with many powerful blows. Jaspen will then be free to climb out of this pit, find Kama, then locate a strong vine to lower down to Bogg. And Bogg's life-debt will be paid in full."

"It is a fine plan, Bog—"

"Sh. Mudkin come. Bogg hides now. Jaspen should do the same."

A metal key clanked into what sounded to be an outer door's lock. Iron bars creaked open.

Once the pair was sufficiently blanketed, Bogg whispered, "Bogg and Jaspen must wait until the Mudkin draw within an arm's length. This is when Bogg and Jaspen will strike. Not a moment soon—"

Another metallic *chink* was followed by a whining squeal of hinges—the inner gate had swung open.

Into the Gort hole stepped the Mudkin.

Jaspen and Bogg halted all motion. They calmed their breathing, opened wide their ears, and listened through the dark.

The Mudkin were slow to move from their post near the inner gate. From their snuffling and groaning—like Five-Claw during its wet-season slumber—Jaspen estimated there were at least two, probably three Mudkin within the Gort pit. Chains jangled behind the Mudkin as new slaves, retrieved from other Gort holes nearby, shuffled their manacled feet and wrung their fettered hands.

Time passed but the Mudkin remained near the entrance, patient. The leaves, pelts, and feathers camouflaging Jaspen and Bogg appeared to be working. But the longer the Mudkin lingered, the more anxious Jaspen grew.

Jaspen wriggled a toe, hoping the noise would coax the Mudkin to step toward him in search of the sound's origin. The heavy grunts of the Mudkin stopped instantly upon hearing the quiet rustle. A low growl from one of the Mudkin warned the shackled prisoners to cease their edgy twitching, to halt the rattle of their cuffs.

Silence ensued. Moments passed, noiseless and still.

Jaspen flexed his toes and the Mudkin promptly unleashed something into the pit.

Whatever creatures they had loosed, Jaspen could hear them swiftly stealing across the leaves and feathers, in the manner of Slither-Belly, toward him. Jaspen's heart thumped and his muscles tensed in anticipation.

"Now!" cried Bogg.

Yet the moment Jaspen bounded to his feet, something cool and vine-like twined about his ankle. The beast-thing coiled tighter and yanked Jaspen's leg toward the iron gate with so much vigor that he was thrown back down to the pit's floor. A second creature found Jaspen's wrist while a third wrapped around his free ankle. Jaspen kicked and twisted and fought and strained . . . yet the bonds would not yield.

"Bogg!" A fourth coil tautened around Jaspen's other wrist. "Get th—"

A vine slipped between Jaspen's lips and he clamped shut his teeth with all the force he could muster. The tendril extended. Its end slid over Jaspen's gums and out the other side of his mouth, over his ear then around his head to form a noose. All the while, the vine's thickest part continued its quest to break through Jaspen's clenched teeth. The woody cord cinched tighter and tighter until it prevailed in parting Jaspen's teeth and burrowing into his mouth. Though Jaspen feared the interloper would slither down his throat and tear apart his innards before bursting up and out of his chest, the vine settled snugly between Jaspen's back teeth: its only goal to gag its victim.

Bogg's frantic huffing and struggling told Jaspen that the Udok, too, was losing his battle with a similar foe.

Soon, the sinewy vines were towing Jaspen across the Gort pit and to the Mudkin. He and Bogg were shackled with wrist cuffs and ankle fetters then chained to the other slaves.

And the pair's one hundred moons as vassals to the Gort had begun.

27

The Dome

"Strip the prisoner." Sorazin grinned at the sight of his uncle pacing anxiously within The Dome, three guards trailing his every step.

Twenty Cove warriors flanked their Mutahn on an elevated stage overlooking a domed structure composed of long, thin, lethally thorned limbs of the Green-Branch-Tree. The branches arched and flexed and crisscrossed in a shape that evoked a huge, open-weave basket turned upside down. The height of two men at its center, The Dome was fifty strides across and braced in various places with animal horns and thick runs of bone lashed to the wood. The construct also boasted a solid band of Gort steel that girdled its base where timber met earth.

A guard near Ertu tore from the old man his tunic, leaving him naked.

"What is the man's crime to deserve this?" objected a Cove from just beyond the torches that rimmed the exterior of The Dome.

"Have you no mercy?" shouted another.

Sorazin's eyes flashed to two of his forty soldiers stationed amongst the crowd. The guards seized the pair of dissidents, dragged them to The Dome and hurled them against the pointed thorns standing out in every direction from the structure.

Shrieks rose and blood spilled from the gashes pitting the backs of the two agitators. They twisted and squirmed and whenever one drew close to freeing himself from the wooded spurs, a guard would shove him deeper into the barbs.

The crowd quieted, fear quashing their protests.

"The man before you has been found guilty of insurrection," Sorazin said to the crowd. "Let this be a lesson to you all." Sorazin's narrow gaze roved the crowd. "Any opposing me, the Cove's rightful sovereign, will suffer a most heinous end."

"I've committed no crime!" cried Ertu, eyes stern. "This *child* Mutahn is—"

The hilt of a soldier's sword struck the old man in the mouth; felling him and knocking clear two of his teeth. Ertu's face slapped into the dirt at The Dome's edge; where a large wooden crate was joined to the outside of the edifice.

A terrible grunt-snuffle rose from inside the crate.

Ertu's eyes darted to the timber cage. Yet the cloudy night conspired with the crate's covered roof to keep the monster inside hidden from view. Another grunt from the cage was followed by a powerful outbreath that sent a plume of dust spiraling up from between two wooden slats of the crate's roof.

A guard prodded Ertu to his feet and the fleshy, old man backed away from whatever forest brute was snorting and bellowing within the crate.

The creature rocked its coop again. A thick hoof kicked out to splinter a plank at one side of the cage while a long, curved tusk slashed upward to fragment a slat on the crate's opposite side.

Smiling, Sorazin sat down upon the royal seat and motioned to his man near the timber cage to carry out his duty.

The door of the cage slid open and Spike-Jaw trotted into The Dome. Proud and confident, the monster's dark, wet eyes found its prey and its hackles flared.

Ertu froze with fear, gawping in awe at the tusked savage before him.

"May Levaioth be with you!" came the encouraging words from the crowd.

Spike-Jaw stood waist-high and possessed the same barrel-chested shape as Charging-Two-Horns. The beast had a thick bristled neck and four piked tusks jutting skyward from its snout: two from the lower jaw and two from the upper. Each tusk grew in a manner that pushed Spike-Jaw's top lip up and back to lay bare its black and pink mottled gums, like Howling-Moon on the brink of attack.

Sorazin grinned at the animal's cold, black stare. A part of the Mutahn wished it were he who was dueling with Spike-Jaw. It had always given him great pleasure to dominate another—whether animal, Udok, Huntressi, Treef, Faijen, or Cove.

Spike-Jaw snuffled and its damp nostrils shivered as they sniffed the air, establishing a better fix on its quarry. The beast lowered its scarred head and charged.

Ertu threw off his paralysis and veered to the side, scarcely evading a tusk.

Spike-Jaw slammed into the steel strip that encircled The Dome's base.

Ertu lifted his face to the moon and clasped his hands together in prayer, openly beseeching Levaioth to provide him with the wits and strength to triumph over Spike-Jaw. For the rules of The Dome were clear: one combatant would be declared champion when the other was declared dead. The winner, if previously accused of wrongdoing, would also be exonerated of all charges; the victory viewed as a pronouncement of innocence from Levaioth himself.

"Well don't just stand there, you fat oaf," muttered Sorazin. "Entertain us!"

Hoofbeats closed in and Ertu leapt, latching onto a beam just as Spike-Jaw thrust upward its tusks with a force so mighty its entire body vaulted from the earth. The beast writhed in the air, whipping like a banner in the wind.

"Bravo, Uncle," mumbled Sorazin, surprised by the old man's sudden agility.

Ertu shouted in pain and grimaced at a thorn boring through the flap of skin between his thumb and forefinger. The old man's grip would not last long.

Spike-Jaw snorted, chest puffed, impatient for its prey to drop.

Ertu's desperate gaze found Sorazin's, the elder's eyes begging his nephew to call off the slaughter.

The coward cannot even die with honor, thought Sorazin. *Come now, Uncle. Return to earth and fight like a man. You sully the family name.*

Ertu drew a breath and prepared himself for what must be done. He pumped his plump legs, back and forth, and his body swung, gaining momentum to propel himself as far from his foe as possible.

The monster below grunted and back-stepped, eyes fixed upon the man above.

Ertu flung his legs forward and released the crossbeam. He bawled in agony as his hand tore free of the thorn skewering it. His feet met the ground running and he raced for a section of The Dome that appeared to hold the thinnest of the green timbers.

His intent was evident: to crash into The Dome's weakest members in an effort to rent a gap through which to escape.

Ertu tilted his shoulder and readied for impact.

Two paces behind, Spike-Jaw lowered its great head.

Ertu launched into the air, his heavy shoulder targeting the slimmest beams.

Yet Spike-Jaw also leapt. The beast threw its massive head forward and up.

Ertu was still airborne when one of the brute's tusks grazed his inner thigh, missing the meat of his leg by a finger's length.

Finally reaching The Dome's branches, Ertu's prodigious weight crashed into the timber enclosure. A pair of dagger-sharp thorns ripped into the wise man's shoulder while another tore into the side of his neck. The tree limbs were flexing and straining and creaking, stretching outward and outward, more and more, as Ertu's momentum continued to press against The Dome.

The assemblage held its breath, every eye broad with the hope that Ertu would regain his freedom.

"It's breaking!" screamed a woman.

And when a few of The Dome's limbs splintered due to the great force of Ertu's heft and momentum, an eruption of buoyant cheers burst from the onlookers.

Yet for every thorned bough that split, two nearby limbs held.

Flung back into The Dome, Ertu crumpled to the earth at the structure's base.

Spike-Jaw struck at once, goring all four tusks into the old man's ample belly.

Ertu cried out in agony, his blood gushing generously over the beast's head and face to drip from its awful jaws.

With its horns still punching into Ertu's belly, the monster thrust itself forward again, snorting and grunting while stabbing its back hooves into the dirt for better traction. The muscles of its hind legs rippled as the creature lodged its tusks deeper into Ertu. Once the beast had buried each of its horns into its quarry, to the hilt, the animal uplifted its massive head.

The old man's body slumped, soft and slack, his innards flowing out to dangle from Spike-Jaw's snout like a limp mass of Slither-Bellies roasting on a spit.

Spike-Jaw trotted in a wide circle with Ertu still impaled on its tusks. Upon finishing its victory lap, the beast began pitching its face and snout side to side, up and down, slashing and gouging—violent, frenzied, grunting—until the gash in Ertu's abdomen was the length of a child's arm and nearly as wide. Gore poured from the old man's belly to drench the monster's brow and head in a cascade of glossy red lymph.

Shortly after unseating the old man from its tusks, Spike-Jaw converged on the gruesome flesh heap that was Ertu. The monstrosity nudged him with its snout, confirming the death. Grunting, satisfied, the savage moved on to snuff about the corpse, its damp nostrils lingering at Ertu's mouth, nose, ears, and armpits.

Sorazin alone applauded.

28

Skeervog

THE MUDKIN SLAVERS VISITED three additional Gort holes after adding Jaspen and Bogg to their number. Upon finally moving out of the gloomy, subterranean corridors between Gort holes, the group emerged into a sprawling common area bustling with the sights, sounds, and smells of life in the UnderDown. The sunless marketplace was lit by an array of torches as well as fires hanging in pots, burning in pits, and glowing in hearths and ovens. Shadows ebbed and flowed over the dirt floor and climbed the earthen walls to dance like dark phantoms, growing and shrinking, stretching and contracting. Food vendors hawked their comestibles from brushed steel carts as well as the short, metal outbuildings that surrounded the square. Mothers called after their straying children. And rhythmic hammering rang from the fiery craters over which blacksmiths pounded heated iron into the swords and blades for which the Gort were renowned.

Jaspen observed the goings-on with keen eyes as the Mudkin navigated their prisoners slowly through the masses. He did not know if their sluggish pace was simply the Mudkin way or if the short, plump race was incapable of ambling any faster. Neither did Jaspen learn if Mudkin were actually composed of mud or if their covering was a type of hide or fur. He did discover that the slithering vine-like tendrils that had wrapped themselves around him back in the Gort hole were the extremely pliable and extendible arms and fingers of the Mudkin.

Kama . . . thought Jaspen and his heart clutched again.

Numb and angry and flooded with sorrow, Jaspen stumbled, his feet heavy. Legs failing, he would have fallen if it hadn't been for Bogg's supporting hand.

It was Sorazin who slayed her, thought Jaspen.

The few other culprits that could have taken Kama's life—animal attack, climbing accident, forest poison, Huntressi arrow—were unlikely.

*If only you had stay*ed, Jaspen chastened himself, *she would be alive. To touch and hold and kiss.* His heart drained, sinking even lower. *I am not worthy of life. Strike me down, my Always. Take me to Kama.*

A sudden clamor of whoops and shouts drew the Mudkin slavers to an eager mob forming around an impromptu event of some kind. The Mudkin shouldered their way to the front of the growing throng, dragging their chained cargo behind them.

Jaspen, dull with depression, weak with hopelessness, was indifferent to his coveted post in the second row. Though his damp eyes were aimed at the earth, he could still perceive two Gort contenders before him. A large patch of dirt separated the pair and it appeared they were about to duel. Each held in their fingers a small, colorful gemstone—one a deep, vibrant green and the other a shimmering purple. Squaring off, they placed the jewels in their palms and began to rub at them; first with a thumb then with the flats of their hands. Each scrubbed at the jewel faster and faster, all while keeping their eyes set upon the other.

The friction produced a glow that shone so brightly that every bone of each Gort's hand was visible beneath the thick skin. When sparks began to spring from their fingers, the rabble grew frenzied. Cheers and jeers erupted in equal measure and Jaspen lifted his dead eyes, just a little. Money and goods were wagered with wild cries and feverish gestures, each bettor desperate to secure their stakes before the conflict commenced.

By now each competitor had raised an orb of burning fire the size of an island melon. They pulled, stretched, and compacted the flames as if endeavoring to mold their individual blazes into some sort of final shape.

The mob sensed the contest was about to begin and they chanted with great anticipation: "*Skeervog! Skeervog!*

A countdown followed. As the numbers descended, each combatant labored furiously to perfect the shape of his fire-creation. They wrestled with their flames—spinning, twisting, grappling—struggling to control the feral infernos twining about the legs, hips, torsos, and arms of the Gort who had created them.

The image of the angry flames lashing and scorching their authors ushered Jaspen back to the Hoodoah's cave—the last time he had seen Kama alive. A figment of her appeared before him.

"Kama . . . " said Jaspen, smiling at her.

But when he reached out to stroke her face, to brush her lips, she dissolved.

The Gort competitors finally tamed their fires. Each contained their small ball of flames in a loose fist. There was only the last number to recite and the onlookers shouted it in unison, loud and resonant.

Silence fell. The only noise was the hissing of the orbs of fire enclosed within the two Gort fists. All watched, rapt, greedy for the confrontation to begin.

The rivals began their dance, circling one another while waiting for the opportune moment to unleash the fires pulsing in their palms. Then each of them suddenly slung his fireball to the earth at his feet and a flare flashed hot and bright.

The fires swirled and leapt and fattened while spitting pellets of flame in all directions. Taller and stronger they grew until each blaze formed into a distinctive fire-creature—one exhibiting a purple hue, the other a greenish tint. The two Gort backed away from their *skeervog*, as these flame-beasts were known. Both watched, smug, confident that theirs would soon reign victorious over the other.

The pair of *skeervog* faced off, inspecting one another for strengths and frailties. Yet just as the fire-beasts burst towards each other, Jaspen was flung rearward—his chains yanked by the Mudkin.

The Shepherd of Fish complied without objection. His misery was so enfeebling that even if Jaspen had wanted to fight to remain near the *skeervog* battle, his lack of will made him incapable.

Jaspen, Bogg, and the other prisoners soon reached a holding tank where each was scrubbed and shorn. They were fed a meal and provided with a sleeping pallet.

Come morning, they were groomed and freshened then dressed in the drab brown garment, thick leather belt, and large iron buckle identifying them as slaves.

29

Gryffud

"My friend, Bogg, and I are here by mistake." Jaspen glanced at the dozen other incoming slaves in the stale, dirt room.

Gryffud—the gruff Gort in charge of the induction of slaves into UnderDown society—snorted. Like most males of his race, he was short and wide with stubby bowlegs and curly orange-red hair.

"The Gort hole into which we fell—" Jaspen cleared his throat, scratchy with grit and dust, then coughed—"was unmarked."

"Forward your case, I will," said Gryffud, "to Justice Glylok."

Of the seven slaves who had previously introduced themselves, four had claimed that they, too, stumbled upon an inconspicuous Gort pit.

"Contact you, we will," said Gryffud, "when our enquiry is complete." Yet his dismissive expression implied there would be no probe into the unmarked Gort hole.

"Thank you, sir." Jaspen held Gryffud's stare, defiant at first, then took his place next to Bogg and the others on the single bench of packed earth that ran around the inside of the dusty, dirt quarters.

But Gryffud's mocking snigger and smug gaze forced Jaspen to his feet again.

"No offense, sir . . . " Jaspen's eyes looked upon the others who had claimed that they, too, had fallen into a camouflaged Gort pit, "but what if Justice Glylok was the foul-heart who decreed the Gort hole into which I fell to stand unmarked?"

Gryffud rounded on Jaspen, his wiry orange eyebrows low. "Over-step, you do. Now sit . . . "—he drove a hard, heavy fist into Jaspen's belly—"slave."

The sharp blow wrang all breath from the Shepherd's lungs. Crash-ing back down to his seat, Jaspen hacked and wheezed, fighting for breath, throat dry with grainy sand and gritty dirt.

Glimpsing Bogg's hands clench, Jaspen took hold of the Udok's leg and shook his head slightly, bidding his friend not to meddle.

When Gryffud turned and paced toward a Gort clanmate calling for him at the room's entry, Bogg whispered to Jaspen, "Fret no more. Bogg has a cunning plan to make happy the heart of this short, angry Gort fellow."

Bogg was next to announce himself and, upon Gryffud's return, the Udok stood up brightly.

"Bogg is thrilled to tell everyone about the Always and how he turned a young Huntressi into wind."

Gryffud squinted at the Udok. "And who be the Always?"

"The Always is the most powerful of our island gods." Bogg's grin widened.

Moments earlier, sensing the danger of the topic, Jaspen might have risen to steer the coming words onto another path. Yet the Shepherd had fallen into a deep mire of grief for the fate of Kama and his ears were blunted to all beyond the knell of his own anguish.

"The Gort believe, we do," said Gryffud to Bogg, "that Fire-Breath is the greatest of gods."

"The Gort are mistaken." Bogg's innocent smile remained.

"Pardon?" Gryffud's flaming, orange eyebrows lowered again.

"Jaspen told Bogg at first meal this very day that the Always rules over every mountain, tree, and river as well as each creature that walks upon Jirvallan sands or swims in the seas that bound our island."

Gryffud's thick bowlegs took another step toward Bogg and he leered up at the Udok. "Implying, are you, that the Always rules the UnderDown?"

"Yes!" Bogg beamed. "And the Always made the Miracle of the Wind so that every Jirvallan tribe would develop a strong trust in the Always. It is a marvel even more astounding than Bogg's father's Hot Coal and Talon Pie."

"Careful, Udok." Gryffud gnashed his teeth and rolled his neck in an effort to check his escalating fury.

Last night, Jaspen and Bogg had heard from another slave that it had been two, long seasons since anyone had been sacrificed to Fire-Breath. For the past moon, the fearsome beast-god's ravenous hunger was a growing concern for every Gort. If the deity were not paid a proper blood tribute soon, Fire-Breath's anger would boil over to destroy a large portion, if not all, of the UnderDown.

"When Bogg introduces Gryffud to the Always, Gryffud's angry, burning red face and squinting eyes will cease. Gryffud will find joy aga—"

"Enough!" Gryffud turned to Jaspen. "And what say you, Cove? You seem a flicker brighter than this sputtering, little short-wick." Gryffud glanced at Bogg.

Jaspen, heeding only the roar of his own anguish, had not heard a thing the Gort had said. *I fool myself to believe that Kama lives*, he had been thinking, sorrow spreading within him like a killing sickness.

Bogg nudged him.

Jaspen ears perked and his eyes sharpened.

"Believe, do you," said Gryffud to Jaspen, "that your god, this *Always*, is ruler of the UnderDown?"

Observing the Gort's rubied cheeks and forehead, Jaspen feared that any positive words regarding the Always would only add to Gryffud's ire.

"Answer, slave," Gryffud pressed, "or it will be to the Black Deep with you."

The Black Deep, as described to Bogg and Jaspen earlier, was a brutal work camp reserved for the UnderDown's most vile criminals. It was sited forty fathoms beneath the dirt lodge where Gryffud was presently scowling at Jaspen.

"Bogg and I do not belong here, sir," said Jaspen. "The hole was unmark—"

"Out with it, boy!" thundered Gryffud.

He seemed intent upon coercing Jaspen to blurt something slanderous about Fire-Breath. The Gort was desperate to find a blood tribute, proper or not, to slake his god's hunger and thereby rescue his race from the wrath of their god.

"Is Fire-Breath worthy of praise or not?" Gryffud asked.

I have no wish to belittle you, my Always, Jaspen shut his eyes, *but you have taken Kama from me.*

"Yes or no, slave?" pushed Gryffud. "Is Fire-Breath worthy—"

"Fire-Breath has yet to show to me any power, sir," said Jaspen, struggling to remain seated. "How is one to worship a deity he does not know. How can I . . . "

It struck Jaspen that his next utterance held great possibilities. A shrewd response could result in Jaspen's freedom from the UnderDown, from slavery, from his terrible misery. If he answered wisely, Jaspen could reunite with Kama before the rising of the next moon. And live with her forever in the Lands of Kiriath-Dae.

Disregarding the urge within that warned him to hold his tongue, Jaspen said, "Is it true that your Fire-Breath is made up of the bones of what were once a very large, fire-breathing Long-Wing?" This was the rumor amongst the Cove.

"The bones to which you refer, boy, breathe fire to this very day, they do."

"Perhaps if mine eyes bore witness to these dry bones vomiting fire, sir, I would bow to your god."

Gryffud listened carefully, as if sifting Jaspen's words for something profane he could use to charge the slave with blasphemy.

"However . . . " Jaspen stood.

Forgive me for defying your voice within me, my Always. But these are the only means by which I can see Kama again . . . in the Everlasting Lands.

" . . . if I discover Fire-Breath to be as pathetic as that ugly fish, Levaioth," Jaspen rose taller, glaring down at Gryffud, "then far be it from me to kneel before a rotting carcass of two moldering wings and a beak so decayed I could shatter it with a finger's flick."

Gryffud's eyes blazed and his red face trembled. His tongue pushed at the inside of one cheek then the other, until . . .

"Blasphemy!" shouted Gryffud, with a tone akin to glee.

Jaspen grinned to himself.

30

Tracker and Faijen

Sᴏʀᴀᴢɪɴ ᴡᴀs ᴇɴɢᴀɢᴇᴅ ɪɴ a bout of instructive swordplay with a new guard when he caught the sight of a thin fellow with hooded eyes posted at the entrance to the Hall of Shells. The Mutahn bobbed his chin, inviting the man to enter while continuing to parry and thrust with his student.

The slight man, his gaze missing nothing, strode with urgent step to Sorazin.

"Sire," said the man, bowing to his Mutahn.

Sorazin neglected to even glance at the Cove's most revered tracker.

"Tell me, Boushi," said Sorazin to the tracker while easily evading his trainee's incoming blade, "that you have returned after two suns away with more than a pair of empty hands and an impatient smile."

Sorazin drove a boot into his new guard's groin.

The recruit groaned, released his sword then fell over, writhing on the alabaster floor.

"For if that is the extent of your gifts," said Sorazin to Boushi while circling the downed student, "you may find yourself at odds with a rather menacing foe in tonight's festivities . . . within The Dome."

The two nights subsequent to Ertu's death had seen three former officials from the Hall of Shells slaughtered by famished forest monsters beneath The Dome's thorned boughs, as their families and friends looked on.

Sorazin was well aware that his brazen elimination of outspoken peacemongers among his tribe would not meet with everyone's approval. But great rulers had always been misunderstood. And once the Udok and

Huntressi tribes were successfully enslaved, even the most shortsighted Cove would come to realize the genius of their new Mutahn.

Boushi said, "There are tidings, indeed, good Mutahn."

"*Mahkifo* is with your underlings, then?"

"The coward dwells beneath us, with the Gort."

The Gort! It takes moons to barter a slave's release with those grasping swindlers!

Sorazin's boot clashed again with the new guard, this time in the ribs.

"Never discard your weapon!"

The Mutahn belted his student again.

"And what of the girl?" Sorazin asked Boushi. "Did she follow that spineless murderer into slavery?"

"My sources confirm that Kama is not in UnderDown, great one."

"Do I pay you, tracker, to tell me where she is not?"

"We anticipate news by morning."

Morning!

As the trainee reached his feet, Sorazin backhanded the young man across the face. The iron-spiked knuckles of the Mutahn's black glove gouged a deep gash from the edge of the youth's eye to the corner of his lip.

Kama could ruin me by then! Sorazin grinned as the rift in the student's face welled with blood and striped his cheek.

Defeated, the guard's arms fell and he sagged against a pillar, exhausted.

Sorazin glowered at him. "Am I to understand this as a posture of surrender?"

The guard nodded.

With a flash, Sorazin's blade separated the guard's sword arm from his shoulder. "The Cove do *not* surrender!"

Collapsing to a knee, the trainee peered to the blood coursing from his armless shoulder then looked to Sorazin, bewildered.

And mahkifo . . .

Sorazin gutted the young man. Innards spilled.

He is surely spouting the tale of my blade racing towards the Hoodoah's neck even now.

Sorazin thrust his sword's tip down through the top of the guard's skull until it jutted from his chin.

Even if others take it as false, their hearts retain a seed of doubt.

The Mutahn's grip on the filigreed handle of his sword kept the guard's head and neck upright and facing forward. The golden hilt atop the dying man's head appeared as a small crown.

A seed that may bud into rebellion.

Sorazin withdrew the blade and the guard slumped to the floor, gurgling and wheezing until going slack.

Sheathing his weapon, Sorazin instructed a nearby servant to conduct the corpse into the woodland and offer it as a gift to those of fang and claw. A gesture of respect from the Cove's new Mutahn.

Sorazin took his place on the Throne of Pearls and removed his black gloves, one finger at a time, while gazing at Boushi. After studying the tracker, Sorazin's eyes drifted to the sun-browned face of a striking servant girl. She was clad in a palm frond about the waist with a string of five, rainbow-colored shells spanning from one breast to the other like an iridescent footbridge. Sorazin's eyes flashed to a decanter of island wine poised on a small table next to him then back to the girl. The servant moved to the wine, filled a pair of goblets, and offered the larger vessel to Sorazin, the other to Boushi.

"To *mahkifo* and the girl's capture." Sorazin raised his jeweled chalice. "I am certain you will manage to return them both by sunfall tomorrow."

Boushi lifted his cup. "Consider it done, great Mutahn."

The pair sipped while discussing a few particulars regarding the search for Jaspen and Kama. Soon, each goblet was empty.

"It does not sit well with me, tracker," said Sorazin, curt, "that my first directive as Mutahn will go down in the annals of Cove history as a failure."

"What failure, sir?" Boushi swabbed a stippling of sweat from his brow. "By moonrise tomorrow, my team—"

"You have grown soft, Boushi, and I cannot abide any servant performing at less than the pinnacle of their powers."

"Honorable Mutahn," the tracker dabbed again at the growing perspiration wetting his face, "I can assure you that my skills are—"

"No longer required. However, if you overcome the venom of Puffer-Thorn that I placed in your wine, the position of cupbearer to the Mutahn is yours."

"Venom?" Boushi's eye twitched and he suddenly creased at the waist.

Sorazin grinned as the tracker dropped to the floor. He watched Boushi thrashing in torment—sweating, mouth foaming, spittle spewing—until he went soft and breathed his last.

A sentry with a thin, dead man draped over his shoulder was exiting the Hall of Shells as a Faijen flew into the royal residence.

"I am the Footman Rollik of the Upper Water." The Faijen set down near the Throne of Pearls and bowed his chin to Sorazin. "Rivers of peace to you and the Cove, young Mutahn."

The water creature stood but half of Sorazin's height and as he folded his gauzy wings—a large pair on his back and a smaller pair above each ankle—all of them ruffled while settling into their places.

"Our tribe's Great Hydron, master Rill, sent me the moment your message reached his sovereign seat. I am at your service."

31

Fire-Breath

"DID BOGG SPEAK WRONGLY?" he whispered to Jaspen as Gryffud hauled the two slaves by their wrist chains out of the dirt room and toward Fire-Breath's shrine.

"It is never wrong to speak truth." Then to Gryffud, Jaspen said, "Free the Udok. It is I, alone, who have spoken blasphemy."

The Gort grinned. "Perhaps, Cove. But a double sacrifice is certain, it is, to doubly please the great Fire-Breath."

Jaspen asked, "Name what I must do to earn for the Udok his freedom? I—"

"His fate is sealed, it is," said Gryffud. "As is yours."

First I abandon Kama in the Hoodoah's cave, now this. Free Bogg, my Always, please. I deserve not to live, but this kindly Udok does.

As Gryffud steered his cargo toward Fire-Breath, he cried out to his fellow UnderDowners: "Sacrifice! Sacrifice! To the shrine of Fire-Breath! All are invited! Invited are all! To the shrine with a *pair* of blood tributes!"

All hearing the report rejoiced and fell in behind Gryffud, Jaspen, and Bogg. Soon, the growing horde was chanting out the name of their god in three distinct syllables: *Fy-er Breath*! *Fy-er Breath*!

Rounding a bend, those trailing Gryffud and the two slaves, hundreds and hundreds now, shouted out in praise as they laid eyes on Fire-Breath's sacred shrine.

Gryffud tugged Jaspen and Bogg through the narrow entrance and into the place of worship, their heavy slave-chains clinking. A large, oval stretch of earth was lit by dozens of magnificent golden torches that circuited the oval's perimeter. Rows and rows of ornate silver benches surrounded the spacious dirt ring and sloped upward from the floor to the earthen ceiling.

Thirty-six Gort priests chanted to their god in unison—a sinister *shoo-hoo-HO, shoo-hoo-HA, shoo-hoo-HO* . . . To signify rank, each holy man wore a robe of orange, yellow or white, with the High Priest dressed entirely in gold.

The enormous skeleton of Fire-Breath loomed frightening and grim at the far end of the dirt oval. The monster-bird was partially-excavated from a pillar of earth. The dirt column stretched from beneath the bird-god's talons to surge up through its belly and spine before continuing through the back half of the huge skull and, finally, to the rafters that upheld the dirt ceiling.

Jaspen and Bogg gazed in wordless astonishment at the deity's gruesome, white jawbones. They were fierce and gaping with razored teeth. It was as if the creature had just defeated an enemy and was shrieking out its ghoulish victory call for all to hear. Two great holes near the tip of the beak were ringed in soot to give the impression that the monster-god had recently fired a blast of flame from its bony nostrils. Huge ribs protruded out from the earthen cylinder like the skeletal fingers of two grasping hands. And the colossal wingspan was nearly the length of Levaioth—from its seven eyes to its timeworn tail.

Fragments of bone crunched beneath Jaspen and Bogg's feet as they crossed the wasteland of scorched earth leading to Fire-Breath. The slaves were unshackled and told to remain on the black, singed earth before Fire-Breath while Gryffud stumped to the burnished golden throne of the High Priest.

The High Priest and Gryffud stepped to the side to speak in private. As they did, the priest occasionally peeked back at Jaspen and Bogg, lips tense.

Shortly, the High Priest nodded. Facing the crowd, he said, "Let us kneel and offer our unrivaled god our highest praise." He sneered at Jaspen, superior. "So that we might earn the protection and favor of the invincible Fire-Breath."

The crowd slid from their silver benches to kneel in the dirt. They spread their arms, lifted their faces, and upraised their palms in worship of the vast carcass of Fire-Breath. All honored the sacred bones . . . save Jaspen and Bogg.

A gong sounded, three bellowing tolls, and the worshipers rose to sit again upon their benches.

"Look!" A Huntressi slave thrust her finger at Fire-Breath.

The crowd swung their heads to the skeleton. The pillar behind the god's eyes and jaws was glowing red. Eager, the mob stamped its feet and broke into the chant they had been longing to utter for so many moons: *Sa-cri-fice! Sa-cri-fice!* As the mantra grew in volume, the blaze within the column burned with more ferocity.

"Kneel now or die!" shouted the High Priest to the two blood tributes.

"What should Jaspen and Bogg do?" asked Bogg, fright creasing his brow.

Head bowed, Jaspen said, "Whatever your heart tells you, my friend. And I am sorry, Bogg. Never did I intend for my tongue to incriminate you."

Fire-Breath's jaws and snout flared. Glowing embers shot from the nostrils.

"Save yourself!" cried a yellow-robed priest.

Nervous, Bogg gaped at Fire-Breath. The entire skeleton reddened with heat.

"Are Bogg and Jaspen to die now?"

"If it is my time to join Kama in the Lands of Kiriath-Dae, then so be it. But I suggest that you break through the guards that surround us and vanish into the crowd. Save yourself, Bogg. This is my journey, not yours. Go. Please."

The blaze within Fire-Breath grew hotter and Jaspen could see Bogg shifting nervously from one foot to the other. One of the half-giant's knees even bent a bit toward the earth.

Jaspen said, "If your heart instructs you to kneel, Bogg, then you may do so."

Bogg thought for a moment. "If Jaspen stands, Bogg stands."

Jaspen could not help but smile at Bogg's endearing loyalty. Turning back to Fire-Breath, he caught sight of something curious in the pillar at the rear of the skeleton's jaws. Jaspen stalked closer, scorched bones crunching beneath his feet.

"Look to where the earth meets the back of the beast's throat," he said to Bogg. "Two openings in the dirt look to be a secret entry into a hidden tunnel."

Bogg squinted at the monster's jaws. "Bogg sees two additional tunnel holes behind the ugly black nose." He drew forward, even with Jaspen. "Bogg also sees shadows of fire dancing inside of the dirty column."

Jaspen looked carefully at the four shadowy shapes in the pillar. "It is more than fire dancing there, Bogg. It is a hoax! And we alone can see it."

"Only Jaspen and Bogg can see what?"

"Four Gort hiding in Fire-Breath's throat. In the dirt pillar."

Flames licked at the inside of the skeleton's nostrils and mouth, each tongue of fire growing bigger and longer by the moment.

"Only from our vantage, Bogg, in front of these bones, can one spy those Gort in there creating their *skeervog*."

"*Skeervog*? Bogg does not know this word."

"The fire creatures those Gort made with their hands, earlier. Remember?"

As flames began to pulse out of Fire-Breath's nose and jaw, the crowd cheered at the prospect of the impending sacrifice.

"*Skeervog* reminds Bogg of an Udok word: *skifoth*. It is a sumptuous after-supper sweet. Baked mud with boiled—"

"Bogg, if we can reach the Gort dancing within the bones, we can defeat Fire-Breath. We can prove to all that their deity is a ruse!"

"Bogg knows for certain that Jaspen and Bogg can subdue the four dancing Gort. Bogg knows this because Bogg has just now recalled that the Always came—"

"Ho!" cried Jaspen, leaping for Bogg, as an arrow of flame shot from Fire-Breath's jaw on a bead for the Udok's chest.

Jaspen knocked Bogg out of harm's way, the fire narrowly missing him.

"Up! Quick!" Jaspen helped Bogg to his feet.

Jaspen glanced at the flames growing in Fire-Breath's mouth then quickly to the shrine's entry doors, the ones through which Gryffud had tugged them. He was hoping the exit would be unmanned, providing a chance for Bogg to escape. Yet the two narrow doors stood closed and locked, three guards protecting each exit.

"Jaspen!" shouted Bogg and yanked him away from an oncoming jet of fire.

Jaspen stumbled out of danger. Though the flames had passed, the heat that hung in the air near Jaspen's head was so intense that it singed the Shepherd's hair.

"A thousand thanks, Bogg." Jaspen peered to the thirty-six robed priests, each sitting upon his own throne of gold.

Jaspen hoped to detect a veiled exit behind the thrones through which Bogg could flee. Yet there was only a sheer earthen wall rising from floor the ceiling.

A globe of lava burst into a thousand pellets of flame as it struck the dirt at Bogg's feet. Though Bogg had leapt, a spray of sizzling liquid spouted up and onto his ankle and set it aflame. The blaze was only alight for a moment before Bogg snuffed it with a fistful of dirt.

"How did you . . . " Jaspen looked with awe at Bogg's lower leg, barely burned. "If it were my ankle that was assailed by such heat, I would be unable to stand."

"Udok possess much thicker flesh than Jaspen or any Cove man. Bogg has also had the good fortune, as it turns out, to have dropped many hot skillets filled with boiling broth onto his feet. Fire-Breath will have to do much better to defeat Boggfroggbiggbogganbiggle. Now, if it pleases Jaspen, Bogg would like to finish the tale regarding the information that the Always told to Bogg in his night-story—"

"We must draw nearer!" Jaspen pulled Bogg closer to the monster.

With each advancing stride, the clearer the shadows of the four Gort inside the pillar became . . . until Jaspen and Bogg could spy the short, thick-set Gort shaping their fire creations, preparing to finish off the two slaves in grand fashion.

"Bogg," said Jaspen, "cast me into the beast's maw at once. I will over-whelm the four Gort, expel them from the beak and ruin their *skeervog*."

"Bogg is sorry." He hung his head. "Bogg cannot fulfill Jaspen's request."

"Why not?"

"Because Bogg has seen the moment Jaspen and Bogg are presently living in a night-story. Very early this morning, near the end of Bogg's time on the sleeping pallet, the Always imparted to Bogg a number of notable words. Bogg has been attempting for some time now to commu-nicate to Jaspen exactly what the Always had said. But fireballs, lava-jets and other interruptions have thwarted Bogg's—"

The pair dodged another stream of flame.

"Interruptions much like that one," continued Bogg, "have prevent-ed Bogg from telling to Jaspen what the Always has instructed Bogg and Jaspen to do."

"The Always spoke to you last night?"

"Yes." Bogg smiled and his hairless, white eyebrows raised toward his hairless, white scalp. "The Always told Bogg that when Jaspen and Bogg are close enough to see the Gort men clearly composing their fire beasts—which is this very moment, Jaspen—Bogg and Jaspen are to stop. Then stand in one place. Then wait."

"Wait? Wait for what?"

"This is a detail Bogg does not know. The Always said it will be made clear to Bogg and Jaspen when the waiting is no longer required."

Inside the pillar, the fire-creatures grew bigger, angrier—torturing their creators as Jaspen had seen when chained to the Mudkin, just prior to the *skeervog* taking their final shapes.

Jaspen evaded another fiery dart and thought, *How can I challenge Bogg's counsel when the morning before this one he spoke of a night-story directing him to the Hoodoah's cave-place, to meet a new friend called King Crusher?*

Bogg asked, "If Jaspen would like to make believe that the Always did not—"

"It's okay, Bogg." Jaspen smiled at him. "As reckless as standing still seems to me, only a fool would quarrel with the one true god of Jirvalla."

The Gort inside the pillar tamed their orbs of fire and compacted them to fit into their fists. Soon, they would sling them out of Fire-Breath's nostrils and jaws and four rampaging *skeervog* would overrun the slaves, burning them to ash.

"I trust you, Bogg," said Jaspen. "And I trust the Always. So, we wait . . ."

. . . *though it is beyond all logic*, thought Jaspen, wanting nothing more than to race to the earthen pillar and scale it.

"Bogg is very excited to learn how the Always will rescue Jaspen and Bogg from a terrible situation that promises to end only in death." He smiled. "Even the Udok's most fearsome warrior, Mushcrushkilljuggen-filler, would either attack or flee. Mushcrush would not have the patience, nor the humility, to stand and wai—"

"Must we talk?" asked Jaspen.

"A morsel nervous, Bogg is. Apologies. Even when it is only a snack-sized portion of apprehension, Bogg tends to over-speak." He patted his lips to quiet them.

And the pair of slaves faced Fire-Breath, peered again into its fiery beak . . . and waited.

32

Footman Rollik

"Before we babble of tasks and favor-bonds, young Mutahn," said Rollik, the Faijen, as he reached into his beautiful satchel, composed entirely of shimmering fish scales, "master sage Rill extends a gift of rare worth to the new leader of our noble allies."

Rollik's face, like most Faijen, was similar to Slither-Belly's but kinder, with large, sapphire-blue eyes, two slits for a nose and small, sharp teeth set into a wide, lipless mouth.

"From the fountainhead of Lillit Springs," said Rollik, proud, "a realm restricted to all but the Faijen."

A short, spiny fin beginning just above Rollik's nose flared. The membranous ridge stood taller, its spines sharper, as it ranged over the crown of his smooth head and down the back of his neck.

"I present to you . . . " Rollik outstretched his hand to offer Sorazin a small, sky-blue egg, " . . . the youthing brine of Mount Everwater."

Unlike the majority of his tribemates, Rollik was the color of clear water— almost see-through—rather than the pale blue and soft green of most Faijen.

Rollik said, "Not that a tadpole as you requires it any time soon."

Tadpole? Sorazin clenched his sword.

"On behalf of the Cove, Rollik," the Mutahn relaxed his grip on the blade's hilt, "I thank you." Sorazin thought it wiser to use the Faijen rather than slay him. "Give my regards to old Rill. It is a gift beyond measure."

"Indeed it is." Rollik puffed his chest and stood taller. Even at his full height, the top of the Faijen's head reached only to Sorazin's upper thigh.

"Now, shall we immerse ourselves in the business of favor-bonds fulfilled and new ones to be struck? Let the island ledger show that my coming to the Hall of Shells this day has satisfied the Faijen's favor-bond given to Mutahn Pehlni nineteen seasons ago."

Clever little bug, thought Sorazin. *To test the waters so early in his first dialogue with the Cove's new Mutahn.*

"A favor-bond satisfied by the arrival of a single Faijen at my hall? You insult the Cove, as well as its Mutahn, Footman Rollik."

Best to show this flea who determines the rules of engagement. Sorazin grinned to himself, his acumen for politics so natural, so cunning.

"Mutahn Pehlni paid to the Udok a costly ransom to prevent those giants from crushing your entire race," said Sorazin. "You would have been born a slave had it not been for the mighty Cove."

"No offense, Sorazin, but a sliver of Cove land is hardly a costly ranso—"

"To call the meadowlands between Horn Rock and Smoke Mountain a sliver is akin to likening the Faijen to a cloud of irritating Buzz-Wings."

Rollik's mouth tightened and the upper row of his pointed teeth showed. "Let us begin anew. What does the youngest Mutahn in Cove history deem as fair recompense for the favor-bond our venerable tribe owes to yours?"

"Two of our clan are missing. I fear for their safety. One is reportedly with the Gort. The other was last seen at the Hoodoah's cave, two suns past. Her whereabouts remain a mystery. Return my tribe-mates to their homes by the next moon and the Faijen's debt to the Cove will be settled."

"As a stream relies on the lake to give it life, so do the Cove rely on the Faijen. I am happy to assist, young Sorazin, but you have much to learn. *Two* exhaustive searches and *two* perilous rescue missions to fulfill *one* favor-bond is an offer steeped in greed, little Covie. Are the Faijen and Cove not allies? Yet I have faced calmer waters negotiating with that foul Huntressi Queen, Ifipo."

Sorazin had always viewed compromise as weakness.

Ertu was adept at negotiating, he thought. *Perhaps I killed him too quickly.*

"You may be right, good Rollik." Sorazin smiled, friendly, humble. "Forgive me my . . . my unintentional . . . "

The right word . . . he thought. *A delicate one that will admit no fault on my behalf but not so timid as to imply weakness.*

" . . . overreaching."

Perfect, thought the Mutahn.

"These are new grounds I tread," said Sorazin, striving for modesty.

The Faijen softened and Sorazin watched with pleasure as Rollik's face and manner grow more agreeable.

Deliberations went back and forth for nearly two hands. Though the converse was not without tension, the disputes were each settled, eventually, with a modicum of civility and even mild comradeship. The Cove and Faijen were allies after all.

Sorazin had, however, been forced to briefly part company with Rollik twice, as a means to regain his composure and fortify his amicable façade. The Mutahn praised himself for managing his emotions so masterfully. For he had not stalked off in a violent tempest but calmly removed himself from the presence of the irritatingly polite and politically savvy Faijen. And upon his return, Sorazin was swift to recover Rollik's trust by offering just the right amount of feigned respect for the water bug's nimble diplomacy and expertise in Island Law.

Yet a moment after the Faijen bowed and bade his farewell, Sorazin promptly lowered his gentlemanly pretense. He sneered at the sound of the vermin's purring wings.

Drawing his dagger, Sorazin ran a finger over its cutting edge. He wondered if he had not been stern enough in his dealings with the pathetic footman.

The pair had ultimately agreed that Rollik would simply *locate* Jaspen and Kama to honor the Faijen's favor-bond owed to the Cove.

I should not have wavered! Sorazin chided himself and cast his dagger at a painting on the wall of two Faijen at play.

The artwork's iridescent shells burst into a thousand shards and plinked to the floor like fragments of a broken sword.

How dare that worthless insect speak to me like that! Sorazin paced to the shattered shells and yanked his dagger from the wall, a few more slivers of seashell tinkling to the alabaster upon which he stood.

The return of either Jaspen or Kama would result in the Cove owing a new favor-bond to the Faijen.

But if the Faijen do succeed in retrieving mahkifo and his whore, what a glorious victory it shall be! A winning stroke for the Cove's new Mutahn.

A further favor-bond to the Faijen would be granted if Rollik, while searching the UnderDown, could provide Sorazin with one hundred, newly minted Gort swords.

"And if Rollik fails," muttered Sorazin, "that haughty, little bug will pay for his inadequacy . . . " he stabbed the wall again, "with his life."

33

Baby Wool-Back

THE CONGREGATION WITHIN FIRE-BREATH'S shrine hushed. The two slaves were seconds from incineration. The Gort god would finally have his sacrifice and the UnderDown could rest easy once again, at least for the next two or three moons.

Jaspen and Bogg remained standing tall with their heads held high and their eyes peering into Fire-Breath's glowing red maw. The Gort inside the dirt pillar were each applying the finishing touches to his *skeer-vog*. In a moment, four flame-beasts would burst from the monster's beak to reduce the slaves to cinders. Yet while hovering there on the brink of death, Jaspen welled with inexplicable hope. It was the same unquenchable feeling he had experienced upon discovering Shokku had been turned into wind.

Erupting in a sudden gale of spirited laughter, long and loud, Jaspen clapped Bogg on the back and exclaimed, "Dance, Bogg! Dance!"

Confused, the Udok stared at Jaspen and shook his face. "Was Bogg unclear when relaying to Jaspen the message from the Always during Bogg's night-story? The instructions were to *stand still* and wait."

"But to dance in the face of certain peril, Bogg, is an act of faith, honor and trust in our god. Come on! Dance with me, Bogg! In praise of the Always!"

Jaspen leapt and swayed and hopped and twirled with such mirth and abandon that Bogg could not help but join him. The Udok howled in hysterics as he, too, began to bob and whirl.

The multitude watched, baffled, as the slaves giggled and gyred. Never had any witnessed such unchecked joy in the face of death; such freedom from fear or self-pity. Whispers raced amongst them:

"Inebriated on mole blood," they said. "Giddy with too much shrew tail."

The High Priest launched from his throne. "Sacrilege! Stop this instant or I—"

"Let them be!" cried a voice from the crowd.

"I will not!" blared the priest, striding toward the slaves. "I command you to halt this clownery at once!"

Jaspen and Bogg glanced at the High Priest then to each other. With nothing to lose, they grinned, mischievous . . . then pranced and pranked and purled and larked with even more revelry.

Incensed, the priest spun his face to Fire-Breath. He stretched wide his arms and said, "Great and glorious Fire-Breath, god of gods," resonated his baritone. "Show us now your might! Display your righteous anger for these faithless infidels!"

Jaspen knew at once that the High Priest was instructing the Gort to unleash their *skeervog* and put an end to the slaves. The four Gort responded by drawing back their arms and slinging their flame-beasts into the arena.

The crowd roared as a ball of flame erupted from each nostril, two more hurtling from the monster's jaws. Cheering now, the bloodthirsty mob had forgotten all about the fearless dance of the slaves.

Jaspen and Bogg continued to spring and whirl merrily as the four orbs of fire blazed toward them.

The burning globes joined as one and flames leapt in every direction from the immense fireball. A moment before colliding into Jaspen and Bogg, the ball of fire split in two and came together again behind the slaves. The burning sphere swirled like a tornado, circling its prey while lengthening and growing hotter.

Jaspen and Bogg pondered the fire with cool reserve as the hideous fire-faces of Laughing-Roar, Slither-Belly, Scavenger-Beak, and Fire-Breath himself formed within the flames. The heat was searing and sweat built on the brows of the two slaves, streaming down their faces. Each fire-image struck out at Jaspen and Bogg with flashing teeth, just missing them. But the efforts of the *skeervog* to frighten them were futile.

The tornado divided into four balls of flame and each separate blaze stretched and fattened until a fully forged fire-beast sprang from the flames. Laughing-Roar approached first, predatorial, snapping its horrific jaws at the slaves, wagging its stumpy tail, and yipping its awful high-pitched cackle.

Slither-Belly came next, hissing and spitting fire as its long flame-body slinked toward its quarry. The towering serpent rose to a striking position, fanned its neck and displayed its wicked fangs, waiting impatiently for the command to kill.

Scavenger-Beak shrieked from behind and the slaves covered their ears against the beast's strident bawl. It hopped toward them, its color changing from smoke-gray to black to crimson, and spread its dark, flaming wings. The sharp beak opened and closed and the *skeervog* seemed to smile when the heat grew so intense that Jaspen's flesh began to blister.

The imposing image of Fire-Breath soared above, spitting small spheres of fire at the slaves until a short wall of flames surrounded them. Alighting on the blackened earth, the monster screeched and beat its long wings, whipping up a firestorm of wind and shards of bone that chinked the faces, arms, and chests of Jaspen and Bogg.

The four *skeervog* prowled about the slaves, taunting them, in hopes of inciting a paralyzing fear that would prove them cowards in front of all. Yet the courage of the slaves never waned.

The High Priest, zealous for death, signaled the Gort hiding within the earthen column to complete the sacrifice.

In unison, the four Gort pulled back their arms then thrust them forward until each pair of hands met with a shrill clap.

Each *skeervog* doubled in size.

"We are coming to you, my Always!" shouted Jaspen, grinning.

The four *skeervog* charged, flame-trails stretching behind. Molten pellets sprayed, charring those in the front rows. Laughing-Roar led the pack, racing toward the slaves with ears laid flat and jaws dripping with flaming saliva. Behind the leader, Slither-Belly sped over the earth as if skating on air. Above, Fire-Breath and Scavenger-Beak descended, shrieking, their faces clear and vicious, globs of flame spewing from the wings. Though each *skeervog* rushed to reach Jaspen and Bogg first, it appeared all would arrive at the same moment.

An instant before the flame-beasts fell upon the slaves, a small, strange fire—of purest white—slowly rose from the singed earth at Jaspen and Bogg's feet. The unexpected flare startled the *skeervog* and each slewed to a halt, wary.

The High Priest looked to the Gort in the earthen pillar, perplexed, as if he had never before seen a flame so perfectly white, so beautifully lustrous.

The silvery-white fire fashioned itself into the image of an immaculate, newborn Wool-Back. It nestled at the feet of the slaves, with its hooves tucked neatly beneath its body. The detail was incredible—the soft ears, adorable face and texture of the animal's woolen fleece were clearly the work of a superior *skeervog* craftsman. Lifting its head, the baby Wool-Back flicked its fiery-white tail and bleated, plaintive and tender, as its large, innocent eyes peered at the four fire-monsters glaring down upon it.

Laughing-Roar and the others scoffed at what appeared to be an uninvited guest. Shrieking as one, each reared back its head and readied to strike the newcomer dead.

"The Always!" cried Bogg, grinning from ear to ear. "The Always has come!"

34

Long-Mane

Slither-Belly's molten fangs were a hair's breadth from the newborn Wool-Back's throat. An instant before the long, curved teeth impaled the little, white *skeervog*, Wool-Back jerked upward its head and a mighty roar issued from its tiny mouth. In a blink, the meek animal at Jaspen's feet transformed into a ferocious Long-Mane.

The massive *skeervog* attacked Slither-Belly at the neck and shook the serpent between its jaws until severing it in two. Each half squirmed in the dirt, fire dwindling, until every flame extinguished, leaving nothing behind but a shiny, black gemstone and two plumes of smoke.

Laughing-Roar champed at the air where the Wool-Back once lay. The beast, confused where its prey had fled, turned to search for it. Long-Mane pounced upon Laughing-Roar, slashing and tearing with tooth and claw. The cur whined, pathetic, in a high-pitched wail, as Long-Mane shredded the fiend into a mass of tiny flames.

Long-Mane rolled its great head to find Scavenger-Beak at the opposite end of the arena. Sauntering toward the *skeervog*, Long-Mane snarled and fixed the winged beast with a stare so vicious it put a chill up the necks of both Jaspen and Bogg. Long-Mane swiped at the earth beneath him, menacing, his broad paw spraying earth and chips of bones toward the thirty-six shrine priests upon their golden thrones.

Scavenger-Beak backed away, frightened, and beat its wings until lifting into the safety of the air. But Long-Mane vaulted high, shooting toward Scavenger-Beak with its forelegs and paws spread wide. Panicked, the beaked one screeched, flapping its wings in a desperate effort to escape the coming fangs. Yet Long-Mane, closing in, widened its gaping jaws and took Scavenger-Beak by the breast.

Long-Mane landed with a heavy whump, its adversary convulsing between his jaws. He pinned Scavenger-Beak's wings to the earth and tore the fiery head from its body. The carcass jerked and twitched while its flames dwindled to nothing.

Long-Mane growled, the head and neck of Scavenger-Beak still hanging from its jaws. Striding to the shrine priests, Long-Mane stalked back and forth in front of them, looking over each of the thirty-six. The *skeervog* stopped in front of the High Priest and flung the head of Scavenger-Beak to the foot of his throne. Yet instead of extinguishing, like the rest of Scavenger-Beak had done, the creature's head burned hotter, until the High Priest's throne burst into flame.

The priest sprang from his seat and shouted, "Devil!" glaring at Long-Mane. He turned to his skeletal god. "Free us of this demon, great Fire-Breath!" he cried then ousted a fellow priest sitting in an adjacent throne and sat down upon it.

Long-Mane peered up to see the *skeervog* of Fire-Breath hovering above. The blazing god blasted a jet of fire that completely enshrouded its target. Long-Mane roared, whether in pain or anger it was too difficult to discern. Sensing victory, Fire-Breath loosed another torrent of flames. Then another.

Jaspen and Bogg looked to each other, troubled, as there was nothing to be seen or heard from the midst of the fire. Those upon the benches also seemed keen to discover if Long-Mane had survived the holocaust.

The *skeervog* of Fire-Breath cried, triumphant, while sailing to and fro about the arena. The shrine priests grinned, nodded: smug. All but a white-robed novice.

Standing, the novice lifted a shaky finger to the fire. "The slaves's god!"

The flames that blazed where Fire-Breath had incinerated Long-Mane were suddenly flaring higher. From the fire's center, something began to rise, until Long-Mane swaggered out of the inferno, even bigger and more terrifying than before.

Long-Mane's roar shook the arena and Fire-Breath's eyes stretched with dread at the figure of the giant *skeervog*. The beast sprang at the winged god. Fire-Breath swerved, frenetic wings beating, and discharged another blast at the incoming foe.

Unimpeded, Long-Mane drew back a paw and swiped. Fiery claws cut through the *skeervog*'s neck, shearing off Fire-Breath's head in its entirety.

Fire-Breath vanished in a puff of smoke and the shiny amber-gold gemstone that was the seed of its life fell to the earth at Jaspen's feet.

The furious High Priest marched across the arena to glare into the skeleton of Fire-Breath. "Kill it!" he shouted to the Gort within the earthen pillar.

The angry priest was mumbling irreverences against Long-Mane until an eerie growl from overhead halted his tongue. The priest glanced up to spy Long-Mane directly above him, plummeting swiftly. Paralyzed, the holy man's mouth dropped open and his eyes froze at the sight of the *skeervog*'s fiery teeth.

Long-Mane crashed down upon the High Priest and tore from him his legs and arms before rampaging through the remaining shrine priests. All were dispatched but one: the novice in the white robe who was bowed low, in praise of Long-Mane.

Turning to Jaspen and Bogg, Long-Mane looked upon them tenderly.

Gazing into the eyes of the Always, Jaspen had never felt such joy, such love, such wholeness and fulfillment.

The Shepherd glanced at Bogg and saw that he, too, had never encountered such bliss, such wellbeing, such friendship . . . Overjoyed, Jaspen filled with gratitude for having a friend to share in this divine feeling, this beautiful otherworldly love.

Long-Mane drew his eyes away from Jaspen and Bogg to glimpse briefly at the bony jaws of Fire-Breath and the four Gort within. Turning back to the two slaves, the Always gave them a small nod.

"Jaspen!" cried Bogg. "The Always has just revealed to Bogg that it is time for *what*!"

"Pardon?"

"Has Jaspen unremembered the words the Always spoke to Bogg in Bogg's night-story? When Bogg said to Jaspen that the Always said 'to stand still and wait', Jaspen asked 'wait for what?' This is *what*! Bogg and Jaspen are to wait no longer!"

Jaspen grinned. "So you can—"

Yet before Jaspen could finish, Bogg had taken hold of him and hurled Jaspen up and into Fire-Breath's bony jaws.

Jaspen landed softly on the floor of Fire-Breath's jaw. None of the four Gort noted the newcomer. Two of the *skeervog*-makers were climbing feet-first into the secret tunnels that had been burrowed into the dirt at the back the skeleton's throat. The others were impatiently waiting their turns to escape through one of the two hidden shafts.

Bolting to the departing hoaxers, each already halfway into their respective crawlways, Jaspen knocked aside the two waiting Gort and seized each of the tunnel-bound cowards by their long, orange hair. He yanked them backwards and out of their warrens, then pitched them out of Fire-Breath's beak.

The piercing screams of the plummeting Gort were eclipsed by a thunderous roar from Long-Mane. And the crowd's collective gasp was likely due to the revelation that Fire-Breath's power was no more divine than a *skeervog* composed by the dirty fists of an ordinary Gort.

Jaspen glanced at his hands, puzzled. Then to Fire-Breath's jaws.

Was it really I who tossed those rogue Gort so far? he thought.

He looked away from the bone beak and back to his palms and fingers, marveling at his inexplicable strength.

It is you, my Always, who empowers me for this task.

He peered to the remaining two Gort. Each had leapt headlong into a tunnel. Only their shaggy-haired ankles and large bare feet showed, kicking, as if the manic fluttering would help speed their descent.

Jaspen darted to the escapees with a footspeed twice as fast and thrice as sure as he had ever known. He seized each Gort by a furry ankle and hauled the deceitful pair from their holes as if they weighed no more than a couple of Rope-Tails. He wheeled in a double circle before slinging the twosome through Fire-Breath's bony maw and into the open air.

Climbing down the skeleton, Jaspen worked the bird-god's ribs like rungs of a ladder. He touched down onto the ground just as Long-Mane leapt onto Fire-Breath's beak, shattering it with a single bite. Then the Always incinerated the carcass's every bone and talon so thoroughly that nothing of the Gort deity remained.

Long-Mane sauntered back to the slaves and stood before them, majestic.

"Witchcraft!" yelled a Huntressi.

"Devilry!" shouted a Gort.

"Levaioth forever!" bellowed a Cove.

Long-Mane's fiery eyes paused on each of those who had cried aloud the name of their false god. An ominous growl in his throat grew into a roar so vigorous that every bench overturned and the arena's ceiling of packed dirt shivered.

A light haze of dust descended from the trembling ceiling, as fine as mist. Slowly it fell. Yet as the cracks above lengthened and widened and deepened, the dust-fall increased. Soon, the earthen dome above was pouring forth pillars of dirt as dense as tree trunks. Horrific screams gained in volume as heaps of earth continued to gush, covering the toppled benches, burying the crowd alive, and muting each screamer as grit and gravel filled their throats.

When the large, domed ceiling finally collapsed in full, its bulk crashed into the arena floor with a muffled thump. A billowing cloud of filth burst upward to blind Jaspen and Bogg to everything but the suffocating, swirling debris.

An eerie silence ensued. The gagging coughs of the two slaves were the only noise beyond the soft hush of shifting sands and grains of earth tumbling down the sides of pyramidal mounds.

A smothered sob came from somewhere above them. A teardrop of flame—the Always!—appeared near a Huntressi warrioress digging her way out of a mountain of dirt. Two additional moans, strangled and faint, sent Jaspen's eyes searching through the pitch. The flame above the Huntressi split into three. The two new flickers travelled through the wreckage. One came to hover over a Cove man's hand jutting up from the top of a sand dune, like a war-torn flag; pocked and scarred but still waving. The other small torch paused in the air, snapping and spitting, above a rippling patch of earth. The crown of a head emerged from the soil, followed by the face of a Gort woman, then her shoulders.

Jaspen and Bogg went on to pull nine Gort, three Cove, two Huntressi and an Udok from the heavy banks of sand. Each of the seventeen survivors was audited for injuries. There was nothing beyond minor burns and scratches.

"Did any of you feel it as I did?" a Gort asked the others. "When first putting eyes on the baby Wool-Back."

A Cove woman said, "Warm burning in the heart. So much joy." She smiled.

"Ay," said another Gort. "And the head tingled, it did. Then . . . floated."

"Clear to me," said the Huntressi, "was that our isle is not six tribes, but one."

Others agreed and further claimed a sense of indescribable comfort and stout inner strength. But above all, back when they had first gazed at the pure, white *skeervog* nestling at Jaspen's feet, each survivor had been struck by an unshakable conviction that the fiery, baby Wool-Back was the one true god of all Jirvalla.

35

False Totem

"Your request, fulfilled," said Rollik, placing a newly minted Gort sword at the foot of the Throne of Pearls.

The Faijen motioned to a wheeled timber cart that was resting outside the front archway leading into the Hall of Shells. It was filled with Gort blades.

"One hundred Gort swords," said Rollik. "Let the island ledger show that the Cove hereby pledge to make good on one new favor-bond to the Faijen."

Sorazin lifted the weapon at his feet and inspected it, nodding his satisfaction. "Plenty of Gort steel, I see, but where is the flesh you promised? Three moons have passed since we have spoken."

"Indeed. Three moons filled with much effort and peril. All for your benefit, young Mutahn. And I am pleased to share the tidings regarding your lost clanmates. Perhaps while sipping the island tea and nibbling at the Cove cakes you were surely about to offer a distinguished ally such as myself."

Sorazin's eyes narrowed at Rollik before glancing to an attractive servant girl. Scurrying away, the girl returned carrying a platter heavy with piping tea steeping in a lustrous pearl pot, two beautifully sculpted shell cups, and freshly baked Cove cakes carefully arranged on a large, shiny, green leaf. She served her Mutahn and the Faijen as they sat upon the lavish courtyard overlooking a vast, luxuriant, green lawn rimmed by manicured trees, bright flowers, fragrant herbs, and flourishing shrubs.

Musical cheeps, hoots, chirrups, and twitters breezed into the courtyard from the lush forest that lay just beyond the pristine gardens.

"Regarding the girl, Kama," Rollik peered to the many warriors sparring on a distant hillside, swords clanking, "it is safe to presume she is dead."

"Yet, once again, you come without evidence."

"She has surely been consumed by forest beak and island fang."

"And *mahkifo*?"

"I have located the Day-Night Cove in the—" the crack of a falling tree drew Rollik's eyes toward the clamor. In the distance, a dozen Cove were erecting a mountainous weapon of wood, steel, and stone. "Do the tides of war loom close?"

"My sources inform me it is imminent," lied Sorazin.

"The Great Rill has mentioned nothing of—"

"Where is *mahkifo*?"

"The Shepherd of Fish dwells in the Black Deep."

"Pray tell, Faijen, if you know his place then why are you without him?"

"Clearly your feet, young Mutahn, have never trod the dirt of the Black Deep. Nor your hands burrowed into the soil of that lightless pit in which slaves are made to work, eat, sleep, and die without ever again laying eyes upon another soul."

Sorazin smirked. *Exaggerating again, this minnow.*

"Clearly your only food has never been the worm, root, or rotting flesh your digging fingers can unearth while scratching at the dirt of the Black Deep in hopes of meeting your daily quota of gold nuggets and gemstones."

Sorazin rolled his eyes.

"Clearly your ears have never jumped to the sound of an Eyeless-Snout-Face tunneling into your pit to feed on your innards while you slumber."

The Mutahn held Rollik's stare, hating the Faijen. In two moons—three at most—Sorazin will have trained the proper number of troops to capture the whole of his arrogant, winged race.

How I long to watch them quiver, thought Sorazin, *when I offer them to Levaioth, one by one by one.*

"And clearly, young Mutahn, the shrieks of those driven to lunacy have no—"

"If you are incapable of returning to me my missing tribesman then simply say it, Faijen, instead of boring me with this ridiculous fiction of the Black Deep."

"The Black Deep is no fable, Sorazin. This I assure you. And no Cove, Treef, Udok, Huntressi or even Faijen descending to its miserable depths has ever reached sun-side again. Perhaps if you increased your reward for the Day-Night Cove you would find favor with Vykon. The Gort King-Lord alone can emancipate a slave from the Deep. In the many moons of his Lordship, however, he has yet to enact this power."

"If the Faijen are too feeble to liberate one simple Cove from the UnderDown, can you at least manage the modest chore of securing for me an interview with the Gort King? Or is even this small errand beyond your power?"

"Vykon fails to acknowledge your claim to the Throne of Pearls, Sorazin. Rumors are rife amongst all island tribes that the totem you presented to Ertu upon returning from the Hoodoah's cave was inauthentic."

"Gossip and speculation, from a jealous few."

"Master Sage Rill was offered information regarding the Hoodoah's totem from an eyewitness."

Sorazin's lip twitched and his back flexed straight and rigid.

He lies, thought Sorazin, calming his face and easing his shoulders.

"Two moons ago, a strange, entirely white Cave-Wing arrived at our royal palace. Master sage Rill, of course, speaks the Cave-Wing tongue."

Sorazin gnashed his teeth and his cheek tremored.

"Hydron Rill did not share much of what was spoken between he and the Cave-Wing. But my master did assure me that the Hoodoah's totem you are endeavoring to pass off as authentic is anything but."

If news of the mock totem has reached Rill, thought Sorazin, *what other secrets have been made known to him?*

Sorazin said, "When there are no other contenders for the Throne of Pearls, Cove law states that—"

" . . . the eldest son of the former Mutahn is to be appointed ruler," said Rollik.

"Precisely." Sorazin sniffed. "So where lay the problem?"

"You have fabricated an untruth pertaining to the validity of your rule, Sorazin. Hydron Rill has been cogitating for many suns the reasons behind your—"

"Enough of this petty frivolity, Faijen."

I am King-Slayer! thought Sorazin, his gloved fingers squeezing into a fist.

"Can you or can you not," Sorazin loosened his hand, calming, "arrange for me a conference with Vykon?"

"Without a proper totem from the Hoodoah, Sorazin, you are to the King-Lord as any common thief who seeks asylum in his realm. Even with me in your company I could not prevent Lord Vykon from enslaving you for a hundred moons."

Sorazin's nose flared. He looked to the many swordsmen in the distance, eager for the day his warriors would storm the UnderDown and capture every last Gort.

"However," Rollik grinned, superior, "as the Faijen are the most beloved and powerful of the Cove's allies, I will go to the trouble of meeting with King-Lord Vykon on your behalf."

"That is very much appreciated, Rollik." Sorazin softened, until . . .

"The price is but one favor-bond."

36

The Black Deep

AFTER SIXTY MARKS ON the inward-sloping wall of his earthen pit in the Black Deep, Jaspen no longer kept a tally of his attempts to climb out of the dark, stretching abyss that was his prison.

After eighty marks on another portion of the circular wall, Jaspen no longer registered the number of suns he had missed since falling into the Gort hole over three, round moons ago.

After ninety grooves on the wall's lowest section, he no longer scored a daily notch into the dirt to indicate when he had last seen, or heard from, the Always.

Jaspen collapsed to the floor of his hole, filthy and exhausted from a day spent like all others—rooting into his pit's walls with nothing but bare hands and naked feet. He untethered the band about his head and removed the clear glass orb from his brow. Four of the Glow-Wings inside the globe had expired. These, Jaspen ate. Two others clung to life, their bodies glowing from time to time to illuminate a small area of Jaspen's otherwise pitch-black burrow.

By the light of the Glow-Wings, Jaspen inspected his fingers. The webbing between them was ragged and torn. He moved the orb to his feet. The flaps of skin joining his toes were also marred from his excava-tions. Even his unique coloring was fading; the black of his back growing lighter and his milky front darkening to hues similar to the damp sand of the Cove beaches he missed so dearly.

I am not myself without the sea, he thought.

Each of Jaspen's workdays began with a small satchel of Glow-Wings landing upon the floor of his pit. When the insects were placed in the glass globe and fitted around his head, the Glow-Wings emitted enough light to locate the gemstones, nuggets, ore, and other items that counted toward the near-impossible quota demanded by the Gort slave masters.

The names of those slaves failing to reach their goals would be entered into a drawing to fight another Black Deep denizen for the entertainment of King-Lord Vykon and his invited guests. The winning combatant of the Nether Pit War, as these contests were called, was the slave whose heart was still beating at battle's end.

Jaspen set the orb on a low, dirt shelf.

"Is this the moment?" he whispered to the Glow-Wings and gathered into his cupped hands a mound of dirt. "Would this be enough to suffocate me until death?"

Eight of the seventeen survivors of the destruction of Fire-Breath's shrine had been consigned to the Black Deep. UnderDown officials were desperate to prevent the spread of gossip regarding the mysterious *skeervog* of Long-Mane that had defeated Fire-Breath, killed all but one of the shrine priests and completely razed the bird-god's shrine. Yet the nine survivors who successfully remained a secret to Gort authorities had been carefully disseminating the truth about what had occurred inside the shrine on the day of its obliteration. Tales regarding the valor of the Day-Night Cove and his Udok companion as well as the inimitable power of their saving god, the Always, had become especially popular amongst children.

Jaspen tilted back his head. Closing his eyes, he suspended the load of dirt above his lips.

"I'm sorry, my Always," he whispered, "but I can wait for you no longer."

He opened wide his mouth, lifted high his dirt-filled hands, and spilled their contents toward his waiting throat. But as the first grains met his tongue, Jaspen clamped shut his lips and the sandy grains poured harmlessly over his nose, mouth, and chin.

"Why can't I do it?" he whispered. Then cried, "Bogg!" into the narrow, black chute above him that extended ever upwards. "Do you live, Bogg? Tell me you live!"

To lose both you and Kama . . . he thought, *would be too much to bear.*

"For once, Bogg, please," he muttered into his hands, "tell me you live." Then, brightening, Jaspen cried upward again: "What a dance we danced that day, my friend!" Jaspen swayed and leapt and gyred as he had in Fire-Breath's shrine.

Yet this time, tears dampened his eyes.

The shining glass globe dimmed and Jaspen rushed to it, grabbing it to peer inside. Another Glow-Wings had died, leaving but one.

"Quick!" He groped about the pit in the failing light until coming to a natural cavity in the rock-ribbed wall. Reaching in, he retrieved the gold-colored gemstone that had fallen to his feet after the Always snuffed the *skeervog* of Fire-Breath.

He stroked the stone as if it were a pet Wag-Tail. "How was your day, my pretty, little Gold-Fins? Did you turn yourself into White-Horn and escape to sun-side when I wasn't looking? Did you visit the Cove? How is Shim? And Plimpoc? Baby Azo must be growing, eh? Or is he—"

The night shrieks began. These were the cries of the Black Deep slaves—of pain and loneliness, of starvation and disease, of death and lunacy.

Jaspen raised his voice against the keening of the Treef, the inconsolable moans of the Udok, the wailing of the Huntressi and the heart-rending dirge of the wing-clipped Faijen: "Cling to hope, my brothers!" he shouted. "Learn, my sisters, from the tiny Glow-Wing. So small her light but oh! how much darkness she scatters! Find your light and let it beam, friends! Only together can we melt the darkness."

Jaspen continued with his words of inspiration until the forlorn squalls subsided.

Returning to the amber gemstone, Jaspen lifted it to his lips and whispered, "Will this be the eve you reveal to me your secret? Please make it so, little Gold-Fins."

He rubbed the jewel between his palms, as the two Gort had done on Jaspen's first day in the marketplace of the UnderDown, when he saw his first *skeervog*.

"Just once, show me what I do wrong."

Directly following their escapes from the flattened shrine of Fire-Breath, Jaspen and Bogg had secreted themselves in a forge owned by one of the other survivors. Gort rulers wasted no time in offering extravagant rewards for information leading to the capture of the Day-Night Cove and his Udok comrade. Jaspen and Bogg stayed but one night hiding in the forge. They feared if their presence was discovered while inside the smith's foundry, the forge's owner would pay with his life for his part in concealing the pair of desperados.

Jaspen and Bogg were apprehended the next day. Subsequent to a severe lashing with scourges barbed with sharp beaks, jagged stones and ripping talons, the slaves were dispatched to the Black Deep.

Continuing to scrub the amber gemstone in his palm, Jaspen stroked it faster and faster. He hoped to raise a powerful fire-creation that would help him find Bogg, break out of the UnderDown and get them both sun-side. Only once since Jaspen's confinement to the Black Deep did the rubbing of the stone produce something unusual: Three workdays ago, the gem began to flare like a Glow-Wing. Yet the small blaze at the stone's center faded as quickly as it had kindled.

He opened his rubbing hands and peeked at the pebble. It remained a simple amber gemstone.

"Damn you!" he cried. Again, Jaspen chafed together his palms—nimbly, quickly. "Please, little Gold-Fins, I beg you."

Looking in on the gem again, it showed no signs of the extraordinary.

"I hate you!" he yelled and hurled the stone into the wall.

Jaspen's eyes followed the suddenly glowing stone as it cut through the dark, a trail of light shimmering behind it. The jewel pelted the wall and fell to the floor, still glowing. Scrambling to it, Jaspen seized the stone and resumed rubbing it between his palms as rapidly as he could.

When the heat of the gem cooled and its glow diminished, Jaspen yelled, "I hate you!"

The stone flared.

It requires anger, he thought.

"I hate you!" he roared again and the gem flashed brighter. "*Skeer-vog* need anger." Jaspen grinned.

A thick twine of rope slapped against Jaspen's forearms then thudded to the dirt at his feet.

From above came a voice: "Identify yourself."

"Jaspen of the Cove," he blared into the pit's long shaft.

"Around your chest place the rope and grip it tight," said the Gort slave master. "Pull you up, I will."

"Why?" asked Jaspen.

"Drawing names. Eligible, you are."

Eligible? Jaspen looped the rope around his torso and tightened it.

"Eligible for what?" he called as the slave master began to haul him upward.

"The Nether Pit War."

37

River Night-Mud

"Opahlua," said the Gort overseer, reading the name from a scrap of parchment and looking at the twenty-nine slaves before him. "Is there an Opahl—"

"I am Opahlua."

The woman took one step toward the center of the ring of slaves. She was tall and formidable with long limbs and cords of lean muscle that stood up on her light brown skin with her every movement.

Huntressi, thought Jaspen, watching her along with the others who had failed to meet their quotas. Yet upon noting that she lacked the Huntressi's large eyes as well as the pupils that dilated vertically, like the jungle's Night-Claw, Jaspen reasoned that she might be a Cove crossbreed.

Opahlua browsed the others before her, calm and confident. Yet when her gaze fell to Jaspen, her eyes narrowed, seething with fury. Her lips tensed and a muscle on her upper arm twitched. She flared her nose at Jaspen before resuming her appraisal of the others.

The Gort overseer nodded to Opahlua then plunged his hand back into the old, corroded vat to draw from it another snatch of parchment.

"Meezul," said the overseer and his eyes knew exactly where to find the Cove chosen to battle Opahlua in the upcoming death match. "Step forward, please."

The frail man took a lethargic step toward the middle of the circle while pushing his glasses higher on his nose. He was small of stature and of an age nearer to death than birth. Meezul's shoulders stooped, his hands trembled and his eyes darted with the nervous air of a misbehaving child caught in the act.

Though Jaspen felt pity for the aged man, he breathed in relief at his own good fortune for having been passed over.

"Opahlua." The overseer faced the woman and bent his chin to her. "Meezul." He turned to the Cove and did the same. "You two will be—"

With a sudden burst, Meezul broke through the circle of slaves and dashed into the dark, toward the lazy, sloshing hum of the River Night-Mud.

"Halt!" commanded the overseer and signaled two torchbearers to pursue the runaway.

The pair gave chase, cracking their whips while instructing the escapee to stop at once. Yet the Gort's stumpy legs and poor foot-speed foiled their endeavors to capture the aged Cove.

A few slaves shouted out their encouragements. Yet upon Meezul's arrival at the banks of the River Night-Mud, the crowd fell silent as the man's grim intention became clear.

Glancing behind him at the Gort torchbearers closing in, Meezul bent his elderly knees, swung back his feeble arms, and cast himself into the viscous, slow-moving bog before him. He plashed down just beyond the range of his pursuers and began to sink immediately, his slow descent illuminated by the fires of the two torches.

"The whip, take it!" A Gort tossed the switch of his flagellum into the swampy mire, well within Meezul's grasp.

Yet even when the thick tail of Dagger-Back slapped the sludgy surface and propelled itself toward Meezul, the Cove turned his face away from the saving whip.

The Black Deep echoed with the grisly caterwauls of Meezul and the splash, growl, and gnash of Dagger-Back taking its time with the unexpected meal.

After calling for the torchbearers to return, the overseer placed his hand back into the vat. He withdrew a snip of parchment. Yet before his eyes could determine the name upon the slip, a slave stepped forward.

The overseer asked, "Do you have a question?"

"No," said Jaspen, suppressing a smile . . . for the spirit of the Always, at long last, was upon him.

"Then why have you—"

"Jaspen of the Cove. Is that not what the scrap in your fist reads?"

The overseer peeked at the parchment, then to Jaspen. "H-how did you—"

"It only matters that I who speak to you am he."

38

Favor-Bonds

"KING-LORD VYKON HAS APPROVED my request to attend the Nether Pit War, two suns hence." Rollik puffed his chest. "When the tide of excitement crests, good Mutahn, I shall slip away into the Black Deep to save your lost tribesman."

Sorazin rubbed his chin. "Surely old Rill has not sent you this great distance only to acquaint me with a flimsy plot to retrieve my missing clansman."

This blood-sucking water-weed is after something, thought the Mutahn.

"Deliver *mahkifo* to the Hall of Shells, Footman. I care nothing of your stratagems if they do not produce what I seek."

Rollik feigned offense. "Your tone with me, young Mutahn, gives me pause. If the Faijen's many efforts on the Cove's behalf have not met with your satisfaction, then perhaps we should sever our previous accord. You are more than welcome to search for the Day-Night Cove yourself."

Sorazin sneered. *I should cut him down where he stands.*

"Apologies for my coarse manner," said Sorazin to the Faijen.

Sorazin's quick eyes flashed to a pair of young servant girls posted but a few paces away, each clutching a large, green leaf from an Arrow-Bark tree. They rushed forward on bare feet. Placing themselves on either side of their Mutahn's throne, they began waving the greenery to generate a breeze to cool Sorazin and his guest.

"It has been a trying day, fair Rollik," Sorazin continued. "The Cove value the Faijen's aid in this matter and depend upon their further assistance. We are allies, are we not?"

"We are indeed. And as such, the Faij—"

A *crack!* in the distance commanded Rollik's attention. He peered through a large window to the hillside from where the clamor had come.

"Those fettered Udok," Rollik motioned to the hill, "why do they toil upon a Cove construction? Has the Jirvallan law prohibiting slavery been lifted?"

Sorazin glanced to the five half-giants. A scorching sun beat upon their bald pates and massive, white-fleshed shoulders and bare backs. They were hauling one oversized log after another out of the forest, each pouring with sweat.

"Those good fellows approached me eight suns ago," lied the Mutahn. "During one of our military exercises."

In truth, Sorazin had captured the half-giants on a recent raid.

"So impressed were they with the might and discipline of the Cove," continued Sorazin, "that they beseeched me to incorporate them into our ranks. This is their trial period, hence the fetters. I have yet to determine if I shall welcome them into Jirvalla's most powerful army."

"Five enemy Udok trespassing on Cove lands?" The fin on Rollik's head flared, suspicious. "And you did not engage them in combat?"

"They came in peace, bearing gifts. If even one had exhibited a trace of hostility, I would have slain all five myself."

On the hillside, a Cove foreman dug the tip of his spear into an Udok's shoulder blade. The half-giant threw back his head, mouth open, spine jerking into an arch.

"And what type of structure, exactly, are your Udok servants erecting? If I may be so bold?"

"Battle catapults, good Rollik. Unlike anything Jirvalla has ever known. My own invention, of course. Royal scouts have informed me that the coming war is to arrive on Cove shores earlier than anticipated. Thus, the swift construction. But I fail to see how that is your concern. Unless old Rill has sent you here with a secret agenda: to glimpse my most recent innovation so he can re-create it for himself."

"You have much to learn, little Covie." Rollik grinned, smug. "Master sage Rill is our island's most ingenious war strategist. Does the water jug instruct the river which way to flow?"

Sorazin scowled at the Faijen.

"But your instincts are admirable, Sorazin, especially for one so young. The *primary* reason for today's visit relates to your tribe's favor-bond owed to mine. The great Rill seeks payment."

"And what, exactly, does the greatest war strategist in our history seek as payment?"

"The one hundred Gort blades I bequeathed to you three moons ago, the Faijen require them at once."

Sorazin's lip jumped and his fists clenched. "I am afraid that is quite impossible. As I mentioned, war comes. The Cove require every weapon—"

"The customary amount of time to make good on a favor-bond is three suns."

"Fair Rollik, the days in which we live are far from customary. If the Faijen could see fit to grant their most trustworthy ally an extension of, say, twelve suns . . . "

My war machines shall be finished by then, thought Sorazin. *And Rollik has just earned for his tribe a private demonstration of their power.*

"Hydron Rill has never before waited more than five suns for the fulfillment of a favor-bond."

If I work the Udok night and day, thought Sorazin, *and enslave another ten . . .*

"Five suns it is. Seven at the most. You have my thanks, good Rollik."

And when your one hundred Gort blades return, Footman, they shall be impaled into the necks of a hundred of your Faijen kin.

39

King-Lord Vykon

JASPEN PUSHED ASIDE HIS plate of fire-grilled game, salted Three-Leaf, fresh vegetables, and double baked Heart-Seed cake.

"I refuse to dine on fare gained by the bitter sweat of slaves."

Sitting alone at his dining table—bathed, scrubbed, and oiled—Jaspen looked with disdain upon the lavish quarters provided for all Nether Pit War competitors.

He eyed the female attendant appointed to him and added, "Neither will I slumber on feathers plucked by the flesh-torn fingers of a fellow prisoner." He waved a hand toward the plush sleeping pallet in the adjoining room. "I would like to return to my pit, if you don't min—"

"And if I do mind?" King-Lord Vykon suddenly appeared at the entrance to Jaspen's dwelling.

Jaspen's eyes broadened in shock at the sight of the Gort's King-Lord entering his quarters.

"Unaware, are you," said Vykon, "that refusing a gift from the King-Lord is a sign of disrespect?" He gazed in approval at the soft pillows, luxurious blankets, spotless stone floors, and scented candles burning in every corner.

"Ap-pologies," stuttered Jaspen, without thinking.

Jaspen stood, instinctively, as the tall, thickly muscled King-Lord stepped nearer. The slave even creased at the waist, bowing reverently, but caught himself and halted the gesture. Counterfeiting a cough, Jaspen straightened, as if the slight fold at his middle had been nothing more than a response to his irritated throat.

The Gort ruler sank into a soft, overstuffed chair and signaled his two royal guards to post themselves at the door.

"Fortunately for you, Jaspen of the Cove," Vykon stroked the fanged head of his pet—a long, brawny Coil-Killer—draped over his enormous shoulders, "I admire one's contempt for hollow comforts." His fingers flicked at the surrounds. "Strength, it shows. And strength," he squeezed his huge fist, "is our greatest virtue. Is it not?"

Vykon uplifted his square chin to Jaspen's attendant and she quickly filled two chalices with Jirvalla's finest wine. She delivered the larger vessel to King-Lord Vykon and the smaller to Jaspen.

"Far too many cowards and weaklings have I seen." The King-Lord swirled his ruby-hued wine, sniffing it. "There is no honor in such things."

"Honor?" Jaspen studied the tall, long-legged King-Lord and contemplated just how little of his blood, if any at all, was of Gort stock. "And what of this lightless, underground death-pit you promote as a haven for refugees? Is that your definition of an *honorable* enterprise, King-Lord?" Only the fiery orange of Vykon's hair and wild beard suggested any ancestral link to the UnderDown race. "With all due respect, how dare you speak to me of honor."

"So fearless!" Vykon chuckled and tipped his flagon toward Jaspen. "I like him already. Pray tell, great Shepherd of Fish, what further traits define the assassin of the Hoodoah, the destroyer of Fire-Breath? It would be deceit to claim that I have not been looking forward to our conference."

"Sorry to disappoint, King-Lord, but it was not I who cut down Fire-Breath. That distinction belongs to the Always. Nor did I smite the Hoodoah."

"He lives then, does he?" asked King-Lord Vykon.

Jaspen shook his head. He explained how the holy man had stopped Sorazin's slashing blade with his bare hand. He then described the Hoodoah's willful march into the blaze of his cave's bonfire. How the flames had twined about the man's legs. How the Hoodoah had disintegrated before Jaspen's eyes, becoming one with the fire.

"Prior to his exodus, however," said Jaspen, "the Hoodoah announced that 'I must become less, so that . . . so that . . . '" Jaspen could not say what he could not believe, " . . . so that the Always could become more," he lied.

King-Lord Vykon studied Jaspen, searching the youth's face and posture for signs of deception. "Believe you, I do, little Covie," he admitted. "Yet without proof, truth is nothing. Sun-side tongues have been wagging, they have, each proclaiming with all confidence that it was the Day-Night Cove who struck down the Hoodoah. And who could lay fault upon them? But a few hands after the Hoodoah's demise, my Mudkin happen upon you lounging in the protective confines of a Gort hole. Suspicious, would you not agree? For it is precisely what the guilty have been doing for ten thousand moons."

"It was not my will to enter that unmarked Gort hole. A friend dear to me, an Udok called Bogg, he too arrived in your kingdom without intention. It is your duty as King-Lord to free the pair of us from the Black Deep. Jirvallan law is clear."

"My duty? What pluck, this brazen little sinew!" Vykon laughed, hearty, then sipped his wine. "Your candor has earned for you my favor, slave."

"Then free me from the UnderDown at once. Along with my Udok comrade."

"Too cruel, it would be, to rob my guests of what has become the most anticipated Nether Pit War in over a hundred seasons."

"The law demands that you restore to me my freedom. I have duties requiring my attention sun-side."

"And he is dutiful too!" Vykon stroked the scaled nose and jaw of his pet and the Coil-Killer's long body tightened with affection around Vykon's torso. "An offer for you I have, Shepherd. But first, pray tell, what treasures lie sun-side that my Kingdom cannot yield?"

"My parents. My people. The isle of my birth. Once sun-side, after avenging my Forever-One's murder, I will trek to the ocean's end to find my homeland. Jirvalla no longer holds anything of value for me."

"A respectable quest." Vykon gestured for more wine. "Freedom is yours, slave, if you but produce for me this *splendid* deity about whom the UnderDown cannot stop speaking . . . "—the King-Lord's face creased with displeasure—"this *god* of yours to whom so many have turned since Fire-Breath's demise . . . "—his teeth gnashed—"this damnable *Always*!"

"Conjure the Always? There is not a force on Jirvalla with power enough to call forth the mighty Always. He comes when he comes. But to all who seek him with a true heart, the Always promises to show himself."

"And what of those of us who seek your god with only the intent to slay him?"

Jaspen chuckled. "You can no more extinguish the Always than you can extinguish the sky. Or slay the ocean. None can lay a hand upon him. The Always is immortal."

"Summon him now and we shall see." Vykon's fingers played, the gold and jeweled rings upon them glinting in the torchlight. "I must prove to my subjects that there is but one god of the UnderDown: Me."

The King-Lord narrowed his eyes at Jaspen, thinking.

"What say you, boy, if I were to attack you this instant? Would your precious Always rush to protect you as he did in the shrine of Fire-Breath? Perhaps if the speaker for the Always perishes, so does his deity?"

"Perhaps." Thoughts of Kama charged into Jaspen's heart, unbidden. Sorrow swamped him and his face fell. So lost was he without her. "There is but one sure way to solve your riddle, King-Lord: Lift your dagger against me and let destiny decide who perishes—you or the Always."

"Oh, ho! How daring, this child!" Vykon laughed. "Such trust!" He stood.

At the door, the two Gort guards snapped to attention.

"Jaspen of the Cove." Vykon shook his head and gazed into the Shepherd's face, smiling. "In all of my seasons, never have I met one so deserving of freedom as you."

The King-Lord's large hands squeezed at the youth's shoulders, fatherly.

"But no one escapes the Black Deep."

40

Preparing for War

JASPEN WOKE TO THE delicate weight of a satchel of Glow-Wings touching down upon his breast. A skin of water slapped into the floor of his pit a moment later.

It was the third sun since King-Lord Vykon acquiesced to Jaspen's petition to slumber in his pit instead of the lodgings offered to all Nether Pit War combatants.

Opening his eyes to the impenetrable dark, Jaspen quickly shut them again.

"Kama," he whispered, longing to return to the pleasant dreamland from which he had been torn.

Yet Kama—her face, hands, voice, smile, eyes . . . —was lost to wakefulness.

"Tell me she lives, my Always," whispered Jaspen. "Show her to me. Please." He rose to his feet.

Closing tighter his eyes Jaspen strove to retrieve the image of Kama. Yet all he could summon were crimson flashes and twinkling lights—like the Night-Sparks upon which he and Kama used to gaze, connecting the glimmering flecks to make animal shapes in the dark sky.

Jaspen soon abandoned the effort and scooped up the Glow-Wings. He placed them in his glass orb and exploited their light to locate the amber-colored gemstone. Shutting his eyes again, Jaspen set his mind to the invention of images malevolent and unjust; the very ingredients required to build for himself a powerful *skeervog*.

Yet Jaspen could not dispel his yearning to bring back the lovely face and form of Kama.

"Are you a Cloaker yet?" muttered Jaspen, absently caressing the stone in his palm. "Oh, how I hope you have achieved your heart's wish." He pictured Kama emerging from a boulder to recapture her shiny dark hair, tanned skin, and green eyes. "How are your parents and Shim?" he continued, lost in daydream.

Though he did not perceive it, the gem in his hand was growing colder instead of hotter.

"You're taller," he said to Kama, his Forever-One smiling back at him.

As Jaspen's fingers rubbed the stone, the gem began to slicken with moisture.

"Have I grown too?" Jaspen imagined his flat hand measuring out how much taller he was than Kama.

So rapt was Jaspen with his make-believe converse that his senses overlooked the gemstone's increasing damp.

"Day-Night Cove," interrupted a voice from above.

Jaspen unshut his eyes. Returning to the present, he suddenly felt the strange cool of the stone in his grip. He moved the Glow-Wings's prison to his palm. In the light of the glass orb, Jaspen saw the amber gem half immersed in a shallow pool of water that had, somehow, filled the hollow of Jaspen's cupped hand. He peered closer and watched in awe as drops of water pushed out from the gemstone to deepen the little puddle within his palm.

How . . . he thought. *How did this—*

"A rope descends," said the slave master above.

Yet Jaspen scarcely heard him. For he was gazing in disbelief at the water that was now overfilling his hand to drip onto his knees and feet.

"Today is the day," stated the voice above.

Jaspen lifted his hand and splashed his face with the water. He laughed. And when the seawater springing from the gemstone refilled the void of his cupped hand, Jaspen splashed his face a second time.

"My skeervog . . . " whispered Jaspen, staring at the amber gem, "perhaps it is to be composed of water instead of fire."

He swabbed his lips with his tongue until it tingled with the briny tang of the sea. Oh, how he missed the ocean.

A thick rope chafed against Jaspen's cheek as it lowered toward his thighs.

"A day's pay I have wagered on you, Jaspen of the Cove," said the slave master. "I pray that your god give you the strength to claim victory."

Strength? thought Jaspen. *Victory?* It dawned on him. *The Nether Pit War.*

With the rope girding his torso, Jaspen ascended to the pit's mouth. He buried the amber gemstone beneath his tongue for fear the slave master would confiscate it.

It was my thoughts of Kama that made the seawater flow. For me it is not rage, but love, that is required to create a skeervog.

The slave master hoisted Jaspen up and out of the pit and smiled at him while unraveling the rope about the Cove's waist and trunk. "Fine, you will do!" He slapped Jaspen on the back. "Anyone who can slay Fire-Breath can surely defeat Opahlua."

Jaspen was ushered to a comfortable accommodation near the entrance to the Nether Pit War arena. A prick of fear for what lay ahead jabbed at Jaspen's neck as he entered the quarters.

An aged Gort woman stood with folded arms, frowning at the filthy state of the Cove. She conducted Jaspen to a back room where a polished stone tub, sculpted from a boulder, was filled with steaming water. The woman reached out toward the Shepherd, grimacing at the touch of Jaspen's grimy garment.

Once undressed, Jaspen was thrust into the tub by the sturdy Gort woman. She scoured every inch of the boy's flesh with a rough-bristled brush. After drying him, she thoroughly oiled Jaspen for battle then produced a sleeveless knee-length tunic. She pulled it over the slave's head then cinctured the loose-fitting garment with a rope belt. To his chest, she strapped a protective sheath of leather, billeted with thin strips of iron. A long timber staff was the final accoutrement.

"Come." She led Jaspen to a small dining area. "Eat, drink."

Jaspen sat at the table and furtively transferred the gemstone from his mouth to his fist. While picking at the rich game, seeds, nuts, and grains before him, he was overcome with a great and daunting angst.

Is this my final day, my Always? Will You allow Opahlua to best me in combat?

"Your fingers shake," said the Gort woman.

"They do not."

"Answer any questions, I can, about the Nether Pit War," offered the woman. "The King-Lord has permitted it."

"Opahlua," Jaspen's lip quivered, "what do you know of her?"

"Six times she has battled in the arena and killed, she did, five men and one woman. Bred for battle, this Opahlua, strong of arm and fleet of foot with sharp Huntressi eyes and the might of an Udok. Some say she has the eye that sees into the morrow. Inherited from her father."

"Father?"

"The prophet whose head you clove from his body."

"Not the . . . "

No wonder! Jaspen recalled how fiercely Opahlua stared at him during the drawing of names.

"Opahlua's father was the Hoodoah?" asked Jaspen.

"Never have I seen one so angry at another as Opahlua is with you."

Jaspen's face sagged. *I fear death, my Always.* He bowed his head. *Am I not too young to die? Yet to join Kama in the Lands of Kiriath-Dae . . . it may—*

"Cove," said the Gort. "A visitor, you have. A gift from King-Lord Vykon."

Jaspen peeked, with bleary eyes, to the entrance to spy a large, blurred figure.

Opahlua, thought Jaspen. *Coming to crow about the excruciating methods with which she intends to kill me.*

"I did not slay your father." Jaspen blinked away his foggy vision.

The visitor came into focus and Jaspen's eyes broadened. He rose to his feet.

"Bogg?"

41

Axyd

THE TREEF ROYAL PALACE was a dazzling effusion of lush, vibrant flora. Trees, shoots, flowers, leaves, moss, and other thriving verdure arched high above a velvety carpet of bright green grass, pink and white clover, feathery reeds, and tiny florets of blue, red, orange, and purple. Chatter-Tails chirped while to-ing and fro-ing over the luxuriant walls and branched ceiling, chasing one another as children at play. Song-Beaks trilled and whistled from boughs above, a few soaring through the palace in search of new roosts from which to warble. There were colorful Hover-Wings, Croak-Necks, Flop-Ears, Tree-Horns, and a pair of Hooting-Long-Arms that were swinging through the fingers of sun that pierced the canopy to stripe the palace from ceiling to floor in long poles of light.

Sorazin, however, remained indifferent to the splendor. He had eyes only for Axyd, the revered Kaliphae of the Treef, who was glaring at him with bulbous eyes—furious.

"From what I know of *mahkifo*," said the Mutahn, "that murdering black-heart has no god but himself. Whatever this *miracle* your rangers believed they witnessed, I can assure you it was nothing more than sorcery and illusion."

Axyd sprang from his throne to stand tall and menacing before Sorazin and the ten Cove warriors that flanked their Mutahn.

"To demeeeean our Treeeeeef god"—the Kaliphae's sharp mandibles came together with a threatening *clack!*—"is to demeeeeean all Treeeeeeef!"

A hundred royal Treef soldiers emerged from the forested walls and dropped from the ceiling to surround Sorazin and his troops.

"I intend no offense, wise Axyd." Sorazin lifted his empty palms, appeasing. "I simply offer my opinion."

"The hive mind doesss not liiiiieeee! What one Treeeeef seeees, all Treeeeef seeeeee." Axyd sat upon the artistically hewn tree trunk that was the Kaliphae's living throne. "Weee Treeeeef stand in defense of Jassspenn. Were it not for the Day-Niiight Cove, the Treeeeef would not know the truuuth of the Alwaaayyyss."

Axyd glowered hard at Sorazin, letting the silence grow between them. Then:

"We have seeeen what you have done to the Udok in the Flame Landsss and to the Huntressssii on the plainsss beneeeeath Arrowhead Peak. I have alssso ssspoken with Hydron Riiillll about your spuriousss totem, falssse Mutahn. A Council of All Tribes we have ssset for the next round mooooon. To discussssss what to dooo with yoooou, Ssssorraziinnn."

This maggot-eater bluffs, thought Sorazin.

"In your quesssst to locate Jassspenn, the Cove will receeeive no help from the Treeeeeef."

The pincers of each Treef soldier snapped together with a sharp *clap*!

"Now, go. Yoooou are no longer welcome heeeeere."

"As you wish, good Kaliphae." Sorazin grinned, arrogant.

The Mutahn and his contingent bowed as one and departed. Once the company was a safe distance from the Treef palace, Sorazin whistled out the signal.

A Cove of unscrupulous character stepped out from behind a nearby tree.

"Prepare the battle catapult," said Sorazin to his shifty tribemate, glancing at the Treef guards posted at the palace's entry. "Set each load aflame and continue the firestorm until every last bough, leaf, and twig of the Treef's royal shed is ash."

"You look well!" Jaspen beamed while scanning Bogg head to foot. "Strong."

"Bogg is healthy." A grin spanned his face. "Though the eating-dirt here is too soft and the supper-bones Bogg quarries for each day are dry, Bogg manages."

Jaspen laughed and rapped Bogg on the shoulder then embraced him. "How good to see you, my friend. I thank the Always you're here."

The pair was not long in friendly discourse when Jaspen noticed that Bogg, too, was attired in a knee-length tunic and leather breastplate. He had also been oiled for battle. In the Udok's hand was a timber staff.

Jaspen asked, "Why are y-you dressed so?" hoping that Vykon had called for all of his guests to dress in the garb of the Nether Pit combatants.

"Bogg has been invited to compete in a very dignified contest called the Nether Pit Game!" He smiled, proud. "King-Lord Vykon assured Bogg that it is a great honor to be chosen as a contestant."

What a fool I am! thought Jaspen.

"Has Jaspen been selected to play as well? Is this the reason for Jaspen's tunic and breastplate similar to Bogg's?"

Jaspen explained that the Nether Pit War was a battle until death. He also apprised the Udok of what had occurred between he and Vykon, three days ago.

"The fault is mine." Jaspen's face fell. "I am sorry, Bogg. When the moment comes, I will not lift a hand against you. Now, listen," his pleading eyes looked into Bogg's, "when they place us within the arena, promise that you will slay me."

"Slay Jaspen? Never would Bogg do such a thing. Jaspen is Bogg's friend."

"One of us must die, Bogg. That is what the Nether Pit War requires. If we refuse to fight, Vykon will put us both to death."

"If the Always wants Bogg and Jaspen to die as one then Bogg and Jaspen shall die as one. As Jaspen so bravely stood by Bogg in the shrine of Fire-Breath, so Bogg will stand by Jaspen in the Nether Pit Game arena."

"No, Bogg. Please. You must—"

A gong was struck.

Two more resonant peals followed.

Jaspen's heart clutched and his hands ran with sweat.

Four armed guards—two brawny Gort, a Huntressi, and an Udok— entered Jaspen's quarters.

"Come," said a guard to Jaspen and Bogg. "Follow now."

42

A Gate Lifts

"Ten!" chanted King-Lord Vykon, along with his two thousand guests—nearly half of the UnderDown.

The amphitheater overlooking the Nether Pit War arena was crowded to capacity.

Jaspen faced Opahlua through a tall, thick, iron gate that separated the two combatants and split the battle arena into equal halves.

"Nine!" roared the audience.

Hundreds of blazing torches edged the perimeter of the large dome of heavy steel bars that encircled Jaspen and the tall, fearsome warrioress.

Opahlua thrust a fist through the bars in a ploy to seize Jaspen's tunic, drag him toward her, and throttle him until he breathed no more.

"Eight!"

Jaspen eluded her grasping hand and said, "I didn't kill your father!"

Opahlua sneered at him. "Yaaaa!" she shouted in frustration and gripped the gate's bars with both of her fists, heaving them upward. Her muscles rippled and bulged. So great was Opahlua's strength that the immense gate lifted from the earth.

"Seven!"

Though enough space had been created for Opahlua to slip underneath the gate, the warrioress could not manage to both hold aloft the heavy iron bars and slither beneath them.

"Six!"

Jaspen peered to the ceiling, webbed with bars. Two Udok stood guard atop the huge cage.

"Five!"

At the count of zero, the half-giants would work the winch's lever to raise the iron bars and the death match would commence.

Opahlua released the gate and it crashed down to the earth with a strident clang.

"Four!" blared the mob.

"Run Jaspen!" cried someone amidst the crowd.

Jaspen scanned the spectators. Vykon had divided the Huntressi and Udok from the Faijen, Treef, and Cove, to keep the conflicting tribes separate.

To heighten their loathing for each other, thought Jaspen.

The Gort onlookers were diplomatically scattered throughout all tribes.

Jaspen's eyes finally landed upon a familiar face. "Perpeht?" he whispered.

"Three!"

"Run! Quick!" The Cove flute-carver directed a finger toward the maze of dirt mounds, steel columns, and heaps of refuse that lay piled behind his tribe-mate. "Hide!"

"Where's Bogg?" yelled Jaspen to Perpeht. "The Udok fighter?"

"Two!"

Perpeht shook his head.

Jaspen dashed away and through the labyrinth of dunes, rubbish, and steel.

"One!"

Taking the amber stone from its hiding place, Jaspen set it in his palm. "Come on, little Gold-Fins," he said to it, stroking the gem.

"Zero!" boomed the audience.

The two Udok atop the cage strained at the metal crank and the gate began to rise.

"Show me a *skeervog*," begged Jaspen, "one made of seawater." He scrubbed at the gemstone, frantic.

The chains hauling the gate rattled and groaned as the barrier reared upward, little by little.

Opahlua clinched the bars again, endeavoring to hasten the gate's slow ascent.

"Help me, my Always!" cried Jaspen. "Please."

Opahlua ducked beneath the bars and bolted toward Jaspen amid wild shouts from the horde: *Kill the shrine-razer! He smote the Hoodoah! Praise to Fire-Breath!*

Jaspen chafed desperately at the amber gem. "Come on, come on, come on! Please Gold-Fins. Please!"

Yet so distracted was Jaspen that he could not conjure the love necessary to generate even a drop of seawater from the stone.

"Jaspen?" The quivering voice was near.

No! he thought, recognizing the speaker's timbre. Jaspen fisted the stone and raced out from the earthen dune that had been shielding him.

Bogg stood trembling before Jaspen. Opahlua was restraining the half-giant from behind—her staff pressing firmly into the Udok's throat.

43

Unannounced Visitor

"I DID NOT KILL the Hoodoah," said Jaspen to Opahlua.

"To escape the tortures I have plotted, you would claim anything."

"Bogg played no part in your father's death." Jaspen angled his staff toward the warrioress, aggressive. "Free him."

"Two men against one woman, eh?" Vykon emerged from behind a pillar. "It hardly seems fair." The King-Lord bowed his head in greeting. "Opahlua."

The manner in which Vykon spoke the name of the warrioress placed emphasis on the middle portion of the word: *pah-loo*.

Jaspen's ear reviewed the King-Lord's utterance. His gaze traveled from Vykon to the warrioress. *My Pahlu . . .* He recalled the Hoodoah's words. *Of course!*

"'My Pahlu,'" said Jaspen to Opahlua. "That is what he called you, your father."

"What did you say?" The warrioress narrowed her eyes at Jaspen, suspicious, and choked her staff deeper into Bogg's throat.

"'Tell my Pahlu it is time.' This is the message your father requested that I pass to you."

Joy-Tears welled in Opahlua's eyes. Her face softened and she eased her grip on the staff at Bogg's neck.

Jaspen's heart surged with compassion for the warrioress. Without his knowing it, the stone in Jaspen's palm grew damp.

"Be not fooled by this enchanter," said Vykon to Opahlua. "He is—"

"What more did he say, my father?" Opahlua asked Jaspen.

Jaspen shook his head. "He stepped into his cave's fire before—"

"Heed him not, Opahlua." Vykon clasped her shoulder. "Slew your father, this one did. And now he seeks only to cheat justice. Are his lies not made evident by the volume of sweat leaking from his palms?"

Jaspen glimpsed the steady trickle of seawater seeping from the gemstone in his grasp.

Grinning, Jaspen thought, *Now to compose a* skeervog.

"My guests, they grow restless." Vykon cuffed Opahlua lightly on the back, rousing her from her daze. "They are eager for blood." He browsed the benches. "Let us not disappoint them."

Opahlua's eyes drifted to Jaspen's dripping hand. "My King-Lord speaks true. You bewitched me, warlock." She glared at Jaspen. "Prepare to die. Directly after this one." She wrenched the staff tighter against Bogg's throat.

Bogg clutched at the pole—squirming, squealing—desperate to loosen the rod at his windpipe.

"Hey Two-Tone!" The voice came from but a few steps to the rear of Vykon.

Opahlua loosened her stranglehold on the Udok and swung her head toward the sound. "Who spoke?" Her eyes swept the area, but saw no one. She looked to Vykon. "Another joins us."

Two-Tone? thought Jaspen.

Only one person had ever called him by that name.

King-Lord Vykon scanned the region from whence the voice had come. There was only dirt, iron bars, and heaps of rubble.

Opahlua asked, "What say you, King-Lord?"

"Let us finish with these two." Vykon turned to Jaspen. "We shall dispense with the intruder thereafter."

"As you wish." Opahlua tautened her staff against Bogg's neck.

Bogg howled, calling for help.

Jaspen, however, had been rendered insensate to everything but the sight of something emerging from the hill of garbage behind his opponents.

Vykon said to Jaspen, "Time to bid us farewell, mighty Slayer of Fire-Breath, Shepherd of Fish."

The King-Lord grinned . . . then pounced.

Yet Jaspen remained motionless, spellbound by the figure of a girl drawing closer while changing her texture and hue to match whatever she happened to touch. His every sense was so enthralled with the mirage of loveliness striding toward him that he failed to take note of Vykon's swift and deadly approach.

It took the whole of Jaspen's strength and focus to mutter but one word:

"Kama."

44

A Cloaker Emerges

HAVE I GONE TO the Lands of Kiriath-Dae, my Always? thought Jaspen, warm and smiling at the illusion of Kama advancing toward him. *Has the King-Lord smote me so soon? Is that why I see her? Or is she but a wraith?*

"Jaspen!" shouted Kama. "Look out!"

At the sweet ring of Kama's voice in his ear, Jaspen buoyed with a love and yearning so powerful that two thick jets of seawater gushed from the amber stone in his grip, bursting out from between his fisted fingers.

Vykon and Opahlua instinctively jerked their eyes toward the foreign voice that had cried out from between them. In the next moment, each was pounded by a shaft of water so breakneck and heavy that both were sent sprawling to the dirt as if pummeled by a prodigious ocean wave.

"Kama?" Jaspen's eyes broadened, mistrusting the truth of the image before him. But, soon, hope flared to pull the corners of his mouth into a smile.

"Why were you just standing there?" Kama folded her arms and shook her head. "They were going to kill you! Geez." She grinned at him, her bright green eyes shining. "I have no idea how you get by without me."

"But I thought you were . . . " Jaspen stared at her, stunned, his stomach overturning. "At the tree, I watched you bleeding."

Heart drumming, louder and louder, Jaspen trembled with joy, confusion, and dizzy amazement. He stumbled toward Kama and threw his arms around her.

"You live!" cried Jaspen, embracing Kama tighter.

"Of course I do," Kama smirked. "Who else is—"

Jaspen kissed her. Tender and deep. Soft and loving and soulful. With a wish, he would have asked that this moment abide forever.

Each lover's hands drew the other closer and closer, tighter and tighter . . . until their thighs, hips, abdomens, torsos, hearts, and lips were all joined as one.

All the while, the rivers of seawater flowing from Jaspen's fist never ebbed.

"Kama, I love with ev-very . . . " Jaspen's eyes suddenly broke from hers and peered about . . .

at the iron dome . . .

at the crowd upon the benches . . .

at Vykon and Opahlua striving against the tempest of seawater.

"You cannot linger!" cried Jaspen to Kama, placing himself between her and his foes. "The peril is— Flee, Kama! Now, please. We will unite again sun-si—"

"Too dangerous?" objected Kama. "For you maybe. I just saved your— Your h-hand . . . " Kama stepped back, astonished by the streams of water shooting forth from her Forever One's fingers.

Jaspen glanced to his watery palm. *My* skeervog . . . he thought. *It has come*!

He pushed the gemstone in his hand toward Vykon and Opahlua and a surge of seawater overwhelmed his rivals, pressing them back another ten paces.

"Hallo hay, Kama!" Bogg smiled and strode toward her, extending his hand in a relaxed manner that seemed more suited to a holiday feast than a battle to the death. "Boggfrogg is very pleased to meet Jaspen's Forev—"

"Bogg," interrupted Jaspen. "This is Kama."

Jaspen took her hand in his and peered into Kama's vibrant, new-leaf gaze sparkling in the torchlight. They were the loveliest eyes he had ever beheld.

He continued, "She has been my h-heart's Forever-One since the day we m-met."

Jaspen's voice betrayed him, shaking. His knees turned traitor and went hollow and wobbly. And his lips revolted, jumping then squeezing then stretching then refusing to move at all.

"That was fourteen rain seasons ago," he managed.

"Fifteen." Kama's eyes glistened with building tears.

Blind to Vykon and Opahlua struggling against the swirling, swelling rapids, Jaspen held Kama's gaze and said:

"When I saw you curled and dying at the foot of that tree, I was certain that fate had stolen you from me, forevermore. I swore an oath then and there—to you, to myself, and to the Always."

The ocean in Jaspen's fist continued to pour into the arena like the spouting blowholes of a thousand Gray-Mountain Fish, keeping Vykon and Opahlua at bay.

Jaspen descended to a quivering knee, his nerves nearly capsizing him. "It is untimely, of this I am aware, but I am bound by my heart's vow and nothing shall sway me from it. Kama of the Cove." His voice, by turns, was quavery then assured. "On this day, with Boggfrogg and the Always as my witnesses, I vow to love and care for you until time's last breath." A tear striped his cheek. "Come what may. Throughout every sun and moon in this life and the next. If only you will make me your dwelling-mate, your Soul-Sharer, your Forever-One. Will you, Kama? Please say—"

"Yes!" She launched into his arms, sending them tumbling over the earth. In between chuckling pecks, overjoyed embraces, and the pleasant press of their hips, one atop the other, Kama cried, "Yes! Yes! Yes! A thousand times, yes!"

They finally kissed, long and soft and deep and moist and awkward and perfect.

Watching them, Bogg choked with emotion and tears drained from his eyes. He wrapped his fleshy arms about them both and a fit of sniffling and sobbing and throat-clearing ensued.

Parting from their kiss, Jaspen and Kama stared at one another—euphoric, rapturous, complete.

"Oh." Kama blinked, recalling something. "Here." She removed from her torso a leather strap with a pouch dangling from it. "From the Hoodoah's cave." Kama reached into the quiver and withdrew the item within.

"My pearl knife." Jaspen took it. How right it felt in his grip. "But I . . . "

Jaspen peeked over Kama's shoulder at Vykon and Opahlua approaching through the roiling water. Nudging Kama aside, Jaspen stationed himself between Kama and the King-Lord.

"I can handle myself." Kama stepped forward to post herself at her Forever-One's side. "Did I not break into the Black Deep?" She glared at

Vykon and Opahlua. "And sneak into this stupid iron jail without any-body seeing me?"

"How very noble." Vykon planted his feet to stand firm in the swift river, just steps from Jaspen, Bogg, and Kama. "A brave knight and his fair maiden standing as one in the face of certain death. Charming. Poetic even. Yet nothing can save you now." He looked back at Opahlua, two paces behind. "Shall we?" he asked.

The warrioress's face furrowed with apprehension. It was clear the torrents issuing from the Day-Night Cove's fist were alive. The gushing seawater possessed intention, purpose. It appeared to be defending the two Cove and the Udok while attacking her and the King-Lord. None-theless, Opahlua's pride urged her to nod at Vykon. She gripped her staff tighter.

Jaspen looked to Kama then Bogg then smiled at his fist and the abundance of water cascading from it. He thrust his knuckles toward Vykon and the warrioress. With a grin, Jaspen flung open his hand, eager for a cataract of seawater to crash upon the King-Lord and Opahlua as it had before.

Yet not a single spout rose from the amber stone. Instead, a soft cur-tain of seawater fell from Jaspen's palm to splash harmlessly to the earth at his feet. The puddle of water grew into a circle the width of a man's shoulders. A column formed, thickening as it ascended, calmly climbing from the earth—like a glass tree trunk—until it settled a staff's length above Jaspen's head.

The crowd hushed and the Black Deep fell into silence as all eyes bored into the mystical cylinder of seawater, spinning and churning and growing thicker.

"Jaspen?" Kama asked, nervous. "What's going—"

"It is the Always, Kama," said Bogg, grinning with anticipation.

Curious, Vykon poked a finger into the undulating, liquid column. "So this is your almighty god? The Always?" He chuckled while glancing at Jaspen then slapped the seawater, once then twice, spattering harmless drops. "Such a savage, he is." The King-Lord struck the watery pillar with his staff, again and again. "And his counterblows are among the most powerful I've ever suffered." Howling with laughter, Vykon clouted the Always again.

The onlookers laughed, nervous, deriving a modicum of comfort from the King-Lord's ease and cool assurance. Convincing themselves that normalcy had returned, they sighed in relief.

"An underground wellspring." Vykon shouted to his guests. "Nothing exceptional at all. As terrifying as bathwater, no?" Vykon glared at Jaspen. "It appears your evil magic has died, boy. Seems only appropriate . . . " he pulled back his staff and readied to split Jaspen's skull with it, "that you die too."

The King-Lord's pole swung for Jaspen's head.

As the cane sped forward, a bolt of water pounced from the wet cylinder. It flew toward Vykon's staff, transfiguring into something else as it stretched toward the King-Lord. It appeared as an animal's limb, yet one forged entirely of seawater. The dripping appendage grew more and more defined with every small length it advanced, until even the smallest detail had the clarity of a statue wrought by a master sculptor.

The animal's appendage was corded with tendon and muscle. The liquid even seemed to be mantled in fur. A vague hoof or foot of some sort hung down from the foreleg. It soon fashioned itself into a large paw. The paw straightened and flexed, spreading its pads to expose a set of long, curved claws. The great paw swiped at Vykon's staff and splintered the rod of wood as if it were a twig.

Then, as quickly as the beast's foreleg had rushed forward, it retracted to vanish back into its watery home.

Bogg smiled at the staff's fragments scattered over the surface of the shallow lake that was now growing deeper all over the Black Deep. He nudged Kama and bounced his eyebrows, nodding emphatically.

Vykon returned to himself and smirked at the column of water. "Finally," he said, "a worthy opponent. Show yourself, coward!" He struck the pillar with one fist then the other.

"All hail King-Lord Vykon!" roared an onlooker.

A liquid protuberance slowly emerged from the column to gradually shape itself into the muzzle and whiskers of a very large Long-Mane. Once formed, the water beast's terrible, toothed maw burst forward with the haste of a slashing whip to champ down on Vykon's skull, face, and neck. Similar to the forepaw just moments ago, the animal's head quickly disappeared back into the pillar of water.

Vykon stood wobbling before the cylinder of seawater, headless. Blood gurgled from his shorn neck to spill down the King-Lord's wide chest, back, and shoulders. His arms and torso swayed as he tottered, until the beheaded body splashed down into the lake that was rapidly rising beneath it.

A storm of frightened outcries fractured the quiet.

Strange bubbling near the center of the fluid cylinder drew the crowd's attention away from Vykon's decapitated body, drifting aimlessly upon the water's surface.

Then out from the liquid pillar shot the King-Lord's severed head.

It arched upward and through a square in the dome's iron bars, seawater spraying in every direction from Vykon's wildly spinning red hair. Descending upon the spectators, the King-Lord's gruesome skull drove the mob beneath it from their benches and sent them racing every which way to evade contact with the gory oval.

The liquid muzzle of Long-Mane pushed out again from the water's column, followed by a pair of watchful eyes and a beautiful mane that shone gold in the torchlight. The creature's brawny chest and silken back emerged next. A moment later the majestic image of Long-Mane stood on all fours like a living ice sculpture thawed and come to life. The magnificent water-beast passed through the dome's bars to stride back and forth in front of the crowd, from one side of the cage to the other. Never once did Long-Mane turn its fierce glare from the chaotic throng. Nor did the horrible snarl in its throat diminish for even a moment.

Jaspen watched Long-Mane with utter wonderment and, in jest, thought, *What a cunning weaver of skeervogs I have become!*

Then he laughed at himself, knowing that everything of import that he had ever accomplished in his life was a gift from the hand of the Always.

Long-Mane halted with its tail to Jaspen, Kama, and Bogg while surveying the horde of corrupt power brokers, crooked Gort officials, merciless Mudkin bounty hunters, and the other malefactors upon the benches.

It was evident to Jaspen that the Always was peering into the hearts and souls of those on the benches, searching for a few humble, honest persons worthy of life.

Peeling back its watery lips to reveal awful teeth, Long-Mane roared with so much force and volume that the iron dome trembled and the lake-top sprang upward in a thousand, watery fingers. As the echo faded, Jaspen's god stilled, the only movement was its muscled haunches sliding back over bent rear legs.

Leaping, Long-Mane dove upon the assembly and rampaged through it—teeth tearing, claws slashing, blood raining.

45

Betrayer

SORAZIN INSPECTED THE COVE's new blacksmithing forge. It had been completed two suns ago, built by five Gort laborers recently captured when the UnderDowners ventured sun-side to sell their prized blades. The Mutahn smiled while examining the furnaces, anvils, hammers, and tongs. His grin widened upon sighting the twenty rough blades that had been crafted yesterday, each awaiting the sharpening and polishing process.

Four Cove sentries, one at each of the two entrances and two roving the forge, stood at attention as Sorazin tested the weight and balance of the crude swords.

"Sir," said a sentinel, bowing low. "The new slaves have arrived."

Sorazin nodded his thanks and exited the forge. He strode past his towering weapon of war before coming to the trio of Treef slaves with whom he had ordered a meeting. Six Cove guards tended to the shackled captives.

"You." Sorazin directed the largest Treef to step forward. "I have been intrigued with the notion of your tribe's hive mind since my recent visit with your Kaliphae. I search for a Cove girl who is thought to have perished, four or five moons ago. Her name is Kama and she is reputed for her skills as a Cloaker. As your master, Treef, I command you to make available to me all images from the hive mind regarding her, whether she be dead or alive."

"Falsssse Mutahn," sneered the slave, "not all Treeeeeeef possess the ssskills to present the hiiive mind to those outsiiide our trrriibe."

Sorazin glanced to the Cove guard directly behind the large Treef.

The slave continued, "Trrraining for such a tassssk is long annnnd . . . "

The Treef's ear caught a hushed hiss from behind, a sword pulling away from its scabbard. The large Treef quickly spun to evade the oncoming blade. In a flash, the insectile slave—though cuffed—had put the guard on his back and disarmed him of his weapon.

Leering down at the sentry, the Treef said, "A noisy warrrrior issss a—"

Sorazin's blade sundered the slave's head in two. The Treef crumpled, facedown, an expanding ring of purple blood staining the soil around the rent skull.

The Mutahn called forth the next slave. "As your master, Treef, I command you to show me the hive mind. I search for a Cove girl who—"

"Neverr wiiill I beetray my trrriiibe as yooouu have betrayed yo— Hrrrr . . . "

The Treef peered down at the bloody sword-tip protruding from his torso.

The Cove sentry who had lanced him kicked the dying Treef forward, off of his blade, and returned his weapon to its sheath.

Sorazin nodded to the guard then addressed the final slave. "As your master, Treef, I command you to show me the hive mind. I search for a Cove girl—"

"Spare this sorry Treef, good Mutahn." An elderly Huntressi slave limped toward Sorazin and the Treef, a Cove guard two steps behind her. "I have seen this Kama you hunt."

Sorazin excused the Treef and advanced toward the Huntressi. "And you are willing to share what you know of her?"

"Under one condition, great Mutahn."

"Making demands of your master is not often a wise—"

"That you kill the witch!"

"She lives, then?" Sorazin grinned. "This Kama?"

I knew it!

"Yes, my chief," said the woman. "I was with the girl the day before your men plucked my daughter and me from the Huntressi tribe."

"And why is it that you want her dead, woman?"

"Your Kama spreads lies among my people about a new god. Far too many of my sisters have flown from the protection of the true goddess of the Huntressi, Thaliana, to follow this false demon. The Always she called him."

"You have my word, good woman, that upon locating Kama I shall sacrifice her to our mighty Levaioth. But pray tell, how is it that a Cove girl, enemy to the Huntressi, came to be accepted among your tribe?"

"The evil Cove-witch was brought to our Huntressi shamaness by two of our sisters who found her in the forest. One of them, Shokku, told us that your Kama, together with the Day-Night-Cove, saved her life from the Treef. On the brink of death, your Kama was. If only they had left her to die in those woods!"

"And was your shamaness successful, in her healing of Kama?"

"A scar spans her hips but she sprints and leaps as I suppose most Cove girls do—slow and clumsily."

"You have my thanks, good woman. Tovvuh," Sorazin called to a nearby guard. "Release this noble soul from her bonds and relocate her to the hut nearest to the Hall of Shells. Assign to her a caretaker as well. Then gather the troops." Sorazin grinned. "We attack at moonrise."

46

A Warrioress Reconsiders

OPAHLUA'S MOUTH FELL AGAPE at the sight of the watery Long-Mane storming through the Black Deep, slaughtering all in its path.

Plunging to her knees in the waist-deep water, the warrioress cried, "Have mercy on me, god most high! The Always alone is my master!"

Jaspen spun toward Opahlua's praise just as a stack of rubble and steel shifted in the rising water to topple down upon her, enveloping her to the chin.

She strained to break free. Her corded neck worked up and down, side to side. Her teeth gnashed. Yet no matter how Opahlua wrestled and writhed, she could unfetter but one arm from the ponderous mound of refuse.

Jaspen rushed through the rapids toward her. "Take the end!" he shouted over the howls and mayhem while stretching his staff toward Opahlua.

She stared at Jaspen in awe, in humility. "Cruel have I treated you," she admitted, penitence in her voice. "Unfairly have I judged you." With her one free hand, she pushed away Jaspen's staff. "Leave me to drown here, Day-Night Cove. My actions merit death not life."

Jaspen knew how forlorn the warrioress must have felt. She was alone in a strange land, without family, void of hope. Perhaps Opahlua was coping with a suffering similar to that Jaspen had faced during the days prior to his first encounter with the Always. The Shepherd recalled the evening he had considered ending his own life, by seeking out and ingesting the red-spotted Killing-Leaf.

"I forgive you, Opahlua, daughter of the Hoodoah," said Jaspen. "Your every word and deed against me is forgotten. Now take the staff, please." He pushed his cane closer to her. "And let your new life with the Always begin afresh this day."

She looked to Jaspen, then to the staff, just a finger's length from her. She glanced to the clear, liquid image of Long-Mane.

The god was gazing upon her with eyes as caring and tender as Jaspen had ever observed.

The water swelled to bury the warrioress completely beneath its churning whitecaps.

"Opahlua!" Jaspen waded toward her. He thrust a hand into the shadowy seawater, hunting for her free arm. "Opahlua!"

A strong, dark fist shot up from the depths and clutched the staff.

Jaspen pulled Opahlua free.

Between gasps, the warrioress said, "You have my thanks."

"Help!" cried a nearby voice. "Heelllp!"

Jaspen moved toward the scream. "Perpeht!"

"Hurry," begged the flute-carver, battling with something beneath the surface. "He's dragging me down. I—"

Tugged downward, Perpeht vanished into the lake.

"I got it!" Kama dove through a gap in the iron bars toward her tribe-mate.

The rising flood extinguished another torch. Only two fires remained alight. The sizzle of the doused blaze reminded the twenty-six survivors that the waters would soon reach the Black Deep's earthen ceiling.

A silent panic broke out: for the only exit up and into the Under-Down was the narrow chute employed by Vykon's guests to descend into, and ascend from, the Black Deep. The small, caged dome was equipped to ferry but five persons at once.

Worse, at the onset of the flood three slave masters had risen to safety in the iron pen. The threesome had chained the cage into its place at the top of the chute to obstruct the opening, fearing vengeance from any escaping slaves to whom they had been overly cruel.

Despite the impasse, the bulk of survivors gathered in a small circle of light that shone upon the waters directly beneath the chute's opening. They warred with one other for the most strategic positions in hopes that the rising waters would eventually convey them toward the small, iron cage above.

"Bogg does not feel it is wise to engage in combat with those fighting to remain in the light. There must be another way to escape the Black Deep."

"They are easy prey," said Opahlua. "Frightened, weak. It is our only choice."

"Bogg would rather drown than drown another."

The final two torches sputtered and hissed, then snuffed, overtaken by the flood. The only light remaining was the fire-glow filtering down through the chute to describe a shimmering wheel on the surface of the waters beneath the opening.

Perpeht said, "I side with—"

"Shh." Opahlua bent her ear toward an unseen something in the distance.

"What is it?" asked Jaspen.

"A strange purr. A call of distress." She listened with more intent. "It sounds again."

Perpeht's trained ears perked. "It rises from there." He motioned to the source of the soft mewling.

Jaspen sensed the stir of the Always within his heart, urging him to seek out the distressed caller.

"Follow me." Opahlua waded through the black toward the faint noise, in the opposite direction of those sparring for position in the chute's light.

The others, directed by the hushed plash of Opahlua passing through the waters, fell in behind her.

Halting abruptly, Opahlua asked for quiet.

The company floated in silence, listening.

"It's over here now," said Perpeht, his minstrel's ear attuning to the pitch as they drifted toward it. "The timbre is deeper than before. I think it's—"

"It's here," said Jaspen and pulled the injured being toward him.

Whatever it was, it was small, no longer than Jaspen's arm. He ran his fingers and hands blindly over the body to find that it had two legs, two arms, thin wings, and needle-like spikes down its back.

"A Faijen." Jaspen pressed an ear to the creature's chest. "The heart beats."

Opahlua said, "Never in all my suns have I laid eyes upon a Faijen worthy of trust. Leave it where it lay. They are a water race. It will survive."

"The Faijen are friend to the Cove," said Jaspen. "And this one will perish without our care. Are we not all children of the Always?"

"I can help," said Kama.

Kama . . . thought Jaspen, grinning at the sound of her voice in the dark, his heart lightened by her presence, his mind and soul awestruck by the miracle of her advent in the Black Deep.

Perpeht said, "The Faijen's water songs are famously atmospheric. It would be a pleasure to hear them."

Bogg added, "The Faijen's fine fingers will be a great help in locating the tiny seeds and thin roots known to spice up even the blandest meal. Perhaps the Faijen will agree to become Bogg's assistant chef."

A piercing scream tore through the Black Deep.

Jaspen drew his pearl knife.

From the ring of light beneath the chute came another shriek. Two more followed. Frenzied hands flailed as bodies were jerked downward by a hidden savage below.

"They have turned on one other," said Opahlua.

"Could it be the Always? asked Kama.

The harrowing screams grew thicker, the atrocities more appalling.

"There is none but one in the Black Deep that incites such terror," said Perpeht. "None but one that growls with such ferocity."

Blood welled amongst the illumined mob to stain the lighted circle with a crimson hue.

"None but one who's hunger never slakes."

A moment later, all within the chute's light had perished.

"None but Dagger-Back."

47

Unwelcome Return

"I HAVE SLAIN MUCH larger," said Jaspen, the seawater and pearl knife emboldening him. "I will make of Dagger-Back as I did of Spear-Snout and Slither-Tail."

"It's too dark," said Kama. "How can you kill what you can't see?"

Bogg said, "And why would Jaspen attack something that is not attacking Jaspen?"

A squeak shrilled in the distance.

"Another survives," said Perpeht. "This way." He made toward the high-pitched shriek. "And tarry not. Dagger-Back will not be long."

The next cry was as clear as a Red-Wing's caw.

"Look," said Jaspen, peering in the direction of the creature that was calling to them. "Light."

A thin beam streamed through a pinhole in the ceiling to paint a small white moon upon the water beneath.

"Another path to the UnderDown!"

As the company advanced toward the bird-like call, the slender reed of light grew thicker, stronger.

"Something digs overhead," said Opahlua.

"It's making the hole bigger," said Kama.

Small talons were burrowing through the ceiling, less than an arm's length above the water's surface.

"Make haste!" Opahlua glanced upward.

The rising waters had lifted them to a hand's breadth from the earthen roof.

They hurried to the slim, luminous shaft and set out at once to scratch and claw at the ceiling, toiling to widen the gap before the waters engulfed them. The earth was no match for the hard, calloused fingers of Jaspen, Bogg, and Opahlua and it came away quickly. Soon the aperture was a size through which even Bogg could wedge himself.

They peered into the airy cavern above them. It was much roomier than expected. There were solid ledges, akin to dirt benches, and a flight of crude, dusty stairs that curved and circled up into the UnderDown.

Behind them, in the filtered glow beneath the chute, Dagger-Back's tail slashed at the surface.

"Kama, you first." Jaspen peeked again at Dagger-Back. "Go!"

"Why me? Because I'm a girl? Forget it."

"Kama, please, it is not the time to argue. Just—"

"The Faijen's hurt," said Kama. "He should go first. Perpeht, lay him near the edge, then you go up."

A grunt from Dagger-Back turned their faces to the plate of light beneath the chute. The monster's ghastly head sat atop the water, as still as stone. Its black gaze seemed to study the six survivors. Weighing their weaknesses.

"Move not a muscle," said Opahlua. "Though Dagger-Back does not see well, any motion in the water will beckon the beast to us."

The limp hand of the unconscious Faijen slid free from Perpeht's arm to slap into the water. Though scarcely audible to the troop, Dagger-Back appeared to have heard the gentle splash as clearly as a boulder crashing into a lake.

The animal's wide snout jerked toward the hushed spatter of water. Snuffling and sniffing in the direction of Jaspen and the others, the beast honed in on the location of the intruders.

And shot toward them.

48

The Grotto

PERPEHT QUICKLY PLACED THE Faijen safely into the cavern then scrabbled into the hollow. "Make haste!" He lowered a hand to help the next to ascend.

"Kama go!" Jaspen nudged her toward the opening.

"Opahlua." Kama brushed away Jaspen's hand. "You're up. Then you Bogg."

Jaspen huffed at Kama's defiance and his eyes prowled the waters.

The warrioress climbed into the cavern, followed by Bogg.

Frantic, Jaspen seized Kama.

"Hey," she objected. "I can—"

"Bogg, catch!"

Jaspen heaved Kama upward and into Bogg's waiting hands.

Turning to Jaspen, Kama watched as he suddenly burst left to plunge deep into the rising flood.

"Jaspen!" Kama angled her face over the grotto's opening to search for him.

"Draw back!" Opahlua tugged Kama out of harm's way. "If Dagger-Back should make a bid to join us, it would not be—"

Whoosh! The waters below broke and something was leaping up and into the grotto.

Hhhrr! Kama's breath caught in her throat as she imagined Dagger-Back hurtling toward her, teeth champing.

Yet the intruder was but a minnow, the length of a finger.

"A Mud-Fin." Kama chuckled. Facing Opahlua, she said, "Good thing you pulled me out of the—"

Dagger-Back stormed into the cavern, doubling the perimeter of the gap in the floor. The monster's hard, broad jaws snapped as they lurched back and forth in quest of flesh.

Kama swiftly drew her arms and legs in close to her body, scarcely evading Dagger-Back's piked teeth. The giant climbed higher, its massive tail propelling it skyward. The beast's deadly maw clamped down so near to Kama's face that she caught its rancid, sour-fish breath in her nose, glimpsed fresh gobbets of gore in its teeth.

Infuriated at its failure to win a mouthful of flesh, the behemoth clawed at the air with its short forelegs in the direction of a larger meal—Bogg.

Opahlua gouged the broken tip of her timber staff into the gills along Dagger-Back's side.

Yet the scales proved impenetrable, rending the wooden rod in two.

Dagger-Back rounded on the warrioress and bucked itself toward Opahlua's outstretched hand. The monster's teeth gnashed down on what remained of the staff, splintering it. Spreading wide its terrible jaws again, Dagger-Back pitched forward.

The warrioress watched, frozen, as the beast's snout advanced to envelop her entire arm.

The seawater embraced Jaspen like a friend. He had finally returned home.

Superior to any physic, the saltwater began at once to soothe Jaspen's many wounds. His hands tingled as the restorative waters set about treating his tattered fingers and healing the threadbare webbing that joined them together. His feet, too, prickled as the waters worked like a magic elixir to mend the small veils of skin between each toe.

Jaspen gaped through the dark until his eyes sharpened and his surroundings grew light enough to navigate the dim depths. Soon, he was aware of each small shift in the undercurrents, each slight rise or fall of the water's temperature, each subtle shadow above and beneath.

Spying Dagger-Back, Jaspen panicked—the beast was gathering momentum to erupt into the cavern.

Kama! he thought.

Jaspen tore through the water, gaining speed with each stroke. Nearing Dagger-Back's tail, the only portion of the animal still submerged, Jaspen pulled at the sea with added strength until he shot from the surface.

Jaspen soared into the grotto beside Dagger-Back. His eyes made a quick sweep of the area. Finding Kama, cowering with her knees huddled to her chest, unhurt.

Thank you, my Always, thought Jaspen then returned his focus to Dagger-Back.

The creature's teeth were about to shear Opahlua's arm from her shoulder. Jaspen thrust his pearl knife into the savage's dull-black eye.

The monster screeched and jerked back its head, freeing Opahlua's arm and leaving it with only a few jagged furrows.

Jaspen drove the pearl knife deeper before withdrawing the blade, only to punch it again into Dagger-Back's throat. Descending now, Jaspen held fast the knife as it sliced into the beast's windpipe and all the way down to where the killer's tail met the body.

A tumble of blood and guts coursed from the long cleft in Dagger-Back's underside. Falling, the monster slapped into the dirt floor of the grotto. It remained there for a moment—gasping, panting—before slipping into the water and sinking into the dark brume of the Black Deep.

49

Reunion

Bogg, Perpeht, and Opahlua stood as one, spellbound by Dagger-Back's slow decline into the depths. It was as if their attentive eyes were the nails in the monster's coffin and that without the mandatory ritual of *watching the dead descend*, the beast might reanimate to torment its killers for the remainder of their lives.

As the others fulfilled the ceremonial duty, Jaspen and Kama secreted themselves into a hugger-mugger nook in which to kiss and cuddle and share whispered words of love everlasting.

A strident squeak from above sent every hand in the grotto to its own weapon.

Each gaped in wonder as a white-winged creature came tottering toward them in a stumbling zigzag that was more of an awkward plummet than an elegant flight.

"Flumflum?" Opahlua watched in disbelief as the albino Cave-Wing settled upon her muscled shoulder. "Come to liberate me from the Black Deep, have you?" The warrioress laughed while running a finger over Flum's outstretched wing.

The beloved pet responded by nuzzling her snowy face into the crook of Opahlua's neck.

"Never have I met a Cave-Wing." Perpeht gently stroked Flumflum's soft, downy head. "How did you become familiar with this exceptional being?" Perpeht drew air in between his teeth to cheep in emulation of the Cave-Wing, hoping to communicate with her.

Yet Flumflum simply looked at the flute-carver, puzzled.

Opahlua said, "Flumflum has been a friend since childhood."

"Do most Cave-Wings live so long?"

"My father was not without magic. How do you imagine this one found me?"

Jaspen told Perpeht, "Opahlua is the Hoodoah's daughter."

Kama placed a hand on Opahlua's. "I'm sorry about what happened." She dipped her face. "He had such a fantastic laugh, your father. So full and whole and . . . " she thought about her next word, "complete, I guess. He was a great man."

"Thank you, Kama." Opahlua smiled. "How did you know him?"

"I was with Jaspen . . . " Kama looked at him and her face rouged at the thought of their hidden hugs, quiet words, and delicious fondling. She cleared her throat. " . . . when your father vanished into the fire. After Sorazin tried to kill him."

The Cave-Wing cawed and bounded up and down on Opahlua's shoulder. Stretching out her leathery wings, she beat them urgently.

"Flumflum assures me that you speak true, Kama of the Cove," said Opahlua.

Jaspen and Kama went on to explain how the Hoodoah had root-led in the ash of the fire, spoken about the boy in the bones then called Jaspen to show himself. They told her the details of how Sorazin had cut away the antlers that pinned him to the cave then attempted to sever the Hoodoah's head from his neck.

"I will take this Sorazin apart," vowed Opahlua, "one limb at a time. With my slowest knife."

Flumflum squawked in alarm.

Opahlua stood, concerned. "Flum says we must vacate the Under-Down at once." She followed her pet to the dirt stairs, crossing the deepening pond that had flooded the cavern's floor. "She will lead us sun-side."

The grotto's crude stairs led up and into a vacant region of the UnderDown.

Flumflum arrived in the dry, Gort realm well ahead of Jaspen and the others. The Cave-Wing screaked impatiently as the ensemble emerged from the Black Deep.

"Sorry Flum," said Opahlua, "but we have not wings. In the forty round moons since I have been gone, have you yet to master patience?"

Flumflum narrowed her tiny eyes at the warrioress before turning away to soar into a narrow passageway—locating a savory Buzz-Wing along the way.

"It's them!" A Gort slave master rounded a bend and scuttled toward the escapees on his short, bowed legs. "Murdered the King-Lord, this one." He indicated Jaspen to the dozens of Gort who came streaming out of the corridor behind the slave master. "Seize them!"

"Go!" Jaspen shepherded Kama and others into the shadowy passage, placing himself at the rear. "Faster!" he urged, trailing behind them.

The fleeing band hurried as best they could through the thin path and uneven terrain. Blindly they chased Flum, directed by her anxious squeaking. They pursued the Cave-Wing into an enclosed space similar in size and shape to the Gort hole into which Jaspen and Bogg had fallen all those moons ago.

With the angry mob closing in, Perpeht snatched the iron bars and slammed them shut. The metal tongue of the latch clanked, declaring to each that they were sealed fast within the Gort hole.

"No!" Opahlua raced to the bars and shook them, confirming their imprisonment. "Fool!" She wheeled on Perpeht.

"What? You'd rather face that Gort mob?"

"The Gort are poor combatants. I alone could slay them al—"

Flumflum screeched from above.

Each peered up to see the Cave-Wing circling the narrow space within the long earthen chute that led sun-side.

"She advises haste." Opahlua mimicked Flumflum's squeak.

The Cave-Wing answered.

"Darkness falls. Forest dwellers will soon emerge. A Tree-Horns or Long-Claw plummeting upon us will do us no favors."

"The keys." The Gort slave master shook the bars from outside the door. "Foglud will have them." He turned to a comrade. "If not in the tavern, you will find him at the gin mill near the iron mound. Go!"

"It is nigh impossible to climb out." Jaspen ran his hands over the dirt walls. "Bogg and I strove and failed a hundred time—"

"Yet Bogg watches Opahlua do what Jaspen and Bogg could not." He stared up at her in awe.

The warrioress clambered over the ceiling and into the Gort hole's long shaft.

Perpeht, too, was gaping in amazement. "How are you doing that?"

"Seventy-four seasons I lived with my mother and father in our cave-place over the waves. After a thousand journeys up and down the sheer seaway that led to our burrow, the cliffs became to me as flat land."

"Opahlua climbs with no less skill than Circle-Horn." Bogg marveled at the skill of the ascending warrioress. "The hoof of Circle-Horn is among Jirvalla's tastiest treasures. When properly seasoned then added to a Hoot-Beak's talon, it is bliss. Perhaps the toes of Opahlua are equally as piquant. Bogg very much longs to taste them." He smiled at the thought. His stomach grumbled.

"Udok." Opahlua stopped to peer down at Bogg from half way up the Gort hole. "If ever I find your lips near my feet, even if it is to place a kiss on such lovely soles," she lifted a foot and wiggled her toes to show off her incredible instep and astonishing arch, "my beautiful hooves shall be the last thing your eyes behold before my fists close them forever."

"He jokes," said Jaspen.

"Never does Bogg jest when it comes to fine cuisine."

After a moment of uncomfortable silence, Opahlua roared with mirth.

"Laugh while you can, slaves." The Gort glanced backward, in search of Foglud with the keys. "It is likely your last chance, it is."

50

Stretching Vines

"Good Mutahn." A Cove commander rushed into the Hall of Shells and bowed before his sovereign.

Sorazin lounged upon the Throne of Pearls, enjoying fresh island fruit from the fingers of a scantily attired servant girl.

"Speak." Sorazin glanced briefly at the officer before returning his gaze to the exquisite young woman in his employ, his eyes roaming every inch of her exposed flesh.

"There is trouble in the UnderDown."

Sorazin's back straightened and he slanted forward. With a sweep of his hand, he dismissed the female servant. To the commander, he said, "Continue."

"A flood has swamped the Black Deep. Even now it swells to threaten the whole of the UnderDown. Thousands are dead. Perhaps fifty have made it out alive."

"Fifty?" Sorazin brought his elbows to his knees. "Any word on whether our wayward tribemate is amongst them?"

"Doubtful, but not impossible. The Day-Night Cove's aquatic skills are legend."

"Yes, legend." Sorazin sneered.

"Witnesses claim the same god responsible for annihilating the shrine of Fire-Breath is father to the UnderDown flood. Some are calling this deity the Always."

Sorazin's lip jumped. He recalled where he had first heard the name of *mahkifo*'s god. It had been in the Hoodoah's cave. From the mouth of the holy man.

"The Always is a fable," said Sorazin. "A fiction invented by a shattered mind. This so-called god was fabricated by *mahkifo*, the Hoodoah's assassin. The madman conjured the Always to lend false virtue to his villainous act. For whom among us, if bidden by their deity to smite another, would dare disobey?"

"No one," answered the commander.

"Precisely." Sorazin's eyes squinted in thought. "It is our Levaioth who is at the source of the UnderDown's destruction. Our god seeks justice. *Mahkifo* will answer for striking down the Hoodoah. The flood beneath us was arranged for the purpose of flushing that coward from his dirty hideaway. So that I might lay hold of him and do what is upright."

"If the Day-Night Cove walks Jirvalla, my scouts will apprehend him."

"For your sake, commander, I hope so. Post a sentry at every Gort hole on Cove, Treef, and Faijen land. Send your finest men into the UnderDown at once. I want three search parties hunting for that gutless butcher. And let it be known that the one who brings to me *mahkifo*, dead or alive—no matter from which tribe they hail—will have earned for themselves a great treasure."

"Right away, good Mutahn."

"For Levaioth's act of kindness to me and to the Cove, we will provide for our god a half-dozen *polog*, together, as one. The tribute will take place at high sun on the day following the round moon, three days hence."

And, thought Sorazin, *if* mahkifo *escapes Cove chains due to your inefficiency, commander, it will be you lashed to The Thumb in his stead.*

Opahlua had escaped the Gort hole and returned to its opening with three long, thick vines twisted as one. Kama, holding the injured Faijen in one arm, was the first to be uplifted out of the pit. Perpeht followed.

As Bogg took hold of the vines, the voice of the slave master blared from the opposing side of the iron bars:

"Foglud!" bellowed the Gort. "Have you the key?"

The clink of a key entering the lock drew the eyes of both Bogg and Jaspen.

"Go!" said Jaspen to Bogg. "I will manage them," and he dashed to the bars to hold them fast.

Yet no matter how mightily Jaspen strove against the many Gort pushing their weight against him, he could not prevent the door from creaking open.

Suddenly, the iron bars slammed shut.

"Will Jaspen never learn?" Bogg's huge hands wrapped around the bars. "Bogg does not abandon a friend."

Opahlua's vantage at the mouth of the Gort hole prohibited her from observing the affairs below. "Why do you linger?" she asked. "Darkness falls. Take the cord. Quick!"

The slave master and his horde beat at Bogg and Jaspen's fists on the bars while some struck out through the rods to batter the pair's feet, knees, and thighs.

"Shortly, Opahlua," shouted Jaspen.

Bogg said, "If Jaspen possesses a plan to overcome these nettlesome little devils, Bogg recommends that Jaspen implement it at once."

"On my count of three," said Jaspen, "press into the bars with the might of your most powerful Udok warrior."

"Bogg is small and could never match the—"

"Prepare to lift us!" Jaspen called into the chute. "We will ascend together."

"Attempt it not!" replied Opahlua. "The line will rend."

"Ready?" Jaspen asked Bogg.

"Confirm that you have heard me," shouted Opahlua to Jaspen. Then to Perpeht: "Retrieve for me another vine."

After a nod of assent from Bogg, Jaspen said, "One . . . "

Opahlua cried again into the Gort hole, "Do not uprise together!" She listened for a response. None came. "Scale the vine one after another. Again: one *after* another."

"Two . . . " counted Jaspen.

When Perpeht returned with a vine, Opahlua instructed him, "Secure the end to that tree. Kama, lash the new vine to this one."

"Three!" yelled Jaspen. "Heave!"

The pair dug their feet into the earth and cast themselves into the bars with renewed force. The hinges groaned and the packed dirt along each side of the door began to crack and crumble. Fine clouds of dust puffed into the Gort hole.

Opahlua said, "I repeat . . . "

"Harder!" urged Jaspen and they drove their shoulders into the iron rods with greater might.

" . . . ascend *not* as one."

The metal door burst free of its moors. The bars crashed into the Gort, thrusting their entire number across the narrow corridor and into the dirt of the far wall.

Bogg and Jaspen, too, careered across the hall to crash into the bars, their weight and momentum driving the iron door deeper into the enemy heap of tangled limbs and contorted faces.

Opahlua bellowed, "The Udok alone will test the tether."

Jaspen and Bogg mustered one final emphatic thrust into the bars then bolted for the vine swaying beneath the chute.

"The cord," reiterated Opahlua, "will not hold the both of— Rrrrrrrrrrrrr!"

The two climbers hurled themselves onto the braided rope and began to scale it.

Opahlua stabbed her heels into the earth and tightened her fists firmly around the vine. Pulling and straining, muscles bulging, back arching, the warrioress tugged and heaved. Yet no matter her strength, the weight of Bogg and Jaspen was proving too much. Slowly, Opahlua was being drawn toward the Gort hole's entrance.

"Tie it off!" called Opahlua to Kama.

"Nearly there," cried Kama, still laboring with the knot she was fixing.

"Perpeht!" yelled Opahlua, her feet at the brink of the hole. "Assist her!"

Several Gort unburied themselves from the pile of bodies. They shrugged off the iron door and scrambled into the pit, splashing through the waters that were now flooding through the corridors and into the Gort holes. They leapt up at Bogg and Jaspen's escalating feet, unable to find purchase.

"Done!" called Kama to Opahlua, confirming the knot's resolve.

Little by little, Opahlua loosened her grip on the cord.

The vine trembled and stretched—whining, groaning, threatening to snap—under the great strain of Bogg and Jaspen's collective heft . . . yet the tether did hold.

And for the first time in far too many moons, Jaspen and Bogg stepped sun-side once again.

51

The Faijen Awakens

JASPEN AND BOGG STOOD wide-eyed and breathless at the myriad splendors of the forest before them. After so many suns imprisoned in the dim murk of the Black Deep, each had forgotten the exhilarating beauty these woodlands held: The deep green of the foliage . . . the rich, brown bark of the tree trunks . . . the echoing chirp of Chatter-Tails at play and the sweet perfume of flowering buds mixed with the earthy musk of forest soil. Their faces creased with smiles of wonder. A stream of wordless praise emerged from their swelling hearts in the form of rapturous sighs and murmurs of gratitude and appreciation.

Jaspen's ear hearkened to the distant waves. They crashed upon the shore, rhythmic and comforting. Thoughts of the ocean broke upon his heart like a mother's want. His legs moved unbidden toward the siren song.

Yet something more essential than the sea was suddenly embracing him:

Kama.

The Forever-Ones held each other close, their bodies melding into one another's dips and hollows. They stood locked in an extended hug, holding hands and whispering and kissing and giggling as if they were the only two inhabitants on the whole of Jirvalla.

A cough from the Faijen drew their eyes.

Perpeht rushed over and assisted the creature to an upright position.

Gaping at those before him, confounded, the Faijen wheezed while clearing his lungs of water.

"How do you fare?" asked Perpeht. "Do you know where you lie?"

The Faijen gazed about him. "It appears a Treef forest. Why is an enemy Udok among the Cove?" His eyes found Opahlua. "And what, pray tell, is that?"

"That is Opahlua," said Jaspen. "And I am—"

"The Day-Night Cove." The Faijen's eyes perused Jaspen, noting his unusual coloring, faded as it was from his time in the Black Deep. "Sora-zin sent me to . . . " The past few hands caught up with the Faijen. With his eye still upon Jaspen, he said, "Not even master sage Rill controls water as you did this day. Are you certain your veins do not flow with Faijen blood?"

"That was not I," said Jaspen. "The Always, alone, can perform such feats."

"The Always, yes. Our tribe has been told of your god. Was it he who delivered me from the Black Deep? I recall a knock upon my brow . . . " he touched a lump on his head. "Very near drowning, I must have been."

"You were." Kama gestured to the flute-carver. "Perpeht saved you."

"Afloat in the Black Deep like a dead Gold-Fins," said Opahlua. "Until this kind soul fished you out. Some would have preferred that he hadn't."

"Fished me out?" The Faijen was coming to himself. "A Faijen born on the proud shores of the River Squee," he puffed his chest, "and raised on the mossed rocks of Lake Lokken does not get *fished out* of anything."

"Helped a bit, that is all." Perpeht played a lively run of notes on his flute.

The Faijen nodded. "No matter how small your effort, Perpeht of the Cove, you have my gratitude." He bowed his face to the musician. "I am at your service."

"Does the crunchy little bug have a name?" asked Bogg.

"Bug! I am no bug!" The Faijen shook himself. "And whether my texture is crunchy or not, Udok, the likes of you shall never discover it." Stretching himself taller, he said, "I am Footman Rollik of the Upper Water." To Bogg, he clarified, "A mighty Faijen."

"Boggfroggbiggbogganbiggle." Bogg crouched down and extended an enormous hand to the diminutive being. "It is a pleasure to meet Foot-man Rollik of the Upper Water a mighty Faijen."

"We call him Bogg," said Kama to Rollik.

"And he is no enemy to us," said Jaspen, "but a brother. As Opahlua and Kama are our sisters. We five are sons and daughters of the Always. Blood-kith. Members of the same clan."

A disapproving screak shrilled from above: Flumflum's strident objection. She pushed off from a low branch and descended, alighting again upon Opahlua's shoulder.

"Apologies, Flumflum." Jaspen bowed to her. "We *six* are of the same tribe." He grinned at the others. "The clan of the Always."

Flumflum peeped in approval.

"Rollik." Kama squinted at him. "You were saying something about Sorazin. What's he been doing?"

"Aside from his ill attempt to strike down my father." said Opahlua.

In answer to the Faijen's bewildered look, Jaspen explained, "Opahlua's father is the Hoodoah. Sorazin's endeavor to slay him failed."

"Slay him?" said Rollik. "Interesting. I will inform Hydron Rill."

Kama said, "Jaspen didn't kill the Hoodoah either."

"We Faijen dismissed the Day-Night Cove as a suspect long ago," said Rollik.

Believing that Jirvalla stood as one against him, Jaspen asked, "On what grounds?"

"Master sage Rill was recently apprised of an untruth spread by Sorazin regarding the validity of the Hoodoah's totem." Rollik grinned at Flumflum. "The Faijen no longer believe a word the young knave utters."

"Yet he continues to sit upon the Throne of Shells?" asked Jaspen.

"It is a matter we Faijen follow with interest. To intercede, however, is forbidden by the decrees of our isle. Until the atrocities wrought by Sorazin reach Mount Everwater, the Faijen—"

"Atrocities?" Jaspen glanced to Kama.

Rollik paused, uncomfortable. "At the height of the last round moon, Cove soldiers overran the Udok, seizing their ancestral lands." Rollik glanced at Bogg, compassion coloring the Faijen's eyes.

Bogg stood from the timber stump upon which he was seated, slowly, as if in a trance. "Does Footman Rollik of the Upper Water a mighty Faijen know how many of Bogg's people Sorazin's men . . . " A tear slid from his eye.

"Three Udok warriors were slain in the brief torrent of violence. For your loss, I offer my sympathies, Bogg. It was later agreed that the Cove would permit the Udok to remain upon their homeland as long as they paid to Sorazin a tariff."

"Tariff?" asked Bogg.

"Each moon the Udok must supply the Cove with three hundred carved arrowheads, two hundred spear-tips, forty large boulders and a dozen young Udok men to be trained as soldiers in the Cove militia."

Bogg hung his head.

Jaspen's heart heaved heavy in his chest. He laid an unsteady hand on his tribemate's shoulder. "My friend. The Always will help us to recapture what was stolen." But a shudder in Jaspen's breath sabotaged his efforts at confidence. "Your kinfolk will regain their lands. This I promise."

"The clan of the Always is six-strong only," said Bogg. "Cove tribe boasts thousands."

"And how many cutthroats did the Always smite in the shrine of Fire-Breath?"

Kama took Bogg's hand. "And how many more were sent to the Everlasting Lands this day alone?"

Bogg held Kama's eyes, then hugged her, pulling Jaspen in to join the embrace.

"What more has this vulgar Mutahn achieved?" Opahlua asked.

"Thirty-two Huntressi have been enslaved along with a small group of Gort. Cove tribe's power has swelled significantly under the new Mutahn's hand. I confess also," Rollik looked to Jaspen and Kama, "that Sorazin desires—"

"The pair of us dead." Jaspen entwined his fingers with Kama's.

A bird's call caught Perpeht's ear. "My friends bring tidings." Unsheathing his flute, he peered to the sky and piped out some notes.

A Red-Beak replied.

"Return shortly, I will." The musician disappeared into the wood.

To Rollik, Kama said, "He talks to animals. Mostly flying ones. Some Slither-Bellies."

"Mask-Face and Rope-Tail too." Jaspen slipped an arm around Kama.

Rollik nodded. "An interesting clan you have here, Jaspen of the—"

"The Always."

Rollik lifted his brow in approval. "Jaspen of the Always it is."

"I am not their leader. The Always is our guide. You are welcome to join us, good Rollik, if you feel so compelled."

Opahlua bristled at the invitation.

"I cannot deny the allure," said Rollik, "but I am Faijen, through and through."

"If ever you should change your mind, we shall be happy to have you."

"Some more than others," grumbled Opahlua and glared at the Faijen while snapping a Rollik-sized stick between her fingers.

"Such grace." Rollik said to Jaspen, ignoring the warrioress. "As your tribe's own Perpeht had a part in saving my life, you have my word that I will never speak ill of the Always clan. Nor will I aid in delivering you or Kama to the Cove's false, black-hearted Mutahn."

"It is my experience," Opahlua stood and drew near to Rollik, "that the word of a Faijen is worth less than the—"

"Kama!" Perpeht scrambled into their midst, out of breath. "Blue-Wing," he gasped, "t-told me— Stink-Tail too. Th-that he has taken . . . h-him."

"He who?" asked Kama.

"Sorazin," breathed Perpeht.

"And who has he taken?"

Perpeht took Kama's hand. "Sh-him."

"Shim?"

Perpeht nodded. Turning to Jaspen, he nodded again.

Kama's lip trembled. Her eyes misted.

"At high sun, two days hence," Perpeht squeezed Kama's hand, "your brother is to be bound to The Thumb, as a *polog*."

52

Deep Scar

"Shim . . . Shim is, is fine." Kama's empty gaze traveled to Jaspen. "He's at home e-eating." She forced a smile. "Or on his s-sleeping pallet."

"We will find him." Jaspen took her in his arms. "And bring him home."

Shim? he thought. *A polog?* He stroked Kama's hair. *It cannot be.*

"He wanted to come with me." Kama stared blankly into the forest. "I told him the UnderDown was too dangerous." A tear striped her cheek. "It's my fault."

"The fault lies with none but Sorazin." Jaspen embraced Kama tighter and her knees buckled. If not for his hold upon her, she would have collapsed to the earth.

Kama's head lolled back and her arms slackened, her face awash in tears.

"We will save him, Kama," said Jaspen. "I promise this with all of my—."

"We go tonight!" Kama shot upright; vigor renewed. "I won't let Shim die."

"No one is to die. But it is too soon. Time is required to—"

"You said you'd kill Levaioth! So do it!"

"Kama, please. I know you—"

"I'm a Cloaker. I'll kidnap him."

"He will be confined to the holding cells. With a guard posted in each—"

"We'll sneak in and break him out."

"Which is precisely what Sorazin anticipates. He has set a snare to entrap us."

"Then I'll take Shim's place on The Thumb," said Kama. "He's a child."

"Shim will not feel The Thumb against his back and neither will you." Jaspen leaned in closer to Kama but she extended a hand to keep him at bay.

Jaspen lifted his palms in surrender. "Kama of the Cove, I have loved you since the day we met. You are my Forever-One and there is no beast that treads the sea, walks the land nor soars the sky that I would not slay for you. But one chance is what we will be granted to set free your Shim. One and no more."

"Then help me now. Tonight." Kama's eyes bounded from Bogg to Perpeht to Opahlua then back to Jaspen. "Shim needs of us."

"The whole of the morrow we have to forge a plan, impervious and without flaw." Jaspen inched toward her. "During MoonFeast, we will strike and— Kama!"

She shot into the forest, her color and texture changing swiftly to those of leaf, bark, earth, and shadow.

"Kama!" Jaspen gave chase, signaling the others to remain in camp. "Stop!"

He charged through the darkening wood, calling out her name, begging Kama to show herself. Yet the Cloaker refused and Jaspen soon lost sight of her. Nonetheless, he continued to sprint in the direction where he had last seen Kama. Time and again, the uneven terrain sent Jaspen tumbling to the forest floor. Yet time and again, he regained his feet to resume his pursuit.

Shim . . . thought Jaspen. *What if we prove unable to save him?*

The night grew darker.

They look to me to lead them. Yet I am but a youth. With nothing.

Jaspen's strides grew shorter.

The Cove are so many. Bogg speaks true. We cannot defeat them.

He continued to call out to Kama.

What if they capture her too?

Tears blurred Jaspen's vision as he considered the probability.

Chancing upon a lush and virginal stretch of woodland that seemed to him familiar, Jaspen slowed. A near-round moon gave light to the trees, plants, flowers, and fallen logs encircling him. Gazing at the flora, listening to the night sounds, feeling the press of earth beneath his bare feet, Jaspen was cast back to the days before he had met the Hoodoah. Before he had come upon Bogg's face half-submerged in Sink-Earth. Before the Gort pit had taken him . . . Jaspen recalled that it was here, in this unsullied swath of forest, that he had first met the young Huntressi, Shokku.

"I recognized it too." Kama stepped out from behind the very same tree where the Always had carried out his Miracle of the Wind. "I'm sorry for screaming at you." Remorse bent her brow. "For letting fear control me." Kama hugged him. "And for doubting that the Always will help us save Shim."

"I, too, have doubted." Jaspen's palm ran to the small of Kama's back. "Even with the miracles I have witnessed, my faith founders. How it shames me."

A welcome silence ensued. Content in Kama's arms, sharing her warmth, Jaspen reflected upon the events of the past few hands. There was much to process: the Nether Pit War . . . reuniting with Kama . . . and then came the Always, appearing this time as the god of water. First, he came as wind. Then as fire. Now, as water. What form would the Always take next?

Kama's sigh, tranquil and pleasant, drew Jaspen from his reverie.

"Tomorrow," he said, "we shall free Shim."

Kama eased from their embrace to look into Jaspen's eyes.

He said, "At high sun the following day, I will appeal to your kin for their blessing, Kama. If you wish it too, the ceremony to bond us as one for the rest of our lives will take place shortly thereafter, at moonrise."

"I wish it," she said. "But . . . " she looked away.

Her brow pleated with tension, with dread.

"What is it?" asked Jaspen, his mood plunging. "Have you second thoughts?"

"Not at all."

Jaspen's shoulders eased.

Kama stepped back, lips tight with concern. "I have to show you something."

She uplifted the bottom of her sleeveless, animal-hide top. A long, ridged scar ran horizontally beneath her navel.

"Sorazin's sword," she said.

"How?" Jaspen's heart galloped, thumping fiercely. "Where? When?"

"After you leapt from the Hoodoah's cave, Sorazin came for me."

Jaspen dizzied and his legs and heart and chest hollowed.

"He never found me," Kama said, "But his blade did."

"I am to blame!" Tears swarmed Jaspen's eyes. "What a fool I was to—"

"No you weren't." Kama took his arm. "We promised not to help each other, remember? My scar is the price I paid for being too proud about my gift. Cloakers are supposed to be humble. And thankful. I was the opposite. Vain. Full of myself."

"You are not the one who abandoned your dwelling mate in a cave, alone with a murderer. My fault far exceeds yours. I would give everything to undo it."

Jaspen spread flat his hand over Kama's scar.

"I am so sorry, Kama. Does it pain you still?"

"No. But," Kama's gaze fell, "the cut was deep." Her eyes eluded Jaspen's. "One of the deepest that the Huntressi shamaness who healed me had ever seen."

Kama explained to Jaspen how Shokku and one of her kin had found her, bleeding at the tree's foot, then rushed her to the tribe of the Huntressi.

"The pain is over now," said Jaspen. "I thank the Always that you have recovered."

"Most of me did. But some of me didn't. And never will." Kama's eyes returned to Jaspen, her gaze serious. "If you don't want me as your Forever-One anymore, I'll understand."

"Kama, there is nothing that will ever—"

"Just let me . . . I've never said it out loud before."

Kama drew herself up, doing her utmost to appear courageous.

Jaspen was unable to bear the sight of Kama's beautiful visage marred by tears. The hush of her muffled sobs split his heart. Reaching out, he took both of her hands in his and gripped them tightly, soothingly. Yet his lips tremored, his arms flexed and his eyes blinked hard and often.

He said, "No matter the gravity of your affliction, Kama, we shall bear it together—the weight of the world shared. Hand in hand, we—"

"I will never bear a child."

53

Cautious Hope

NEVER BEFORE HAD JASPEN encountered heartbreak so dismal, so raw, so comfortless. Before long, the Shepherd's cries were matching Kama's, his eyes likewise echoed hers, tear for tear.

Kama howled and wailed, refusing to stop. So vast was her anguish that she seemed to be withering away before Jaspen's very eyes. With each wretched groan, more and more of Kama's lifeblood appeared to be oozing away.

And when she finally collapsed, still and limp and chill as stone, Jaspen took her for dead.

Long did the Shepherd tend to his Forever-One, calling out her name into the nighted wood, beseeching the Always to comfort her, to retrieve her soul from the edge of the Eternal Lands. At last, Jaspen soothed Kama to wakefulness.

Another wave of miserable sobbing broke. When it passed. Jaspen said:

"Kama of the Cove," his tears ebbing yet still dripping, "the number of sons and daughters that we may or may not usher into this world alters nothing of the perfect joy you have birthed in my heart." Taking her hand, he pressed it to his chest. "Feel it. Never did I know those wild leaping beats before my heart knew yours." Embracing her now, he said, "Never did I know how true love felt until—"

"But after a while, that'll pass. And someday you—"

"There are no buts, Kama. I have been in love with since that moment, thirty seasons ago, on Cliff Rock, when we blew into the Horn-Shell as one. Our lips brushed, unexpectedly, do you not remember? Not even Shim's age, we were. Yet it was then that I knew you were my Forever-One. "Jaspen lifted a finger. "Forever-*One*, Kama. Meaning there is none other to whom I belong but you. Nothing will change that."

"Things do change though."

"*Things*, yes. But *hearts* do not. And if ever yours were to stray from mine, it would beat no more. For it is your grin and touch and gaze and scent and laugh that nourish it. If only you knew how full you have made me, Kama. You are far more than the finest dream I have ever dreamed."

Kama's little smile was a hint that her mood was easing.

"And with the great number of miracles that have been shown to us," Jaspen laid a hand on Kama's wound, "I cannot doubt the possibility of another. Yet even if our futures come and go without children, it is madness to make believe that my love for you is measured by the number of offspring we bear. Is that among your motives for choosing me as your dwelling-mate? To provide for you handsome sons?"

Kama sniffed. "Handsome?" She swiped the back of her hand across her leaking nose, to rid any residuum left from her weeping. "Only if they look more like me."

Jaspen laughed along with Kama and their mirthful chorus had broken the bonds of sorrow, spurring the lovers to cautious hope.

The Forever-Ones embraced and snuggled and sighed. Kisses were soon being placed on necks and fingers and wrists and ribs and ears and shoulders . . . until slumber finally overtook them.

54

Kogobod

SORAZIN PLACED A BLACK-GLOVED hand on The Thumb.

How fortunate you are to have me as your ally, Levaioth, thought the Mutahn, grinning at the prospect of a half-dozen *polog* knotted to the timber post. *Tomorrow at high sun, oh! what a feast I am providing for—*

"Sire." A guard approached his sovereign. "As you requested." He gestured to the gaunt, bedraggled man beside him, four additional guards at the man's flank.

"Kogobod." Sorazin's eyes browsed the fellow with distaste. His threadbare clothing, general filth and cheeks drawn for lack of food were an affront to the ruler. "Is this any way to appear before your Mutahn? I will not brook such disrespect."

At Sorazin's glance, the captain of the guard struck Kogobod across the face.

The starved man stumbled but refused to founder. Lip bloodied, Kogobod raised a proud, determined gaze and fixed it upon Sorazin.

Kama's father said, "You are no Mutahn of mine," and he spat at the planks near Sorazin's feet.

The captain retracted a hand to strike again but Sorazin waved him off.

"As you have most certainly overheard, Kogobod, your only son, Shim, is due to face a grisly fate on the morrow." Sorazin's war boots clumped heavily on the pier as he paced a slow circle around the aged fellow. "Pray tell old man, would you welcome the occasion to deliver your youngest from an end so bleak?"

Kogobod was stunned by the proposition, but his eyes soon narrowed. "At what price?"

"Your daughter, Kama, is sought for questioning with regard to the Hoodoah's murder. Present her to me and neither of your children will suffer mortal harm. Pain, yes, the law requires it. But they will not perish. Of that you have my word."

"Your word, false Mutahn, is worth less to me than that which evacuates the rear exit of squatting Two-Horns. Concerning the Hoodoah's slaughter; every Cove man, woman, and child outside of your perfidious Hall of Shells knows that your hand is a thousand times more likely to have slain the Hoodoah than that of Jaspen or Kama—"

The iron spikes along the back of Sorazin glove met Kogobod's cheek.

Kama's father buckled and fell to the pier.

Sorazin kicked him in the hip, the ribs, before turning to his guards.

Two of them seized Kogobod's legs and drove him across the timbers until his head and torso splashed into the sea. Holding fast to the wiry man's pedaling feet and legs, the guards suspended him upside down in the water.

When Kogobod's submerged thrashing grew sluggish, Sorazin motioned for his guards to draw him from the depths.

"It needn't have been this way." Sorazin unsheathed his sword, calmly. "If only you had acquiesced." He thrust the tip of his blade into Kogobod's open hand, pinning it to the pier. "How your fortunes would have improved."

Kogobod grimaced but refused to give Sorazin the pleasure of seeing his pain.

Kneeling, Sorazin withdrew a long, double-edged dagger from his belt.

"This edge is kept quite dull." Sorazin dragged the blunt blade over the crease of the old man's elbow, blood oozing up to fill the ragged trench. "Yet not entirely toothless."

Writhing, Kogobod bit back his yelps of distress.

The Mutahn continued to scrape and saw at the man's elbow, without hurry, until Kogobod's arm was rent in two. He carried out the same procedure to gradually separate one of the man's legs at the knee and the other at the hip. Only then did Sorazin instruct his guards to return Kogobod to the water.

The morning was new when Jaspen and Kama returned, hand in hand with eyes twinkling, to the camp of the Always clan. They had passed the night near the tree where Shokku had been turned to wind.

Bogg was hunched over the fire, whistling, as was his habit while preparing First Meal over the open flame.

"Hallo hay, Bogg," said Jaspen, curious as to why the Udok seemed so unconcerned about his and Kama's absence the previous night.

Bogg smiled up at the pair and dusted the large skillet's burden of eggs and flesh-meats with a pinch of crushed bark. "Will Jaspen and Kama be joining the Always tribe for First Meal this fine, fine morning?"

"Yes please!" said Kama. "I'm famished. Smells wonderful."

Bogg jiggled the skillet to upend the items so that each would heat through. The frypan sizzled and smoked in response, casting a flavorsome aroma throughout the timberlands.

Glancing again at Kama, Bogg grinned. "Bogg finds Kama's headdress beautiful."

"Headdress— Oh! Thank you." Kama recalled the circlet of tiny, white flowers that adorned her head like a slender tiara. "Jaspen made it for me last night." She gazed at him and they both blushed.

Confounded by Bogg's lighthearted cheer, Jaspen asked, "Are you not surprised to see us? Were none tossed in sleepless angst over the whereabouts of your missing brother and sister?"

Perpeht yawned and sat up from his sleeping place behind a log. He rubbed his eyes and stretched his back. "Flumflum informed us of where the pair of you had taken your sleep. She assured us that you were both well and good."

The Cave-Wing mewled from her upside-down perch on a shaded limb then re-buried her face beneath a wing and returned to slumber.

Though Flumflum had related to Perpeht the insignificancies concerning what had transpired between the Forever-Ones last night, the Cave-Wing had kept private the more poignant subjects. Flum had mentioned nothing of the woeful tears that had spilled from both Kama and Jaspen after Kama had broken the news of her barren womb.

Neither did Flumflum tell Perpeht of the dreams that Jaspen had shared with Kama the following morning. The Shepherd had watched three separate night-stories. The first concerned Black-Wing standing upon Spike-Jaw and pecking bugs off of the larger animal's back. The second saw Fuzzy-Buzz-Wings pushing its face into one open flower after another. The last was a conversation between Tiny-Beggar-Fish and Shell-Back, the former asking just how much he was allowed to consume off of Shell-Back's hard, shield-like covering.

Thinking about the night-stories that Jaspen had divulged to her, Kama had said, "All three dreams are about alliances. The Always wants you to see Rill."

"He does?" Jaspen had cleared his throat. "I mean, yes. He does. Clearly."

Rolling her eyes, Kama had said. "Seriously, what would you do without me?"

Jaspen and Kama sat with the Always tribe, eating First Meal with the others.

"And where be Rollik?" asked Jaspen. "Has he returned to the Faijen?"

"He departed shortly after you pursued Kama into the wood," said Perpeht.

"And good riddance, I say." Opahlua was sitting upon a rock at the edge of the fire holding a large plate of food. "Faijen . . . " She stabbed a tender cube of flesh-meat with her dagger's tip. "What a dream to never lay my eyes upon another."

"Perhaps you should keep them closed then," said Jaspen, casually taking a bite of egg.

"For what reason?" asked Opahlua. "Footman Fish-Breath is no longer—"

"We are to meet Hydron Rill," said Jaspen. "At his royal palace. Directly following this lovely repast. It is speculation, sure, but I suspect that we *may* encounter a small number of Faijen, perhaps a few hundred. At most."

Opahlua's venomous glare was joined by her deep, rumbling, animal growl.

55

Great Hydron Rill

"Come, friends." Great Hydron Rill waved for Jaspen and the others of the Always tribe to draw near his royal throne.

Yet Kama, Bogg, Perpeht, Opahlua, and Jaspen remained upon the rock to which their nervous feet clung. For the floor leading across the Faijen palace to the Fountain Throne appeared to be no more than the surface of a lake dotted with large, cream-colored flowers. Each of the visitors feared that a tread upon the lake would result in being plunged beneath the surface and swept down the cascading waterfall that roared and splashed behind them.

"I promise none will go under," assured Rill.

The palace seemed to be constructed wholly of water. Two-dozen towering pillars of liquid were teeming with every size, shape, and color of fish frisking within. The walls of the residence flowed upward in smooth, rolling waves to culminate in a gracefully rounded ceiling. Within the watery roof, vivid red and deep-blue reeds along with river grasses in every shade of green swayed with the current. And every so often, a Flat-Tail or Croak-Neck would poke its curious face out from the ceiling or walls to consider the newcomers.

"Keep to the petals and all will be fine." Hydron Rill motioned for Rollik, propped at attention near him, to escort his guests across the wet expanse.

Rollik was soon standing upon a creamy flower in the water before the Always clan, encouraging them to step in.

They did and each reached the fabled Fountain Throne without incident.

Master sage Rill was larger than most Faijen. He was nearly as tall as Kama and as thick around as Bogg. In all other ways, the Hydron appeared as the eight Faijen soldiers flanking his throne: a body of transparent blue-green, wings sprouting from the shoulder blades and heels, eyes of sapphire and small, sharp teeth set into a broad, lipless mouth.

Rill bowed his face to Jaspen and the others. "Rivers of peace to all members of Jirvalla's newest tribe." He snickered, pompous and superior.

"Thank you, Great Hydron." Jaspen dipped his chin to him. "Permission to dispense with the pleasantries, your highness. For the sun and moon wait for no one and our tribe is in need of immediate support."

"Your candor is refreshing!" Rill grinned to reveal four rows of piked teeth.

Unfortunately, the Hydron's toothy smile gave the impression that Rill would much rather be dining on his visitors than speaking with them.

"The Always tribe requests the Faijen's aid in retrieving my Forever-One's brother from the Cove's false Mutahn. We will provide the Faijen with three favor-bonds for their assistance in bringing Shim to safety."

At the word *three*, Rill's torso jolted taller.

Calming quickly, the Hydron leaned back to sink into the liquid throne's high back. He ran a hand over the spiny fin atop his head, flattening the spikes that had flared at Jaspen's mention of the number of favor-bonds proffered.

"To oppose the Cove," said Rill, "would break the alliance struck between our tribes nearly four hundred round moons ago. No matter how many favor-bonds our help would win for the Faijen, only a fool would contend against the Cove." He looked Jaspen up and down, disapproving.

"But Sorazin is not the rightful Mutahn."

Bogg stepped forward. "Sorazin has also thieved from the Udok the ancestral lands, killing three of Bogg's kinsmen and enslaving dozens more."

Kama added, "Over thirty Huntressi have also been forced into bondage."

"Pray tell, little half-giant," Rill snorted at Bogg then glanced to Kama, "woman," he looked upon Kama with revulsion, "what concern of mine are the Udok and Huntressi?"

"Take care your tongue, Fish-Face." Opahlua gauged her surrounds, undoubtedly assessing from where a Faijen attack would be launched, should they choose to be so foolish. "To speak insolence to any of my tribe is to do the same to me."

"And who, exactly," smirked Rill, "is this regrettable brown log of a woma—"

"I am one born of sea-rock and ocean spray!" The butt of Opahlua's staff thundered into the flat rock beneath the veneer of water upon which she stood. "Slew a Tusk-Fin before I could speak and took the heart of Split-Hoof on my twenty-eighth moon." She stepped toward Rill, glaring at him. "Before your birth, little tadpole, I was speaking to fire, rain, wind, and sea and reciting incantations that if spoken this day would sink Jirvalla whole."

The Faijen soldiers posted themselves in front of their Hydron, prepared to strike if Opahlua were to venture too close.

"I am bone of my mother, murdered by a Faijen she believed a friend, and flesh of my father, the greatest prophet and holy man our island has ever known." The warrioress lifted her proud chin and stood tall. "I am Opahlua. Daughter of the Hoodoah."

Rill's wings fluttered uncomfortably and a perceptible shiver pranced across his shoulders.

Kama said to Rill, "Might be unwise to trifle with her, eh?"

"My condolences," Rill quickly settled back into his familiar pomposity, "for the loss of your parents. But that has little to do with the issue at hand."

Jaspen said, "Sorazin's attempt to cut down the Hoodoah, then illegitimately place himself on the Throne of Shells is a grave concern for every tribe."

"Perhaps." The Hydron rubbed his neck, seeming to cogitate upon how to proceed. "But perhaps not. None know which way a young river will bend."

Rill stared long and hard at each of the unlikely band before him. He folded his hands and placed them in his lap.

"Though the Always tribe will be wading into uncharted waters," said Rill, "I understand why you must strike out against the Cove. If I were included in your number, I would do the same. Yet no matter how noble your quest to topple Sorazin, the concerns of the Always tribe are not a Faijen matter. My apologies."

"We are but six, Great Hydron. The Cove are thousands. We require help."

"Well, if the rumors are to be believed," mocked Rill, "then your *all-powerful* god should have no trouble subduing the Cove. Any deity who can defeat Fire-Breath, destroy his shrine, dismember Vykon and flood the Under-Down certainly does not require the assistance of little *tadpole* Rill. Does the river ask the puddle for water? With such an *almighty* force behind you, I wonder why have you come to me at all?" The Hydron snickered in derision. "A Long-Mane forged first of fire then of water . . . Preposterous."

"Hundreds of witnesses, sire, would be glad to attest to the truth of—"

"I am Jirvalla's most powerful being!" Rill shot to his feet, every fin flaring. "You tread upon thin ice, guppy, when you dare to create a false god to compete with me!"

Opahlua whispered to Jaspen, "Allow me to split this infernal, little mudworm's head, I beg you."

Catching Rollik's eyes, Jaspen asked, "Permission requested, Great Hydron, to address your servant, Rollik."

Rill calmed, drew a long breath and sat again upon his throne. "Granted."

"Good Footman Rollik," said Jaspen. "You were present when the Always made manifest his might in the Black Deep. You later mentioned that you had never before observed such power."

"It was an incredible display, yes." Rollik glanced at Rill. Quick. Sheepish.

The Hydron tacked a hard stare to his footman.

Jaspen resumed, "Did you not also reveal that the phenomenal control over water you witnessed that day exceeded anything you had ever seen from your Faijen god, Aguille, or any Hydron who has ever graced the Fountain Thron—"

"Do not answer that," ordered Rill, "*former* Footman Rollik."

"*Former*, sire?" Rollik's eyes squeezed toward each other.

"You are hereby dismissed as a court servant, Rollik of the Upper Water."

"But, sire, I have done nothing wron—"

"Let the royal scrivener also make note," Rill caught the eye of a scribe, "that the Faijen known as Rollik is banished from our tribe for the ten round moons to come ."

"Ten! No," pleaded Rollik. "Please, sire, I will—"

Rill lifted a hand to stop him. With a flick of his fingers, the Hydron directed Rollik to depart from his royal presence.

Embarrassed and heartbroken, Rollik's face dropped in shame and he crept away from the Fountain Throne.

Jaspen said, "The Always tribe would be honored to have you stay with us, Rollik of th—"

Opahlua nudged him. She shook her head, lips tight, encouraging Jaspen to withdraw the offer.

Jaspen considered Opahlua's appeal, then the forlorn Faijen.

He said to Rollik, "You are welcome to reside with the Always tribe for as long as you wish."

With nowhere else to go Rollik nodded, morose, and took a place near Kama, who patted his head reassuringly.

"As for you, Lord Fish-Food . . . " Jaspen scowled at Rill.

The Faijen soldiers, four at each side of the Fountain Throne, clapped their spears upon the watery rock floor and swiftly raised them to shoulder height. All eight of the pointed tips targeted Jaspen.

Opahlua growled and prepared to spring.

Jaspen called off the warrioress and spread his empty palms toward Rill, showing them to his court. "Thank you, Hydron, for your time. But we have an innocent child to save from an unjust ruler. Before departing, however, my clan-mate," Jaspen glanced at Opahlua, "has asked that you grant to me one final request on her behalf."

Rill narrowed his eyes at Jaspen then gave the warrioress a short, sidelong look. "Fine. Speak it."

"Thank you." Jaspen bowed his face to the Hydron. "The esteemed daughter of the Hoodoah is eager to know if you would allow her to thrust each of those toothpicks your sentries carry deep into your rearmost cavity?"

56

Gathering of Weapons

"THAT WENT EXCEEDINGLY WELL!" said Opahlua as the Always clan paced away from the Hydropolis. "It may seem poor luck at present but I assure you we will soon be thankful that those slimy, winged fish have decided against supporting us."

Rollik sneered at Opahlua.

She said to the Faijen, "Offense intended."

Downhearted, Kama slumped along beside Jaspen.

Jaspen slid an arm around her. "We will save Shim. You have my word. Axyd will assist. It is only a short journey to the Treef palace. We should be arriving—"

"The Treef royal palace has been reduced to ash," said Rollik. "By Sorazin."

"Have they a temporary gathering place? It is exigent that I see Axyd."

"No Treef has appeared sun-side since their palace was razed three days ago. Rumor suggests the entire tribe has repaired to their underground refuge."

"The Secret Tunnels? Why? It is not Axyd's way to retreat."

"The Kaliphae sustained a near-mortal injury in the fire. The Treef will not reemerge from their burrow until Axyd either heals or dies. As is their custom."

Jaspen asked Rollik, "Do you know the way in? To the Tunnels?"

"No Faijen does."

"But weeeeee do." Three Treef dropped from the branches above.

Jaspen, Kama, Opahlua, Bogg, and Perpeht formed a protective circle, each facing outward. Each prepared to fight.

"Weeee come in the peace of the Alwayyys." The Treef leader bowed to them.

"I remember you." Kama relaxed and stepped toward the black Treef.

"Tarkisss is how they call mee." The black Treef bent at the waist in greeting.

"You were at the Miracle of the Wind. So were you." Kama gestured to the brown Treef.

"And this one as well." Jaspen glanced at the green Treef.

"Yessss," said Tarkis. "We threeee were there. And now all Treeeef have seeeen it in the hiiiive miiind. The one truuue god of Jirvalla, the Alwayyys, is now worshipped by everyyy Treeeeef."

Jaspen asked, "Have you come to help?"

"Yessss."

"The Always tribe thanks you." Jaspen bowed his head to them. "Are there more?" He peered up to the trees, his hopeful eyes searching for further allies.

"Onlyyyy Zirid," Tarkis motioned to the brown Treef, "Calyp," he indicated his green tribe-mate, "and I have beeeeen sent to assisssst the Alwayyys tribe."

Jaspen nodded but his lips pinched in disappointment, wishing that Axyd had sent at least two dozen more soldiers.

Sensing Jaspen's frustration, Tarkis said, "Perhaps when Axyd seeees how much the Alwayyyys tribe needs the Treef, heeeee will send more to helllp."

"My brother, Shim," Kama looked from Tarkis to Zirid to Calyp, "have any of you seen him?"

"Safe within a cell of bars beneeeeaath the Hall of Shells, he isss." Tarkis reached out with a pincer toward Kama's ear.

Opahlua's staff shot forward to push the claw away.

Perplexed, Tarkis turned his bulbous eyes to Opahlua. "Weeee meeeeean no harm. I wiiiish only to show to Kaaamaaa thisss Cove-boy called Shiiiimm."

Kama glanced at Opahlua and nodded.

The warrioress withdrew the staff and returned it to her side, wary.

Tarkis touched Kama above the ear and her eyes flung wide.

"Shim!" she cried.

"What is it?" asked Jaspen.

"I see him," said Kama, her eyes faraway. "He eats a Peel-Fruit in his cell."

Tarkis took back his pincer. "Zirid saw thisssss five hannds ago."

Jaspen asked the brown Treef, "Have you knowledge of a way into the dungeon beneath the Hall of Shells?"

"Yesssssss. Zirid and Calyp wiiiiiilll help." Tarkis clacked out an order to his underlings and the pair of Treef rangers hurried toward the Hall of Shells.

Kama smiled at Jaspen. "We're going to save him."

"Perpeht." Jaspen turned to him. "Is it possible to send a Rope-Tail to confirm that Shim has not been transferred to another cell over the past five hands?"

A few notes rose from the musician's flute. "It is done."

The sun was falling and the Always tribe, along with Tarkis, were lying in secret within a hillside thicket of brushwood overlooking the Cove's new forge.

"Two longswords, four shields, and five daggers, as a minimum," said Opahlua to Kama. "If you can bear them, seven shields is a better number."

"My back is broad," said Kama. "Like Charging-Two-Horns."

Opahlua passed an eye over Kama's thin arms and slender frame then said to Jaspen, "Perhaps it is I who should seize the weapons."

Shortly after the three Treef had met the Always tribe near the Hydropolis, Tarkis, Calyp, and Zirid had apprised Jaspen of Sorazin's new foundry. Perpeht then sent a Song-Beak into the forge to estimate the number of weapons available within it. Opahlua thought it a good idea to raid the blacksmithing plant at the first opportune moment.

"Udok are very well made for carrying many items," said Bogg. "Bogg's friend Zagfragg can carry eight shields in Zagfragg's right hand alone and three upon the skull. If only Bogg had been trained as a thief like Zaggfragg."

Flumflum soared out of the forge to ascend the hillside. She circled the treetops four times prior to descending upon the Always tribe, to confound any unwanted eyes that might be upon her. Alighting upon Opahlua's shoulder, the Cave-Wing screaked happily and folded her wings, her tiny feet stepping up and down in excitement on the warrioress's dark flesh.

Opahlua translated Flumflum's message. "Inside are one Gort met-alsmith, an Udok apprentice, and two Cove guards."

"No Cloakers?" asked Kama.

Opahlua squeaked out the query to Flumflum.

"She says no."

Jaspen whispered to Kama, "Still, beware that another may be in attendance. Disguised amongst them. Perhaps even two."

Flum took umbrage and cheeped at Jaspen, insulted.

"Come on, Perpeht," said Kama. "Let's get in there." Kama rose to her hands and knees. Her flesh instantly mimicked the texture and color of mountain flora.

"Wait," said Jaspen. "I will accompany you."

"You don't trust me?" Kama asked Jaspen.

"Of course I do. It's just . . . "

"Jaspen frets. How adorable to watch one Forever-One worry about the safety of the other." Bogg smiled. "Bogg's heart grows with a fond warmth whenever Bogg is witness to one of love's many wonders."

Rollik said, "I can be of assistance."

"To what end, Faijen?" asked Opahlua. "To nettle the enemy with your vexing demeanor? A flea as you could not ferry even a single gem to adorn the hilt of a—"

"Opahlua," said Jaspen. "He wants only to help. Rollik, you may speak."

"Thank you." Rollik bowed to Jaspen while glaring at Opahlua. "Some Faijen, myself included," he puffed up taller, "enjoy a rare power. As the Always tribe has shown to me undue kindness, I feel your clan has earned the right to employ my unusual talent however you see fit."

Rollik closed his eyes and applied the whole of his force to his task. Mist began to issue from his head, hands, wings, and feet. Thickening, the vapory fog spread to mantle him so thoroughly that none could distinguish his form amid the blurry haze.

"It is termed the Faijen Mist," said Rollik, the cloud diminishing around him. "As I have held previous converse with Sorazin, my presence among the Cove will not be viewed as exceptional."

Opahlua presented Perpeht with two sharp darts that appeared as twigs. "For the Cove guards. Place them in your—"

Perpeht drew back a finger to test the honed point of one of the lances.

"Ho!" Opahlua halted Perpeht's hand prior to it reaching the dart's envenomed tip. "The poison of a red-spotted Croak-Neck is among Jirvalla's most lethal. A single drop would send the whole of us to Kiriath-Dae."

Perpeht carefully loaded the dart into the end of his flute.

"If the enemy approaches," said Opahlua to Kama and Perpeht, "I will caution you." Pressing her cupped hands to her lips, the warrioress rendered the strident call of a Blue-Wing.

"Got it." Kama looked from Opahlua to Jaspen. Her eyebrows lifted and a mischievous grin made a lovely bridge between her cheeks. "A kiss for luck?"

Jaspen smiled. "*A* kiss? My hope was for five hundred."

As Kama and her Forever-One nuzzled, pecked and giggled, Opahlua sniffed in derision.

"What fools love makes of us!" The warrioress shook her head. "May it remain forever afar from me."

57

Defectors

W<small>HILE LOOKING UPON</small> K<small>AMA</small> and Perpeht stealing down the hillslope toward the Cove forge, Jaspen asked Opahlua: "Your converse with Hydron Rill; is there truth to your words? Can you indeed utter in the tongues of fire, wind, earth, and sea?"

"In seasons gone, there were entire days I would pass in discourse with the trees, the rain, the waves, clouds, and sun. Yet after many moons locked within earth's womb, I fear the skills once possessing me have withered. Since my rebirth sun-side, I have heard naught from flower, wind, or water. Thankfully," Opahlua stroked her Cave-Wing's soft head, "I still grasp every word of my little Flumflum."

"Perhaps the Always will restore your powers when the time is right."

"It is my hope and prayer."

"Your time in the UnderDown," said Jaspen, his eyes still following Perpeht and Kama, "how did you come to be trapped there?"

"Never was I trapped. Did you fail to see me float out of the Gort hole? I could have escaped at any moment. But when my father suggested that I seek shelter in the UnderDown, he also told me to wait there until receiving his message."

"The one that I brought to you? During the Nether-Pit War?"

"The very one." Opahlua gestured to Kama.

She was slipping into the foundry, Perpeht behind her. The musician peeped into the forge from the door's threshold, Rollik at hover above him. A moment later, Perpeht placed the flute to his lips and readied it to dispatch the blow dart within.

Kama, cloaked, pressed her spine and shoulders deeper into a stony wall
and took a quick inventory of her surrounds.

A Gort ironsmith was hunched over a fire at the room's center. He
removed a stretch of white-hot steel from the flames and placed the sizzling metal strip upon an anvil. The smith hammered at the sword-to-be,
again and again, a shower of glowing orange sparks arcing into the air
with each strike.

Three timber barrels, each filled with water, stood near the Gort.
Ten newly minted swords cooled in one barrel while several spears were
immersed in another. A smaller, half-barrel held a goodly sum of finished
daggers. An Udok apprentice was stacking shields on the floor as well as
upon some upper shelves.

One Cove guard stood with his back to a far wall, battling to keep
his eyes aloft, while another was packing the bowl of his pipe with cut-
and-dried Brown-Leaf.

With many a dark nook in which to hide, a Cloaker might be concealed in any of them. Erratic shadows cast by the fire made detection
near impossible. Kama's eye probed the inky spaces, vigilant. She spotted
no one else veiled within the forge.

The slumberous guard stretched his neck before moving from
the wall to a barrel. He submersed his hands, scooped some water and
splashed his face with it.

As the second guard labored in vain to stoke his pipe, Perpeht
targeted the Cove at the water barrel and launched the blow dart. The
poisoned tip struck the watchman just below the ear as he was scrubbing
his eyes with damp hands. The toxin dizzied him almost instantly and he
collapsed, dead, before reaching the door.

The dead sentry's thud upon the floor drew the second guard away
from his pipe. He lifted his eyes to see the large fist of the Udok apprentice
speeding toward them. The half-giant's knuckles met their mark and the
watchman's head snapped back with a crack like two boulders colliding.
The sentry lurched forward then fell, unconscious, his chin breaking
upon an anvil before his torso hit the earth.

A Cloaker shot out from behind a barrel and raced for the exit.
Kama dashed to the cask of daggers and plunged her hand into the wa-
ter. Returning with a blade, she drew back the knife and hurled it at the
Mutahn's Cloaker.

The dagger found purchase in the man's shoulder. Yet it was not enough to prevent him from escaping the forge.

Leering at Sorazin's Master-at-Arms, Opahlua blew into her hands a second time. The urgent call of a Blue-Wing came forth.

The warrioress noted three additional Cove soldiers advancing upon the forge.

"Four trained combatants," said Opahlua. "This does not bode well."

"Why do they linger?" Jaspen's hand struck the ground. "They should already be free of the rear exit! Call again, Opahlua. Something is amiss."

As the warrioress lifted her hands for a third time, the whisper of a stretching bowstring murmured from a few paces behind Opahlua, Jaspen, Bogg, and Tarkis.

Jaspen and Opahlua peeked to one other, sidelong, alarm widening their eyes.

The breeze of a speeding arrow ruffled the hair on Jaspen's head as it passed by on a path toward the Cove forge.

The bolt bored deep into the neck of a sprinting Cloaker who had just emerged from the foundry with a dagger jutting from his shoulder. A second arrow speared into the torso of the Master-at-Arms. Three darts later, the trio of soldiers who had just arrived at the forge slumped to the earth, dead.

Jaspen spun to see Shokku and another Huntressi approaching.

"Man with beard take my Huntressi friend to be Cove slave." Shokku gestured to one of the felled guards. "Other dead man, he got in way." She shrugged.

"I like her very much," said Opahlua.

"This Yetahni." Shokku introduced her cousin. "We receive Kama message and seek to join her in Always tribe. Help save Shim. Kill Sorazin."

Bogg, his eyes on the forge, said, "Kama and Perpeht approach, with friends."

The Gort sword-maker and Udok apprentice were scrabbling up the hill behind Kama and Perpeht. Each was laden with as many swords, daggers, spears, and shields as they could ferry. What they could not manage had been placed in a wooden barrel the Udok was carrying in one of his enormous fists.

The four of them arrived, gasping from exertion, and unburdened their freight, a bulk of blades and shields clattering at Jaspen and Opahlua's feet.

"Did you get the Cloaker too?" Kama asked Shokku.

"Arrow to neck," said Shokku and gestured to the Cloaker's dead body.

Kama sighed in relief. "So good to see you." She hugged the two Huntressi. "Did Queen Ifipo get my message?"

"Queen no help." Shokku returned a pair of unused arrows to her quiver. "Ifipo fear if help Always tribe, anger Thaliana, goddess of Huntressi."

Yetahni added, "Many Huntressi have temper for you, Kama. They say Always god is invent by you and Shokku and Shepherd of Fish. But few Huntressi believe like Shokku and me. They come in morning. Twenty."

"Twenty!" Kama embraced Shokku and Yetahni again. "Thank you."

The Udok from the forge was wiping clean his face when Bogg approached. Blinking away the water in his eyes, the Udok apprentice gaped in surprise at the face before him. "Boggfrogg?"

"Muggfrugg!"

The half-giants greeted one another in the Udok manner then exchanged some words in their native tongue.

"Muggfrugg is a friend of Bogg's," said Bogg to the others.

Muggfrugg had a hairless head, fleshy cheeks, thick lips, and hands as big as the paws of Black-Claw. The most prominent variance between Bogg and his friend was the latter's size; he was two heads taller and an arm's length broader than Bogg.

Muggfrugg bowed in greeting to each of the Always tribe.

Jaspen said, "Is Rollik not with you? The Faijen?"

"Muggfrugg has seen no Faijen," said Muggfrugg.

Each looked around. Rollik was not among them.

"Coward," huffed Opahlua. "Did I not caution you? Fawning before Rill this very moment, Rollik is." She rooted through the barrel of swords. "Petitioning Fish-Face to return him to his former employ as footman. We are stronger without him."

Muggfrugg led Bogg to the Gort metalsmith and introduced him.

"Fynndir, I am," said the Gort, his bearded chin nodding to Bogg.

Fynndir was half Bogg's height and bore the common hallmarks of his race: bowed legs, thick forearms and wiry, red hair coating his chest, shoulders and back.

"Did Fynndir build all of these swords?" Bogg indicated the scattering of blades that lay on the earth near the barrel through which Opahlua was searching.

"I did, yes. To select one for you, may I? It would be my pleasure, it would."

Bogg nodded his assent and the Gort ironsmith lifted one sword then another. Yet chose a third, the largest of all. He presented the hilt to Bogg and said:

"Among the few, you are, with the brawn to master a weapon of such heft."

Bogg received the blade with gratitude. "A thousand thanks to Fynndir. Bogg will use it to carve only the finest game."

Fynndir glanced at him curiously, uncertain if Bogg was speaking in jest.

Chuckling, he said, "Finest game!" Fynndir's laugh grew in hilarity. "A pranking man, is Bogg!" He mumbled, "Finest game . . ." then slapped his own leg.

The Gort went on to handpick the individual swords and daggers that were best-suited for Muggfrugg, Perpeht, Kama, Shokku, Yetahni, Tarkis, and Jaspen.

Observing Opahlua sifting through the barrel of blades, Fynndir said, "Find it soon, you will. Upon discovery, your hand will take to it like that of an old friend."

Opahlua's arm was shoulder-deep in the barrel when she suddenly halted all movement. Her eyes lit with delight. Slowly, she drew out a magnificent, black-and-silver war-axe. Looking it up and down, in worshipful admiration, she grinned.

Forged from a single run of superior Gort steel, the battle-axe boasted an artfully scrolled handle crowned by a heavy head with a long, crescent-shaped blade on one side and a square hammer-face on the other. Jutting upward from the top of the axe was a sharp pike the length of a man's outstretched hand.

Fynndir said of the weapon, "Of my grandest achievements, for certain."

Opahlua swung the axe back and forth, up and down, acclimating to its size, weight, and balance. Turning abruptly, she hurled the weapon at a distant tree. The axe spun, pike over hilt, in perfect revolutions, glinting in the dim light, until slicing into the thick trunk. The blade split the tree nearly in half, lengthwise, as if struck by lightning.

All watched as a Cove Cloaker fell away from the tree, head sundered in two.

"Bound for the Hall of Shells to tattle our whereabouts, no doubt." Pacing to the dead man, Opahlua removed her axe from the trunk. "In all of my suns," she nodded to Fynndir, "this be the finest blade I have ever brandished."

"We should seek safety." Perpeht peered to the forge, anxious, then to the dead Cloaker near the tree. "Where there is a Cloaker, there are soldiers."

The tribe collected the weapons and hurried into the forest.

Kama asked, "Does anybody know where we're go—"

"Take cover!" Opahlua leapt for Jaspen and Kama, shoving them out of the path of a huge fireball.

The blazing globe crashed to the earth where Jaspen had just stepped.

"Sorazin's catapult." Muggfrugg watched as the fiery sphere tore through the forest to scorch into ash every tree, shrub, and flower it hurtled past.

"Incoming!" shouted Kama and the Always tribe scattered before the next searing orb exploded nearby to set another swath of forest alight.

The ball of flame was followed by the blaring clangor of three hundred clubs and swords clashing into one another. The thunder of a savage war-cry drew the eyes of the Always tribe . . . and they watched as a battalion of enslaved Udok came charging over the rise, in full battle regalia.

58

Cogglogg's Army

OPAHLUA GRINNED AT THE oncoming horde, spinning her war-axe. "The first twenty to arrive are mine." The weapon whirled in deft circles, swiftly orbiting her forearm, wrist, shoulder, and waist. "Whoever touches even one, you die too."

"Bogg sees by the eyes of each Udok warrior that all have been chewing the Mountain Blue Root."

Muggfrugg explained, "Mountain Blue Root increases Udok strength, eliminates Udok pain and makes each Udok chewing it nearly invincible in battle."

"My axe shall prove otherwise," said the warrioress.

"They are but slaves, Opahlua," said Jaspen. "Fighting not of their own volition. Sorazin alone has coerced them into battle. None of them deserve death."

"Perhaps Cogglogg does," said Bogg. "Cogglogg is chief of Udok warriors. Cogglogg is in front now, the tallest battleman, the Udok presently snorting like Snout-Horn while advancing upon the Always tribe. Cogglogg has bullied Bogg always."

"Muggfrugg, too, is bullied by Cogglogg, almost every day."

"Bogg grants permission for Opahlua to cut away Cogglogg's hands."

"Muggfrugg would enjoy seeing a foot severed as well."

Jaspen looked out at the tall, raging giant, lumbering toward them. "The choice is yours. I do not command this tribe. But my view is that it would be folly to engage the Udok at close range. If the Always has compelled you to strike down Cogglogg, arrows seem a much wiser cho—"

Two arrows shot past Jaspen and toward the Udok leader, one from the bow of Shokku and the other from Yetahni. Swiftly they flew, side by side, at equal height and speed. Each arrow picked its way through a narrow slit in the iron, battle visor that Cogglogg had lowered to protect his face. Shokku's lance bored into Cogglogg's left eye just as Yetahni's flinty tip obliterated his right.

The giant's head was thrown rearward with such force and momentum that the Udok's feet were thrust forward, sweeping out in front of him, toes skyward, parallel to the earth. Cogglogg's sword and shield took to the air. The Udok leader thudded to the ground, facing skyward, two Huntressi arrows rising from his battle visor.

Unimpeded by Cogglogg's death, the mad Udok throng continued forward.

"That's it . . . " said Opahlua, readying her war-axe for combat. "Come to me."

"My friend," said Jaspen, "It is not yet the time to battle them."

"You are not my shepherd," said Opahlua.

The Udok's rumbling, heavy strides and clanking shields grew nearer.

"Nor do I intend to be. I only recall to your mind that delivering Shim from Sorazin is our chief mission."

Opahlua growled at Jaspen.

"Your axe will gorge on Cove blood, Opahlua, plenty of it. But I implore you, let not the feast begin this day."

"For Shim." Opahlua grunted through gritted teeth and lowered her axe.

"This way!" Perpeht dashed into the trees while blowing into his flute.

Jaspen and Opahlua raced into the forest after Kama, Bogg, Fynndir, Muggfrugg, Shokku, Yetahni, and Perpeht. As the clan pressed deeper into the wood, an angry swarm of Red-Beak, Blue-Wing, Long-Wing, Song-Beak, Hoot-Beak, and Cave-Wing—all led by Flumflum—sped past the Always tribe and toward the marauding Udok. Following closely behind the airborne fleet came a ground force of Rope-Tail, Mask-Face, Stink-Tail, and Chatter-Tail.

"Well done, Perpeht," said Jaspen. "Well done indeed!"

59

Shim's Cell

THE ALWAYS TRIBE WAS gathered in a dank cave sited along the seaside border of the Treef forest, its entrance shrouded with bush and bough. All were accounted for. Only a few weapons had been made forfeit in the Udok attack.

"No," said Kama, huddling around a small fire with the others. "I have to see Shim *before* MoonFeast." She pushed aside a plate of game with forest fruits that Bogg had prepared.

"Seeee him, you can," said Tarkis, "in the hiiive miiind whenever you plea—"

"*He* needs to see me, Tarkis. And soon. I won't let Shim fall asleep thinking he's going to die tomorrow."

"Kama." Jaspen took her hand. "We spoke of this. Our plot is to free Shim *after* MoonFeast."

"He needs me before then." Kama turned her spring-green eyes to Jaspen and his heart ached at the sight of them dewing with tears.

"I . . . I do understand." Jaspen felt Kama's pain, sharp in his breast, cramping his abdomen. "I love him too." There was nothing to utter that would alter Kama's position. "We shall reach Shim before MoonFeast."

Kama clasped her arms about Jaspen's neck and kissed him.

"It is madness!" Opahlua shot to her feet. "Our ploy is contingent upon—"

"Kama will simply take her place beneath the Hall of Shells two hands earlier than proposed," said Jaspen. "That is the whole of it. The balance of our stratagem will progress as planned. We shall win Shim's freedom shortly *after* MoonFeast."

Though disgruntled, Opahlua acquiesced.

Kama edged along a stony wall encrusted with every size and shape of shell the sea had to offer. Her coloring emulated her background of brown stripes, white rondures, green spirals, red speckles, and a further myriad of diverse hues and patterns. The Cloaker's texture, too, would shift from fluted to ridged to smooth; whatever was required to twin the mass of shells into which her back was pressed.

She looked up, slowly, to spy Zirid camouflaged against the beamed, timber ceiling. The brown Treef had infiltrated this bank of prison cells beneath the Hall of Shells moments after sunfall, at the behest of Tarkis (who was crouched alongside Jaspen and Opahlua within a dense thicket of brushwood a hundred paces from the Cove's royal hall.)

Kama grinned at her unwitting brother from the better side of the iron bars that separated the siblings. There was not a mark on him. While Shim applied his fork to the task of rearranging the supper upon his plate, he hummed a cradlesong that Kama's mother had enjoyed singing to her children when they had been new. Behind Shim was a sleeping pallet with a pair of pillows and a mound of blankets upon it. Though Kama was pleased that it appeared to be a comfortable prison cell, it was a prison nonetheless. And when thoughts of the morrow broke into Kama's head—Shim lashed to The Thumb, waves rising as Levaioth approached—a shudder ran through her.

A large guard bearing a sword was posted outside of Shim's cell and, three cells away, a Cloaker reclined as still as death in the shadow where floor met wall. Staring at the Cloaker, Kama was certain he was ignorant of her presence.

Kama turned over many plots within her mind prior to striking upon one to gain Shim's notice without rousing enemy suspicion. Her patient fingers crept along the wall behind her, furtive and diligent, in search of a slender shell projecting from the others. Upon locating a thin edge of a jutting shell, Kama pinched a small part of it and quietly snapped it off of the wall. She balanced the white fragment on her thumb, lingered until the guard and Cloaker were otherwise occupied and flicked the shard with her finger to send it whirling between the bars and into her brother's cell.

The little flake tinkled to the stone floor near Shim's plate and skittered into his leg. The large guard's face jolted toward the sound but he quickly dismissed the soft knell as nothing out of the ordinary—the boy's spoon and plate clinking against one another, perhaps.

Kama was unable to discern whether Shim had registered the arrival of the tiny visitor. The boy continued to hum his mother's lullaby while pushing his supper to and fro across his plate. When the guard turned his face away, however, Shim reached out and took up the broken shell. He peeked at it slyly and smiled. Stealthily, he scanned the wall opposite his cell, beyond the bars. Though Shim's eyes roved the rocky wall, they never once passed over Kama's camouflaged face.

Kama yearned to twitch a finger or toe to draw Shim's gaze. Yet she could not risk divulging her position to the guard or Cloaker.

Finally, Shim lowered his face, defeated.

Kama quickly identified a second protuberant shell and was about to uncouple it from the wall when she heard Shim muttering to himself.

"Yaaahhh," he said quietly, feigning dread. "The tree's eating me! Mom! Mohhhmmm!"

Kama snickered to herself. She recalled the game of hide-and-seek—moons ago—when she, while cloaked as an Arrow-Bark tree, secretly extended her hand to latch on to Shim's so as to startle him.

That little waigu *saw me the whole time*, she thought, still grinning.

Satisfied, Kama sighed. Her heart, at last, could settle. Her stance softened. For Shim knew that his sister was near, plotting his deliverance.

Kama's only duty at present was to lie in wait while remaining unseen until Jaspen and the others achieved their positions. With nearly two hands in which to tarry, Kama reviewed the plan to free Shim from his cell. She was revisiting her part of the stratagem for the third time when, at the upper edge of her vision, a strange haze began to gather directly above her. It was as if the low, crawling fog of the forest floor had pressed through a rift in the outer wall to seep into the underground prison. Growing more and more ample, the dank haze began to descend upon her.

The guard posted at Shim's cell watched the vapory murk swell from the wall above Kama with an anxious gaze. He clanged the hilt of his sword against the iron bars.

Almost immediately, drops of deep purple blood splashed upon the floor at Kama's feet. She held her breath as Zirid, the brown Treef, dropped from the rafters to clatter like kindling upon the stone floor; dead.

A previously unseen Cloaker, his drawn knife bathed in Zirid's purple lymph, leapt down from overhead to alight upon the floor near Zirid's skull. He stood but an arm's span from Kama.

The short sword Fynndir had selected for Kama was at her waist. Impulse and vengeance drove Kama's fingers toward the blade. Though it would be a simple matter to dispatch the Cloaker before her, doing so would reveal her position. And all hope of rescuing Shim would be lost. She stopped her fingers, returning them to perfect stillness.

From Shim's chamber rose a sudden whine of hinges. A small hatch door hidden in the floor's rear corner pushed upward. A figure, shaded by shadows, climbed up and into Shim's prison cell, a dagger in hand. Once free of the hatch, the figure stood up tall and proud and strode from the dim: Sorazin.

60

Traitor Revealed

TARKIS LAY IN THE undergrowth next to Jaspen with his pincer resting softly upon Jaspen's head, just above the ear.

"The cloud above Kama?" asked Jaspen, viewing the events in progress near Shim's cell by way of the hive mind. "From where does it emerge?"

"It iiiis not cleeeearr."

"And for what reason does the guard—"

The hive mind stuttered, blurred, then blinked, before all went black.

"What has—" asked Jaspen. "I no longer see."

"Ziriiid." Tarkis bowed his head, mournful. "Zirid wasss dissscoverrred."

"Killed?"

"Death issss the only way to break the hiiiive miiiiiind." And an insectile keening, hushed and forlorn, moaned in Tarkis's chest.

"I'm sorry, Tarkis." Jaspen placed a hand on the Treef's shoulder. "Zirid—"

Kama! thought Jaspen and he welled with dread. *Has she, too, been revealed?* He drew his pearl knife.

"I must see to Kama." Though Jaspen endeavored to impart sympathy, to respectfully grant the honor due a departed tribemate, his knife twitched, his cheeks rubied, and the cords of his neck bulged with agitation. "With haste." His teeth grit.

"It would be folly." Opahlua held fast to Jaspen's arm. "None but Kama is to enter the Hall of Shells. That is what we agreed. We know not if she is in peril."

"She needs me." Jaspen vied with the warrioress. "Free my arm!"

"Ten soldiers with daggers, twelve brandishing spears, and twenty more slung with swords block our path. That is to say nothing of the archers upon the roof. We three could, perhaps, cut down half of them before—"

"Kama requires me! There is no more to be said."

"As you wish." Opahlua released Jaspen. "Ahead of our imminent deaths, however, if you would be so kind. Do you recall Kama's words upon discovering that Shim had been taken?"

"Of course."

"Tell them to me."

"Kama said she would go to the Thumb in her brother's stead."

"And if that incident should unfold, which of us is host to certain talents that seem ideally matched to save her? Out there." Opahlua's eyes traveled to the long path of planks perching over the sea. "On the tip of that timber pier? Surrounded by all that *ocean*?"

Jaspen stared at the warrioress, his eyes hard.

"Who?" pressed Opahlua.

Jaspen sighed and relented. "I am."

"Do not forget it."

Kama watched in numb terror as Sorazin, with a smile like a scythe, pressed his dagger to Shim's throat.

The false Mutahn browsed the wall of shells. "Show yourself, Cloaker." He pushed his blade deeper into the boy's flesh. "Or I split your brother's neck."

Shim's whimpers and sobs reverberated about the dungeon.

When Kama failed to surface, Sorazin pulled Shim to his feet and thrust him roughly into the iron bars. "On my count of three then." He snatched the boy's hair and yanked back Shim's head to expose the little boy's soft, smooth neck. "One." Sorazin returned the dagger to Shim's throat. "Show yourself and your kin goes free. He is nothing to me. It is you I have been chasing since the beginning."

Sorazin's dark eyes studied the walls.

"Two . . . " He forced the keen, knife edge deeper into Shim's flesh. "Remain hidden, Cloaker, and, well . . . "

Shim squirmed and kicked and squalled as Sorazin drew his blade inward and inward . . . until the bright silver steel of it glistened with the boy's oozing blood.

"Free him!" Kama pushed away from the wall, sword drawn.

The large guard advanced upon her, his weapon ready. "Drop your— Hrrr!"

Kama dipped and spun, her short sword biting into the guard's leg. She stood over the fallen sentry, her blade's tip at his eye.

"Finish him, please." Sorazin's hand called off the two Cloakers who were converging upon Kama. "Show to us how ruthless and savage Kama of the Cove has become."

"Kama of the Always," she corrected, sneering at Sorazin.

She looked to her brother. He appeared so small. Never before had she seen him so terrified, so hopeless.

He'll probably kill Shim anyway. Tears smeared her vision.

Kama's head drooped and her arms went slack. Her sword clanked to the floor.

Sorazin grinned, then peered to a recess in the craggy wall above Kama.

"You have my gratitude." The Mutahn bowed his face to the creature above Kama, hiding within a small, thin hollow nooked into the wall.

The creature responsible for producing the strange mist—the murky haze through which Zirid fell just moments ago—began to take shape as the spy passed from the shadows and into the light of the dungeon.

"For your assistance in the capture of this enemy of Jirvalla," Sorazin indicated Kama, "I hereby pledge to your tribe the previously agreed upon sum of two favor-bonds."

Kama snapped her face to the hollow above. She eyed the saboteur, furious. "After all we did for you," her voice charged with malice.

Rollik hung his head in shame and retreated into the shadowy void from which he had come, a few curls of the Faijen Mist still rising from his wings.

61

Mutineer, Captured

JASPEN STARED INTO THE fire, eyes blank. The flames were blurred and their color flat. The crisp pop and snap of the logs arrived muted in his ear. He felt hollow and cold, from top to bottom, inside and out—his senses deadened to every sight, sound, and smell; his heart and lungs empty of life.

After a Rope-Tail had informed Perpeht of Kama's capture, the Always tribe had returned, dejected, to their hidden lair in the Treef forest. Though Bogg had prepared a meal to comfort them, none partook.

A new intrigue was required. The previous plot to return Shim to freedom hinged upon Kama's cloaking prowess. Without her, the tribe was ill-suited to penetrate the Hall of Shells, sneak into its dungeons and uncage Jaspen's Forever-One. And now that Kama, in place of Shim, was counted among tomorrow's *polog* awaiting death, the number of soldiers and spies safeguarding the Cove's most treasured prisoner would be trebled, at least.

The hard blow of Kama's capture, coupled with the failure to rescue Shim, had thieved the tribe of their capacity to focus on anything beyond the hopelessness of the task that lay before them. As urgent as it was to compose a new stratagem to save Kama, none could summon a correlating thought.

Even the advent of Calyp storming into the cave won nothing but mere glances from Jaspen, Opahlua, Bogg, Muggfrugg, Shokku, Fynndir, and Yetahni.

The green Treef said, "I have hiiiiiiim."

Tarkis stood and clicked out a short reply.

"To a treeee outside is he leeeashed," said Calyp. "Come, let us bleeeed him."

Torn from his stupor, Jaspen turned to Calyp and drew his pearl knife. He rose and tread from the cave, vengeance darkening his brow.

The tribe hastened after him.

"Hallo hay, Rollik." Jaspen glared at the Faijen.

The Rope-Tail that had notified Perpeht of Kama's imprisonment had also disclosed to the musician the identity of Kama's betrayer.

Jaspen clenched tighter the pearl knife, his hands and arms shaking with outrage. "Kama risked her life to save you from the Black Deep and this is how—"

Thhwwk! Wood chips flew as an axe slashed into the bark a hair's breadth from Rollik's ear.

Opahlua approached. Scowling at Rollik, her close-fisted backhand whipped across the Faijen's jaw. A spatter of green blood sprayed from Rollik's lips.

"A Slither-Belly as this one has not the decency to merit a quick death." Opahlua spat in Rollik's face. "Let us kill this filth slowly." She snatched the fin atop Rollik's head and heaved it upward. "Shall we commence the cutting here?"

Shhwwpptt! An arrow pierced the tree near the Faijen's shoulder.

"Hhrrr!" Rollik winced in pain at the bolt pinning his wing to the tree.

Shokku came forth. "Or clip the wing, do we?"

"What of your tribe, Tarkis?" Jaspen called him forward. "How do the Treef dispatch a turncoat?"

"To a tall treeeee's top we bind him." *Clllkkk!* The Treef's pincers snapped shut a sliver's length from Rollik's face. "Thennn to the face and neck we smeeeeear the favored foooood of Long-Wiiing."

Calyp added, "At the eye, is where the beeeak begiiins its feeeeeassst."

Yetahni said, "Huntressi tie lawbreaker to tree. Little ones practice arrow shooting at. Three days and many arrows, before die."

"And the Udok?" asked Jaspen.

Muggfrugg said, "Udok crush betrayers between boulders."

Bogg added, "In a very slow manner."

"I have not the patience for those." Jaspen glowered at Rollik. "You stole from me my Forever-One." His face trembled. Tears, hot with spite, burned in his gaze. "And now my eyes may never see her again."

Jaspen drew back his knife.

The others gathered near, eager for justice.

"Have you any last words, Faijen?"

Rollik peered up at Jaspen, pathetic. "I'm . . . I'm sorry."

The pearl knife shot forward, swift and powerful.

Its keen tip splintered the bark a finger's width above Rollik's head. Impaled in the tree, the knife's pearlescent hues glimmered in the moonlight, eerie.

All quieted. Each waited with wide eyes and short breaths for Jaspen to withdraw his knife and thrust it into the Faijen.

Rollik's head lolled forward, limp, in grim anticipation for the killing stroke.

In the distance, a Hoot-Beak called, woeful and lonely.

Jaspen seized the hilt of his knife, yanked it from the bark, and drew it back once more. He tensed his hold on the weapon. The muscles of his arm and shoulder thickened in preparation for the mortal strike. His pulse raced and his eyesight sharpened, targeting the small creature's deceitful heart.

"Bogg would very much enjoy sharing a night-story that Bogg watched earlier this morning while still slumbering." His smile was typically bright.

Perpeht whispered, "Another time, perhaps, would better suit."

"Bogg believes that this is the ideal moment to tell the thrilling tale."

"Opahlua, however," growled the warrioress, "does not."

"Bogg also believes it was the Always who gave to Bogg the night-story and is presently encouraging Bogg to regale the whole of the Always tribe with it." His bald eyebrows bounced and his grin was as pure as it was naïve.

Jaspen drew an exasperated breath and lowered his pearl knife.

"Tell it, Bogg," sighed Jaspen, "if you must."

"Bogg must, yes!"

Bogg nodded, took a full breath, and began.

"In Bogg's night-story, Bogg watched an Udok do something terrible, something that deserved a death sentence. The Udok's name was Cuttgutt. When Cuttgutt told the Udok Chieftain the terrible thing that had happened, the Chieftain was surprised. Even though Cuttgutt was having the worst life-day ever when the horrible deed occurred, the Chieftain would never have expected Cuttgutt to carry out such an abominable act. For Cuttgutt was known as a good Udok who had never done anything nearly as bad as this to any Udok before.

"The Chieftain said that Cuttgutt must be put to death immediately for the terrible misdeed. But Cuttgutt begged the Chieftain for three more days.

"Since this crime was the only serious offense that Cuttgutt had ever committed, the Chieftain allowed the condemned Udok three more days to live.

"That very same day, Cuttgutt happened upon a young Udok girl drowning in the river. Cuttgutt plucked the little thing from the rapids, wrung the water from the child's lungs then breathed life back in the girl's body.

"The following sun, Cuttgutt was praying on the mountaintop when the doomed Udok spotted enemy warriors in the distance advancing in haste to attack the Udok tribe. Cuttgutt ran swiftly to the Chieftain and reported the news. This gave the Chieftain time enough to prepare for battle and the Udok claimed a great victory over the tribe's foes.

"During the next sun, the day before Cuttgutt was to be crushed between two boulders, the Udok overheard three tribemates plotting to kill the Udok Chieftain. Cuttgutt decided to hide in the Chieftain's sleeping hut and leap out in surprise just as the evil Udok plotters rushed forward with lifted knives to slay the Chieftain.

"Cuttgutt succeeded in vanquishing all three of the Udok conspirators while the Chieftain watched in amazement from the royal bed.

"The next morning, while the ropes were being looped around Cuttgutt's hands and feet, the Chieftain came striding forward and stood directly in front of the condemned Udok. Facing the entire tribe, the Chieftain said:

"'How many Udok here today have carried out a deplorable deed while having the worst life-day ever? Lift a fist if this is true.'

"All in attendance raised up a clenched hand, including the Chieftain. Even the Udok whom Cuttgutt had acted against was standing with a high fist.

"The Chieftain then told the crowd the good things Cuttgutt had done over the last three days. Then the Chieftain said, 'To cast a vote to smite Cuttgutt today for a deed carried out on this Udok's worst life-day ever, raise up a fist at once.'

"There were lots of Udok eyes looking back and forth at other Udok eyes, wondering what to do. Many Udok were retreating from the platform where Cuttgutt was still being tied up, backing away from the convicted Udok until vanishing into the timberlands. Yet Cuttgutt did not know this, due to closed eyes. For Cuttgutt was certain that a mortal crushing was coming. It would only make it worse to watch the fists of many friends raised in favor of the guilty Udok's sentence of death.

"Finally, the Chieftain spoke: 'Look up, Cuttgutt, and see what the tribe has resolved to do.'

"Cuttgutt slowly peeked, one eye at a time. Not one tribemate had lifted up a fist. Tears came leaking down Cuttgutt's face.

"The Chieftain smiled and said, 'If none here condemns Cuttgutt then neither does the Udok Chieftain. Cuttgutt is hereby forgiven and set free. For there are times when mercy is more powerful than justice.'"

62

To Heed or Defy

THE ENTIRE WOODLANDS FELL into an otherworldly hush, as if every tree, shrub, and bush had stilled its boughs and branchlets in honor of the parable's moral truth.

The Always tribe, too, was rendered silent by Bogg's unthinkable message of mercy. The night-story's conclusion was so startling that none knew how to proceed. The story's point was also opposed to the Island Law stating that it is right and just for traitors to suffer death for their crimes.

Jaspen knew beyond question that Bogg's night-story was indeed a gift to him from the Always. No island-born king, queen, Mutahn, prince, soldier, cook, hunter, or poet-musician possessed the great stores of mercy to consider allowing a traitor to go on living. Yet *knowing* the moral of Bogg's fable was true did little to abate the Always clan's frenzied lust to dispense mortal justice.

It is not proper, thought Jaspen, *to permit this rogue to go free*. His face fell.

The tribe's uneasy quiet was finally broken when Bogg announced:

"The end." He smiled, as unaffected and well-meaning as a baby Wag-Tail.

Jaspen's pearl knife was still trembling in his fist. How he yearned to impale Rollik's breast and cut from the Faijen his disloyal heart.

Lifting his eyes, Jaspen glared at Rollik. "You deserve not to live, foul Faijen. Were it left to me," he upraised the pearl blade and held it before Rollik's pitiful face, "you would have already have been carven into sixths."

"An arm," said Opahlua, her fist squeezing then loosening at the handle of her war ax. "Not even all of it." She, too, was scowling at Rollik. "I will take it at the elbow." Her teeth gnashed. "Fine! A finger. He will be marked by vengeance! By justice!" She glanced at the others. "All in favor, say aye."

"Aye!" cried Jaspen, Shokku, Yetahni, Tarkis, Calyp, Fynndir, and Muggfrugg.

Yet Bogg said, "All of Cuttgutt, even the tip of the criminal's smallest finger, was pardoned by the Chieftain."

Perpeht added, "We either heed Bogg's story as the will of the Always and set Rollik free . . . or we deliberately defy the wishes of our god."

The words hung in the air, gaining weight with each moment, until finally pressing into the reluctant ears of those who would have preferred that Bogg had kept his night-story to himself.

"Unleash him." Jaspen slackened his fist, letting fall from it his pearl knife.

He could scarcely believe the words that had issued from his lips.

"Rollik of the Upper Water," said Jaspen, "the Always tribe forgives you."

The Faijen uplifted his face, incredulous.

"Some of us, yes, but not all." Opahlua strode forward and pushed her forehead close to Rollik's. "I would be well within my rights as stated in the Law of All Flesh to flay every patch of wing and fin—"

"Yet the Always tribe," said Jaspen, "adheres to a higher set of a laws than that of our island brethren. And our latest decree is one of mercy. Of love. We now abide by a Law *Beyond* All Flesh."

The warrioress leered at Rollik, yearning still for the mutineer's blood. At long last, she softened. Looking to Jaspen, Opahlua nodded; curt.

"Ask yourself, Faijen," said the warrioress, "would your great Rill have done as much?"

Weeping, Rollik shook his head. "Never."

While Fynndir was trimming away Rollik's binding cords, Bogg said, "It has struck Bogg that the Always tribe presently is made up of at least three previous Cove, two previous Udok, two previous Huntressi, two previous Treef, one previous Gort and one previous other tribe . . . " he glanced at Opahlua, "as well as one Winged-Folk."

Flumflum squeaked in appreciation.

"Since the Always tribe is currently lacking a former clan-member of the Faijen, Bogg believes the Always tribe should invite Footman Rollik of the Upper Water to be counted among Jirvalla's newest clan."

The thought of sharing the Always tribe with the monster responsible for Kama's capture was inconceivable. Rollik's presence among them would only damage the tribe's character, integrity, reputation, and unity.

Yet when a quiet whisper within counseled Jaspen to humbly yield to Bogg's bidding, he knew it was voice of the Always.

If I only speak *of forgiveness yet refuse to pardon, even if it be my enemy*, thought Jaspen, *then I am but a jarring gong, a broken flute. All noise and no music.*

Jaspen said to Rollik, "You are free to do as you wish." Somehow, he found a grin for the Faijen and smiled it at him, reassuring. "If you choose to remain among us, our tribe would be pleased to welcome you. If otherwise, we will pray the Always bless your every thought, word, and deed, whichever way the wind may carry you."

Tears streaked Rollik's face. "I deserve not your kindness. So treacherous my actions!" He threw himself upon Jaspen, the Faijen's slender arms straining to grip the Shepherd closer, tighter.

Bogg approached and placed a friendly hand on Rollik's back. One by one, the others came forward to do the same. Opahlua was last to arrive, spreading wide her fingers and pressing the heat of her palm into the Faijen's finned scalp.

Drawing himself away from Jaspen, Rollik squeezed his wrists where they had been yoked. His eyes travelled from one clan member to the next, holding the gaze of each for a few moments before moving on—Rollik's face and smile conveying a gratitude so profound that none could argue the purity of his remorse.

"Though I am honored by your offer to include me as part of your tribe, your family," said Rollik, "I must decline. For until I take some time alone, to uproot the strutting pride and hollow vanity that drove me to act so hideously toward those who have shown to me only love, I am of no use to anyone. Only after slaughtering these inner demons can I, in good conscience, choose my place. I hope that is acceptable."

"Our door is ever open to you, good Rollik." Jaspen smiled. "Whenever you may find your way back, whether after the passing of one moon or a thousand, you are welcome as a member the Always tribe."

The Faijen extended his thanks to each of them before taking wing into the forest, soaring away in search of answers, in search of himself.

While watching Rollik fade into the night, Jaspen was suddenly set upon by a kindling warmth in his torso. A strange, tingling rush followed and the wild current of it surged up to his brow and down to his arched feet, flooding the whole of him with a thrilling, prickling heat. The buoyant vitality charged Jaspen with so much hope, cheer, and confidence that he felt as if he were glowing.

Moments ago, there was only grief, failure, and heartbreak as dim as Jaspen had ever known. He questioned how such vim could rise amidst his former deflation. How was it possible that a single candleflame of unexpected light could disperse so much darkness? There was but one force on the whole of Jirvalla that could spawn such marvels.

Turning to the others, Jaspen clapped his hands and said, "Let us speak of the morrow." He rubbed together his palms, bright and eager. Smiling, he said, "The Always and I have lit upon a plan to save Kama."

63

Fangs and Talons

"Perhaps I was unclear." Sorazin paced around the bed of fangs, talons, and pronged seashells upon which Kama was tethered. "It is the *command* of your sovereign to call to your *mahkifo*. At once."

Kama turned her eyes to Sorazin, defiant, then closed tight her mouth. She glared at him with unblinking severity before returning her gaze to the night sky. She had been leashed to the jabbing table shortly after reuniting with Shim, who was to remain in his cell until Jaspen's capture. A team of royal guards had conducted Kama to the beach sands near Three Rocks moments ago.

"A final chance," said the false Mutahn to Kama and plucked from the guards encircling him the largest man. "Call to him," ordered Sorazin and grinned at the girl's anxious squirming on the piked bed, her blood beginning to flow.

Yet Kama held his stare, undaunted, and uttered not a word.

Sorazin signaled to the hulking sentry and the man drove his brawny fists deep into the front of Kama's shoulders with the whole of his heft and strength.

Kama's hips jolted skyward and Sorazin smirked at her torment. Her neck strained against the strap binding her head to the barbed cot. Blood spilled from her neck's nape and shoulder blades to soak the toothed bed and pour from its edge. Kama's unclad feet were bearing the brunt of her weight and Sorazin took in the sight of her shredded heels with pleasure, each new furrow adding to the deep motes of blood dappling her back, spine, and buttocks.

For all this, Kama's voice never once lifted beyond a hushed groan.

"Your determination shows grit." Sorazin called forth three sentries to join their fellow guard near Kama. "Seems a shame to dispel such valor." He passed a hand over the rows of piercing teeth and pointed shells, pleased with their deadly tips. "Yet, I feel it my duty to make the effort."

To the four sentries, Sorazin extended a flat hand, his palm toward the ground. He then inverted it so as to face the knuckles earthward.

The guards hoisted the table. Overturning the bed, they lowered Kama's tethered body to the soil. Each dutifully obeyed their Mutahn's directive to make certain that Kama's nose and mouth were the first of her body parts to sink into the soft beach sands.

Sorazin snickered at the pathetic sound of Kama's muffled cries and chuckled at the bucking and lurching of the capsized bed. What mirth to see his enemy strive for breath and find but dust.

"Cease this indignity at once!" A tall, sturdy Tharsool drove his way through the guards toward Sorazin. "I demand you to right this pallet at once!"

Three additional Tharsool joined their chief priest near the upended table.

Sorazin's hand directed his sentries to leave the torture bed as it lay, with Kama struggling beneath its weight, her face still pressed into the earth.

Calmly, Sorazin asked, "And by what authority do you seek to overrule a command of your Mutahn?"

"By the divine order of Levaioth himself!" thundered the chief priest and he instructed the trio of Tharsool to restore the table to its upright state.

A growing crowd of Cove villagers frustrated Sorazin's wish to draw his blade and cleave the chief priest into a dozen bloody fragments.

"How dare you treat a holy sacrifice to our god with such contempt!" bellowed the priest. "You border on the blasphemous, son."

A Tharsool brushed away the sand from Kama's eyes and face. He cleared her throat of debris and unbound her from the fanged bed before carefully lifting her from the keen-tipped talons, shells, and teeth.

Sorazin drew near the chief priest and inclined his face close to the holy man's. "If I discover you have overstepped in this affair, Tharsool, I will—"

"The moment you designated this young woman as *polog* is the moment you bestowed upon me and my brethren the honor to act as her caretakers. She is no longer your concern, no matter your title."

"Take heed your tongue, servant, before I—"

"We will do our utmost to cleanse her wounds," the priest glared at Sorazin, "to mend her flesh and to remake her body into a temple worthy of Levaioth. But if you have marred her beyond repair then let the island ledger show that I—chief priest and high prophet of the Tharsool—have proclaimed that you alone, Sorazin, have stained that which was spotless and thus profaned a sacred gift to our god. And in so doing, you alone, Sorazin, have imperiled not only your own life but the lives of every brother and sister who calls the Cove their own."

64

Plans Hatched, Vows Forged

"WE MUSTN'T BE DRAWN into battle with Sorazin and his troops." Jaspen loaded another log upon the cave's fire. "At high sun on the morrow, our every effort will be given to rescuing Kama from The Thumb."

"Yet if an enemy archer, blade-fighter, or catapult-man seeks to thwart our mission," said Opahlua, whetting her axe upon a smooth stone, "hesitate not to cut him down."

"Sorraazziiiinn leans much on brute ssstrenngth to winnn connflictssss," said Tarkis. "A sound ssstrategy will defeeeeeat him."

Perpeht said, "My forest friends inform me that the Cove have entered into combat a dozen times over the past four moons. A poor pupil, Sorazin is not. He will have learned much."

Jaspen nodded. "It is imperative that we meet the Cove army with battle tactics they have yet to encounter."

"Bogg supposes that Perpeht's talent with a wooden blow-flute will be a great surprise to Sorazin." He placed a stone between his large square teeth and bit into it. "Bogg suspects that Cove tribe does not regularly practice contending against Rope-Tail and Mask-Face." He champed a fist-sized rock into fourths and offered the pieces to his tribemates. "Pebble anyone?"

Muggfrugg alone partook.

"But when the Alwayysss tribe battled againsssst the Udok warriorsss, Red-Beeeak and Cave-Wing did come. Soraazzzinnn will have hearrrd of it."

Jaspen paced the cave, in thought. "We must introduce a new element of surprise every moment from the time the drums first beckon Levaioth until Kama is returned safely to us."

"With one hundred trained fighters," said Opahlua, "your ruse would have but a faint chance. We are eleven in number. Four of us warriors. And one of those is a Cave-Wing."

"I concede that for any other Jirvallan tribe, the task would be hopeless," said Jaspen. "But we are not any other tribe. Success will be ours by putting to use our differences. If we merge the Huntressi instruments of war with Treef combat strategies as well as Gort steel with Udok battle methods, the Always tribe will create a new art of warfare, one with which Sorazin has never before engaged. This is how we will prove victorious."

Hope spread throughout the cave, followed by grins and nodding chins.

"Fynndir," said Jaspen to the Gort. "Have you the talent to compose a *skeervog*?"

"In my youth I dabbled. Yet many seasons it has been since my stone was lost to one who bested me in a contest. Not every pebble has the power to produce a flame-beast. Rare they are to chance upon. Never did I find another after I—"

Jaspen's amber gem arced over the fire toward Fynndir. The Gort snatched it from the air with unusual swiftness. Opening his fist, he peered at the stone in awe.

"In the shrine of Fire-Breath," Jaspen glanced at Bogg and smiled at the memory, "the stone in your hand fell from a *skeervog* defeated by the Always."

Fynndir turned the gem over in his palm, examining it. Smiling, he chafed the jewel between his palms. "It may take many suns to recapture my former skill."

"We have only what remains of this night and until high sun tomorrow. Do for us your best, Fynndir. That is all any of us can ask."

Excitement colored the Gort's face. "May I be off to practice?"

"Go."

Grinning wide, Fynndir exited the cave while scrubbing at the stone and giggling with glee.

Jaspen asked, "Who else claims an aptitude for something uncommon?"

Bogg raised his hand.

"Bogg," said Jaspen, "you need not raise your hand. We are family."

He lowered his hand, embarrassed for having raised it, and said, "While Bogg is known for his expertise in cooking sumptuous meals, it must be said that Bogg is also gifted at preparing very toothsome after-supper sweets."

Jaspen nodded and ran an uncomfortable hand over his head.

"Bogg speaks truth," said Muggfrugg. "Muggfrugg has enjoyed a great many of Bogg's confections. From Black Bark Mud Cake to Sweet Dirt Pie with Fungus."

Opahlua whispered to Jaspen, "Perhaps Sorazin will show us mercy if we hand ourselves to him tonight."

Three hands passed and the tribe was weary after having explored in detail each clan-member's unique battle skills. They had agreed upon a plot to save Kama, though Jaspen and Opahlua had both voiced their concern that a few particulars had not been resolved to their satisfaction. Yet late was the hour and their bodies required rest, for the events to come would push each to their utmost limit.

"There is something that remains," said Jaspen. "There is a chance, though slight, that come tomorrow Kama and I may both be slain."

Shuffling feet and uneasy grumbling ensued.

Jaspen's eyes traveled from one ember-lit face to the next. He was suddenly overcome by the diversity of, and his great love for, this strange new tribe.

"Look at us," he said. "Two Udok, two Huntressi, two Treef, a Cave-Wing, a Cove, and a Gort. As well as the two unknown bloodstocks from which Opahlua and I hail. All bound as one. Each with faith in the same, loving god. Brothers and sisters, all." He smiled.

"Many seasons ago, when the waves first ferried me to Jirvallan shores, I felt as a stranger. An outcast. Every place to which I ventured, I searched for others who were painted as my flesh was painted, who could swim as I could swim, who felt an affection for the sea as I did. There were none. I was alone. As dear as my adopted mother, the Widow Yadha, was to me, and I to her, even she did not understand me as I craved to be understood. I felt much like the insulting name Sorazin calls me, *mahkifo*, the unwelcome, dirty sea-foam that is looked upon by all with disgust.

"What a blessing it would have been to have founded this tribe when in my youth." Jaspen stared into the orange glow of the dying cinders. "I would have felt that I belonged somewhere, would have felt that I had, at last, found my lost home."

"Bogg, too, has never felt understood by any," said the Udok. "Not until Bogg met Jaspen and then the Always did Bogg feel known. Bogg has a life-debt to pay to Jaspen. And if Jaspen is to die tomorrow," he stood and tilted high his chin, "Bogg, too, will die."

"It is not my wish to die on the morrow, Bogg. But if that is what the Always has willed for me, to depart Jirvalla for the Everlasting Lands of Kiriath-Dae, I will do so with a smile upon my lips. For I will leave knowing that the Always would rather have me living together with him than living upon Jirvalla. No matter what comes to pass, I trust that the Always shapes events that are best for us, best for him, and best for Jirvalla."

"Worry not about death, Jaspen." Opahlua placed a firm hand upon his shoulder. "We will each fight until our last breath to ensure that you and Kama return to us."

"Ay," said Shokku.

"Untiiill my laaasssst breath," said Tarkis.

Calyp's green-hued mandibles clacked in agreement.

Yetahni nodded. "Fight with all arrow, we do."

"I have every intention of returning," said Jaspen. "But no matter my will, I may not. If I fail to rejoin you, I ask each of you to make an oath that you will not disband this tribe. That you will gather others to the Always clan. Others who feel as outcasts. Like *mahkifo*. You must avow to remain faithful to the Always, trusting in him, and doing whatever he tells you. Promise to me and to the Always that you will tell your children, and your children's children, of the Miracle of the Wind. Of what the Always did for Bogg and me in the shrine of Fire-Breath. You must share with others the flood of the Black Deep and how the Always delivered from death Opahlua, Perpeht, Bogg, Kama, Rollik, and myself."

A squeak from Flumflum indicated her displeasure at being omitted.

"Apologies, dear Flum." Jaspen laughed. "And, of course, Flumflum too, most majestic of all Cave-Wings."

Opahlua grinned and stroked her pet's soft, bouncing head.

Jaspen gripped Opahlua's hand, to his left, and Bogg's, to his right. "Promise me now, with an oath-bond stronger than any you have ever forged, that each of you will abide by the words I have spoken. Swear on your lives that you will keep the vows made this night."

65

Barriers

JASPEN'S SLUMBER WAS INTERMITTENT, unsettled, his thoughts pushing him from one side of his sleeping place to the other. The images in his mind arced wildly from one side of the pendulum to its opposite: each picture of a winning stratagem that aided in Kama's rescue was quickly overthrown by a despairing image of a tactic that had gone awry.

Surrendering to his sleeplessness, Jaspen lifted his inner voice to the Always, asking for strength of heart, body, mind, and soul. For quick re-flexes and speed in the water. He prayed that the Always protect him and his tribe-mates. He entreated him for great leaping ability when the in-stant came for him to erupt out of the ocean, quickly cut Kama free from the Thumb then return to the sea as swiftly as possible. He beseeched the Always to provide dreams or visions that would prepare him and his tribe-mates for unexpected turns.

Yet dreams remained as far off as sleep and Jaspen crept from the cave while the island was still draped in darkness.

A large, perfectly round moon hovered so close to the top of Smoke Mountain it seemed Jaspen could run to it in just a couple of hands. Gaz-ing at it for a long while, he smiled at its mysteriously glowing beauty. How he had missed the sight of the great, night light during his seasons in the Black Deep: its rising and falling, its dark stains, and different shapes—from thin smile to the full, round eye it was this morning. He could scarcely believe this was only his third sun since being freed from the UnderDown.

Pacing toward the sea, accompanied by the caroling of Song-Beaks and Chatter-Tails, Jaspen happened upon a mother Tree-Horns with her frolicsome calf. He froze, loath to spook the pair, and his heart warmed at the tenderness with which the mother attended to her fawn. Jaspen recalled his own parents and the lone memory of them replayed in his head—he, as a little boy, running over the shore to bound up and into his mother and father's loving arms.

He arrived at a smooth, flat boulder jutting out a few arm-lengths over the sea. The ocean spread out before him—a dark, sleeping blanket—as far as he could see. The water was nearly flat; calm and still. The small incoming swells produced only the slightest plash when they finally tumbled over upon themselves to slap upon the shore's white sands.

The sun was still leashed within the ocean depths but near enough the surface to disperse its pink and purple rays into the lower sky. Jaspen peered to the brightening horizon and his eye followed the orderly flight of seven Bucket-Beaks, their long wings close to the water. He wondered how the Lands of Kiriath-Dae could be any lovelier than this.

Soon the sun peeked up to form a small, white hill upon the water. As the rising knoll grew taller and wider, Jaspen took to the sea. His body tingled at the soothing touch of the salted ocean. The squawks, howls, and moans of the sea-folk were everywhere. He immersed himself in their conversations, unraveling their accents and separating the different tongues of the various shoals. After a short while savoring the myriad undersea languages, he announced his presence, uncertain if his past acquaintances would recall his voice after so many moons away. Most did, the majority of them hushing for a moment before replying with a tactful morning greeting.

Jaspen recognized the area through which he was passing and halted to plunge into the deep. There, half-shrouded by the shifting sands of the ocean floor, were the skeletal remains of the Slither-Tail Jaspen had defeated the day prior to his descent into the Gort hole. His bone spear rose from the broad jaws as strong and straight as it had ever been. He drew the lance from the ocean bed, lashed it to his back with a length of kelp, and ascended to fill his lungs with air.

The Shepherd of Fish swam quietly now with his eyes scarcely cresting the surface, moving slowly as to leave the water undisturbed. The pier and crescent-shaped shore from which it extended came into view. The Tharsool were already arriving with their drums.

Why so early? thought Jaspen. It was five hands, at least, until high sun.

Jaspen submerged and was proceeding toward the pier when the sight of a Dagger-Back halted his advance. Near the beast dangled the stringy tentacles of a Killing-Vine-Legs. Though Dagger-Back glared at Jaspen, the beast did not move toward him. Jaspen cautiously continued toward the pier, giving Dagger-Back a wide berth should the monster decide to strike.

A Wide-Eye appeared near Dagger-Back, then Slither-Tail, then the flowing, transparent bodies of two additional Killing-Vine-Legs drifted across the surface above them. It was unusual for beasts as these to huddle so closely together in the open ocean.

With his next stroke, Jaspen discovered the creatures swimming before him were not traversing the open ocean at all: for they were each enclosed within a long fence of Gort steel.

The pier stood a fair distance away and Jaspen was determined to assess the strength of the wooden posts upon which the pier was built. His hope was to locate a structural weakness he could exploit during his rescue mission. As a last resort, he could apply himself to pounding and knocking against the weak member until felling the timber jetty. He would then snatch Kama and speed away with her through the sea to a faraway shore. If the great horde of murderous sea creatures remained so near The Thumb, however, the plot would be unfeasible.

Jaspen swam the cage's edge, searching for an opening or, perhaps, a parcel of sea between fence and pier that was not so thronged with savages.

Yet the fence extended on and on until reaching land, on both sides of the pier. The Gort steel bars stretched from the sea bottom to a short-arm's length above the surface to form an impenetrable, half-circle that protected The Thumb from unwanted intruders. Any would-be saviors wishing to reach the pier—and its forthcoming *polog*—via the ocean would find it inaccessible.

To make matters even darker, not one stretch of sea within the enclosure was void of Killing-Vine-Legs, Puffer-Thorn, Wide-Eye, Spike-Tail, Dagger-Back, and a host of other deadly ocean beasts.

Jaspen dizzied and his body numbed.

The success of the Always tribe's plan was contingent upon gaining access to The Thumb by sea. Winning the pier from shore would be impossible. The beach would soon be swarming with Sorazin's troops, as thick as a thousand colonies of Stinging-Red-Legs with many a snare, trap, and Cloaker lying in wait. Though it struck Jaspen that he could leap over the bars protecting the pier, he would never reach Kama before a Slither-Tail, Dagger-Back or Killing-Vine-Legs reached him.

It dawned upon the Shepherd that Kama would indeed be sacrificed to Levaioth, just has Sorazin had planned.

And there was nothing Jaspen could do to prevent it.

66

Feet, Bronze, Ocean

DAZED, JASPEN PLUMMETED DOWN through the water until his back touched down onto the sea-bed as softly as a feather upon forest soil. A cloud of sediment plumed up from beneath him to describe upon the sandy ocean bottom an outline of Jaspen's head, arms, shoulders, torso, and legs.

I have failed my tribe, he thought. *And I have failed you, Kama, my Forever-One.*

As the floating silt drifted down to rest again upon the ocean floor, Jaspen stared up through the water—eyes blank—into the blurred sky beyond the surface.

If she dies, he thought, *I die too. You alone can save her now, my Always.*

He pictured Levaioth bursting through the iron fence to arrive at The Thumb. Looking over the *polog*, the monster would enjoy their twitching, screaming discomfort. Its seven gruesome eyes would stalk Kama's body, lustful for a taste of her flesh. Jaspen imagined the behemoth's black nostrils so close to Kama that she could smell the beast's rancid, fish breath. He could hear Kama wailing, *Jaspen! Jaspen! Where are you?* In his mind he watched her tears flow, helpless, as she strained against her bonds.

Then Levaioth's teeth would sever her in half.

It was too much to bear.

Jaspen could not allow his Forever-One to perish while he still drew breath.

He sprang from the sea-bed, broke the surface, and raced through the ocean. Once upon land, he sped to the cave and burst in to find his tribe-mates sleeping.

"Up!" he cried, gasping. "Rise up! All of you! At once!"

Hurrying from one to another, Jaspen jostled each of them awake.

"A new plot, we require! Now!" he panted.

The tribe wakened in haste and Jaspen apprised them of the fence that encircled the pier as well as the multitude of grisly sea creatures contained within it.

"Three hands, we have, at most," said Jaspen, his breath returning, "to forge another plan. High sun will be upon us shortly and time is needed to gather our weapons and take positions."

Yetahni said, "Weapons prepared. All position only thousand stride away."

"Good. But . . . " Jaspen's lips knit. "Kama. How are we to save her?"

The tribe regarded each other, each shaking his or her head.

"Opahlua?" urged Jaspen.

"Our sleep has just been broken." The warrioress added some dry leaves and twigs to the warm embers of last night's fire. "The best of my thoughts remain in slumber." She blew upon the leaves until they kindled to flame. "Perhaps a few more tree limbs and a small meal will spur—"

"We have not the time!" Jaspen paced around the budding fire. "If it is beyond us to draft a new— Last night!" Suddenly hopeful, he said, "I beseeched the Always to deliver to each of us night-visions. To benefit us in our combat, should something go amiss during our quest to save Kama. Did the night bring to anyone new counsel?"

Shokku shrugged. "I was young, skip through bright forest. Happy. Then rain. I still skip. Over puddle. Over ditch fill with rain. Skip over water like earth."

The tribe discussed it but found Shokku's dream without value.

"Bogg had a night-vision. There was a great feast. All were eating at the same table. The cuisine was savory and delicious."

Each gazed at the Udok, expecting more.

Bogg said, "Then Bogg chased a Croak-Neck that was hopping over a lake, from one Floating-Green-Leaf to the next. Bogg wanted the Croak-Neck to add to a beautiful Braised Beak and Claw Hash. But Bogg could not catch the Croak-Neck."

Jaspen deflated.

None of the others could recall anything of their night-visions.

"I remember now," said Fynndir. "Hammering at a great shield, I am, smoothing out the hollow, shaping it like a shallow bowl. A Cove master is suddenly before me. He snatches the shield and casts it into the sea. The shield floats upon the water's top for a long while. Then, as seawater floods into the hollow, it sinks."

After a moment of silence, Jaspen asked the Gort, "Nothing more?"

Fynndir shook his head.

"Calyp? Tarkis?" Jaspen asked the two Treef.

"Nothiiiinnggg," said Tarkis.

"Fruitless are these night-visions." Opahlua prodded the twigs and logs with the tip of a sword to encourage the flames to grow. "We must attack by land. It is the only way to make the pier our own. Unless any of us have wings to fly."

"Fynndir's shield . . . " said Perpeht, "in his night-vision. If it is a symbol of Sorazin, it is a fortuitous vision. He is on top now, leader of the Cove. But soon he will sink."

Muggfrugg said, "But what if the shield of Fynndir represents the Always tribe?"

"Huntressi arrow help get Jaspen to pier," Yetahni said.

"It would require five-hundred bolts," said Jaspen.

"Have you that number?" asked Opahlua.

Shokku shook her head.

"Your friends," asked Jaspen, "the twenty Huntressi you spoke of."

Shokku said, "To arrive three hand before high sun."

The sudden beat of Tharsool drums thumped in the distance.

"The calllll to Levaiiiioth!" said Tarkis.

"It is four hands from high sun!" Jaspen shot to his feet.

"Sorazinnnn feeeears us," said Calyp. "The more time he lingerssss . . . "

"The more time we have to outwit him," finished Perpeht.

Jaspen rubbed his eyes, thinking, struggling for a new ruse to rescue Kama . . . until he dropped his hands in resignation.

"I will offer myself to Sorazin," he said. "To be placed upon The Thumb in Kama's stead."

Bogg stood. "If Jaspen goes, Bogg goes."

"Bogg, please," said Jaspen. "This path is mine alone, not yours. It is the only solution."

"We have time," said Opahlua to Jaspen, her eye following the sword's tip as it etched symbols in the fire's ash.

Watching Opahlua's sword, Jaspen was thrust back to the Hoodo-ah's cave, when the holy man had spoken of the boy in the bones, the King-Crusher.

My fears have been realized, thought Jaspen, *I am no more a De-stroyer of Thrones than I am a God-Slayer.*

As the Tharsool drums gained in volume, Jaspen turned to Opahlua and said:

"Levaioth could arrive at any moment. I must depart before he en-ters the harbor."

"We go as one." Opahlua stood, battle ready.

"Sorazin will only kill the whole of us then. The Always tribe must survive. Remember your promises to me." Jaspen looked to each of his clan-mates, grave. "To keep this tribe together." He took a shield from the pile of them in the corner as well as the Gort sword Fynndir had pre-sented to him. "To love one another like the Always loves us." He strode to the cave's exit.

"Bogg does not want Jaspen to go. Bogg fears that Jaspen will not return." Tears streamed his face. "Can Jaspen not have one more meal with the Always tribe?"

"Are you certain there is no other way?" asked Perpeht. "Must you go?"

"The drumbeats grow stronger," said Jaspen, his eyes watching the pier in the distance. "Even now, they lash my Kama to The Thumb." He turned his face, one last time, to his tribe. "Pray to the Always that he be close to me this day." Jaspen's heart was climbing out of chest; he grit his teeth to keep it in. "That he be close to all of us. Should I fail to return, hasten not to join me the Everlasting Lands, my brothers, my sisters." He dipped his chin to them and was away.

"No!" said Bogg and leapt up, dashing after him. "Wait for Bogg!"

It took the full strength of Opahlua, Tarkis, Fynndir, and Mugg-frugg to keep Bogg from bursting out of the cave.

After calming Bogg, and curbing two additional attempts to escape, the tribe seated themselves around the bonfire, each staring dismally into the flames.

"Opahlua." Perpeht peered to the warrioress but her pensive gaze was fixed upon the flickers, flares, and sparks of fire. "What are we to do?"

"The dreams . . . " Opahlua whispered to herself while the tip of her sword absently drew in the ash.

Perpeht kept on," Is there a—"

The warrioress uplifted a hand to quiet Perpeht. She stood and viewed the symbols she had scribed in the soot and cinders. Squinting at them, hushed and still, Opahlua focused every whit of her concentration on the odd scratchings in the ash. She stepped over Fynndir, seemingly unaware of the Gort's presence, to observe the curling, twining flames and the jumbled engravings beneath them from another vantage. Gently, silently, Flumflum alighted upon Opahlua's shoulder.

None dared to interrupt the warrioress's fierce contemplation.

Time wore on as Opahlua remained in frozen rumination.

Tarkis was the first to notice, due to an opportune shift in the fire's light, the faint beginnings of a smile widening Opahlua's lips. Just a smidgen.

Then, still gripped by the fire and the ash-drawn shapes, Opahlua mumbled, "Flumflum." It was barely audible. "Tell me you see it too," she whispered.

The Cave-Wing examined the flames, thoughtful, penetrating . . . Then she bobbed her white head and stepped from foot to foot before trumpeting forth a long, assenting *cheeeeeeeeeep-cheeeeeeeeeeeeeep!*

Opahlua laughed, loud and gleeful. "I knew you would!" Smiling at Flumflum, the warrioress said, "Bogg. Perpeht. Retrieve Jaspen at once."

Bogg beat the flute-carver to the cave's exit by four strides.

"Fire, earth, and ash have spoken," said Opahlua to the others. "It is by way of foot, bronze, and ocean that we shall save Kama."

67

Logs, Boulders, Mirage

SORAZIN MARCHED OUT OF the Hall of Shells and toward the pier, a wall of guards—four deep—surrounding him. Approaching a place prepared for him near the foot of the pier, the Mutahn tread over a lush carpet of red island flowers and vibrant green fronds that led to a throne of stone, timber, coral, and bone that had been carved and crafted explicitly for this occasion.

Each Cove, Huntressi, and Udok in attendance descended to a knee and bowed his or her head as the monarch passed. To a fortunate few, Sorazin extended a hand and permitted the humble subject to press their lips to one of the iron pyramids that adorned the knuckles of the Mutahn's dark, leather gloves.

Reaching his throne, Sorazin waved to the crowd in acknowledgment of their adulation. He sat upon the sovereign seat and motioned for the armed escort before him to part so that he might enjoy the struggling of the six *polog* fettered to The Thumb.

Sorazin grinned at the hopeless manner and pathetic whimpering of those being offered to Levaioth. There were two Huntressi, an aged Udok, a Cove man and woman, both destitute, and the most prized *polog* in over fifty seasons: Kama.

A capital day! thought Sorazin and when the tail of a Dagger-Back slapped the water just beyond the end of the pier, directly in front of Kama, a thrilling tingle ranged Sorazin's spine. *How powerless you must feel*, mahkifo, *knowing there is naught you can do to deliver your precious one from death.*

The false Mutahn glanced up and to his rear at the forty archers lining the roof of the Hall of Shells, bows and arrows at the ready. Beyond them, in a clearing on the hillside, stood a squadron of war catapults, each armed with one destructive projectile or another.

Sorazin peeked through the barrier of sentinels protecting him and smiled at the sight of hundreds of soldiers in every direction. Their shields, helmets, swords, and war-axes glinted in the morning sun. He shifted his eyes to spy the camouflaged outlines of a great many hidden Cloakers, posted at strategic stations throughout the village, beach, and surrounding wood.

He called for his guards to clear a space so as to view the Tharsool kneeling upon the beach. He clapped his hands, thrice—the signal for the Cove holy men to commence the blood-tithe ceremony.

The drumming commenced.

It is a few hands earlier than you anticipated, eh mahkifo? thought Sorazin.

He wrapped his gloved fingers about the hilt of his sword and whispered. "Because you will come to me and die only when *I* command it."

Kama peered at the ocean stretching before her as far as the eye could see. The rising sun was bright in her eyes. She had been placed at the pier's very tip in hopes that this would be the site where Levaioth would strike first. *View it as a privilege,* Sorazin had said. *For Levaioth's grand feast is to begin with you.*

The previous night, prior to pinning Kama to the bed of teeth and talons, the false Mutahn and his guards had paraded her to each village's MoonFeast celebration. *"The accomplice to the Hoodoah's murder,"* is how Sorazin had introduced her. *"For her crime, she is to be presented to Levaioth as a blood-tithe. Tomorrow, we shall witness her punishment together."* The gag between Kama's teeth had prevented her from objecting.

"Are you coming, my Forever-One?" Kama's eyes patrolled the sea.

The pounding of drums commenced, followed by the sinister chanting of the Tharsool, beckoning Levaioth.

"If you cannot, I understand." Tears streaked her face. "But if you are, then you must hurr—"

Something crashed into the ocean and a great splash rose, then another. Two thick walls of water spouted upward near the shore on each side of the pier, blocking Sorazin and his army's view of the sea beyond the watery veil.

"Go!" cried a distant voice from the far shore to Kama's left.

Her eyes snapped to the place where the outcry had come, far from Sorazin's catapults, archers, and other men of war. The trunk of a cut tree shot up through the lush green canopy that rimmed the faraway seashore. Arcing through the sky, the timber pillar soared toward the pier.

Then came a boulder.

With neither enroute to crush her, Kama breathed in relief.

Jaspen, she thought.

Another shout from the timbered shore drew Kama's gaze back to where the mighty trunk and boulder had been heaved. Her eyes broadened with shock, then incredulity. For the marvel at which Kama could not stop staring was one more likely to be encountered in a fireside fable than a field of war.

Whispering to herself, she muttered, "Looks like a . . . "

She narrowed her eyes, desperate to make sense of the impossible image.

Wishful thinking, Kama convinced herself. *A mirage.*

For it appeared that someone was racing toward her.

Speeding on foot . . .

. . . atop the ocean's surface.

68

Skipping Stones

SORAZIN'S EYES DARTED TOWARD a large and sudden splash near the pier. The tallest edge of the screen of water was visible above the guards that stood at attention between the Mutahn and The Thumb.

Bolting up from his throne, Sorazin cried, "Levaioth!"

Another thundering eruption followed and Sorazin pressed through his sentries in a bid to glimpse the Cove deity at close range.

Yet upon spying what must have been a second boulder and second tree trunk plow into the sea to raise two more hedges of water, it was clear the cause behind the shuddering ocean was not Levaioth at all.

It was the Always tribe.

"To arms!" shouted Sorazin to his troops. "Ready the catapults! Archers—bend your bows!"

He turned to his soldiers on the beach, intending to rouse them to battle when, suddenly, a shadow drew itself upon the sand amidst their number . . .

The Mutahn knew that form—the step of the figure advancing calmly past the chanting Tharsool, the familiar hands laid open in surrender.

The enemy's name fell from Sorazin's lips like an answered prayer.

"*Mahkifo* . . . " he whispered, grinning at a dozen spear-tips and sword-points prodding Jaspen toward Sorazin, toward certain death.

"There is not much to amend." Opahlua was seated upon a stone near the cave's fire. "Only one or two matters. Kama will be set free."

"The night-visions," Jaspen added a log to the fire. "What are their meanings?"

The eyes of the entire Always tribe were fixed to Opahlua.

"Shokku saw herself skipping upon the surface of water, as if it were hard earth." Opahlua glanced at the Huntressi. "You shall see your vision come to pass this very day."

"How?" asked Shokku.

"Shields. More than forty, we have." Opahlua gestured to the stacks of them about the cave. "They float. Just as Fynndir saw in his night-vision."

"For a short time, yes, atop the water they will stay," said Fynndir. "But they will not support the weight of any of us. Boats they are not."

"Boats, no," Opahlua grinned. "But stepping stones, yes."

Opahlua placed a shield on the ground with its hollow facing upward, as a shallow bowl. She stepped back and dashed toward the shield.

Jaspen grinned as the ball of Opahlua's foot lightly touched down in the center of the shield's hollow before quickly pushing off again to continue sprinting without breaking stride.

Opahlua said, "Who among us has not tossed a flat stone over the water to watch it skip across the surface?"

"A fine plan, Opahlua!" Jaspen smiled at the warrioress.

Opahlua said, "It was Bogg's night-vision of the Croak-Neck hopping across the Floating-Green-Leaf that confirmed the fire's message."

"The visions of an Udok, Huntressi, and Gort combining to save a Cove girl." Jaspen laughed. "It is more than perfect. You cast the shields and I shall run upon them to reach Kama and free her."

"The night-vision was Shokku's," said Opahlua to Jaspen. "Not yours. She is also the smallest of us."

"And fastest," said the Huntressi.

"I will require another to cast shields beside me." Opahlua looked to Yetahni. "Faultless aim is imperative. Along with unfailing strength."

"I can do." Yetahni stepped forward.

"What of the ocean fence?" asked Perpeht "It juts from the water. Will it not halt our stepping stones?"

"An arm's length above the surface, it was." Jaspen's hands measured out the distance. "The sea has been rising since." His palms came closer together. "At present I would wager that the fence is a hand's-breadth, at most, above the ocean's top. And it sinks deeper into the water with each moment. The uppermost part of each stake also curls in toward the pier. To keep the Fin-Folk within their pen."

"And to assist our shields to skim over it."

"We will neeeed a further diversionnn," said Tarkis. "Sssomethiiing more than logs and boulderrsss to hold Soraazzziinnn's attention. Only heee can order his archerrssss to shoot at Shok-k-k-uuu."

"Leave Sorazin to me," said Jaspen. "None can capture his attention as I."

"What is Jaspen's plan?" asked Bogg.

"It matters not. Place your efforts upon saving Kama. I will tend to the rest."

Opahlua said, "And should your ruse succeed with Sorazin, how is it you intend to make your way back to us?"

"I do not yet know. Once Kama is set free and my mind is at rest, once I set foot upon the battlefield and survey our enemy's weakness, a plot will avail itself—"

"To quit this cave without a scheme to return is madness."

The drums of the Tharsool beat louder.

"Does your ear not heed the call to Levaioth, Opahlua? We have not the time to devise a stratagem to make safe my homecoming. It is all we can do to put our trust in the Always. In the Law Beyond All Flesh."

Considering Jaspen's words, ruminant, the warrioress said. "This new law of yours has been with me since the instant you uttered it, last night. I concur that the Law Beyond All Flesh holds merit. Yet this new code is not a replacement of Jirvalla's older writ. It is meant to strengthen it. The Law of All Flesh is a rule of reason that is as valuable this day as it was yestermoon. And our old statutes confirm that if you land on the wrong side of my blade, you will bleed. That if you leap into Smoke Mountain, you, too, will become smoke. And that if you enter a war without a strategy, you will be conquered."

"It is a point well-made, my friend." Jaspen smiled. "You will make a very fine Hoodoah, indeed. If only we had three or four hands to deliberate, an ironclad stratagem would be won and my return assured. But my Forever-One, at this very moment, is enchained to The Thumb. Awaiting death. Alone."

The distant drums continued, their echoing peals gaining in volume.

"You are a master of battle," resumed Jaspen to Opahlua. "As is Tarkis. I trust you both with my life and will leave to you the tactics that will lead to my safe passage home."

The warrioress looked to Tarkis. "We will do our utmost to open up for you a way of retreat. When the time of your escape draws near, look to the forest. It is a route Sorazin will least expect."

"Agreeee, I doo," said Tarkis.

"Yet keep wide your eyes, Shepherd of the Always tribe, for if a safer path presents itself—a passage by sea or shore—we will amend our gambit at a moment's notice."

"Ten thousand thanks." Jaspen bowed his head to Opahlua and the others.

"My troops are standing by." Perpeht lifted high his flute.

"Arrows ready too." Yetahni grinned at Shokku, keen to let fly the bolts.

"Muggfrugg's catapult is in position," said Muggfrugg.

"We have a catapult?" asked Jaspen.

"Soon after Jaspen vacated the cave this very morning," said Bogg, "Muggfrugg and Boggfrogg borrowed one of Sorazin's throwing machines."

"Many Huntressi sister come soon," said Shokku.

"Muggfrugg sent smoke words asking the Udok for help as well," said Muggfrugg. "Many Udok are prepared to fight to regain the ancestral lands."

Bogg added, "Bogg also asked the Always to come." He smiled. "The Always said yes."

"All excellent news!" Yet Jaspen's grin suddenly faded when his ear caught a faraway sound. "But whosoever intends to abet our tribe . . . " he pressed an ear nearer the sea, "should make haste."

Straining to interpret the unsettling noise in the distance, Jaspen angled toward the cave's mouth. His knees began to wilt, more and more with each stride, and apprehension slurred his vision.

My return to this cave . . . he thought, his flesh growing damp, *I fear the half-cooked plot to bring me back will end in my demise.*

Reaching the cavern's exit, Jaspen closed his eyes and directed his ears to the sea's unusual rustling.

The time has come, he thought as the source of the strange murmur became apparent.

"Levaioth nears."

69

Foot Meets Shield

"Please relieve MAHKIFO of his sword, shield, and bone spear," said Sorazin to the warriors flanking Jaspen. "That little, child's blade," he indicated Jaspen's pearl knife, "he can keep."

"Set Kama free," said Jaspen. "Take me in her stead."

"Do they not kneel to their sovereigns from whence your kind hail?" Sorazin's eyes flashed to a guard behind Jaspen.

The butt of the sentry's spear struck Jaspen's knee.

The Shepherd crumpled to the earth in what looked to be a posture of allegiance to the Cove's Mutahn.

"I accept your apology," bellowed Sorazin, loud enough to draw every eye in the vicinity toward Jaspen hunched on the beach at the Mutahn's feet.

Rising, Jaspen stood tall and gazed at the many enemy faces glowering at him.

Another boulder and log crashed into the sea near The Thumb.

"To save your Forever-One," Sorazin pressed the tip of his sword to Jaspen's throat, "I will offer to you the same as I did Kama. Simply confess to the Cove that you killed the Hoodoah a moment after he declared me as their rightful monarch."

"That is all I must do to save Kama?" Jaspen peeked to The Thumb.

With the masses of splashing water as well as a strange ocean-mist rising up from the feet of the six *polog*, Jaspen could not establish whether Shokku had reached Kama or not. He would tarry a bit longer before progressing to the next stage of his plan.

Bogg stood masked behind a huddle of trees, four hundred paces from the chanting Tharsool and the scores of foot soldiers surrounding the pier. The catapult stood armed and ready, loaded with one of the fifteen boulders borrowed from Sorazin . . . boulders that were about to be returned.

Muggfrugg was stationed thirty paces nearer the sea than Bogg. A dozen neatly cut tree trunks lay close by, waiting to be hurled through the air toward The Thumb. The larger Udok clanked together the two, great hooks he was gripping in his fists, eager to begin launching the logs into the sea.

Last night, Fynndir had dismantled a sword, spear, and shield to forge two large hooks, each with an attached handle. The Gort had shown Muggfrugg where to impale each log with the two hooks—a hand's breadth down from the shorn end. Once the hook-tips were in place, Fynndir counseled the half-giant to lean back and revolve in a circle while holding the hooks at arm's length. The faster Muggfrugg could spin, the farther the log would fly when released. It was evident after one preparatory throw (upcoast, far from the pier) that this new method enabled Muggfrugg to pitch each tree trunk much farther than with only the pushing force of his arms and legs.

Tarkis's role was to reset the catapult after each toss, at which time Bogg would place another boulder into the weapon's wooden nest as quickly as he could. Once the cargo was ready, Tarkis would trigger the catapult and the timber arm would spring forward to unleash the stone.

Opahlua trilled out the call of a Blue-Wing and Muggfrugg squatted to stab the two hooks into a cut tree trunk. The warrioress followed her imitation of the Blue-Wing with the shrieking cry of a Chatter-Tail.

Muggfrugg gripped tighter the log and began whirling like a Funnel-Wind. The half-giant's muscles rippled and bunched, his arms and shoulders massive, as the log swept out in a huge, sweeping circle in front of him with a *whoosh! whoosh! whoosh!* During his third circuit, Muggfrugg twisted the hooks free of the timber and the tree trunk sailed up and out of the woods toward the pier.

When the ascending log reached a certain height, Tarkis discharged the first boulder.

Opahlua grinned at the long pole of timber and great stone, both on a course to crash into the sea near The Thumb. She glanced at Shokku.

The Huntressi was poised and ready to burst forward and rush into the ocean the moment Opahlua gave the signal. Shokku looked briefly at the warrioress, twenty paces to her left, then faced forward again. She listened out for Opahlua's cue while watching for a shield to come skimming across the water in front of her. Peeking to her right, Shokku grinned, nervous, at Yetahni, posted opposite Opahlua. Yetahni made a few hand gestures to Shokku—a prayer that the Always be with them in their quest to save Kama.

Behind Yetahni stood Perpeht. Fidgety, the flute-carver rolled his neck and decided to execute one final practice test of his task. He snatched a shield from the pile at his feet and quickly fed it to Yetahni. Yet the shield slid from Perpeht's perspiring hands before reaching the Huntressi. The musician's face fell, hopeless.

Calyp, Opahlua's shield bearer, shook his head at Perpeht's blunder and instructed him where to hold each shield, via a few simple gestures, to prevent the metal disc from slipping free of his hands.

Perpeht nodded his thanks to Calyp. Yet before he could rehearse the new technique, Opahlua had shouted "*Go!*"

Shokku shot for the ocean, fast and powerful. She had placed five colorful shells in the sand to mark where each of her strides were to land in order for the ball of her foot to meet the center of the first shield. Strides one, two, three, and four were perfect.

From the corner of her vision, a split second before Shokku was due to streak into the sea, the first shield came shooting toward her from her left. It was nearly impossible for her to keep her eyes fixed on The Thumb, as Opahlua had ordered. But Shokku managed to resist the temptation to turn her face to the approaching shield.

And when the ball of Shokku's foot kissed the shield, it was as if she were running on dry earth.

70

Return of Rollik

ROLLIK WAS PERCHED UPON a branch of a tree overhanging the Hall of Shells. He was peering out at the ocean in search of Levaioth when the first log splashed down. Soon after, a boulder crashed into the water on the pier's other side. The Faijen hastened toward the commotion.

Hovering above the six *polog*, Rollik glanced to his left to witness Shokku running fleetly across the water's surface. It took him but a moment to ascertain how the Huntressi was accomplishing such a feat. Shields continued to blast out from the trees from two locations along the shoreline to skip over the water, each accurately anticipating exactly where Shokku's next stride would touch down.

Marvelous! thought Rollik as his eyes traveled ahead to Shokku's apparent destination: The Thumb.

Shortly after Rollik had been set free by Jaspen, he drifted through the nighted forest, deep in thought. The Faijen was both humbled and astounded by the Always tribe's pardon. Every other Jirvallan tribe would have slain Rollik for a crime akin to the one he had waged against Kama.

Nevertheless, Rollik was compelled by pride and well-worn habits to visit the Faijen Hydropolis. He was anxious to know whether the two favor-bonds earned by Rollik from the Cove were adequate for Great Hydron Rill to accept the former footman back into the fold of the Faijen.

What an honor to be reinstated to my royal post, he had thought.

Yet as Rollik had advanced through the dark toward the Hydron's royal palace, a pang of guilt stung his heart. He was driven to shroud himself in a nearby stand of reeds upon spying a Faijen night guard in the distance, on his rounds.

Concealed in the reeds, waiting for the night guard to pass by, Rollik had thought, *As much as I dislike her, that dark woman speaks true.* Tears shone in the Faijen's eyes. *Even Rill, who has known me since birth, who has dined at my mother and father's home, would not extend the kindness and mercy that the Always tribe has shown to me this very eve.*

"What a fool I am," he murmured into the night.

My only hope is that Jaspen's offer to welcome me into the Always tribe still stands.

Alighting from the reeds, Rollik was stopped at once by a voice behind him.

"Halt!" the night guard had commanded. "And apprise me as to why a Faijen is hiding amongst the reeds so proximate to the entrance of our Hydropolis."

"I am no Faijen!" Rollik turned to face the guard. "I am Rollik of the Always tribe. Servant to the mighty Jaspen and worshipper of Jirvalla's most powerful god!"

"Rollik?" the guard had whispered.

"Scupper . . . How grand to see you!"

The watchman's eye roved in search of others who might be near. He had signaled for Rollik to quickly descend with him back into the protection of the reeds.

"You must depart." Scupper's eyes were still roving for danger. "At once."

"But the favor-bonds—"

"Did naught to soften Rill's heart against you. Our orders still stand: Kill—"

The hum of whirring wings had stopped him. Scupper lifted a finger to his lips. Hovering just above Scupper and Rollik was a second night guard. The sentry's watchful eyes prowled the trees and shrubs, his spear and dagger at the ready.

At long last, the guard had deemed the area safe and flitted away.

"Please, Rollik," Scupper had begged in a hushed voice. "Go, and do not return."

Rollik nodded, at once pained by his expulsion and joyful at the notion of becoming a committed member of the Always tribe. Rollik had winged away toward the bush-and-bough shrouded cave near the seaside border of the Treef forest.

Arriving at the hideout, Rollik had hidden himself behind a rock at the cave's ingress. The Always tribe was deep in converse, weaving together a plot to save Kama. Their scheme was daring and extraordinarily imaginative. Slender were the odds of carrying it off, however. Still, Rollik had longed to be a part of it. As unorthodox and unlikely as their ploy seemed, it was certainly no more outlandish than what had occurred in the UnderDown.

But what if I am rejected? he had thought. *What if Jaspen has reversed his opinion of me?*

After a moment, Rollik had lifted high his head and whispered, "Far be it from the Day-Night Shepherd to do such a thing. Too honorable is he."

Rollik had emerged from behind the boulder and was about to enter the cave when the drums of the Tharsool sounded. The former Faijen had peered back toward the beach where the Cove holy men were calling forth their sea god.

Perhaps, Rollik had thought, *I could be of better use if I . . .* he pondered the notion and nodded. *Yes, I believe I would.*

After casting one last look into the cavern, Rollik had turned away. Moments later, he had alighted upon a slim tree bough near the Hall of Shells.

Rollik was still floating above the *polog* when a loud *crack!* pealed from the shore to his left. His eyes flashed to the place from whence the sound had come. A boulder rose slowly out of the trees to barely make it into the ocean, a great distance from where the others had been crashing into the sea.

Whatever contraption was hurling the rocks has failed, thought Rollik.

His supposition was confirmed when no further boulders sprang from the trees to splash down near the pier. The logs, however, continued.

Rollik looked to the Hall of Shells. Archers crowded the corner of the roof nearest the sea. From their new position, without the crashing boulders to build a screen of water, the bowmen had a clear view of The Thumb.

Below, more archers hurried to the places along the shore where they too could fire directly upon the *polog* without interference.

"They will kill Shokku . . . " muttered Rollik and he looked to the Huntressi.

Shokku was approaching swiftly from behind the watery barrier provided by the tree trunks. Two more skimming shields and she would arrive at the pier's tip.

Rollik darted to the planks and set down on the pier midway between the archers and The Thumb. He closed his eyes and riveted his every sense on eliciting as much Faijen Mist as he could muster.

As the archers notched their arrows and awaited instruction from Sorazin, a thick haze began to rise from the pier, blocking the bowmen's view of The Thumb.

Shokku dashed over the water. With the breeze cutting through her hair and her eyes half-shut and streaming from the wind, she laughed. At both herself and the implausibility of the endeavor at which she was so gallantly succeeding. Oh! the feeling of racing over the water! It was as if she was Bucket-Beak in flight just a hair's breadth above the sea-top.

With only a few strides before she was due to leap onto the pier, Shokku noticed the boulders were no longer pounding into the ocean to upheave a protective curtain of water.

"Only you, my Always, can shield me now," she prayed in her native tongue and bounded off the next shield to win the pier near Kama.

"You were amazing!" said Kama, her eyes wide with astonishment.

"No time for chat." Shokku's knife sawed through Kama's tethers. The Huntressi then freed the other five *polog*.

"Incoming!" Kama gawped at two arrows arching toward them, both of them loosed from the same shore from where the shields had been coming.

"No worry." Shokku grinned at the descending bolts, each carrying a small sack tied near the arrow's tip. "Yetahni never miss."

The darts stabbed into the planks between Rollik and the guards manning the pier. The viscous contents of the sacks splattered across the timber.

"You see what I do on water, yes?" asked Shokku.

Kama nodded while rubbing her wrists where they had been tied.

Shokku said, "Now you do same. Two shields only. Then dive over fence."

"Run on the water? No way, I—"

"Mist." Shokku noted the cloud rising about them. "From where come?"

Kama sneered in the Faijen's direction. "Rollik. I don't know why but he—"

"Fell the Faijen!" commanded Sorazin from the shore. "It is that cheating water bug who makes the fog!"

"No time more!" said Shokku.

"Archers!" Sorazin peered through the thickening brume to spot Kama and Shokku. "Fire!" He indicated for his arrow-men on the roof to slay them.

"Follow me!" Shokku spun toward the shore where the shield-throwers were awaiting her signal then chirped out a short, strident whistle.

Thwack! A spray of splinters burst from The Thumb as an arrow bored into the wood between Kama and the *polog* next to her.

"Guards!" Sorazin roared to his men on the pier. "Cut them down, every *polog*. Now!"

The guards unsheathed their swords and approached The Thumb.

"Hrrrrr . . . " A bolt found purchase in the throat of a *polog* an arm's length from Kama.

Though all had been cut free, the *polog* lacked a safe place to shelter themselves from Sorazin's men and their weapons. Guards drew nearer to them from the base of the pier while the fenced-in sea beasts gathered beneath the jetty's tip. The *polog* were stranded near The Thumb, marooned in the open air.

A shield came scudding over the water toward the pier. Then another.

"What keeps you from them?" Sorazin bellowed to his guards on the pier. "Kill them! Make haste!"

"Trust shields," said Shokku to Kama.

"Our boots are caught," replied a guard to the Mutahn, his feet bonded to the timber beneath him by a tacky substance.

Kama glanced at the approaching shields. "Trust the shields," she whispered to herself then nodded at Shokku. "Will do."

Shokku peeked to the guards. Each was held fast to the planks by a viscous ooze that Tarkis had named Forest-Stick-Trail—the gooey resin that had burst from the pouches tied to Yetahni's arrows.

Sorazin glimpsed through a diminishing hedge of water to spy a shield skipping over the ocean's surface. He quickly solved how Shokku had reached the pier.

"Send a fireball!" demanded the Mutahn. "Now!" He trained a finger at the far shore where more shields were being launched.

Shokku retreated a few steps to gain the proper footspeed. To Kama, she said, "No look down."

At the mouth of the harbor, the dark tattered tail of Levaioth ascended from the sea—enormous, foreboding, dreadful.

71

To Sacrifice All

JASPEN GRINNED AT THE image of Fynndir's *skeervog*, a Glow-Wing the size of a child's thumb. The small, sizzling flame bounded through the archers on the roof of the Hall of Shells, scorching the eyes and faces and fingers of every bowman it met. The *skeervog* then sped to the beach and burned through the archers posted on the sand about the pier.

Sorazin viewed the vexing flare in frustration before returning to the Faijen Mist, the murk continuing to broaden around the *polog*. He shouted at his whimpering archers, chastening them for their poor aim, upbraiding them for pausing their onslaught due to piddling finger burns from that tiny flicker.

Irate, he caught the eye of a guard behind Jaspen. "Spear!" he demanded.

Sorazin seized the lance and narrowed his eyes at the bank of fog billowing up from the timber planks. He drew back his arm, shifted his grip, then sent the spear whistling into the swirling Mist.

Almost instantly, the haze wavered and thinned. Soon, only a few lingering wisps clung to the air, stretching in the wind like threads unwoven . . . until nothing but clear sky lay between Sorazin and The Thumb.

Kama and Shokku came into view. They were sprinting across the pier, heading for the ocean.

Rollik was hesitant to unshut his eyes. What if he had expended the entirety of his Faijen Mist last night—when perpetrating the most heinous act of his life: the mutinous betrayal of Kama? What if he could manage but a single, vaporous puff?

"How sorry I am, dear Kama," he whispered, tears leaking from his closed eyes. "Oh! the distaste with which you looked upon me last night. So foul! Yet I deserved worse."

An arrow cut through the swelling fog just above Rollik's head to bore into The Thumb. A metallic hiss followed—a nearby guard unsheathing his sword.

"Even if you cannot forgive me, Kama," Rollik forced open his eyes, "I vow to spend the rest of my suns making up for my error against you." Gazing through the dense haze, Rollik spied Kama standing next to Shokku.

She is safe! he thought. *And this Mist . . . never in my life have I conjured clouds so thick! Thank you, my Always.*

An overwhelming sense of accomplishment took hold of Rollik and a surge of excitement, of triumph, spread up from his heart to push into his throat.

Helpless against such growing enthusiasm, Rollik cried out, "FOR THE ALWAYS TRIBE!"

Rollik tingled with joy as the haze about him and the *polog* multiplied all the more, extending upward and outward.

Perhaps this one honest act is enough for Kama to pardon my trespass against her, he thought. Eyes shining with hope, he grinned at the notion.

"Perhaps a day will come," he whispered to himself, "when we will even call each other frien— Uhhhhrrrrr . . . "

A spear pierced into Rollik's breast and the tip of it traveled through him until exiting out of his back, the butt of the lance extending from his chest. The force flung the Faijen across the pier, past Shokku and Kama and into the waters beneath.

Kama caught sight of Rollik sliding past her feet to slip into the ocean next to her, a Cove spear running through him. The sea-beasts converged upon the Faijen at once, tearing Rollik into pieces before devouring every last shred of him.

Yet before Rollik was lost to the teeth of the Fin-Folk and to the depths of the sea, Kama saw upon his face a grin so tranquil and an aspect so joyful she could not contain her smile. Rollik's sapphirine eyes peered heavenward and they beamed with the wondrous quality of a grand purpose finally fulfilled. The radiating glow from his face plainly stated that he had died willingly, gloriously, in service of another.

The Faijen Mist, thought Kama. *He was doing it to hide Shokku and me from Sorazin.*

And Kama made an oath that if ever she were to see Perpeht again, she would tell him of Rollik's selfless sacrifice, of his luminous mien, and the divine luster of his sparkling blue eyes, so that the flute-carver could compose an ode in memorandum of the traitorous Faijen who redeemed himself by giving his own life to save the lives of two others.

In the distance far beyond where Rollik had perished, closing in on the pier, came Levaioth. Kama watched in awe as the monstrosity's ragged black tail slapped down into the water, her eyes broad, her heart thudding.

"Kama, look only at shore where going." Shokku indicated their destination.

"The shore. Got it." She fell in line beside Shokku.

The Faijen Mist around them was subsiding, rapidly.

"Ready?" Shokku crouched, eager to burst forth and cross the timbers.

Kama nodded and dug her bare feet into the pier.

Skating toward them over the water came the shields.

"Another spear!" shouted Sorazin from the foot of the pier. "Make haste!"

Shokku cried, "Now!" and the Huntressi and Kama bolted across the planks.

Sorazin, spear in hand, targeted Kama.

"No!" Jaspen lunged for Sorazin but was pounced upon immediately by three guards.

The Mutahn's dart flew, swift and sure.

Shokku leapt off the pier toward her shield, Kama a step behind.

Sorazin grinned at his soaring shaft, its speed and flight and aim faultless.

From the edge of her vision, Kama glimpsed the spear pelting for her. She had not the time to gauge whether the pike was on a course to impale her or not. For if she removed her eyes from the shield, or made even the slightest maneuver to evade the spear, Kama's foot would fail to meet the center of the shield; a misstep that would end in Kama splashing into the sea amongst the caged devils therein.

Kama sent up a short prayer to the Always, closed her eyes and sprang from the pier.

72

Spear Versus Cave-Wing

S<small>ORAZIN'S GRIN WIDENED AS</small> the lance sped to an arm's length from its target.

Jaspen watched from the sand, yearning to cry out Kama's name, to warn her. Yet he bit back the inclination. If Jaspen's voice were to rise, his Forever-One would turn toward it. Even a small quiver in his direction would cause Kama to miss the coming shield and thereby become a morning repast for Wide-Eye, Spike-Tail, and Dagger-Back.

With his eyes locked to Kama, leaping now, Jaspen glimpsed a strange ivory-winged blur speeding toward his Forever-One. The white fuzzy creature hurled itself into the spear's path to collide into the shaft just behind its keen tip. Thrown off its course, Sorazin's dart plummeted harmlessly into the ocean.

"No!" cried Sorazin as his javelin went amiss and Kama's foot set down in the hollow of a shield skimming across the ocean's surface.

A victorious, squawk called from above The Thumb and Flumflum circled the pier twice, in proud victory, before fluttering back toward Opahlua and Yetahni on the far shore.

Jaspen whooped with cheer and shouted out in praise of the brave Cave-Wing.

"Fireballs!" Sorazin thrust a finger at the shore where shields were being dealt into the water at perfect intervals. "Now!"

A guard replied, "The warriors tending the catapults are dead, sire. Huntressi arrows."

"All fourteen of them?"

"Twenty-seven. Those arriving to help were also slain."

"Send three battalions to exterminate the Huntressi at once. And fireballs. In the air." Sorazin lifted a finger to the sky. "At once!" He turned to face Jaspen and drew a breath, collecting himself. "She means nothing." Sorazin glanced through a narrow gap in the screen of water to spy Kama scurrying over the water. "We shall recapture her before sunfall. Kama will be hanged in front of the entire tribe for what she did to the—"

"In response to your offer, you perjuring Side-Walker," Jaspen scowled at Sorazin, "I must respectfully decline your request that I bear false witness with regard to the Hoodoah's disappearance."

"Hhhuurrrr!" A guard behind Jaspen, within the outer ring of sentries, slumped to the earth—an arrow in his neck.

"We of the Always tribe," resumed Jaspen, "maintain a stringent code of honor."

The forty guards that now surrounded Jaspen spun toward the coming arrows and raised their shields to defend against the barrage. Yet three more fell over, dead.

Sorazin grinned at Jaspen. "I was hoping you would— Ho!"

Fynndir's fiery Glow-Wing shot into the Mutahn's face to sear Sorazin's cheek. Swatting wildly at the *skeervog*, Sorazin clapped himself on the brow, scarcely missing the pest.

While Sorazin was immersed in battle with Fynndir's *skeervog*, Jaspen snuck his pearl knife from its sheath. He stepped to his rear in hopes of stealing through the mob of soldiers unseen, so occupied were they with the coming arrows. Yet there were too many guards and too little room to squeeze between them and slink away.

Sorazin smirked at the darting little blaze and withdrew his blade. His eyes bounded after the *skeervog*, deftly trailing it. In a flash, Sorazin's sword struck.

The Glow-Wing dimmed as the Mutahn's blade sheared it in half. The *skeervog's* two parts sputtered, sparking pathetically as they pitched and stumbled through the air in opposite directions. Then, in a puff of smoke, the Glow-Wing vanished.

The amber stone dropped to Jaspen's feet. He stepped upon the gem to secrete it from Sorazin.

Five more guards toppled to the sand, blood spewing from the slots in their flesh from where the feathered ends of arrows protruded.

Sorazin said to Jaspen, "The penalty for rejecting my benevolent offer, *mahkifo*, is death."

Levaioth's vast, moth-eaten tail crashed again into the sea, closer this time, the mammoth splash drenching The Thumb.

A crackling fireball sizzled through the sky on course for Opahlua, Yetahni, Perpeht, and the others.

"And so the tide turns." Sorazin pressed his sword's tip to Jaspen's chest.

73

Muggfrugg's Boulder

SHOKKU, YETAHNI, OPAHLUA, AND Kama were plunging through the trees at a breakneck pace while notching and firing arrows at the guards surrounding Jaspen.

"Clear a path for Jaspen on the woodland side!" cried Opahlua.

Directly above the tribe's female brigade, Tarkis and Calyp swung through the branches toward Jaspen. As they advanced, they called out in their strange, native tongue urging all Treef in the area to join the assault on Sorazin, to take revenge upon the man who torched the Treef's royal court and injured their honorable Kaliphae.

Muggfrugg, with but a single log remaining, redirected his aim. He sunk the hooks into the timber and spun. A spray of perspiration broadened in a widening ring as the velocity of his whirling increased. Vaulting from the earth, he gave a great shout and let fly the tree trunk.

The log sailed higher, farther, than any of the Udok's previous casts. When it struck the roof of the Hall of Shells, thirty Cove archers were crushed upon impact.

And by the time Sorazin's fireball touched down, the Always tribe had already fled their former post.

Jaspen deflected Sorazin's blade with his pearl knife. He was happy to bide his time until Kama, Opahlua, Bogg, Perpeht, Tarkis, Calyp, Fynndir,

Yetahni, and Shokku broke through the Cove militia. Or forged for him a path of escape.

"He is mine!" blared Sorazin to a soldier who was drawing back his sword in response to Jaspen's show of aggression. "I alone will slaughter this worthless cutthroat." The Mutahn glowered at his sentries.

Nine additional Cove troops, each positioned on the forest side of Jaspen, took mortal arrows.

Levaioth's tail splashed down once more, seawater erupting to dampen the sandy shores about the pier.

Yet Sorazin had eyes for nothing and no one but Jaspen. He flashed a haughty grin and the pair began to circle one another, blades swiping.

Opahlua had dispensed with her bow in favor of the black-and-silver war-axe. The warrioress had finally returned to her element and she hammered, stabbed, butted, kneed, kicked, and rammed her way through the Cove swordsmen, her axe cutting them down like a scythe through grass.

Yet no matter how bloody or wide the swath of slain enemies behind the warrioress, more and more Cove continued to emerge. If Opahlua, Tarkis, and the others were to succeed in clearing a route to the forest, they would require more assistance.

Opahlua caught Shokku's eye and directed her to commandeer the lone remnant of roof that remained intact upon the Hall of Shells. The warrioress then called out in strident mimicry of a Chatter-Tail in distress.

At Opahlua's signal, Perpeht clambered out from the hollow log within which he had been obscured.

"Reporting for duty," he whispered to himself and pressed the timber flute to his lips.

Yet after a short burst . . .

"Well, if it isn't the banished whistle-maker."

The smaller of two Cove soldiers, each equipped with dagger and sword, glared at the musician.

"Flute-carver," corrected Perpeht. "And minstrel."

"And dead." The larger Cove reached for his dagger.

"Dead?" Perpeht drew back a step. "Is that the wage for writing a new ballad these days?" A string of notes streamed from his flute. "Death?"

"Cove law states that any banished, former tribe-member trespassing on Sorazin's land is to be executed on sight."

Perpeht piped three more notes. "Is there not a battle you blood-thirsty dullards should be joining?" He puffed into the instrument again, his fingers dancing over the holes. "In that direction, perhaps?"

"Dullards?"

"As blunt-witted as they come, I'm afraid." A melody sprang from the flute as Perpeht back-stepped over a log.

The sentries, weapons drawn, advanced upon the bard.

The larger of the two grinned and said, "This is going to be fun—"

Furious rustling from a nearby bramble stopped the pair's advance.

A trio of Stink-Tails emerged from the underbrush.

"Would you look at that?" Perpeht whistled while stretching wide his eyes.

The animals glared at the guards and hissed at them, white-striped tails high.

"Rare to see them so bold. And disgruntled." Perpeht examined his fingernails, casual. "Whatever did you do to them? Dine upon their young?"

The fighting men backed away with quickened step, huffing in alarm.

Perpeht blew into the mouthpiece and the Stink-Tails burst for the soldiers, teeth bared.

The soldiers barely kept their feet while turning to scurry away.

Behind and all around Perpeht came the crash and clamor of his stampeding forest friends.

"Help comes, Opahlua." Perpeht hurried after the storming band of Rope-Tail, Mask-Face, Red-Beak, Slither-Belly, Chatter-Tail, and every other animal within earshot of Perpeht's flute.

Bogg and Muggfrugg grinned as the band of frenzied creatures rushed past them enroute to the enemy Cove. The two half-giants were each rolling a boulder before them.

"Bogg wonders how Jaspen is doing," he said to Muggfrugg.

He strained to squint through the thick ring of Cove warriors encircling Sorazin and Jaspen. Yet their number was too great to glimpse anything beyond the many spear-tips, bronze helmets, and large shields.

"Bogg would like to offer Muggfrugg the honor of the first toss."

"How kind Bogg is to Muggfrugg," said Muggfrugg. "To the tree side?"

"Indeed." Bogg hopped up and down in a continued effort to determine how Jaspen was faring in his duel with the Mutahn. "Bogg and Muggfrugg must open a trail for Jaspen to reach the forest."

"Muggfrugg will do." He squatted down and twined his long, amply muscled arms about the boulder.

"Does Muggfrugg see Shokku on the rooftop of the Hall of Shells? And Tarkis, Calyp, and Opahlua in combat upon the shore?"

Muggfrugg grunted in affirmation.

"Bogg does not imagine it would be good to squash any of the Always tribe."

Muggfrugg hoisted the boulder over his head. "Worry not, Bogg. The boulder will fly true."

"Bogg will take a position there." He gestured ahead, along the timberline, forty strides away. "Bogg will cast the last granite stone a moment after Muggfrugg."

Muggfrugg walked toward the fighting, faster and faster, to gain the proper momentum, then broke into a jog; all while balancing the boulder above his head.

Bogg crept closer and closer to his new post while scanning the area for an enemy presence. Concealed behind a thick tree trunk, he peered into the undergrowth, squinted for hidden Cloakers, and examined the boughs above for any foes that may be lurking overhead. While peeking upward, he noted a few hazy billows rising from a mountain in the distance: smoke words.

Bogg read the ascending clouds, whispering, "Fifty Udok. On way to fight."

He turned to share the news with Muggfrugg. Yet upon seeing his tribe-mate, Bogg stepped back in dread.

"No . . . " Bogg murmured at the image of Muggfrugg wobbling beneath his boulder, two Cove arrows jutting from his torso.

Three enemy archers were creeping toward their injured adversary, firing bolt after bolt as they drew near.

"Muggfruuuuuggg!" bellowed Bogg, a tear in his eye.

Muggfrugg glanced to Bogg, streams of blood flowing from his wounds.

A spearman buried his pike into the back of Muggfrugg's leg and the half-giant stumbled, faltering to a knee.

An arrow sideswiped his upper arm, taking with it a wedge of flesh.

Though striving mightily to keep the boulder aloft, Muggfrugg's muscles finally gave way and the granite came down upon him to crush him beneath its colossal weight.

Amidst tears of rage and grief, Bogg pressed his boulder high above his bald pate and took careful aim.

"MUGGGFRRUUUUUGG!" he boomed and hurled his burden to the appointed site.

The boulder pounded onto the beach to mash a dozen enemy upon touching down. The hurtling globe bowled over another seventy Cove before slowing to a halt near the Hall of Shells.

Yet Bogg was blind to the ruin that lay in the wake of the great stone. For he had been laboring to tear from its earthen nest a strapping oak, one that he was now employing to club into extinction the bowmen who had struck down his dear, longtime friend.

Once finished with the archers, Bogg turned toward the pier.

"Jaaaasspen!" he yelled and sprinted toward the shore. "Bogg is coming!"

74

Arrival of Levaioth

SORAZIN AND JASPEN CIRCLED and feigned, thrust and dodged. As their blades clashed, Sorazin noted the brunt of the Always tribe's attack was falling upon those posted between Jaspen and the nearest tree line.

Quickly intuiting his enemy's stratagem, Sorazin shouted over the battle to a proximate commander: "One hundred soldiers between myself and the near forest, now! And add forty to my personal guard."

While Sorazin barked orders, Jaspen spied an opening on the Mutahn's left. He struck with the pearl knife, swift and powerful.

Sorazin parried the hopeful lunge with ease.

Jaspen gnashed his teeth in frustration. *I am overmatched*, he thought.

"Drive us toward the water," Sorazin commanded the seventy warriors that now wreathed the two fighters.

Again and again, Sorazin's heavy blows rained upon Jaspen while the soldiers maneuvered the duelists toward the lethal beasts within the sea-fence.

Help me, my Always, prayed Jaspen, struggling to evade the many strikes of Sorazin's siege. *For without your strength, this day is certain to be my last.*

"Where I cut Kama," Sorazin grinned, "I now cut you."

His blade raced for Jaspen's middle.

Jaspen turned away the sword but was late in spying Sorazin's incoming fist.

The Mutahn crushed Jaspen in the ear, the iron points of his black-gloved knuckles scoring a trio of deep pits in the side of Jaspen's head.

"Jaaaasspen!" roared a voice in the distance. "Bogg is coming!"

Yet Jaspen failed to mark his tribe-mate's call. For he lay unconscious on the shore with one bloody ear facing Sorazin and the other buried in the watery shallows near the pier.

Perpeht's army of wing and fang burst onto the beach and tore into the Cove with a ferocity and bloodthirst as savage as Jirvalla had ever seen. Sharp beaks gouged into cheeks and eyes. Claws carved out long, crimson furrows down torsos and thighs. And champing teeth sunk into enemy bellies, necks, and shoulders.

Opahlua grinned at the sight . . . then ducked beneath a sword before cutting down three Cove soldiers. "May the Always bless you, good Perpeht." Her war-axe cleaved through two more enemy heads. "And please, my little Love-Flum," Opahlua watched with concern as the Cave-Wing slapped and bit at a variety of Cove faces, "tread carefully."

Tarkis and Calyp stabbed and slashed while snapping off enemy body parts with their lethal pincers and sharp mandibles. When Yetahni was not filling the enemy with arrows, she was slinging pouches bulging with Stinging-Red-Legs and Blinding-Powder at enemy strongholds. And Kama was sneaking over the beach on her elbows and knees, twinning the hue and quality of sand, toward her Forever-One.

Bogg's thunderous call turned Opahlua toward the half-giant. She watched him streak onto the sand and toward Jaspen. The warrioress whistled an instruction to Shokku, Yetahni, Kama, Tarkis, and Calyp to muster all their forces to make clear a pathway for Bogg. Though reckless and unplanned, the former Udok's mad dash to save Jaspen seemed to be meeting with success as he barreled through the enemy at a brisk pace.

Opahlua noted a sudden rise in the number of friendly arrows flying overhead and she glanced to Shokku atop the Hall of Shells. The warrioress's eyes rested, pleased, at the seven additional Huntressi joining Shokku upon her perch. Four more crouched upon the boulder that had settled near the Cove palace, each commanding arrows enough to slay a hundred.

With Jaspen sprawled at Sorazin's feet, bloody and harmless, the Mutahn ordered the ring of guards about him to part so he could gaze with pride upon his valiant troops trouncing the Always tribe.

Instead, the Mutahn looked with disdain upon feral hordes of Red-Beaks, Blue-Wings, White-Wings, and Hook-Beaks gashing and clawing at his Cove militia. A pack of Howling-Moons chased down his swordsmen and spearmen to tear into their legs, backs, and throats. Tree-Horns were goring, Slither-Bellies were striking. A Black-Claw was slaughtering. And a few, long, ropy Coil-Killers had braided themselves about some of the Mutahn's best guards and archers to throttle and squeeze until they breathed no more.

Mounds of dead—Cove soldiers riddled with arrows, Cove guards impaled with spears—covered the bloodstained beach. Many were retreating apace into the woods. Still more were foundering to the sand to spread wide their arms and legs in a humiliating posture of surrender.

Sorazin's eye caught upon a company of two hundred Treef soldiers veiling themselves in the trees that rimmed the beach, awaiting the command to attack. Two dozen Huntressi lay in wait behind boulders and trees, every bow notched with an arrow. In the near distance, the deep-voiced war cry of the Udok chieftain chilled Sorazin's neck. The animalistic rumble was followed by the clamor of rampaging giants crashing through the woods—snapping boughs and cracking tree trunks as they descended upon the Hall of Shells.

Sorazin called out to a nearby captain, "Launch the flaming arrows! And busy the catapults. I want fireballs!"

"Toward the north, south or west, sire?"

"All. Torch the island, captain. To the last twig."

Sensing his impending defeat, Sorazin thought, *As I gave you my word so long ago, great Levaioth: When I cease, so does Jirvalla.*

The underwater fence yielded with an eerie metallic moan as Levaioth passed through the barrier as if it were nothing more than a bed of kelp. Approaching The Thumb, the huge, hard-scaled monster held high its great head. The beast's seven, jet eyes ranged the shore, gazing in bewilderment at the untold number of bodies lying motionless in the sand.

Levaioth's nostrils flared and quivered as they drew in long pulls from each direction. The creature hoped the aromas would provide some clarity as to why so many were scattered along the beach. There was perspiration and smoke. Cut wood and burning leaves. Shards of steel and dust from broken boulders. And blood, fresh and flowing, from members of each Jirvallan tribe.

War, thought the monster and its salivary glands responded to the bouquet of severed limbs, burning flesh, soft innards, and other flavorsome viscera.

The sea-beast looked to the pier, drool leaking from its maw. Yet the post at its end was lacking its typical offering. This, too, was unusual. Adding to the curious events, the feet belonging to a group of soldiers seemed to be shackled to the timber planks of the pier. Levaioth's bewilderment was soon replaced by an unbearable lust to bury its teeth into something fleshy and blood-filled.

One by one, Levaioth plucked up the Cove guards from the pier and crunched them between its six rows of peaked teeth.

75

Sea of Dangers

Jᴀꜱᴘᴇɴ ʙʟɪɴᴋᴇᴅ ᴀɴᴅ ꜱʜᴏᴏᴋ his face. Head fogged, vision blurred, he peered up at Sorazin until his enemy came into focus.

Why am I at Sorazin's feet?

He gaped around the shore, puzzled by the mayhem. A fireball sped through the sky. Then another. A piercing shriek near the pier drew his eye—Levaioth.

Kama! Jaspen recalled the image of his Forever-One bound to The Thumb.

The morning came back to him in fragments.

She's safe. Jaspen grinned.

The scent of woodsmoke lured Jaspen's gaze to a distant shore where three, gray-black towers of smoke were belching soot into the sky. The forest was blazing.

Behind the Mutahn, a number of guards fell to Huntressi arrows while others caught spears to the chest and back.

Sorazin said, "Your pathetic Always tribe is no more."

The Mutahn's sword slashed into Jaspen's side, just above the hip.

The Shepherd's howl of sudden, burning pain was eclipsed by another ear-piercing screech from Levaioth.

"Your Kama suffered a dishonorable, if not excruciating death," resumed Sorazin. "But worry not, *mahkifo,* for you are but moments from joining her."

The ocean lapped against Jaspen's injury, cool and soothing. He glanced at Levaioth behind him. Then to the pier. Then to Wide-Eye and

Dagger-Back escaping into open water via the aperture in the fenced-in cage, rent by the dark sea monster.

"Yet prior to your exit from my island, you filthy fish," Sorazin drew back his sword, "you will feel every burrowing inch of my blade. You will taste your own blood as it wells onto the root of your tongue. And you will hear with your own ears the last of your throat's pitiful gasps."

Sorazin's blade shot downward.

Jaspen—senses heightened, muscles twitching—watched the sword-tip driving toward his chest.

He redoubled his grip on the pearl knife, giving rise to a new flow of fresh blood from the gap in his side. His eyes made a rapid sweep of his surrounds, questing for a viable escape route. Yet a dozen guards flanked Sorazin in a tight half-circle and obstructed Jaspen's view of the beach as well as the forest beyond.

Even if the others have been crushed, he thought. *Kama lives. This I know in my bones. I will not leave her.*

It would be folly, Jaspen knew, to continue his duel with Sorazin. The blood loss from the gash at his hip was already weakening him.

I must take to the sea, he thought.

A blinding beam of light speared Sorazin in the eyes. Startled, he recoiled and his plunging sword slowed.

Fynndir! Jaspen grinned. *You have saved my life!*

The Gort had battled his way to the site Jaspen had indicated to him earlier, where the sun's rays could be diverted into enemy faces with a burnished shield slanted at the proper angle.

Jaspen, with only a moment before Sorazin would overcome the sun's glare, glanced to the swath of fenced-in sea behind him. *It is the only way.*

Yet the slapping tail of a nearby Dagger-Back and the smooth fin of Slither-Tail reminded Jaspen of how improbable his goal to reach the safety of a coral reef or dense bed of kelp. But there was no other choice.

Jaspen bucked his body and writhed beyond the path of Sorazin's diving sword.

The Mutahn's blade sunk deep into the sand.

Jaspen, upon his stomach now and peering past Levaioth to the horizon, dug his toes into the beach and coiled, preparing to leap into the perilous waters. The deep gouge at his side thumped and burned and stung, gushing with blood.

It is my home, my haven. His hands tingled as the saltwater bathed them.

Incensed, Sorazin yanked free his blade from the sand's grasp.

Your waters, my Always, have favored me before. Jaspen breathed deep the ocean's briny musk. *Urge them to favor me now.*

Sorazin's sword drove again toward Jaspen.

Closing his eyes, Jaspen murmured, "Kama, I am coming."

And he sprang into the sea, his powerful strokes ferrying him quickly past countless ocean killers and toward the relative safety that unfurled for miles on the opposite side of the iron sea-fence.

76

Captured

A swarm of Huntressi spears and arrows cut the air to punch into the necks, torsos, and abdomens of Cove warriors on all parts of the shore.

Enemy soldiers fell dead on Bogg's every side and the path leading to the guards surrounding Jaspen and Sorazin lay clear before him.

Reaching the wall of shields protecting the Mutahn, Bogg hurled himself into it. The half-giant's heavy fists bludgeoned and chopped, fragmenting skulls. His thick feet shot out to shatter any ribs and sternums they could find.

Soon, Bogg stood face-to-face with Sorazin . . . just as Opahlua, Tarkis, Calyp, and Yetahni plowed through the remaining guards to post themselves next to the former Udok.

"Where be Jaspen?" demanded Opahlua, her eyes scouring the shore and pier.

Sorazin's hand burst to his sword.

An arrow *whooshed* from behind Bogg to split the narrow gap between he and Tarkis.

The feathered shaft bored into Sorazin's thumb, knocking free the blade from his fist.

"Uhhhhrrr!" Sorazin clutched his injured hand with the other, pressing them together, blood streaming from his palms.

A second bolt spiked through the knuckles of Sorazin's good hand and tunneled through both hands until pinning them together.

The false Mutahn plummeted to his knees, gazing in dismay at the arrow joining his two hands as one.

Shokku, bow in her fist, strode to Sorazin and pushed her face close to his.

"You kill my sister—"

"JASPEN!" Kama dashed over the sand toward her Forever-One in the water.

He was stroking fleetly through the sea-beasts all about him. The splash of his hands and feet drew Levaioth's gaze. The monster seemed to observe him with interest, gliding slowly toward the Shepherd of Fish.

Shokku shot an arrow into each of Sorazin's thighs then rushed, along with the others, to stand at Kama's side and watch Jaspen hastening through the sea.

"Bogg believes that Jaspen will make it over the fence."

"He's getting closer." Kama smiled and unwittingly stepped into the water.

"Danger." Shokku took Kama by the elbow and drew her back to shore.

"Make safe his passage!" cried Opahlua and motioned for those skilled with spear and bow—every ally on the beach, in the forest, and atop the Hall of Shells—to let fly their lances at any finned predator converging upon their tribe-mate.

A flock of arrows and spears plunged into the sea behind and on each side of Jaspen.

"Nearly there now!" encouraged Perpeht and puffed a few notes into his flute.

Seemingly blind to the bolts knifing into the water beside and behind him, Jaspen pulled at the water with increasing force, arms wheeling, gaining speed as he neared the limit of the steel enclosure.

"Go!" cried Yetahni.

Jaspen was but a few strokes to the safer environs that lay beyond the crowded waters within the fence.

A company of Treef clacked out their support from high in the trees while their tribe-mates on the shore were already dancing in celebration of what was certain to be Jaspen's triumph.

"Is he . . . s-slowing?" Kama strode again into the sea.

Jaspen's body slackened and he lost velocity, as if an errant spear had struck him.

A terrible hush fell over the Always tribe.

An arm's length from the bars, Jaspen halted all movement.

"No . . . " Kama shifted her eyes from Jaspen to Opahlua. Surprised to see the warrioress's hand locked around her arm.

Jaspen bobbed in the water, stiff and paralyzed. Slowly, his shoulders and torso rotated until his blank, dull eyes beheld the sky above, his mouth agape.

Bogg said, "Perhaps Jaspen feigns death in a ploy to fool Levaioth."

The beast drew closer to the figure floating near the fence, intrigued, drawing a storm of shouts, spears, and arrows; the latter bouncing from Levaioth's impenetrable scales like twigs off a boulder. The monster's seven-eyed face dipped into the water and remained beneath the sea until circling Jaspen thrice. Levaioth then rose again to survey the body from above, its long neck craning to appraise the body before him from various heights and angles.

A slender tentacle, nearly transparent, climbed from the water at Jaspen's side to slap down upon him like a whip.

Jaspen's body jolted at the lash. His muscles flexed then relaxed then flexed once more, then again, in rhythmic spasms.

"What was that?" Kama looked to the others.

Yet none had the heart to tell her it was the numbing limb of a Killing-Vine-Legs.

"I'm going in." Kama strained against Opahlua's grip . . . to no avail. "Let me go!"

Two additional stinging coils slithered around Jaspen's chest and waist.

The Shepherd's body replied with its cadenced response: jolt-stiffen-ease.

"JAASSPPEEENNN!" wailed Kama, tears spilling.

Levaioth's head continued to slip beneath the sea then rise up again as if determining whether the black-and-white being was fit to consume.

More arrows came, each breaking harmlessly against the creature's impervious hide.

"Bogg still believes in Jaspen and in the power of the Always to save him."

Opahlua showed to him an encouraging smile. Yet the slight sway to her jaw, from side to side, betrayed her expression.

"This isn't . . . happening." Kama's fingers curled and she rocked back and forth, back and forth . . . until sagging to her knees. "Jaspen . . . "

Bogg placed a reassuring hand upon her back.

"Bogg . . . " Kama's teary eyes peered up at him. "Tell me he's okay. Tell me Jaspen's swimming back to me right now," she begged. "I need to hear it. Tell me."

Yet the best Bogg could manage was to compress his thick, wide lips together as one and behold Kama with a concerned gaze.

"No. No." Perpeht turned his face away from the sea, his flute slipping absently from his grip to settle into the sand.

Kama and Bogg took their eyes from each other and fixed them to their tribe-mate still floating atop the ocean.

Levaioth's terrible, black snout was descending upon Jaspen.

The thin lips peeled back and the rows of mossy teeth showed.

The deep, wide mouth opened.

And the monster snapped up Jaspen into its great jaws.

77

Larger than Levaioth

"NOOOOOO!" Kama sprang to her feet and leapt for the ocean.

Bogg and Opahlua caught her while still airborne and wrestled her back to shore.

"I have to go to him! He needs me! Let me go!"

Levaioth shrieked in victory and slapped its fins to the sea top. Gliding over the ruined fence, the beast slashed its tattered tail and charged into the open sea.

"Let go! NOW!" Kama squirmed against Opahlua's hold.

The warrioress held Kama's angry stare for a long moment. Then said, "As you wish," and loosened her grasp. "But if your life is made forfeit in pursuing Jaspen, all of his efforts to save you will have been in vain."

"And what would you have me do?" She jerked free her arm. "Nothing?"

Opahlua was still glaring at Kama when the weight of Jaspen's death finally sank into the warrioress's heart. Her lips began to tremble and she stumbled back. Tears rose as despair and heartbreak broke upon her. She tilted her face to heaven, spread wide her long, ropy arms, and burst into tears, howling in lament.

"In the Black Deep," she sobbed, "he delivered me from death." She watched the sea's surface ripple with the movement of Levaioth below. "I failed to accomplish the same for him."

Opahlua let fall her arms and they swung, slow and leaden, at her sides. Feeling the weight of the war-axe, useless in her fist, she peered at the weapon—encrusting in blood—and gave vent to her furor. She tightened her fist upon the axe's handle and looked out to spy Levaioth's black tail vanishing around the curve of shore at the harbor's mouth.

"YYYYAAAAAAHHHHH!" she bellowed and heaved her war-axe after the beast, far into the sea.

"Bogg too has failed." The half-giant gazed out over the ocean. "Moons ago Jaspen saved Bogg from a pool of Sink-Earth. And once again Jaspen saved Bogg in the shrine of Fire-Breath. Yet when Jaspen required Bogg's help, Bogg could not rescue him." His face creased with grief and his shoulders bounced, tears as fat as acorns splattering the sand.

Perpeht, moved by the outpouring of sorrow, picked his flute from the sand and pressed his quivering lips to his instrument. Out of the flute drifted a dirge of such loss and desperation that none hearing the funereal song could prevent the flow of tears.

"But Jaspen isn't dead." Kama stared at the tide lapping the shore before lifting her eyes to her tribe-mates. "He can't be."

The others regarded Kama with pity. They smiled at her with tight lips and nodding chins, wishing her words were true.

"I know you think I'm . . . But . . . " Embers of hope kindled in Kama's eyes. "Don't look at me with your pathetic faces, any of you!" Rounding on Bogg, Kama said, "Jaspen lives. Say it, Bogg. SAY IT!"

"Jaspen lives," mumbled the former Udok, disinclined to cross Kama.

"You're next Opahlua." Kama glared at her. "Say it."

Nodding, Opahlua lifted high her head. "Jaspen lives!" And she seemed to almost believe it.

"That's right he does." Kama looked to Shokku and Tarkis. "He's only gone away for a while. He's coming back. You'll see. Until then," Kama eyed Calyp, Perpeht, Fynndir, and Yetahni, "let no member of the Always clan ever think or say anything to the contrar—"

"*Mahkifo* is as dead as your father," snorted Sorazin, his speared hands quavering with the effort of speech.

Opahlua's foot drove the smile from Sorazin's mouth.

Yet the false Mutahn still managed a chuckle.

Shokku notched an arrow, drew back the bowstring, and leveled the sharp tip between Sorazin's eyes

Shokku glanced at Kama. "May I?" she asked.

"Lash him to The Thumb." Kama withdrew Jaspen's pearl knife from the sand.

Opahlua and Yetahni joined Shokku in shoving the fallen Mutahn across the beach. They forced Sorazin to limp and scuffle through the agony of the arrows in his thighs without the slightest help. To Sorazin's credit, he reached the timber post at the pier's end with few complaints.

Shokku fastened the final tether around Sorazin's ankles. Rising up, she spat in his face. "You kill my sister. Now die like her."

Grinning at her enemy's twitching face, Opahlua seized the arrow jutting from Sorazin's upper leg and shoved it another hand's-breadth into the meat of his thigh.

Sorazin yowled in agony. Drool spilling, sweat streaming, body shivering.

A number of Udok, Huntressi, and Treef had commandeered several of the ceremonial drums of the Tharsool. They sat upon the beach and reproduced the steady thumps and monotonous rhythm with which every Jirvallan was familiar: The haunting call to Levaioth.

"Remember this?" Kama slammed the butt of Jaspen's pearl knife into the bridge of Sorazin's nose. "I think Jaspen would've wanted you to have it . . . right here." Kama buried the piked tip of the knife into the soft tissue at the underside of the Mutahn's chin.

With a grunt, she shoved the blade upward until it broke through the flesh on the floor of Sorazin's mouth, beneath his tongue.

"But Jaspen forgave Rollik," said Bogg.

Shokku, Kama, Yetahni, and Opahlua snapped their faces to the half-giant. Each glared at him, bitter. While contemplating Bogg's words, however, their demeanors softened from rage to irritation.

The other members of the Always tribe—crowded together near The Thumb—regarded each other, perplexed, uncertain of how to proceed.

Opahlua said, "Are you suggesting we pardon this murdering beast?"

"He stole my chance at having children." Kama showed the tribe the scar across her womb. "And what about the island?" She waved a hand at the raging blazes spawned by the catapulted fireballs. "We just let him get away with it?"

"He ssslew Zzzirid." Tarkis clapped together his mandibles with a sharp *click!*

"And Muggfrugg too," added Bogg.

The drums beat louder, adding an ominous weight to the burning island. Black smoke billowed upward as the Treef and Udok began to chant in imitation of the Tharsool.

Perpeht said, "He should pay for what he did."

"Bogg simply states that the Always tribe is not like other tribes. Bogg heard Jaspen confirm this fact more than once. Bogg only—"

An ear-splitting *clap*! thundered at the mouth of the harbor. A towering spout of seawater surged high and broad and thick.

The drummers roared in approval at Levaioth's return.

78

End of a False Mutahn

A DEEP FURROW IN the ocean angled toward The Thumb. Behind it spread an expanding wake that sent great swells to crash upon the rocky shores defining the lateral borders of the harbor.

"Seems Levaioth has grown." Perpeht blew a few uneasy notes into his flute.

"Perhaps it be the mother of the beast that stole our Jaspen," said Fynndir.

None could deny that the trail in the sea behind Levaioth had grown far deeper and spread wider than any had previously witnessed.

"Either way . . . " Kama stepped to the pier's tip and fixed her eyes to the faraway shape beneath the surface, "I'm killing it." She raised high her chin, threw back her shoulders, and drew the pearl knife.

As the monster loomed nearer, Bogg took Kama's arm in an endeavor to draw her away from The Thumb.

"Get off!" Kama yanked free her arm.

"Bogg understands. But Bogg made to Jaspen a vow to protect Kama's life. Even if Kama seeks to dishonor Jaspen's final petition by leaping into Levaioth's mouth, Bogg cannot permit it. Jaspen is the best friend Bogg has ever known. Bogg will not violate the oath-promise made to Jaspen."

Kama scowled into Bogg's innocent gaze for a long moment. Nodding her compliance, she sheathed the pearl knife and trod alongside Bogg until reaching the shore.

In the harbor, the monster's back broke the surface.

Sorazin's eyes widened and he shuddered at the size of the giant.

Yet the beast's dorsal side was not the black, scarred back of Levaioth. It was smooth and as clear as water. With an appearance like fur that shone gold in the sun.

Bogg smiled. He turned to Kama. "Bogg told Kama the Always would come." Eyebrows high, he motioned for his clan-mates to accompany him across the pier to greet their deity at The Thumb.

Kama, Bogg, Opahlua, Flumflum, Shokku, Perpeht, Tarkis, Calyp, Yetahni, and Fynndir—some more hesitant than others—ventured to the pier's terminus. Together, they beheld their god in awestruck wonder as Long-Mane mounted higher and higher out of the sea.

Those who had yet to meet the Always face-to-face—Fynndir, Yetahni, Tarkis, and Calyp—fidgeted and shivered. Their panic grew as the Always neared. What if the god were to find them undeserving?

Midway between the entry to the harbor and The Thumb, Long-Mane's head crested the waves. Forged of seawater, it appeared as it had in the Black Deep, only much, much larger. Every last detail—the round ears, the flowing mane, the golden-hued eyes . . . even the small black dots, in parallel rows, from which the coarse whiskers poked—boasted a definition as rich and clear as the forest animal itself.

Long-Mane rose higher, shaking the sea from his eyes, ears, and muzzle. The thick shock of fur bordering his great face shed heavy globes of water that pocked the ocean from one side of the harbor to the other. Still a good distance from the tribe that bore his name, the Always ascended wholly out of the sea to stride upon its surface toward the pier.

Those upon the shore murmured in wonder and gasped in fear at the creature's otherworldly radiance, majestic bearing, and sheer magnitude: four times the height of Bogg and sevenfold the half-giant's width.

The larger part of those upon the shore were bent in genuflection to show reverence for the Long-Mane striding across the ocean's top. A smaller part, who felt unworthy of such splendor, scurried into the forest to either hide themselves or to watch the fearsome creature from the protection of the trees.

"Jaspen . . ." muttered Kama to herself. To Bogg, she asked, "Do you think the Always brought him back?"

Yet so mesmerized was Bogg by the sight and presence of his beloved deity that he had been rendered deaf to Kama's query.

Sorazin whimpered and veered his eyes from the mountainous beast. "It is-s only a dream," he sniveled. "A child's fancy."

Long-Mane caught sight of the dead and dying sprawled over the beach. His gaze paused on the bloody heaps of battle-torn bodies. The creature's brow pinched and he hung his head in mourning. Lifting his piercing eyes to the tyrant responsible for the carnage, Long-Mane peeled back his lips and a spine-chilling growl rumbled from its great maw, shaking the pier.

Sorazin whined and wheeled his head as far away from the watery behemoth as his fetters would allow.

Turning from the false Mutahn, Long-Mane approached the Always tribe with an approving purr thrumming in his throat. His admiring eyes lingered on each clan-mate before moving to the next.

Gripped by the beast's heavenly gaze, the Always tribe stood as still as frozen boulders; eyes staring, necks tingling, ears drumming, hearts hammering. Save Flumflum. Who, while perched upon Opahlua's shoulder, cooed and ruffled her wings then greeted the Always with a curtsey of sorts, to the deity's great delight.

It was as if a pool of sun was spilling into each of the tribe. The kingly presence of the Always soon warmed their every inch. A sacred and unnamable quality was soon melting away every heartache ever sustained . . . the pain of every lost opportunity . . . All hurt was eased, even that of Jaspen's vanishment, while peering into the benevolent face of the Always.

Long-Mane then tilted toward Sorazin and leveled him with a penetrating glare. Staring long and hard at the disgraced Mutahn, the Always seemed to be laying bare the man's heart; determining its worth.

The deity grew suddenly troubled and dropped his heavy eyes. Tears fell to the pier in large, glistening drops from Long-Mane's sorrowed face. So plainly heartbroken was he that none in his presence could halt their tears from joining his.

At long last, the great Always showed a more hopeful gaze to his tribe. Long-Mane contracted to a size that placed the crown of his luxuriant mane just a head above Bogg's smooth, hairless scalp. Yet even while assuming this smaller stature, Long-Mane lost none of his otherworldly magnificence or sacred grandeur.

Long-Mane leaned his warm mane close to the clan and brushed it against them. His kind eyes bid them to put away their fears and lay a hand upon his tresses.

"Doesn't even feel like water," said Kama, clutching one amber clump of his lavish mane after another.

"It is exactly as fur!" Perpeht's bright eyes consulted the others.

"Bogg believes a few strands of it could do wonders for Gristle and Knee Bone stew."

The Always tribe grew quiet and their faces etched with solemnity. Each of them stared deeply into Long-Mane's fur to encounter mystical images of Sorazin being played to them as if a Night-Vision.

They watched as the deposed Mutahn sat cowering in a jail cell awaiting the Always tribe's final word regarding his sentence. Somehow, a few of Sorazin's former soldiers overthrew the prison guards to free Sorazin. The former Mutahn quickly rose again to power and, in but a few moons, subjected all of Jirvalla to his terrible rule. The island fell into ruin.

Seasons later, Sorazin's son killed his father to take the throne. This awful, new ruler was tainted with more bloodthirst than Jirvalla had ever known.

As the vision reached its end, Long-Mane pulled away from the tribe and dilated to his previous height and breadth. He peered down toward Opahlua's feet.

There on the pier, dripping with water, was the war-axe Opahlua had hurled into the sea. Stunned, the warrioress leaned down and took hold of it.

"The Always . . . " she stammered. "He wishes for us to—"

"Exxxxecuute Sssorrraaazzin." Calyp's pincers came together with a sharp *clack*!

Long-Mane's stern eyes confirmed what the tribe already knew. A moment later, the beast turned to the many fires burning throughout Jirvalla. His expression hurt, he paced onto the shore.

As the beast's watery paws touched the beach, the tawny sands rushed up to fill up the whole of Long-Mane's body. He strode over the shore—an enormous, living, breathing, sand creature—while sniffing in the directions of the individual fires. The grains of earth and slivered shells that formed his haunches rippled as Long-Mane shifted his weight in preparation to pounce. He unleashed an earth-quaking roar and leapt into the sky toward the largest blaze. While airborne, the Always morphed again into seawater and splashed down to douse the inferno. Seven other fires were extinguished in like manner.

When the smoke cleared, Long-Mane—his body now formed completely of sun—was poised atop Jirvalla's loftiest mountain. He peered lovingly upon the island of his creation. Pleased, he looked fondly upon each tribe. Finally, Long-Mane regarded the Always clan, still watching him from The Thumb.

As the tribe peered into those soft, sun-golden eyes, so far away but seeming so close, the Always vaulted into the sky. Soaring upward, Long-Mane transformed into a cloud while holding to his chosen shape—from the great paws spread out before him to the long tail extended behind, curling up at its tufted tip.

Chuckling, Kama nodded and waved at the cloud of Long-Mane as if wishing a happy farewell to a dear friend she expected to visit again soon. She waved and waved until the breeze tugged and twined and re-forged the cloud of Long-Mane into a baby Wool-Back prancing upon a hilltop.

Pivoting away from the fading cloud, Opahlua was quick to convince the others that the Always had plainly selected her to carry out Sorazin's grisly sentence. None could argue that Long-Mane had retrieved Opahlua's war-axe from the deeps and placed it at her feet for this express purpose.

Yet Opahlua did not set about the execution with the vengeful zeal that her tribe-mates expected of her. For the warrioress recalled the woeful eyes of the Always when he looked upon the battlefield's dead. Even more distressing was the crushing pain that had strafed across Long-Mane's face upon discovering that Sorazin had lost everything in his heart worth redeeming.

And so it was that as Opahlua drew back her axe to deliver the killing stroke, a tear dampened her cheek and a pang stabbed at her breast. The warrioress's blade tore into Sorazin nonetheless, severing him at the waist into two distinct halves.

79

The Olden Tongue

Stroking fleetly for the gaping cleft Levaioth had cloven into the steel sea-fence, Jaspen had buoyed with hope.

A few pulls more, he had thought, *and I shall be through!*

He attuned his ears, one final time, to the sea-beasts in the vicinity. The clicks of Wide-Eye, groans of Dagger-Back, squeaks of Spike-Tail, and the whistling trill of Puffer-Thorn announced that none were within striking distance.

A great, lethal rain of arrowheads and spear tips struck the sea around Jaspen in a scatter of white splashes, undoubtedly loosed from the bows and thrown from the fists of Sorazin's fighting men. Ignoring the deadly downpour, Jaspen held that if the hostiles could not pierce him at his previous mark nearer the shore, neither would they succeed in impaling him at this distance, just two body-lengths from the Gort fence.

"I am coming, my Forever-One! A few more kicks and I—

A strange sensation, like a very thin lance, stung Jaspen's ankle. The sharp pain quickly shifted to searing heat.

Toxin, he thought as the poison of the Killing-Vine-Legs spread swiftly.

The numbing palsy frustrated Jaspen's arms and legs. Soon, the venom had thieved his every motion.

JAAASSSSSPENNNN! came a faraway shout, or perhaps an echo, the word faint and worn by the time it had limped into Jaspen's ear.

A foolish hope whispered that the alarmed call had issued from Kama.

Senseless and paralyzed, Jaspen battled to roll over, to face the sky so he could breathe. He waged war against the daze set upon him by Killing-Vine-Legs, fighting against it with the whole of his heart, body, and soul. He willed his fingers to curl, his toes to flex, his arm to flutter, his neck to stretch . . . anything. Yet the Shepherd could not ascertain whether his body was responding to his urgings or not. For he could no longer feel anything at all.

Only Jaspen's eyes, fading but clinging to sight, apprised him that his face was still trapped beneath the sea.

Then, suddenly . . .

Sunlight.

Yet the bright glow upon which his eyes were fixed had lingered but a moment before an inky night-blackness began to creep in from the perimeter of his vision. The dark ring closed like a trapper's noose around a Grey-Wing's throat. The day narrowed and narrowed until a tiny, white feather was bobbing alone in the vast darkness that rose like a dome above and around Jaspen.

Peering up at the dimming light, Jaspen had but one thought: Kama.

He recalled the happy tears in her eyes as he was reciting to her the words that would bond them together as Forever-Ones. It was two nights past, after Kama had dashed into the wood upon learning that Sorazin had captured Shim. When Jaspen had finally found Kama, deep in the forest, he proposed that they should conduct the ceremony that would merge their hearts forever, in this life and the next.

Kama, too, had been eager to take the Oaths Eternal.

They did.

Following the Word-Bonds, Jaspen and Kama had twined together three vines—two to represent the new life-mates and one to symbolize the Always. With the vines braided as one, the Unbreakable Knot was tied to signify their pledge to each other as well as their affirmation that the Always was a chief component of their union.

It was upon the tying of this knot that the Always had arrived.

Or had he? Jaspen's mind was growing foggier. *My thoughts are so . . . Perhaps the entire ceremony had all been no more than a Night-Visio—*

"Could this be the departed child whom I have been seeking?"

A voice had wafted into Jaspen's ear from somewhere undersea. He could not be certain but the fish seemed to be speaking in the sea's Olden Tongue. Jaspen had not heard the ancient language since childhood.

"Oh, yes, yes!" the voice had said. "It is surely he! Surely it is!"

Still pondering the identity of the mysterious speaker, Jaspen thought, *Not even Gray-Mountain-Fish converses in a dialect so primitive as this.*

"For his flesh has been struck with the day-night seal of his royal forebears," the voice had said.

Day-night seal? Though Jaspen had endeavored to untangle the ancient words, his addled wits would not permit it.

"Oh! how pleased his begetters will be!"

Could this speaker be . . . thought Jaspen, *Levaioth?*"

Having been robbed of the power of speech, Jaspen had not the faculty to inquire.

But a flash of memory spiked through Jaspen's bewilderment to bring back to him an event that had occurred shortly after fleeing the Hoodoah's cave. He had reached the shallows along the shore where he had hoped to thwart Sorazin's return to the Cove. A splash far behind Jaspen was that of Levaioth. The Shepherd had plunged his face beneath the sea and chirped out a challenge to old Tatter-Tail. The monster had replied by turning his seven eyes toward the Shepherd of Fish. Levaioth had then answered Jaspen with queries in the Olden Tongue regarding the identity of the challenger. Levaioth had made plain to all Fin-Folk in the area that he had been pursuing the Day-Night Cove for many seasons in order to return the lost child to his parents.

Yet Jaspen had heard nothing of Levaioth's appeal. For prior to the fish's words, the Shepherd had already lifted his ears from the ocean.

"Oh! how very long have I been questing! What a gladsome day this—" The speaker paused and a grumble of concern rose. "A deep notch at the boy's side needs care," the creature had said. "And the mortal sting of Killing-Vine-Legs is upon him! We mustn't tarry! The lost kin must consume his mother's remedy soon!"

Mother? Somewhere in his heart, Jaspen knew the word's meaning.

"Worry no longer, child; an unworthy shepherd Levaioth is not. To your home we travel! Without delay!"

Home . . . It had been Jaspen's last thought before all went black.

For Levaioth had scooped up the Shepherd of Fish and set him lightly on the soft, wide bed of his tongue before racing through the waves, out of the bay, and far out the sea.

80

A New Life

THE FEAST OF ALL Tribes, Jirvalla's first ever, was due to commence with the inaugural toast of island wine at sunfall, just three or four hands away. Tribes from every part of the island had been streaming onto the shores near the half-crushed Hall of Shells since high sun. Each Treef, Udok, Gort, Huntressi, and Faijen arrived to greet the Cove and Always tribes with warm smiles and open hearts.

Several dozen of the younger children who had yet to encounter a member outside of their own clan arrived with their little lips twitching and tiny fingers trembling. They clung tight to the palms of their parents while observing the races they had only heard about in legend and song. The giant Udok, dark-skinned Huntressi, insectile Treef, red-bearded Gort, and the winged Faijen were all sources of both wonder and trepidation. Yet it was not long before their apprehensions were shed. Soon, girls were leaping off the pier while holding hands with those of former enemy tribes to splash into the sea, screaming with mirth, while boys raced across the beach without a care as to the size, shape, or color of their competitors.

Many adults, too, exercised caution when first laying eyes upon those belonging to a formerly unallied bloodstock. Yet after a goblet of island wine, all were happily engaging with one another. Many even learning the rules of a brand-new game, such as the Treef's beloved Leaf Toss or the Gort's silly Mud Spouting.

Perpeht piped song after song: about a Faijen named Rollik, a girl sprinting across the sea-top, a massive Long-Mane emerging from the ocean, and an unlikely hero known only as the Shepherd of Fish. And Shim was happy to show off a small scar he had suffered while in the jails beneath the Hall of Shells—as if his recent mark was a badge of honor.

Sunfall approached and those who had taken it upon themselves to make certain the feast would commence on time bustled about in mad preparation.

"Fish without bones!" Bogg glanced to his new tribe-mate, a former Faijen. "Oh, how Scupper jests!" He added a few jagged pebbles to his Tooth and Split Boulder bisque. "Bones are the best part!" The half-giant chuckled and placed a Spotted-Red-Fin—head, eyes, teeth, fins, bones, guts, and all—into an oiled skillet. "Scupper makes Bogg laugh." He shook his head, still snickering.

Kama was setting alone on the beach, peering out at the horizon, as she often did at day's end. The sun was dipping behind the mountains behind her and its fading rays painted a glimmering path of light along the ocean's surface. The luminous stretch winked and sparkled all the way out of the harbor and to the very end of forever, where the waters tumbled off the world's edge to feed the Everlasting Lands of Kiriath-Dae with seawater and Fin-Folk.

"I dreamt of you again last night," Kama whispered to the sea.

It had been a hundred suns since the Always tribe had freed Kama from the tip of the pier. None had seen nor heard from Jaspen since. Only Bogg and Opahlua had been visited by the Always, in a small number of Night-Visions.

The entire island had undergone myriad changes since the Always had appeared near The Thumb in the form of a colossal, watery Long-Mane.

The Cove and Treef had completely embraced the Always as their new deity. Both tribes merged utterly with the Always clan—the lone tribe on the whole of Jirvalla that existed without a Mutahn, King, Kaliphae or other monarch. The Always was their sole potentate. All boundaries formerly dividing the two tribes had been erased. A goodly number of Treef had already built family mounds along a strip of timberland where forest trees met beach sands. The insectile race had chosen the area due to its proximity to a sacred site, near the pier. This is where a pristine paw print—as big as an Udok's chest—of an immense Long-Mane was impressed into the soft sands, unmarred by devouring tide or pitiless time, as if the great beast had just trodden there seconds ago.

Eight of ten Udok had put their faith in the Always as well. The majestic sight of a huge Long-Mane sitting serenely atop Jirvalla's tallest mountain had made the former deity of the half-giants appear feeble and inattentive by comparison. Even the portion of stubborn-hearted Udok who remained devoted to Vinoko seemed to suffer a sad deflation of their faith.

After the flood that had ravaged the UnderDown and put to drowning over half of its denizens, ninety-two Gort quit life belowground to emigrate sunside (along with three dozen escaped slaves). Each of these new settlers, having personally witnessed the incomparable power of Jaspen's god, pledged happy allegiance to the Always. They, too, chose to raise their new dwelling places within the line of shade trees that rimmed what was once Cove shores.

A great majority of Huntressi and Faijen flatly rejected the Always. They had judged the many wonders credited to the so-called deity as make-believe. Nonetheless, the dozens of Huntressi who had joined Shokku and Yetahni in their quest to free Kama from The Thumb had come to believe in the love, strength, and supreme godship of the Always. Only six Faijen, each a former friend of Rollik's, had placed their faith in the Always. They lived near each other along the River Squee, close to where it emptied into the ocean, a few hundred paces from what the Treef called Katoka-cha, which in their tongue means Footprint of the Always.

Opahlua had moved into her father's cave and took her rightful place of honor as the island's Hoodoah. Flumflum was very pleased to show to her the great many amendments to the living area that the Cave-Wing and Opahlua's father had accomplished since the warrioress had last dwelled there. Unlike her father, Opahlua spent much of her time beyond the walls of her cave-place. She had grown fond of telling children of her riveting tales from her time in the Black Deep, the battle she had waged against Jaspen during the Nether-Pit War, and many other stories about life in the UnderDown. She also shared the island myths and legends of old that had been given to Opahlua by her late parents and grandparents. The many scares and gripping surprises of these fireside fables had always been punctuated by a suddenly snapping flame or flying spark (for Opahlua, like her father, was not without magic).

Bogg had been appointed as the Always tribe's master cook. He had been further entrusted with the storing and preserving of the great quantities of wild game, fruits, vegetables, nuts, and other comestibles that continued to stream into his possession via lavish gifts given to him by generous givers. Along with the influx of Treef, Cove, and Huntressi into the Always tribe came their differing palates. Each race preferred certain herbs, textures, sauces, and tastes with which Bogg was unfamiliar. It required many, many moons for Bogg to master the specialties preferred by his new tribemates.

Kama nuzzled her toes into the sand. "When are you coming home?" she whispered. "I miss you."

A soft, evening breeze brushed at her neck and gently pawed at the tips of her long, dark hair. It brought with it the sweet aroma of island flowers mixed with the savory scents of wild game, fresh fish, and forest fruits sizzling over open flame.

"Hallo hay, Kama." Shokku drew near, extending a flat hand in greeting.

"Hallo hay." Kama pressed the back of her hand to Shokku's palm.

The former Huntressi took a place in the sand next to Kama and they marveled in silence at the beauty of the swaying trees, the lilting birdsong, the sun warm on their backs, and the sea unfurling in a long, rolling, blue blanket before them.

Kama said, "Do you ever wonder if it really happened?" Her finger drew in the soft little dunes, grains tumbling. "If it wasn't for Perpeht and his songs," Kama glanced over at the musician entertaining clusters of children with his music, "I might think the whole thing was a Night-Vision."

Shokku nodded, understanding how slippery the memory of painful events can be. "I cut Kama from Thumb. You and me run on shields upon sea-top. The Always rise from ocean like Long-Mane. These facts I know."

"And Jaspen? Did Levaioth really . . . " Kama's voice trailed off. She clutched a fistful of sand, lifted it then spread wide her fingers to watch the grains sift through them. "Every sun I sit here and look out at the ocean. And every sun I expect to see him walking out of the sea with a basket of fish, smiling at me." Again, she traced on the sand. "But he never comes. Do you think he ever . . . "

A strange tingling ran across the scar that Sorazin had etched between Kama's hips. She placed a hand upon it.

" . . . he ever will?" Kama asked.

"Bogg and Opahlua saw Jaspen. In Night-Vision. Say Jaspen gone for little while only. Jaspen lives. Say it!" Shokku mocked. "Say it!"

Kama chuckled. "Jaspen lives."

Another twinge, stronger this time, tread across Kama's scar. She pushed her fingertips into the strange sensation.

Shokku resumed, "Bogg and Opahlua say Jaspen leave you alone only short time more."

Kama smiled.

"Girl, why you grin like that?"

"Because Jaspen didn't leave me alone." Kama pressed Shokku's open hand to her lower abdomen and held it there.

"Your scar, okay?"

Kama nodded, eyebrows high, a child with a secret.

Shokku's hand suddenly leapt up from Kama's stomach as something prodded at her palm. The former Huntressi's eyes broadened in surprise.

Kama giggled.

"But Isan-Dunugu . . . " Shokku pushed her hand into Kama's abdomen again. "Huntressi shamaness . . . She say you never— It happen again!" She smiled. "It is miracle of Always!"

Kama's grin grew wider.

And for the fourth time in its young life, the baby inside of Kama kicked.

THE END